THE DARKEST POINT

A GRISHAM & SULLIVAN CRIME THRILLER

JOHN HARDY BELL

SECOND
SIGHT
PUBLISHING

ALSO BY JOHN HARDY BELL

THE STRATEGIST

THE OTHER DANIEL

THE LAST GOOD AGENT

THE ROGUE ELEMENT

THE DARKEST POINT

ISBN-13: 9781071285640
ISBN-10: 1071285645

For more, visit www.johnhardybell.com

I am terrified by this dark thing
That sleeps in me;
All day I feel its soft, feathery turnings, its malignity.

Sylvia Plath

PROLOGUE

"IS THE BLINDFOLD TOO TIGHT?"

I hear this question as I feel hands on the back of my head securing the knot even tighter. The hands belong to a woman, as does the voice. I've only caught glimpses of her here and there. She's middle-aged with blondish hair and tan skin. Her mature, gentle face matches her mature, gentle voice. It's a comforting voice, and I sense that she uses it intentionally. She doesn't come right out and say *everything will be okay, this will all be over soon, just do as he asks and you'll walk out of here alive,* but her constantly reassuring tone implies it.

"It's fine," I tell her, even though it obviously isn't. Because she's trying so hard, I feel an odd compulsion not to make her feel bad. I follow up with, "Thank you."

"You're welcome, Jacob. When you're finished, I'll see about getting you something to eat. You must be starving."

I say nothing this time. I haven't had anything approaching an appetite since I was brought here. Even though my ability to measure time is pretty much gone, I estimate that it's been nearly three weeks. Aside from the glimpses of a woman whose name I still don't know, I haven't seen much of where I'm being held captive apart from the room I've been locked in. It's a nondescript ten by twelve-foot space with a cot in one corner, a rusted toilet in the other, and a card table and folding chair in the middle. The floor is carpeted, and the walls are painted lime green, so I know it isn't a prison cell. But it may as well be one.

Before each of these blindfolded sessions (of which this is the fifth), I'm instructed through the door to get on my knees and face the wall. The door is opened, and two men walk in, one on either side of me. I'm told that if I look at either of them, I'll be shot. I believe them, and I comply. As one man handcuffs me, the other puts the blindfold over my eyes. They then hoist me to my feet and out of the room.

After walking approximately sixty-four steps (I count them as a way of confirming that I'm going to the same place each time), I'm placed in a chair and pushed up to a table. A digital voice recorder is put in front of me. Then the men walk out, and the woman walks in. She once referred to one of the men as Ash, but that's all I know about them. I feel like even that's too much.

Each time, the woman pats me on the shoulder as she walks out and closes what sounds like a heavy door. She does the same thing now. Before she leaves this time, she says, "It's getting a little cold out. I think I'll make soup. Chicken noodle sound good?"

She could be anyone's perfect mother. She could be *my* perfect mother. This makes the nightmare of my situation one-hundred times worse.

After what feels like an eternity of silence, the door opens again, and he walks in. I've come to recognize the sound of his footsteps by now. Not heavy like the two men who are my watchdogs. These footsteps are light and easy. Footsteps that are accustomed to moving through spaces quietly and efficiently. I swallow hard as he pulls back his chair to sit across from me.

"Good morning, Jacob." His voice isn't light and airy like the woman's, but it's mature like hers. Stern and unyielding. "Have you found your appetite yet?"

I clear my dry throat. "Not really."

"We'd like for you to eat. The accommodations may not be much, but the food is fantastic. Besides, how are you supposed to write if you don't fuel your brain?"

I say nothing.

I've come to learn two things about this man so far. The first is that he isn't particularly interested in a two-way conversation. He asks questions as a means of making statements, not because he cares about what I'm thinking or feeling.

"Speaking of writing, what do you say we get this session started?" he continues. "We're coming to a fascinating part of the story and I need to get the details out while they're fresh in my mind." With that, I hear the click of the voice recorder. "Do you have any questions before we begin?"

He's never asked me this and I'm not sure how to respond. My question is obvious, or at least it should be, but I'm still afraid to give it voice. Apparently, he senses this.

"It's okay, Jacob. Speak freely."

I attempt to clear my throat again. "I have two questions," I say in a thin, raspy voice.

"Drink this first," he says, and I feel something cold and wet touching my lips.

He tips the bottle and water fills my mouth. I pull at it with frantic chugs until it's gone.

"Better?" he asks when I'm finished.

I nod.

"Good. Now you were saying?"

"I have two questions," I repeat.

"Okay."

"The other man who's here with me. Is he all right?"

"The other man's name is Paul."

"Is Paul all right?"

"You're only asking because you're worried if *you'll* be all right."

He's mostly correct about this. I stay silent rather than lie.

"Paul Grisham is as fine as someone in his circumstance can be. I need him just as much as I need you. Your roles here may be different, but they're equally important."

And that brings me to my second and most important question, the one I'm desperately afraid to ask. He once again senses my hesitation.

"What is it you really want to know, Jacob?"

I take in a deep, painful breath and slowly let it out. The air is stale and thick, and it's difficult to breathe. It doesn't help that I'm hyper-aware of every breath I take. When you're not sure which one will be your last, you don't take any of them for granted.

"When you're finished with us, when I help you write your book and Paul does whatever he's supposed to do, will you let us go?"

The question hangs in the air for more than a few seconds before I hear the click of the voice recorder cutting off.

"The short answer is that it may be impossible to let both of you go. But there's a lot that needs to happen between now and then, so for right now, let's stay focused on the task at hand."

I can't see his face, but I can sense his flat, emotionless expression. It's clear to me that he's already formulated the outcome in his mind, and nothing I say is going to change that. The only thing I can do now is what I've done from the beginning: comply with everything he asks of me.

When I hear the recorder click again, I know his story is about to begin. And when the story begins, my sole job is to listen. As has happened each of the previous times, when he's finished, I'll be escorted back to my cell (as I said, it may as well be a prison). With one of the watchdogs pointing a gun at my head, the other will remove my blindfold and handcuffs. I'll then sit down at the card table that functions as my workstation, and I'll write; all day, all night, until I've transcribed every word he's recorded.

So far, his life story has spanned three hundred and twenty typed pages. The end goal of that story, he tells me, is to reveal the truth about the woman whom he feels is responsible for his daughter's murder; the woman whose father is somewhere in this hell along with me.

The second thing I know about the man who is keeping me captive, more than anything I've ever known in my entire life, is that he wants Camille Grisham to suffer, and is prepared to go to any lengths to make sure that happens. I fear for myself, but I fear for her and her father even more.

"Now we've come to the part of the story where I tell you about my daughter, sweet, innocent girl that she was. She was murdered by Daniel Sykes, the man who was to be the subject of your book. The man you so desperately wanted to turn into a human-interest story. But he's not a human. He's a goddamn animal. And he killed Madison, my daughter, like a goddamned animal."

I keep every fiber in my body still, too afraid to move or speak.

"But he never should have been allowed to kill her. And make no mistake, he was *allowed* to kill her." He pauses for a long time before continuing. "I need you to listen to this next part very carefully because it involves you. It's the entire reason I brought you here. Are you listening, Jacob?"

"Yes."

I can sense him leaning in until he's a few inches from my face.

"Camille Grisham has to pay in the worst way imaginable. For that to happen, I need you to draw her out."

"Draw her out?" I ask with genuine confusion. "How am I supposed to do that?"

"With your words."

He spends the next several minutes speaking my instructions into the voice recorder, down to the size and style of the font I'm to use in composing the text. The first of the three messages, he explains, will contain the reasons for his actions. The second will serve as the impetus for Camille's participation in his objective. The third will be a specific set of instructions for her to follow. Failure to comply with these instructions, he explains, will result in the death of one person every day until she does comply.

After I compose the messages, I'm to make a copy of each and put them in envelopes to be labeled with the addresses that he will supply. My fingerprints, he claims, are a critical piece of the puzzle. From there, we wait for Camille's response.

"Is all of this clear?" he asks as he finally sits back in his chair.

"Yes."

"Good. Now, before you get to it, there's one more thing that I need you to do."

I hold my breath as he stands up and walks behind me.

I keep my eyes shut as he rips the blindfold away from them.

"I think we've officially moved past the stage of pretense. There's no reason you shouldn't see my face. Open your eyes."

I respond by clenching them even tighter, my mind holding firm to the adage that I've heard expressed in every hostage movie ever made: Never let them show you their face. Once you see their face, you're dead.

Pain as he grabs my hair and yanks my scalp. "Open them!"

I comply. I'm briefly blinded by the LED light from the lamp pointed at me. The only image I can make out is his silhouette as I blink away piercing strobes of light.

When my eyes finally adjust, I can see the course details of his face.

He smiles at the sound of my shrieking.

After allowing ample time for my shock to sink in, he leans into my ear and whispers. "Time to get to work, Jacob."

1

BRIEFING

F BI SPECIAL AGENT PETER CRAWLEY was all-too-aware of his reputation. Cold. Aloof. Distant. Robotic. He'd even been given a nickname by certain members of the BAU Team: Doctor Ice. It bothered him more than he cared to admit, but he did his best to take it in stride. Deep down, he understood that the moniker was justified. The twenty-three-year Bureau veteran had many strong suits, but emotional engagement wasn't one of them.

So when tough questions arose about a former special agent's decision to join the task force charged with discovering the whereabouts of her missing father, Crawley addressed them with a forced composure that belied his mounting irritation. In addition to being one of the finest profilers he'd ever encountered, Camille Grisham was also a friend, which made the criticism of her inclusion – an inclusion that he'd insisted on – feel very personal.

But because Doctor Ice's well-earned reputation didn't allow him to take such things personally, he had to ensure that his poker face held up, despite persistent badgering from the two local agents assigned to the task force; agents he didn't know, and based on early results, didn't like.

"Look, I understand that she has a long history in Behavioral Analysis and that the two of you are close. But she quit, remember? And based on everything I've heard, she has no desire to come back."

The most vocal of the pair was a hothead named Gabriel Pratt. As profilers went, Pratt was made of all the right stuff. Crawley could see that the moment he laid eyes on him. Subsequent reviews of his personnel file confirmed it. The problem with Agent Pratt was his ego. His was the classic 'big fish in a small pond' syndrome that afflicted many a D.C. hotshot forced to relocate to a Midwest field office too small to handle the weight of their considerable talent.

"I know what's at stake for her, so I don't want to sound insensitive," he continued, "But I'm not sure what she can bring to this investigation beyond her witness statement."

"He's got a point, sir. How do we know she won't let her emotions get the best of her? It's certainly happened before."

Allison Mendoza was Pratt's less-talkative yet equally presumptuous partner. Like Pratt, Mendoza came highly recommended. And like Pratt, she assumed that her opinion was much more relevant to Crawley than it actually was.

"With all due respect to both of you, it isn't your job to understand Camille Grisham. You're here as my CBI liaisons. And while I can appreciate your experience and ability, your involvement here is procedural. In other words, I didn't have a choice. So before you waste another breath questioning Camille's credentials or my judgment, please put your misguided ego aside long enough to understand the actual flow of things here. You're on this task force because the crime occurred in your city. Camille Grisham is on this task force because Director Spaulding wants her to be. The sooner you can accept that fact, the sooner we can all move forward.

I want Agent Grisham to feel nothing but welcomed here. Is that understood?"

"*Agent* Grisham," Pratt chided.

"Is that understood?"

Pratt and Mendoza looked at one another, their eyes silently communicating a mutual disdain of Crawley, his condescending tone, and their inability to do anything about it.

"Understood," Mendoza answered, her stare still fixed on Pratt.

"Loud and clear," Pratt concurred, wisely taking his partner's cue.

Doctor Ice breathed an undetectable sigh of relief. "Great. Now can we move ahead with the briefing that brought us here in the first place? Camille is on her way, and I want to make sure we're fully up to speed before she arrives."

He opened his briefcase and pulled out three manila folders, two of which he gave to Pratt and Mendoza. He opened his and immediately began reading.

"From page two of the report. There are four dead that we know of so far. All women. Two in Pennsylvania, one in Tennessee, and one in Missouri. In each case, the victims were abducted from their homes, taken to a remote location, sexually assaulted, mutilated, and strangled. The mutilation patterns are consistent with those used by Daniel Sykes. As we know, Sykes is in a federal prison serving out a life sentence. That leaves us with the probability of a serial copycat. We're in Denver because the two latest incidents, the abduction of Paul Grisham and Jacob Deaver, occurred here.

Crawley flipped to the next page of the report. "Daniel MacPherson is the man currently in custody for Deaver's abduction. MacPherson is the brother of Candace MacPherson, Sykes's last victim. Deaver reportedly met MacPherson during his research for a book he was writing about Sykes.

The extent of their relationship during that time is unclear, but we do know that at the time of his arrest, MacPherson was posing as Deaver in an effort to get close to Camille. This obviously makes him a prime person of interest in Deaver's disappearance. Unfortunately, we haven't been able to establish a firm connection between MacPherson and the disappearance of Paul Grisham or the previous murders, even though it's safe to assume they're connected. DPD has interviewed him several times to no avail. I'm counting on us to do better.

He flipped to the next page. "There's scant physical evidence aside from the two notes sent to Paul Grisham's residence and the BAU offices, respectively. The notes were identical in content. DNA from blood found on the paper is a match for Kerrie Wallace and Harley Middleton, two of the victims. But there are no prints, and the writing doesn't match samples taken from MacPherson, Deaver, or Paul Grisham. That basically leaves us at square one."

Crawley closed the report and looked up at Pratt and Mendoza. They were attentive despite already knowing the details of the report. It would have been easy to tune out his summary, but they didn't. He took this as a hopeful sign that they were team players.

"Questions? Concerns?"

"Only about Camille," Pratt said.

Crawley rolled his eyes, the first visible crack in Doctor Ice's armor.

"Specifically as it relates to our suspect," Pratt clarified.

"Go on."

"She believes that MacPherson is involved in her father's disappearance."

"An assumption we're all making at this point."

"But we don't have the skin in this that she does. Her confrontations with Daniel before his arrest were contentious, and she's already assaulted him once. How do we know she won't go after him again?"

"Jesus, Gabe. Can you blame her?" Mendoza said. "I'd want to beat the hell out of him too. And so would you."

"I'd like to think that if either of us were in that position, we'd have enough foresight to remove ourselves from the situation before it escalated to that point."

"You're telling me that you'd sit on the sidelines if it were your mother or sister out there?"

"I'm telling you that for the integrity of the investigation, I'd have to."

Mendoza laughed. "That's bullshit, and you know it."

"Of course it's bullshit."

Pratt and Mendoza spun around at the sound of the new voice in the room. Neither of them said a word when they saw who it was.

For his part, Doctor Ice stood up from his desk and smiled, refusing to suppress the overwhelming emotion that this moment inspired in him.

"Good morning, Camille."

2

THE CONSULTANT

W HEN THE GUY AT THE FRONT DESK clipped the visitor's badge to Camille's jacket, he smiled and asked how long she'd be staying. It wasn't an official question, just polite, everyday conversation. He undoubtedly knew of her reason for being here. He'd been briefed the same as everyone else in the building. Yet he barely blinked as she nervously approached him, choosing to greet her not with reservation, pity, or scorn, but with the warm banality that he would a regular tourist. Camille couldn't have been more appreciative of the gesture. She promptly returned his smile and replied, "Hopefully, not too long."

Then she met Special Agent Stephen Wells from Crawley's BAU task force, and her smile went away.

"I'm so glad you'll be joining us," he said with a solemn gaze. "I just wish it were under better personal circumstances."

Camille bit her lip and nodded as she shook his hand, sparing herself the indignity of saying something that would make this already awkward situation even worse.

"You're still thought of very highly in the BAU," Wells

continued. "They say the place just isn't the same without you."

Agent Wells wasn't around during Camille's tenure, and she wondered if she was staring at her replacement. "Lots of great people there."

"For sure, and they're all rooting for you."

The hush that followed only exacerbated the awkwardness.

"But enough about that," Wells finally said. "Peter and the rest of the team are waiting."

He promptly led Camille down a long corridor of dark cubicles to an open conference room where she happened upon a conversation that seemed to feature her as the main talking point.

She'd wanted to enter the room like a reasonable person and wait for the proper introductions. Instead, she was put in the uncomfortable position of defending herself.

"Of course it's bullshit," she said in response to one of the agents and his insinuation that her presence could compromise the integrity of his investigation.

The look of abject horror on the agent's face as he turned to see her standing behind him almost made up for the sting of his insult, but not entirely.

Peter Crawley's smile was as big as Camille had ever seen it. He clearly relished the timing of her entrance. "Good morning, Camille. Please come in and join us."

She did so, glaring at the agent as she took the seat next to Crawley.

"You've already met Agent Wells from the BAU," he continued. "This is Allison Mendoza and Gabriel Pratt from CBI. They're our local liaisons."

"Nice to meet you, Camille," Agent Mendoza offered with what looked like a genuine smile.

"Likewise."

Agent Pratt's greeting wasn't nearly as genuine. "I apologize if I offended you. That wasn't my intention."

"You did offend me, Agent Pratt. But in the interest of not tainting this working relationship before it begins, I accept your apology."

Pratt's jaw tightened as he turned to Crawley. "Anything else we should know, sir?"

"My briefing is finished, so I'll turn it over to Camille in case she'd like to add anything that the official report didn't cover."

"The official report is thorough enough," Camille replied curtly, refusing to feed Pratt's angst about her emotional vulnerability. In truth, the official report wasn't thorough at all. It didn't mention her anxiety about being here or the fact that she spent every minute of every day thinking about her father, or the reality that she would end the life of the person holding him without hesitation if he wasn't returned to her unharmed. But no one in this room needed to hear that, not even Peter Crawley, the man who would vouch for her until the day he died, no matter what she did. Only her father had more unconditional faith in her ability.

"Okay, since Camille doesn't have anything, let's discuss where we go from here."

"I just got off the horn with DPD admin. We're good to go on the MacPherson interview," Wells reported. "He's been slow to cooperate so far, and he's still refusing counsel, even though he was assigned a public defender two weeks ago. I honestly don't know how much we'll get out of him."

"Time isn't exactly on our side," Crawley replied as he turned a worried eye to Camille. "We'd better get something."

Crawley's expression troubled her, and she looked away. Without saying a word, he'd managed to tell her everything about the current state of their investigation.

It was nowhere.

Nearly three weeks had passed since a true-crime author named Jacob Deaver confronted Camille in a quiet coffee shop, where she was quietly minding her business, to pitch an idea for a biography that would detail her work as an FBI profiler; specifically, her controversial role in the apprehension of serial killer Daniel Sykes. Sykes, Deaver went on to say, was planning his own tell-all, which promised to paint Camille and her deceased partner Andrew Sheridan in the most unflattering light possible. By telling her own story in her own words, she could mitigate the damage from Sykes's book before it could ever see the light of day.

The pitch sounded reasonable, and Camille might have even considered it, were it not for the small matter of the real Jacob Deaver being reported missing one week earlier by his New York-based agent Meredith Park.

The truth, Camille would come to discover, was that the Sykes autobiography never existed, just as her biography would never exist. Daniel MacPherson, posing as Deaver, had used the cover as a means of getting close to her. For what purpose, she wasn't sure.

Then her father went missing, and the purpose became crystal-clear.

Camille sat quietly as the agents discussed the various tactics they would use to elicit MacPherson's thus far elusive cooperation. Agent Pratt seemed especially confident in his abilities.

"The problem is that the local hacks have been coming at this guy the wrong way. They're using GITMO-style tactics on him when he's nothing more than a pawn. The trick is to approach him with some understanding, make him think he's as much of a victim as anyone else."

Camille was about to roll her eyes at the suggestion, but Crawley beat her to it.

"A victim?"

"I know it sounds strange but hear me out. Daniel MacPherson is just a kid. He was angry over his sister's murder, and he wanted revenge. Sykes had already been put away, but that wasn't enough. He needed to make someone pay in a tangible way. I think we can all agree that there's another player involved, and it's that person, not Daniel, who killed those girls and abducted Deaver and Camille's father. Daniel himself admitted that he was merely a cog in the wheel. He was sad, he was pissed-off, he was desperate, and our killer exploited that. No one is saying that Daniel MacPherson is innocent. He's far from it. But if we can get him to believe that he's being used by someone who ultimately doesn't care about him, maybe he'll reconsider the lengths he's willing to go to protect that person's identity."

"You don't think that's been tried already?" Camille asked. "If you assume for a second that you can reverse psychology your way to a confession, especially from someone as calculated as Daniel MacPherson, then you don't have the first clue about what you're dealing with."

Pratt's eyes narrowed as they found Camille. "Well, please enlighten me. What are we dealing with?"

Camille turned to Crawley, who gave her permission to proceed with a nearly imperceptible nod of his head.

"The person you're dealing with isn't some grieving, innocent, exploited pawn. He's deliberate, highly motivated, and very unstable. You're right that he's looking for someone to take his anger out on, and since he can't get to Sykes, I'm the next sensible target. But to think that because he didn't kill those girls he's any less dangerous than the person who did is foolish. I've been face to face with this man. I saw the way his eyes turned black with hatred when he looked at me. If he'd had the opportunity, he would've killed me the moment he saw me."

"From the sound of it, he had the opportunity. Why didn't he take it?" Agent Mendoza asked.

"Because killing me wasn't part of his plan. Not at that moment anyway. So if he had the restraint not to kill me when he could've gotten away with it scot-free, what makes you think you can persuade him to deviate from the plan now?"

"What do you suggest then?" Crawley asked.

Camille took a deep breath. She needed steady nerves for what she was about to say. "Give Daniel exactly what he wants."

"Which is?"

"Me."

The room fell silent. All eyes were on Camille, waiting for clarification, but she suddenly felt hesitant to give it.

From the moment she agreed to join Crawley's task force – a mere two hours after her father's abduction – Camille knew what her role would be, even if no one else did.

Her visitor's badge wouldn't afford her any of the powers of an acting field agent. She wouldn't have an official firearm or shield. She couldn't arrest anyone or give orders to local law enforcement. From the Bureau's standpoint, she was here strictly as a consultant; someone with intimate knowledge of Daniel Sykes's M.O. And because the subject they were looking for was believed to be a Sykes copycat, she would presumably have intimate knowledge of his M.O. as well.

But there was only so much consulting that could occur in a case like this. Consultants talked, they pondered, they hypothesized. Camille wasn't here to hypothesize. She was here to find the person who abducted her father. And as far as she could see, there was only one way to do that.

"He wanted me here for a specific reason. Otherwise, I would be the one you all were searching for right now. I don't know what that specific reason is yet, but I don't think I'll have to wait long to find out."

"So we're just supposed to sit back and wait for you to be attacked?" Mendoza asked incredulously. "That doesn't seem reasonable."

"Especially because we have no idea who we're dealing with or what his plan is," Pratt added.

"We figure out the plan by asking," Camille said.

"You mean I'm just supposed to go in there, ask MacPherson what this plan is, and expect him to tell me?" Pratt asked.

Camille shook her head at his arrogance. "You can ask him questions until you're blue in the face, but you won't get anywhere."

Pratt smiled. "And what makes you so sure about that?"

"Because you're not me."

The smile on Pratt's face was suddenly replaced with something darker. "You're suggesting that it should be *you* who conducts the MacPherson interview?"

"That's exactly what I'm suggesting," Camille answered, her stare matching Pratt's in its intensity. "And I need to be in there alone."

"You've got to be kid—"

"Done," Crawley said, cutting off Pratt's protest. The four of us will monitor Camille and reconvene afterward to discuss. I trust that works for everyone."

"Works for me," Agent Wells said.

Mendoza tentatively nodded her approval while Pratt quietly seethed.

"Great, then let's get to it." Crawley stood up, and the others in the room followed suit. "Camille, you can ride with me."

"Fine," she replied, keeping a wary eye on Agent Pratt as he huffed out of the conference room.

She worried that he would be a problem. Not that she didn't have solutions for blowhards like him. She'd encountered more than her share at Quantico. She just didn't have the mental stamina to deal with him right now. Most of her energy stores had already been used up, and what was left in reserve would have to be saved for Daniel MacPherson. She wondered if even that would be enough.

"You sure you're up for this?" Crawley asked with a pat on Camille's shoulder as they left the conference room.

"If I said no, would you hold it against me?"

Crawley smiled a second time. In Camille's experience, that was a record. "Not at all. As long as you don't hold it against me that I finally sweet-talked you into coming back."

Bullied would be a more apt description, but that was water under the bridge now.

"Just help me find my father, Peter."

"I will." Crawley stopped, his hand still gripping Camille's shoulder. "If it's the last thing I do."

3

ANTICIPATION

A GENT PRATT WAS THE FIRST to enter the DPD Admin Building, followed closely by Agents Mendoza and Wells. Camille and Agent Crawley trailed behind at a considerable distance.

"You were pretty quiet in the car," Crawley said.

"What was I supposed to say?"

"You could've started by telling me how you're feeling."

"About what?"

"Confronting MacPherson. Being back in an interrogation room. Wearing that FBI shield."

"It's not a real FBI shield."

"You know what I mean."

"I'm fine."

Camille didn't need to look at Crawley to sense the doubt on his face.

"How are you really feeling?"

"I told you, I'm fine."

Crawley stopped mid-stride. "Do you remember the last time you were in this situation? The last time you conducted an interrogation?"

The image of Daniel Sykes made Camille stop too. "Of course, I do."

"It didn't turn out so fine."

She shook the memory away. "This is different."

"How?"

"Are you having second thoughts about me going in there?"

"Not at all. I'm simply looking out for you."

"I appreciate that, Peter. I really do. But I can handle myself."

"I know you can. I also know that I'm asking a lot. I just don't want it to be too much. So if it gets to be, you have to promise to tell me."

Camille looked in Crawley's eyes and saw a strain of emotion that was rarely present. He was genuinely worried about her. She hoped her brave face would be enough to allay his concern, even if it wasn't enough to conquer her own. "I promise."

Crawley exhaled quietly. "Okay. Let's go."

Upon entering the Major Crimes Division, the group was greeted by Lieutenant Owen Hitchcock and his team of detectives. Pratt, Mendoza, and Wells had already completed their round of introductions by the time Camille and Crawley caught up to them. The banter seemed friendly.

When Lieutenant Hitchcock saw Camille, he immediately broke away from the group. His arm was extended before he even reached her.

"Good to see you, Camille. I wish the circumstances were better, of course."

From what Camille could recall, she only ever saw Hitchcock under less-than-ideal circumstances. "It's good to see you too, lieutenant. Thank you for accommodating us."

"Not a problem. Your father means the world to this department. Getting him home safely is priority number one." He turned to Crawley. "I don't believe we've met. Lieutenant Owen Hitchcock."

"Special Agent Peter Crawley. Pleasure."

"Likewise."

The two exchanged a cordial handshake. Given Crawley's penchant for swinging his federal authority around like a battle ax, Camille knew the pleasantries wouldn't last.

"I take it you've already met my team." Crawley said.

"I have," Hitchcock confirmed with a smile. If he was at all leery of the group of agents and their sudden invasion of his territory, he didn't show it. "And allow me to introduce my leads, Detectives Alan Krieger and Jim Parsons. They were the first to interview MacPherson following his arrest. I'm sure you've already seen their summary, but I figured you'd want to ask them some follow up questions before you–"

"That won't be necessary," Crawley insisted. "The summary was quite thorough in explaining MacPherson's reluctance to talk. We're hoping that Camille can have more luck."

Hitchcock's smile faded. "What do you mean?"

"She's conducting the interview."

Hitchcock turned a surprised eye to Camille. "I didn't realize you were officially back with the Bureau."

"I'm not."

"Camille is here as a consultant," Crawley explained. "We believe we're dealing with a Daniel Sykes copycat, and there's no one more familiar with Sykes than Camille. She can provide valuable insight."

"She also has a deeply personal connection to one of the victims," Hitchcock said.

"I understand that."

"And you think it's a good idea to grant her access to a suspect that she's already had precarious run-ins with?"

Camille looked at Pratt and detected a hint of smug satisfaction on his face. She shot him a dirty look and turned back to Hitchcock. "That's exactly why I need to be the one in there. I'm the reason all of this is happening in the first place. I'm the one that Daniel wants, which means I'm also the one that my father's abductor wants. Your men have already tried talking to him, and they've gotten nowhere. Meanwhile, Jacob Deaver and my father are still out there, and the more time we waste in here, the harder it'll be to find them.

Camille paused to catch her breath. She knew the only chance she had to sway Hitchcock was to keep her emotions in check. "Yes, this situation is very personal, lieutenant. But I know how to conduct myself in there. I've been face to face with Daniel already. I know how he thinks. I know what his motives are. I know that he hates me. But his hatred makes him more vulnerable to emotion. And if he gets emotional, he's more likely to say something that he doesn't mean to; something that can lead us to the man we're looking for."

The tension in Hitchcock's face began to subside. "Can you assure me that things won't go sideways in there?"

"You have my word."

Hitchcock glanced back at his team. They looked less than convinced. Injured pride, Camille speculated.

"Would you at least like to have Krieger or Parsons sit in with you? They've already spent a good deal of time with him. Maybe they could offer some perspective."

Preservation of the fragile male ego was at the very bottom of Camille's priority list right now, and because of that, she responded with a simple but firm, "No."

Casting aside the terseness of her reply, Hitchcock turned to Crawley. "I hope you can appreciate just how unusual this request is. We're talking about allowing someone with no official law enforcement credentials to question the prime suspect in an ongoing criminal investigation. I don't have to tell you how that would sit with a judge should it go that far."

"No, you don't have to tell me," Crawley said. "But you know as well as I do that everything Camille has said is true."

"Again, lieutenant, it won't go sideways in there," Camille reiterated.

Hitchcock blew out a loud sigh of surrender. "Fine. But if it does, it's not my ass, or theirs." He pointed to Krieger and Parsons. "Understood?"

"Completely," Crawley replied, then turned to Camille for confirmation.

"Understood."

"Okay. If you all want to follow me, MacPherson is this way."

Hitchcock led the group down a short hallway to a monitoring station that had been outfitted with a small bank of computer monitors and several chairs. The monitors were numbered one to five. The only one currently switched on was number three. It was there that she saw him.

Clad in jailhouse orange, his hands and feet bound to a small table that Camille hoped was bolted to the floor, Daniel MacPherson looked small and feeble. But in his case, looks were deceiving. When she honed in on the grainy image of his narrow, bearded face, she noticed something else: a smile of anticipation.

He was waiting for her.

As the rest of the group situated itself inside the room, Hitchcock pulled Camille back into the hallway.

"I'm not going to lie to you, this one's got me a little nervous."

Camille tensed at his words. "Why?"

"We don't know anything about this guy aside from what you've told us. He has no criminal record to speak of, no incidents from his past that would indicate a capacity for

violence, and no clear-cut motive for his involvement in
Deaver's abduction. We can't get a read on him at all, and
frankly, that concerns the hell out of me."

"You're looking at his motive," Camille said flatly.

"What makes you so certain?"

"He thinks I'm responsible for his sister's murder."

"Daniel Sykes is responsible for her murder."

"I didn't capture Sykes before he killed Daniel's sister and
her friend. In his mind, that makes it my fault." Camille
didn't want to admit that there was once a time when she
believed the same thing.

"So what's his endgame? Why abduct your father and
some random crime writer? Why not go after you directly?"

"That's what I need to find out. Whatever the end game
is, I can certainly tell you that it's much bigger than
Daniel."

"What about the murders in Pennsylvania, Missouri, and
Tennessee?"

"Not him."

"How do you know?"

"I just know. Besides, there's nothing in his past that
would indicate violence of that magnitude. You said so
yourself."

"We could've missed something."

"He merely played his part. Someone else is orchestrating
this."

"Including the murders?"

"Yes."

"Your confidence almost has me convinced."

"Almost?"

"He hasn't said five words to my detectives in over three
hours of interview time. What if he decides to play the same
game with you?"

"I'll make him talk to me."

Hitchcock's expression hardened. "You promised it wouldn't go sideways in there."

"It won't. Trust me."

Hitchcock blew out another loud sigh. "At this point, I don't have much of a choice, do I?" He glanced inside the monitoring room. "Can I trust your guy?"

"Agent Crawley?"

"Yes."

"For what it's worth, there's no one aside from my father who I trust more."

"So does that mean you'll go back to work for him when all of this is over?"

Camille bristled at the question but did her best to contain the irritation. "First things first, lieutenant."

Hitchcock nodded his understanding. "We'll get your dad back, Camille."

She didn't doubt the sincerity of his promise for a second, but it wasn't nearly enough to convince her. Before she could voice the thought, Crawley emerged from the monitoring room.

"Are we good to go out here?"

"I believe so," Hitchcock said before turning back to Camille. "We'll be watching closely. If you feel like it's getting out of hand in there and you need someone to come in, look into the camera and give us a nod. Okay?"

Camille knew she wouldn't need Hitchcock or anyone else to back her up, but she thought it best to humor him. "You got it."

"Okay. Good luck in there." With that, the lieutenant made his way inside the monitoring room, leaving Camille and Crawley alone in the hallway.

"You won't be giving us that nod, will you?" Crawley asked with a knowing smile.

"Of course not."

"Didn't think so. Now go in there and do that thing you do."

Camille hadn't done that 'thing' in a long time, and for the first time since agreeing to come back, she wondered if she could ever do it again. Rather than admit that to Crawley, she turned her attention to the closed door of Interview Room Three. "Something tells me Daniel is looking forward to this as much as I am. No need to keep him waiting."

4

BETTER NATURE

THE AIR INSIDE THE INTERVIEW ROOM was considerably cooler than it had been anywhere else on the floor. Camille knew this wasn't an accident. The temperature was likely turned down a few degrees below comfortable. It was a common interrogation tactic meant to keep the interviewee on edge. Daniel didn't so much as flinch when she entered the room, so Camille wasn't sure if the tactic had worked on him. She was a different story.

Doing her best to fight off the chill, she eased into the hard chair opposite him. When she finally settled in, Daniel smiled, sat up straight, and placed his cuffed hands neatly on the table.

"Nice seeing you again."

Just like he did when they first met in the City Perk Café all those weeks ago, he was mocking her with civility. Thankfully, she wouldn't be caught off guard this time when the true monster emerged. For now, she decided to play along.

"Hello, Daniel. Thanks for taking some time to talk."

His smile widened. "I didn't exactly have anyplace else to be. And even if I did, I wouldn't pass up this opportunity."

Camille held his gaze. "Neither would I."

"When they came into my cell this morning to tell me I'd be making the trip over here, I couldn't have been more excited. I knew it would be you."

"Why were you so sure?"

"They knew I wouldn't talk to anyone else, so you were pretty much the only option left. Not to mention, our last meeting ended on a really sour note, you sucker-punching me in the face and all. I figured you had some regret about that and wanted to make amends."

Daniel was right. She regretted not putting enough power in the punch to knock him unconscious. The same mistake wouldn't be made twice. "I'm hoping we can have a more constructive conversation this time."

"Fire away, Agent Grisham."

"Camille."

"But that little badge on your lapel says you're an FBI agent again. I want to be respectful."

"Then call me Camille."

Her narrow eyes communicated a dead seriousness that he was wise not to ignore.

"You're right. With all we've been through, formalities are kind of silly. Where would you like to begin, Camille?"

There were a million places she could have begun, and Daniel had probably anticipated all of them. So she decided to throw him a minor curveball. "I'm curious why you've refused legal counsel."

As expected, the question momentarily stumped him. "I suppose it's like using a tricycle to make a cross country trip. You get nowhere pretty fast."

"But if you really have to get somewhere and that's the only mode of transportation available, you'd do better to use it."

"I'm exactly where I need to be."

"You mean you don't have any designs on getting out of here?"

"I don't have anything left out there that matters to me. You made sure of that."

"It's not my fault that Candace died."

It was here that Camille noticed the first break in his carefully constructed veneer.

"Candace didn't die. Candace was murdered. And if you want this conversation to continue, please don't say her name. You don't have the right."

"You brought it up."

"And I'm telling you to drop it."

Camille put her hands up in mock deference. "Okay." She allowed an extended silence to settle between them before continuing. "So you're prepared to spend the rest of your life in jail?"

Daniel appeared to relax as he sat back in his chair. "I doubt I'll spend the rest of my life here. You normally have to kill someone before they throw that kind of time at you. I haven't killed anyone."

"But you're protecting someone who has. That's as good as committing the crime yourself. Do you really want to carry out someone else's prison sentence?"

"For the right person with the right cause, you'd be willing to do anything."

"Even if that cause involves kidnapping two innocent people and killing four more?"

"I personally would have chosen different means, but I can't argue with the end goal."

"And what's the end goal?"

Daniel's smile returned. "Justice, of course."

"Justice for what you think I've done to you."

"And countless others. I'm sure I'm not the only one with an ax to grind, Camille. There were twenty-six other people killed by Sykes's hand. And of those, nine were killed *after* you and your partner had the chance to catch him. You remember Alexandria, don't you?"

Daniel was referring to the now well-known incident that occurred three months before Sykes was ultimately apprehended. Camille and her partner Andrew Sheridan were part of a search and rescue operation involving an Alexandria, Virginia woman named Sherrie Creswell. A note left at the scene of her disappearance matched letters left by Sykes at previous crime scenes. Camille helped coordinate the effort involving some eighty local volunteers and countless law enforcement officials. Unbeknownst to her, one of those volunteers happened to be Daniel Sykes himself. The two even struck up a friendly conversation about the particulars of the case.

When the search was abruptly called off after Creswell's body was discovered in a ravine over a hundred miles away, Camille thanked the volunteers - Sykes among them - for their time and effort and sent them on their way. She would have never differentiated him from any of the other concerned locals, until his arrest and subsequent interrogation, when he recounted the events of their meeting in detail, right down to the red-soled bison leather boots that she wore to help navigate the area's thick marsh.

Sykes went on to tell Camille that his last nine murders, which included Daniel MacPherson's sister Candace and her friend Jessica Bailey, were committed after their encounter; an encounter he secretly hoped would result in his capture. That was where the interrogation, and Camille's FBI career, ended.

She spent months blaming herself for those murders; the weight of guilt almost crushing her spirit completely. But she fought her way through it and eventually forgave herself. Counseling and intense self-reflection had nearly allowed her to move on completely. Then Daniel MacPherson showed up, bringing all of that guilt and anger back with him.

"Of course I remember Alexandria," Camille said. "But I've moved on. I really think you should too."

Daniel's jaw tightened. "That's easy for you to say. What have you lost in all of this aside from your career and a few nights of sleep?"

"I've lost plenty."

His eyes brightened. "That's right. Your precious Agent Sheridan. But that was your fault too, right?"

Camille's forced composure was beginning to wane. "Why don't you tell me what you want?"

"I've already told you."

"If you truly wanted justice, you had the opportunity. You knew where I lived, where I had my coffee every day. I wasn't hiding. You could've killed me before I even saw you coming."

"If I'd done that, the world would see you as a victim, and that defeats the entire purpose."

"How should the world see me?"

"As the liar and coward that you are."

Camille edged forward in her chair. "None of this has anything to do with my father or Jacob. Tell me where they are."

"I can't do that. Not until you show the world your true self."

"And how am I supposed to do that?"

"He'll tell you."

"Who?"

"You'll see."

She gripped the edge of the table to stop herself from punching him again. "Enough of the games, Daniel. Who abducted my father?"

He paused as if needing to frame his answer properly.

"He'll reveal himself when he's ready. All I can tell you for now is that he's a very noble man, with a very noble cause. And I *will* stay here for the rest of my life if that's what it takes to help accomplish his objective."

Camille knew that Daniel wasn't prepared to say anything more, and her persistence would only cause him to dig his heels in further. So she decided to employ another tactic, part of which she begrudgingly borrowed from Agent Pratt.

"For what it's worth, I'm sorry for all of this."

"I bet you are," he answered through tightly-pressed lips.

"I mean it, Daniel. There's hardly a day that goes by that I don't think about what happened in that basement or the fact that I wasn't able to save your sister. You have every right in the world to be angry. If I were you, I'd want to take my pain out on someone too. I get it."

"Like hell you do."

"Trust me, I do. But I also know something else. No matter what happens to me, or my father, or Jacob Deaver, nothing is going to change. You can get all the vengeance you want. You can embarrass me. You can kill me right here in the most brutal way imaginable. And for a time, it would probably feel good. You'd finally get to bask in the satisfaction of your well-deserved justice. But when you wake up tomorrow, and every day for the rest of your life, that pain you're feeling right now, that sense of loss that lingers in your bones, that longing to hold on to something that's lost forever, it will still be there, just as debilitating and all-consuming as it ever was. And there won't be anyone left to blame but yourself, and the man who put you here. The man you're so hellbent on protecting. He'll go on with his life, probably without giving you another thought. And you'll continue to suffer. All by yourself. That's the only possible outcome right now. But it can be different. If you're honest with yourself, if you look really deep down, you know it should be different."

Daniel immediately broke her gaze, but not before Camille could see the dampness pooling under his eyelids.

"I'm sorry for your loss, Daniel. I'm sorry that Candace isn't here anymore. But you have to ask yourself, would she want this for you? Would she want to see you here? Suffering all alone? Would she want her legacy to include the murders of more innocent people? I didn't know her, but something tells me she wouldn't. It's not too late to change that legacy; hers and yours. It's not too late to stop the real bad guy in this situation; the same bad guy who doesn't care if you rot in your jail cell without any contact from the outside world. Please. Jacob Deaver doesn't deserve this. Neither does my father. Neither do you."

Daniel closed his eyes and turned away. When he opened them, tears were streaming down his face. "What about you, Camille? Do you deserve it?"

She didn't respond.

Daniel wiped the tears away with his shoulder. "That speech was really great. Oscar-worthy. The sad part is that you actually believe it."

"Of course, I do."

"Well, you're right to say that things won't change for me. But they won't change for you either. I'm powerless to stop what's coming. And even if I could stop it, I wouldn't." The cracks of emotion that continued to spread across his face betrayed the words.

"You're not powerless, Daniel. No one else has to die."

"But someone else is going to die. And it's happening soon."

Camille was hit with a sudden surge of adrenaline that momentarily blinded her. "Who?"

The cracks in Daniel's face smoothed out, and his smile returned. "Jacob's agent."

"Meredith Park?"

He nodded. "And she won't be the last. Not unless you comply."

"With what?"

"His instructions. From what I understand, they'll be precise, and you'll have to follow them to the letter. If you don't, someone else dies. Then someone else, until there's no one left in the world that matters to *you*. We'd finally have something in common then, wouldn't we?"

Camille edged forward in her chair again, gripping the table with such force that the almond-colored skin covering her knuckles turned pale white. "If anything happens to Meredith Park, or anyone else–"

"It will be your fault. Now I suggest you take everything I've said to heart. I wasn't entrusted with the specifics of his plans for Meredith. But I do know that she's first. It might be today, it might be next month. For all I know, she could be dead already. If she isn't, you'd better figure out how to stop it."

Camille released her grip on the table and stood up.

"You were obviously trying to appeal to my better nature with that psycho-babble," Daniel continued. "I guess it worked. I wasn't supposed to say anything about Meredith. But my better nature won out. Thank you for inspiring me." Daniel's twisted smile left no doubt about the insincerity of his words.

Camille was on her cell phone before she even left the interview room. She was nearly out the door when Daniel's voice stopped her.

"And just like that, you're leaving? I thought we'd only gotten started."

When she turned back to him, she saw the monster in all its hideous glory. As much as she hoped to be prepared for its return, she wasn't. "I couldn't have been more wrong. You do deserve to rot in here."

"I certainly won't disagree. But that's neither here nor there. What's really important is that this may be the last time I see you. I should at least get a proper goodbye."

Against her better judgment, Camille approached him. Her hand was balled up in a tight fist and ready to be swung with the worst of intentions. Daniel sensed what was coming and closed his eyes, steeling himself for the blow. But before Camille could take proper aim, the echo of Crawley's stern voice ricocheted off the walls.

"Camille, that's enough."

She turned to see him standing in the doorway. He had a cell phone in his hand and a troubled expression on his face.

"Let's go."

She quickly followed him out of the room. As the door closed behind her, she heard Daniel's last words, muffled and distant.

"Good luck, Camille. You're going to need…"

5

A POSSIBLE TARGET

"I'VE TRIED GETTING MEREDITH PARK on the phone, but she's not answering," Crawley said as he and Camille rushed inside the monitoring room. "If we can't reach her, I think we should consider sending a couple of patrols to her hotel to bring her in."

"How do we know MacPherson isn't bluffing?" Hitchcock asked, apparently not so eager to deploy precious department resources where they weren't absolutely necessary.

"Exactly," Pratt added. "It was obvious he wanted to get under Camille's skin from the outset. His tactics weren't working, so he said something that he thought would rile her up. It's highly unlikely that he would be aware of an impending attack against Meredith Park or anyone else. He's completely isolated in there."

"Unless he really is the one pulling strings and arranged something ahead of time," Mendoza countered.

Camille kept an eye on monitor three as two uniformed officers approached Daniel, unshackled him from the table, and led him out of the room. He glanced into the camera as he walked past it. The look of perverse delight present on his face for much of their encounter had suddenly morphed into something more solemn.

"It's impossible to know if he's bluffing or not," Camille said to Hitchcock. "But I'm not willing to risk Meredith's life by assuming he is, and I hope no one else is either."

Crawley responded by redialing her number.

"I'll send a unit out," Hitchcock said. "Where is she staying?"

"The downtown Westin," Camille replied.

The lieutenant nodded and left the room.

"Still no answer," Crawley reported. "When was the last time you spoke with her?"

"Just yesterday," Camille answered. "She's been meeting with the press nonstop since being out here. There's apparently a news conference scheduled for today that she wanted me to be a part of. I politely declined."

"A good idea under the circumstances," Crawley said. "We should advise her to cool it with the media too."

"The constant exposure probably made her a target to begin with," Mendoza theorized. "Now we have the specter of MacPherson's threats. I get that she cares about Jacob, but this seems like an awful lot of trouble to go through. Did she have a relationship with him beyond being his agent?"

Camille shook her head. "She claims it was business and nothing more. I believe her."

"Then why put herself through all of this?" Pratt asked.

"Because she blames herself for Jacob's disappearance. It was her idea to change the focus of the book from Sykes to me. It was her idea to have Jacob come here to pitch the book. Meredith feels that if she hadn't done that, he wouldn't be in the position he's in right now."

"And neither would your father," Pratt added.

Camille stiffened. "None of this is her fault."

"No one thinks it is," Crawley affirmed.

"But Daniel likely blames her for the Sykes biography," Agent Wells chimed in. "As Jacob's agent, she would've known about the book proposal before anyone else. She may have even been the one to encourage him to seek out Daniel and the other family members for the initial interviews. Wasn't that what set this whole thing in motion in the first place?"

Camille immediately thought back to something Daniel said: "*I'm sure I'm not the only one with an ax to grind, Camille. There were twenty-six other people killed by Sykes's hand.*" And for each of those twenty-six, there could have been at least one family member or close friend with the same animus toward Camille that Daniel had. The search for his accomplice would have to begin there. She filed the revelation away for another time and turned back to Wells.

"You're absolutely right. And that makes it even less likely that Daniel is bluffing."

"Which means we'd better find Meredith right now," Crawley added. "Camille, did she tell you where this news conference was supposed to take place?"

"The first two were at her hotel, and I'm assuming this one will be as well. It isn't scheduled to begin until one o'clock." She glanced at her watch, noting the time of ten-forty-six A.M. "That still gives us time to find out for sure. I say we follow the patrol unit to her hotel."

"Agreed," Crawley said. "The last thing we want is for her to show up on television again. Like Allison said, it's only making her more of a target."

"Okay, let's go."

Camille was the first to leave the monitoring room. The others followed closely behind.

She was dialing Meredith's cell phone number as she slid into the passenger's seat of Crawley's car. He hadn't been able to reach her and Camille didn't expect to do any better, but she thought that the message about Daniel would be much better coming from her than Crawley. He wasn't known for having a soft touch when it came to delivering bad news. To her surprise, Meredith answered on the second ring.

"Hi, Camille."

"Meredith, I'm so glad to hear your voice. Agent Crawley has been trying to reach you."

"You mean that joyless stuffed-shirt you're working with? What did he want?"

"We need to see you right away."

The sarcasm in Meredith's tone instantly disappeared. "What's the matter?"

"Where are you now?"

"I'm at the hotel prepping for my news conference, a news conference that I would still like for you to be a part of, by the way."

"I can't do that."

"I really wish you would reconsider."

"I don't think you should do it either."

"Why not?"

"We're on our way."

"Who's *we*?"

"Myself, Agent Crawley, and a patrol unit from the DPD."

Camille heard something that sounded like a gasp come through the phone. "What on earth for?"

"I'll explain everything when I get there. In the meantime, don't leave your hotel room until you know we've arrived."

"You're really freaking me out, Camille."

"Just stay put until we get there."

Camille turned to Crawley after she hung up. "Meredith is at the hotel."

"I gathered. How did she sound?"

"She's scared to death. And I can't really say that I blame her."

6

AN ABUNDANCE OF CAUTION

MEREDITH PARK'S SUITE was a corner unit overlooking downtown's bustling Seventeenth Street. The luxurious space was almost twice the size of Camille's apartment, complete with two bathrooms, a separate bedroom, wrap-around balcony, and two fully functional workspaces that she used to prepare for the two press conferences she'd thus far given. The setup was impressive, and Camille imagined that she was paying an ungodly sum to stay here.

But the stately surroundings suited her. Even in a drape-front blouse and faded blue jeans, Meredith was the definition of Upper East Side elegance. She looked at the group through a pair of gold-rimmed Cartier eyeglasses as nervous hands pulled her dark brown hair into a tight ponytail. "I apologize if I seem a bit out of sorts. I wasn't expecting Camille to arrive with such a formidable entourage." Despite the anxiety that her guests undoubtedly inspired, the composure in her sharp, pretty face didn't falter for a second.

"Sorry to barge in like this," Camille said. "I realize there are an awful lot of us."

"I feel like a bona fide VIP," Meredith replied with a tense smile. "I don't think the president gets this much attention."

"We're here out of an abundance of caution and nothing more," Crawley assured her.

"Is that why there are two police officers standing outside my door?"

Camille motioned to the large couch in the center of the room. "Do you mind if we sit? I'll be happy to explain."

She and Crawley sat down opposite Meredith while the three other agents fanned out to separate corners of the suite. Meredith eyed the trio warily.

"So what's this about?"

"Daniel MacPherson," Camille said.

"What about him?"

"He and I met about an hour ago. As you know, he hasn't said much since he's been in custody. I thought I'd have better luck getting through to him."

"And did you?"

"I pressed for information about who abducted Jacob and my father. He didn't offer any, of course. But in the midst of the conversation, a name did come up."

"Whose?"

"Yours."

Meredith's brown eyes grew wide with concern. "What did he say?"

Camille and Crawley exchanged a glance, each hoping the other would take the question. When Crawley didn't speak, Camille knew that she'd been volunteered.

"He claimed that the person holding them would reach out to me with a specific set of instructions that I'm supposed to follow. He didn't say what I would be instructed to do. But he did say that if I didn't follow those instructions exactly as they were laid out, someone would die."

"Me?"

Camille hesitated before answering. "Yes."

The sound of Meredith's gasp filled the suite.

"But we have no reason to suspect that he or anyone else is prepared to make good on the threat. As Agent Crawley said, we're only here out of an abundance of caution."

"I'm afraid that doesn't sound any more convincing than when Agent Crawley said it."

"Daniel has been closely monitored," Agent Pratt chimed in from across the room. "He hasn't had contact with anyone since being inside. There's a good chance this was simply a ploy to antagonize us."

Meredith looked to Camille for confirmation.

"We certainly have to keep all options on the table at this point. But considering Daniel's unwillingness to give us a straight answer before now, it's difficult to take his claims with anything more than a grain of salt."

Meredith abruptly stood up and began pacing the room, clearly unmoved by the attempts to reassure her. "This can't be happening," she mumbled to herself. "Why would he choose me?"

"We haven't seen evidence to suggest that he has," Crawley said.

"But you know it's likely true. You wouldn't be here otherwise."

"We don't know that it's true," Camille reiterated. "You also have to remember who the source is. Daniel hasn't exactly been a wealth of information before now. And as Agent Pratt said, he's been locked up for nearly three weeks with no communication from the outside world. Does the nature of his threat concern us? Of course it does. But this whole thing has been little more than a game to Daniel. And this threat may simply be more of the same."

"She's right," Pratt said. "He's done what he came here to do and now he considers his work to be finished. Since he no longer has anything to lose, he can toy around with us as much as he wants to with no fear of the consequences. Then he gets to watch from the safety of his jail cell as we scramble for a response. Clearly, he's getting off on this."

As much as Camille wanted to disagree with him on principle alone, she couldn't. Meredith, on the other hand, looked less than convinced.

"So, you come in here with an army of FBI agents, scare the shit out of me with news that a threat has been made against my life, then proceed to tell me that the threat isn't credible? What's next? You leave and tell me to have a nice day?" Meredith addressed the question to Camille, but Crawley took it upon himself to answer.

"Of course not. The officers will monitor you for the rest of the day. After that, we'll assign a detail to stay with you until the threat has been properly assessed. You'll be safe, Mrs. Park. You have our word."

"You also have our word that we'll figure out what's happening," Agent Mendoza added. "We've arranged for the DPD to detain Daniel for further questioning. If they can't get him to talk, we'll step in again. We have the best people working on this." She glanced at Camille before turning back to Meredith, steely conviction in her warm eyes. "We'll get to the truth, one way or another."

It was the first time that Camille had heard Mendoza speak at any length. Her tough talk was clearly more the result of youthful exuberance than seasoned field experience, but Camille appreciated it nonetheless. If she hung around Mendoza long enough, perhaps some of that exuberance would even rub off on her.

"We certainly will," Camille concurred, doing so for her own benefit as much as anyone else's.

Before Meredith could give voice to the relief apparent on

her face, Crawley added, "But there is one other thing we need to discuss first."

Meredith stiffened. "I'm afraid to ask."

"Your news conferences."

"What about them?"

"We feel your recent appearances on television may have put you in a compromised position. It's clear from your statements that you were close to Jacob Deaver and you have a lot invested in his current situation. But we can't rule out your high visibility as a catalyst for Daniel's threat."

"You can't possibly think that I'm responsible for this," Meredith snapped. "I'm doing what I have to do to make sure that Jacob and Paul come home. I won't allow their disappearance to become some back-burner story that no one cares about a week from now. Jacob is in this situation largely because of me, and I refuse to turn my back on him." She looked at Camille. "Or your father."

"No one is asking you to turn your back on them," Crawley emphasized. "We're simply asking you to keep a lower profile until we can figure out what we're dealing with."

"And who will speak on Jacob and Paul's behalf in the meantime? With all due respect, your agency hasn't exactly been burning up the airwaves with updates."

Crawley's jaw tightened. "Our investigation is still in its early stages, Mrs. Park. We only speak to the media when we determine the news is worth reporting. Right now, there isn't anything worth reporting."

"But don't you think it's good for the public to at least know that you're working toward something?"

"Not particularly," Crawley said bluntly.

"Speaking from personal experience, it's rare to see field agents from the Behavioral Analysis team address the media concerning an active investigation," Wells explained. "I'm sure Camille can attest to that based on her time in the Bureau."

"He's right," Camille confirmed, even as she tried to push away memories of the media firestorm directed at her in the aftermath of Daniel Sykes's violent apprehension. In the weeks following, news outlets from around the world jockeyed for the rights to her story. Some offered enough money to cover her Bureau salary for five years. But she granted only a single interview, which turned out to be a front-page feature in the Washington Times. She couldn't help but wonder if it was that interview that proved to be the fuel for Daniel MacPherson and her father's abductor. "Agents do their best to stay out of the public view while they're conducting fieldwork, particularly in cases like this."

"But this case is different," Meredith insisted. "This is your father. Normal rules shouldn't apply."

The statement hit Camille like a baseball bat to the chest. She attempted to respond, but her lungs couldn't find the strength to produce the words.

"We're aware that you asked Camille to join the news conference you've scheduled for today," Crawley said. "She was absolutely right to decline the offer."

"But Camille is the reason this story matters to the public in the first place. People go missing every day, Agent Crawley. There may be a thirty-second blurb about them, what they looked like, or where they were last seen, and usually, that's it. And as I understand it, the FBI isn't in the business of investigating local missing-persons cases. This case matters because one of the missing is a former police officer who happens to be the father of a well-known FBI agent. Hearing from Camille directly will only make the case matter more."

"Or she could make the situation worse by provoking her father's abductor," Pratt speculated.

"But how do you know he can't be reasoned with?" Meredith asked. "Isn't it at least worth taking the chance?"

Crawley shook his head. "We don't know the first thing about who we're dealing with, what his motives are, or what triggers him. What if Camille goes on television and says something he doesn't like? We have no idea how he'd react. Absent that knowledge, it's not worth taking the risk."

"I'm afraid I have to disagree," Camille said, not giving herself a chance to consider the gravity of the spontaneous statement.

Crawley's eyes communicated the gravity for her. "What?"

"Like you said, we have no idea who this guy is. He abducted my father and Jacob over three weeks ago, and the only communication we've received from him are those cryptic letters with the names of his victims. Don't you think it's odd that he hasn't attempted to reach out to us again?"

"What are you suggesting is the reason for that?"

"He may be waiting for us to reach out to him."

"To say what?" Pratt asked with what sounded like genuine curiosity.

"Perhaps it's nothing more than a public acknowledgment that he holds all the cards," Camille answered.

"A personal appeal to his power," Agent Wells added. "There's hardly a person alive who doesn't respond to a good ego stroke. It could certainly be a start."

Crawley looked skeptical. "And how do you plan on framing this acknowledgment of his power? We sure as hell can't coddle him."

"I have no desire to coddle him," Camille responded with a hint of irritation. "But I do think we need to send him some sort of message."

"Whatever that message is, it needs to be subtle," Mendoza asserted.

"And it shouldn't be at all confrontational," Wells added. "At least not yet."

"Do you agree with this approach?" Crawley asked the group.

"Camille has a point about the lack of communication," Mendoza said. "If he is waiting for us to reach out, we should probably oblige."

"There is risk in it, but I have to agree," Wells confirmed.

Crawley looked to the lone holdout. "What about you, Agent Pratt?"

Camille braced herself for the inevitable push-back that had thus far been Pratt's signature reaction. Instead, he eyed her with a gaze that bordered on sympathetic.

"Do you really think you can handle that? You've been through enough of these pressure-cooker situations with the media to know that it rarely ends well. All it takes is one invasive or inappropriate question to send the signal to the rest of the vultures that it's feeding time. I'm sure they'd love nothing more than to goad you into some outburst of emotion, and given the circumstances, that may not be diffi-cult to do. No offense, but we can't afford to have you crack right now. We have a big job ahead of us. All hands are needed."

Camille couldn't decide how to take his statement, so she addressed it as neatly as she could. "I know what's at stake here, not just for me personally, but for the entire scope of this investigation. I can handle it."

Apparently satisfied with the response, Pratt turned to Crawley. "If we can keep her statement tight and control the Q and A, I suppose we can give it a shot."

Camille looked at Pratt. When he looked back, she saw that the hard-edge had softened somewhat. They were still a long way from burying the proverbial hatchet, but it was progress.

"Seeing as I'm grossly outnumbered, I won't even bother casting my vote," Crawley said with a sigh of resignation. "So, let's talk logistics."

"The first thing we need to do is control the environment," Pratt began. "Should we consider staging it at the CBI building?"

Mendoza shook her head. "It's not an official CBI press conference. We might be better off keeping it here, so long as we can thoroughly vet the participants."

"I agree," Crawley said. "Mrs. Park, how large is the media contingent?"

"There's one cameraman from a local telecast, and writers from three local papers, including the Post."

"That number may grow once they learn that Camille will be there," Wells speculated.

"Then we'd better make sure no one finds out," Camille said. "Fewer reporters means fewer questions."

Crawley turned to Meredith. "Tell your contacts that the presser is still on and that you'll be the only one attending. If they ask what you'll be talking about, inform them that you have updates, but try and keep the details as vague as possible. We want them to come, but we don't want them to think it's important enough to bring their friends along."

"I'll start making the calls," Meredith said as she walked to a nearby desk to retrieve her cell phone.

"While she's doing that, we should probably get to work on your statement," Crawley said to Camille.

"If I'm going to talk to him effectively, my words can't sound rehearsed, Camille replied. "I certainly won't say something I shouldn't, but I can't roll out there with some carefully-crafted speech either. He'll see right through it."

"Then let's at least create a framework of what you should and shouldn't say. That way, you still have some room to improvise if you need to."

Camille nodded her understanding, though she had no plans to improvise.

"What about MacPherson?" Pratt asked. "Should one of us head back to Major Crimes to monitor the follow-up interview?"

"Lieutenant Hitchcock insisted that his guys Parsons and Krieger could handle it," Wells reported.

"Parsons and Krieger haven't handled anything so far," Mendoza said. "They've barely gotten two words out of him."

"We have to toe a fine line with the locals," Wells warned. "We go in there and start telling Hitchcock that his people aren't good enough and he may try to shut us out altogether. We have the flashy federal shields, but this is still his town."

"Does anyone have a better suggestion?" Crawley asked.

"I know the perfect person to handle the interview," Camille answered without hesitation. "But it might require a few swings of that battle ax you call an FBI badge."

Crawley allowed a tight half-smile to crease the corner of his face. "No problem at all. You just tell me where to aim."

7

THE COMING STORM

THE ONLY THING IN THE WORLD that Detective Chloe Sullivan hated more than an unsolved case was an unsolved case that she wasn't allowed to work.

When Camille Grisham's father was reported missing three weeks ago, Chloe was the first to respond to the call. It was Chloe who collected the initial statements from Camille and Meredith Park. It was Chloe who drew the first concrete link between Paul Grisham's disappearance and the disappearance of Jacob Deaver. And it was Chloe who rightly concluded that their prime suspect, Daniel MacPherson, was not working alone. But for reasons not explained until much later, the case was abruptly reassigned to another team of detectives before her investigation could gain the proper traction.

Her burgeoning friendship with Camille was the eventual justification. An investigation conducted with personal stakes could hardly be impartial, Lieutenant Hitchcock reasoned. And because Chloe had a personal stake in this investigation, she couldn't be allowed anywhere near it. It didn't matter that half the department shared an association with Paul

Grisham that went beyond professional. In Hitchcock's mind, Chloe was the only one too close to the situation to be of reliable use.

She suspected there were other factors at play, not the least of which was the ongoing Internal Affairs probe of her former partner Walter Graham, and his connection to an alleged murder-for-hire plot involving the mayor's husband Elliott Richmond and Camille's best friend, Julia Leeds. With Graham no longer alive to answer for those charges, Chloe was left to answer questions of her own; namely how much she knew about her partner's dealings. Though she was cleared of any wrongdoing very early on, she couldn't help but wonder how much her reputation had been damaged by the association alone. But without hard evidence that personal bias was to blame for her reassignment, she abandoned the thought; along with any hope that her participation in this still-unsolved case, as desperately as it was needed, would ever be a realistic possibility.

This explained why Chloe found herself at a complete loss for words as she sat inside Lieutenant Hitchcock's office, staring at the case file that had been placed in front of her.

"I'm assuming you know what this is," Hitchcock said as he pointed to the words DANIEL MAC/ COPYCAT written in red ink across the top.

Chloe nodded as her mind scrambled to formulate the proper response. "But I don't understand why I'm looking at it."

"I'd like you to familiarize yourself with its contents. There have been a few developments in the case since you filed the first report, and you need to be completely up to speed before we send you in there."

"Send me in where?"

"Interview Room Three. That's where we're holding him."

"Daniel MacPherson?"

"Yes."

"What's he doing in there?"

"Camille Grisham was here earlier today, along with Special Agent Peter Crawley and the BAU task force. She sat down with MacPherson for a rather interesting interview session."

"From what I've heard, Daniel hasn't talked to anyone."

"Apparently he saved himself for Camille."

It was a surprising development, to say the least, but Chloe maintained a neutral expression.

"Did he disclose anything significant?"

"We believe it's extremely significant."

"What did he say?"

"It's detailed on the last page of the report."

Chloe picked up the file and quickly read its contents. "So where do I come in?"

"Camille and the BAU team are busy following up on the information MacPherson provided, but they want to make sure he doesn't know more than he's telling. I need you to figure that out."

Chloe shuddered at the euphoric surge of adrenaline that coursed through her body. "But this isn't my case. Why not send in Krieger and Parsons?"

"Because they haven't been able to get through to him. It was thought that you might do better."

Chloe wondered if it was Camille who made the recommendation but saw no benefit in asking the question. "Are Krieger and Parsons okay with this?"

"Not really, but they're big boys. They'll get over it. No one here doubts your ability, Chloe."

"Including you?"

"Especially me."

"But you took me off the case before I could even—"

"That was a mistake, and I'm attempting to rectify it. Are you interested in helping?"

Chloe fought to contain her enthusiasm. "Absolutely."

"Then get caught up and meet us inside the monitoring room in ten minutes."

"Can I bring Greer?"

"Bring the Pope if you need to. Just be quick about it."

Ten minutes later, Chloe and her partner Marcus Greer were making their way to the monitoring station where Hitchcock, Krieger, and Parsons had already situated themselves.

"So, what do you think accounts for the lieutenant's change of heart?" Greer asked as he eyed the last page of the file.

"If I had to guess, I'd say he was persuaded by someone higher up the chain."

"Camille Grisham's crew?"

Chloe shrugged. "We'll probably never know. Whoever it was, let's just make sure we don't disappoint them."

"Camille is a friend, so I know this one means more to you than most," Greer said. "I've got your back all the way, sport."

In the short time that he'd been her partner, Greer found ways to prove that on a daily basis. She doubted this day would be any different.

"I don't know what this place would be like without you, Marcus. But I hope I don't have to find out anytime soon."

"If I have my way, we'll still be catching bad guys when we're old enough to swap stories about the great-grandkids."

Chloe smiled at the thought. "You ready to catch one right now?"

"Hell yeah."

They walked into the monitoring room to see Hitchcock, Krieger, and Parsons huddled around a screen. Chloe assumed they were looking at Daniel. "We're here, lieutenant."

"Good," Hitchcock said as he glanced up from the monitor. "Any last-minute questions before you go in?"

Chloe shook her head. "The directive is pretty clear: Find out if he's really telling the truth about Meredith Park, and if he is, figure out what else he knows."

"Easier said than done, but that's the gist of it."

Chloe then looked to Krieger and Parsons. "Any advice about how we should approach him?"

"If the lieutenant's right, you'll end up teaching us a few things," Krieger said with a tight expression. "All we can do is wish you luck."

Chloe nodded, doing her best to empathize with Krieger's wounded ego. She hoped it was nothing that a round or two of beers couldn't eventually smooth over.

"If there are no more questions, it's time to get the show on the road," Hitchcock directed.

When Chloe glanced at monitor three, she saw Daniel staring into a space off-screen. He sat perfectly still, and for a moment, she thought that the feed had been paused. Then she heard the rattle of his leg shackles as he stretched. Chained to the table like the dangerous animal that the world thought him to be, he was a disturbing picture of calm. It was only then that she truly appreciated the weight of the task ahead of her.

If you have any magic in your law enforcement arsenal, now's the time to work it, Chloe mused as she opened the door.

Daniel remained still as she and Greer entered the room. If their sudden presence bothered him, he went to great lengths not to show it.

"Good afternoon," Chloe began as she took a seat in the chair nearest him. "I understand you've been hanging out for a while. Would you like anything before we get started? Coffee? Soda? A bite to eat?"

Daniel's blank expression was briefly colored by irritation as he shifted in his chair.

"Dehydration is no joke, Mr. MacPherson. Let me at least get you some water," Greer offered with overdone exuberance. "You sit tight. I'll be right back."

A hint of amusement flashed across Daniel's face as Greer left the room. By the time he turned to Chloe, his smile had grown cold. "I take it he's the good cop."

She met his icy sneer with one of her own. "We're both good cops."

"Better than those other two? Krieger and the fat one?"

"You've already said more to me than you did to them, so I guess you answered your own question."

"Touché. Detective?"

"Sullivan. My partner's name is Greer."

"You mean the good cop."

Chloe struggled to suppress her sudden irritation. "Sure. Is it okay if I call you Daniel?"

"I don't see why not."

"Thank you." She allowed an extended silence to settle between them as she shuffled the papers inside the file folder.

After a few moments, Daniel broke the silence by placing his chained hands on the table. "So what brings you by, Detective Sullivan?"

"Not much," she said as she casually looked up from the file. "I just want to talk."

"About what?"

"Whatever's on your mind?"

"Why would you assume that something is on my mind?"

Chloe shrugged. "You've been sitting in this cold, empty room by yourself for over three hours. I'm sure you've had questions."

"I know exactly why I'm here if that's what you're getting at."

"You do?"

"Yes. And so do you, so let's not B.S. each other. The fat detective tried that tactic. That's probably why he and his partner have been relegated to watching me through there." Daniel pointed to the camera mounted in the corner. "Please don't drop the ball like they did."

"Fair enough. I'll cut right to the chase then. Tell me about the threat against Meredith Park."

"You weren't kidding when you said you'd cut right to the chase."

"Answer the question."

"And I'm supposed to tell you because?"

"Because deep down, you actually want to do the right thing. Otherwise, you never would've mentioned it."

Daniel's eyes briefly lost their focus as he became lost in thought. He quickly shook it off. "It's nice that you think so highly of me, but I'm worried your faith might be misguided."

Chloe smiled, sensing her first breakthrough. "My hunches are rarely wrong."

Daniel edged forward in his chair. "What else are your hunches telling you?"

"That the information you gave Camille Grisham only represents a fraction of what you actually know."

"So this is about Camille."

"It's about Meredith."

"No, it's actually about Camille."

"Tell me why you think that."

"Why not ask her. You're friends, right?"

"I'd rather hear it from you."

Daniel slid back in his chair. "Maybe I was just trying to

scare her. Maybe none of it is true at all. Did you ever consider that?"

Chloe nodded. "It's been considered. In fact, most of the people looking through that camera think you're lying. They say it's impossible that you'd know any of the things you told Camille. You haven't spoken with anyone since you've been in custody, so in their minds, you couldn't possibly be privy to someone else's plan. And they sure as hell don't think that you could've arranged it yourself."

Something faltered in Daniel's face. "Is that so?"

"Unfortunately, it is," Chloe answered, knowing full well that it wasn't. While there were concerns about the veracity of Daniel's claims, nearly everyone connected to the case, from Hitchcock to Camille's team, had no choice but to operate as if the claims were true. But Daniel didn't need to know that. Not yet, anyway.

"You don't really think that, do you, detective? Otherwise, you wouldn't be here."

"It doesn't matter what I think. I'm simply asking the questions."

Daniel took a deep breath to steady his labored breathing. "Well, they're stupid to think I'm lying."

"Are they?"

"Don't try and play mind games with me. You have no idea what I actually know."

"Then help me understand."

"Where is Camille now?"

"That's none of your concern."

"Is she with Meredith Park?"

"I said that's none of your concern."

"I'll assume that's a yes."

"Assume whatever you'd like."

"You'll understand very soon. And so will Camille. The storm is about to hit."

"The storm?"

Daniel's self-satisfied demeanor made an abrupt and unwelcome return. "That's right. But don't worry. We'll be plenty safe here. We can ride it out together. You, me, and the good cop. Speaking of which, where is Detective Greer with that water? The anticipation suddenly has me feeling parched."

"Who's playing mind games now?"

"You're right," Daniel said with feigned contrition. "That doesn't really serve a purpose."

"But honesty does."

"I am being honest."

"You're speaking in riddles. If you were truly being honest, you'd tell me exactly what's going to happen and when."

"The *what* will speak for itself. As far as the *when*…"

"Yes?"

"What time is it?"

Chloe begrudgingly checked her watch. "Twelve-eighteen."

"If all goes well, it will be in less than an hour."

A sharp current of anxiety stirred inside Chloe's chest. "What happens in less than an hour?"

When Daniel smiled, his light eyes grew dark. "Turn on the television at one o'clock, and you just might find out."

8

THE MESSENGER

THE CURTIS ROOM was a small meeting space located on the mezzanine level of the hotel. It could comfortably accommodate a media pool of twenty-five with plenty of room to spare. But Camille was hoping for a far more modest turnout.

She waited impatiently inside a nearby room with Crawley and Wells while Agents Pratt and Mendoza monitored the activity of the Curtis.

"How much time?" Wells asked.

Camille could sense Crawley's nervousness as he checked his watch.

"It's twelve fifty-seven. Meredith's statement shouldn't last more than two minutes. That gives us five minutes total. Still enough time to call it off, Camille."

"I'm not calling it off."

Crawley nodded. "Once your heels are dug in, there's no moving you. I should know that by now."

"I thought you were one of the few people who actually admired my pathological bullheadedness."

"Indeed."

Camille's thin attempt at humor did nothing to lighten the mood, just as the cup of ginger tea she'd been sipping on for the past half hour did nothing to relax the tightness in her stomach. "What are the chances the statement will be telecast live?"

"Meredith said there would be at least one camera. I doubt they'd have a satellite truck on standby for something this small, but anything's possible."

"Even if they want to go live once you walk in, there won't be enough time to set up," Wells added.

"That's right. You're in there for five minutes, tops. When you're done, we get you out before the first question can be asked."

Crawley's plan sounded good, and Camille really hoped it would play out that way. But she was also prepared for the unexpected. The basics of the statement had been outlined in her head several times, but with nothing written down, she couldn't account for what would actually come out of her mouth once she was in front of a microphone. She hadn't so much as uttered her father's name in public before now, let alone discussed his abduction. Emotions that had been successfully bottled up for the past three weeks suddenly had the potential to burst wide open, like a weakened levy buckling under a relentless water surge. And it could happen in front of the entire world.

But that was the chance she had to take. This statement would possibly be her only chance to control the narrative with her father's abductor, and assuming her hunch was right that he was waiting to hear from her, she couldn't be afraid to let him hear the rawest, most unfiltered version of Camille possible. She couldn't speak to him as an FBI consultant. She had to speak to him as a grieving daughter. And she could only pray that there was enough empathy left in him to listen.

Crawley rechecked his watch. "One o'clock. Should be any minute now."

On cue, Agent Pratt walked in. "We're all set out there."

Crawley nodded. "Numbers?"

"Five so far."

"Meredith said there would only be four," Wells recalled.

"Who are they?" Camille asked.

Pratt looked at the notepad on which he'd written the names. "Sarah Kline from the Post, Amy Bloom from Westword, Mitchell Harris, the cameraman from Seven News, Jeremy Durant from the Denver Daily Mail, and Will Freeman from the Mile-High Dispatch."

"Did they check out?"

"We cross-referenced their credentials with the staff directories of each organization. They're all legit."

Camille turned to Crawley. "Which one is the newbie?"

"No way to know. Maybe Meredith undercounted."

"Maybe," Camille said, unsure why the addition of one would even matter. For reasons she couldn't explain, it did.

Crawley put a hand on her shoulder. "Time to say hello."

Camille took in a deep breath and held it. After a long eight count, she slowly exhaled until there was nothing left of the anxiety that had settled inside her chest. With her focus restored, she led the group out of the room. "Let's do it."

She kept her eyes on Meredith as she entered the Curtis. Aside from a few murmurs upon her arrival, no one in the media contingent spoke.

"And now, Camille Grisham would like to offer a brief statement," Meredith said as she vacated her seat in front of the small cluster of microphones and digital recorders laid out on the table.

Camille turned to survey the faces in the crowd, then took Meredith's seat. Beyond the sea of unfamiliar onlookers, she spotted Pratt and Mendoza in the back of the room. Crawley and Wells stood near the door.

"Thank you, Meredith. I appreciate the chance to speak." She paused to review the outline in her head, but its once familiar contents were suddenly blurred and distant. She closed her eyes to clear the haze.

When she opened them, she was immediately drawn to the man standing on her right. His short, round frame was perched against the wall as if he were using it to keep himself upright. The ID card attached to his lanyard told her that he was just another member of the press. But something was off. His polite smile did little to mask the nervousness in his puffy eyes. Unable to hold her gaze, he looked down at his notepad and attempted to write something, but trembling hands made the task difficult. He looked back at her, then at Crawley and Wells, then behind him at Pratt and Mendoza, as if he was concerned with being noticed. When no one returned his attention, he turned back to his notepad and attempted to write again.

Unsure of what she was seeing, Camille kept her focus on him as she began speaking.

"There was a lot of debate about whether or not I should address the issue of my father's abduction publicly. I've personally gone back and forth on the question several times. But with the current circumstances being what they are, I feel that this is the ideal time to come forward. Many of you may not know this, but I'm working with the FBI and local law enforcement as a consultant on this case. While I can't speak on the particulars of my role, I can tell you that the men and women on the front lines of the investigation are the finest that their agencies have to offer, and I feel fully confident in their ability to bring about the resolution we're all hoping for."

Camille paused to allow the rising swell in her chest to

pass. As she did, she observed the man to her right feverishly scribbling on his notepad. The trembling in his hands had appeared to stop, and his once bulging eyes were narrow and focused. When he finished writing, he checked his watch, then looked at Camille in anticipation of what she'd say next.

Convinced that she may have planted red flags where they weren't necessary, she turned her attention to Crawley, eager to use a friendly face to guide her through the rest of the statement.

"But as of right now, we're a long way from that resolution. That's why I'd like to take this time to address the person or persons who abducted Jacob Deaver and my father, Paul Grisham." With the carefully constructed outline now wholly torn away from her memory, Camille closed her eyes, opened her heart, and allowed the words to flow without the restriction of forethought.

"My father is the wisest, kindest, most decent man to ever walk the planet. I understand that I'm incredibly biased, but I defy anyone who has ever known Paul Anthony Grisham to say otherwise. If you've talked to him for any amount of time, I'm sure you know that too. He was a Denver police officer for twenty-five years. He's experienced the worst that the world has to offer. He's dealt with human beings at their absolute lowest. Yet through it all, he remained committed to seeing only the good. Don't get me wrong, he's no saint. He can't part the seas or turn water into wine – though I think he'd like to sometimes. But Paul is a man who values life; his and everyone else's. He values yours too. But you don't have to take my word for it. Just talk to him. Ask him who he is and what he believes. You'll get to know a man who is the kind of person that I could only dream of being."

When Camille opened her moist eyes, she quickly scanned the room. The reporters, including the man to her right, were all still. No one wrote in their notepads, no one checked their cell phones. All eyes were fixed on her; unprepared for the emotion of the moment, yet completely consumed by it. When she looked further, she saw Agent Mendoza standing in the back, dabbing at the corner of her eye while Pratt nervously looked down at his feet. Crawley, for his part, looked every bit the proud surrogate father as he urged her to continue with a reassuring nod.

Camille cleared the lump of emotion from her throat, found the camera stationed in the corner, and looked directly into it. "If you've done this because of something you have against me, please make it about me. Not them. They don't deserve this. It's not too late to change the outcome for the better. All the power rests with you. You can still do the right thing. I love my father more than anything in the world, and I miss him terribly. But I'm not asking this for myself. I'm asking for him. I'm asking for Jacob Deaver, a kid who hasn't even begun to live life yet. There's been enough suffering. Please, let them go. That's all I ask." She paused to gather her nerves one last time. "Thank you."

As she stood up, she felt a hand on her shoulder. "That was wonderful," Meredith whispered with a strained smile as she wiped a tear from her cheek.

Camille pulled her in for a hug. She'd been through a lot in the weeks since Jacob's disappearance. She grieved just like Camille did. And she did so while maintaining the bravest public face imaginable. After this experience, Camille had an even deeper appreciation for that bravery.

"We should probably go before the questions start," Meredith suggested.

Camille nodded her agreement as they quickly moved away from the table. Unfortunately, they weren't quick enough.

"*Camille, why are you involved in the case? Doesn't it represent a conflict of interest?*"

"Do you have an actual suspect? Or can we take this as a sign of desperation?"

"Is it true that these abductions are connected to the murders of those four college students?"

The barrage of questions hit her with furious efficiency.

Though there were only four reporters in the room, the white noise created by their simultaneous outburst made it feel like four-hundred. Camille suddenly found herself frozen where she stood; a deer caught in the light of an inevitable death that she was powerless to stop.

Before she could attempt to fend off the onslaught, she heard Crawley's booming voice rising above the din.

"As was explained before the press conference began, Camille will not be taking questions."

A tall red-head clad in a Motörhead t-shirt and faded blue jeans quickly responded. "But this is the first time the public has heard from anyone connected to the case. Don't you think they have the right to know where things stand?"

"Of course, and we'll be sure to offer a more thorough briefing when the information warrants."

"Do you at least have a solid suspect?"

Crawley waved off the question as he took Camille by the elbow to lead her out of the room.

Determined to get an answer, the reporter persisted. "What about Daniel MacPherson? Is he still your main person of interest? And if so, why haven't we learned more about him? Are there things you're not telling us?"

"And who exactly are you?" Crawley asked, his frustration finally reaching critical mass.

"Will Freeman with the Mile-High Dispatch."

"Well, Mr. Freeman, I don't know what they teach you at the Mile-High Dispatch about professional etiquette, but when someone respectfully informs you that they won't be answering questions, especially when that someone has been through as much as Camille has, you'd do well to listen, lest you find yourself cut out of the information loop altogether."

The reporter smirked. "Is that a threat, sir?"

"More like a word to the wise."

With that, Crawley continued with Camille toward the door. Just as they crossed the threshold, another voice spoke up.

"You can't leave yet."

Camille turned around to the sight of the reporter whose jittery behavior first got her attention. He was standing only a few feet away, close enough for her to see that the anxiety had returned to his pale, weathered face. He extended a legal-sized piece of paper in her direction. His hand was shaking violently.

"You can't leave yet," he repeated in a cracked voice. "Not until you hear what he has to say."

The fear in his eyes told Camille that he wasn't a physical threat, so she took a step toward him. "Who?"

"Please, just take this," he said as he extended the paper further.

Out of the corner of her eye, Camille saw Pratt and Mendoza edge toward the man from behind. Pratt was reaching inside his jacket.

"No," she said to the pair as she put a hand up.

The man jumped as he spun around to see the agents standing only a few feet away.

Camille quickly redirected his attention. "It's okay. Talk to me."

He let out a heavy groan as he turned back to her. "This isn't my fault. These aren't my words. I need you to know that."

"I understand," Camille responded in the most reassuring voice that she could summon. "Can you tell me whose words they are?"

"I can't tell you because I don't know," he stammered. "But I assume it's the man you're looking for."

Camille looked at the paper in his hand. The thin bond allowed her to see that it contained a small-point text that covered the entire page. Certain words appeared to be typed in all caps for emphasis. "Tell me what it says."

Crawley stepped in front of her. "Absolutely not. And you," he pointed a stern finger at the cameraman. "Turn that off, right now."

"You can't," the man cried. "He explicitly said that if there was a camera present, it needed to record this."

"I don't know who *he* is, but *he* isn't in charge here."

"Maybe he is," Camille said before turning back to the reporter. "What's your name?"

"Jeremy Durant."

"From the Denver Daily Mail?"

He nodded.

"Okay, Jeremy. Can I ask a couple of questions?"

He nodded again.

"The man who wrote this message. Do you know him?"

"No."

"Then how did you receive it?"

"It was delivered to my office via courier."

"Addressed to you personally?"

"Yes."

"Was there more inside the envelope than that message?"

Jeremy hesitated before answering. "There was another note."

"What did it say?"

"To come here."

"Anything else?"

"Yes, but I can't tell you."

"Why not?" Crawley barked.

"Because he said that I couldn't share it with anyone. And if I did..."

"You were threatened?" Camille asked.

Jeremy nodded.

"Okay. I want you to tell me what's on that paper. But first, I need everyone else to take a deep breath and relax." She turned to Crawley. "That includes you."

Crawley's jaw tightened, but a quick nod let her know that he was prepared to stand down.

"Please, I really need you to know that I didn't have a choice," Jeremy reiterated. "He knew things about me. About my wife. I couldn't risk it."

"It's okay, Jeremy. No one is blaming you. Now take another deep breath and tell me what it says."

Jeremy tightened his grip on the letter. Each time he attempted to speak, his breath caught the words before they could escape. Eyes that were once clear and alert had now become soaked with dread and exhaustion as the bleak reality of the moment appeared to sink in. When he looked at the letter again, his breathing quickened into short bursts of spastic energy that he couldn't control.

"You have to calm down," Camille implored him. "If you don't, you're going to hyperventilate."

"My wife. You have to make sure she's sa—" The sudden wheezing in his chest stopped him before he could finish.

"Where's your wife now?"

"I don't know. I tried calling her at work, but she isn't answering."

"Okay, we'll do whatever we can to make sure she's safe," Camille said, not sure how she would actually do such a thing. "In the meantime, I need you to tell me what's in that message."

Jeremy took in a large pull of air and his breathing stabilized. "I'm not the one who's supposed to read it. I'm only supposed to make sure it's delivered."

"Who's supposed to read it?" Crawley asked.

Jeremy extended the paper toward Meredith. "She is." His other hand gestured to the camera. "And he says he'll be watching."

9

GUIDELINES

C AMILLE INSTINCTIVELY REACHED for the letter but stopped herself before she touched it. "Does anyone have gloves?"

"Right here," Wells said as he pulled out a pair from the inside pocket of his suit coat.

Camille took the gloves and slipped them over her hands. "Who else handled that aside from you?" she asked Jeremy.

"It was sealed in an envelope when the courier delivered it. I was the only one who touched the letter."

"We're going to need that envelope. Do you still have it?"

"It's on my desk."

Camille turned to Crawley. "We should have someone escort him back to his office to retrieve it."

"I can do that," Wells volunteered.

"We'll also need print comparisons for Mr. Durant and the courier once we find out who he is," Crawley added.

Camille nodded then turned back to Jeremy. "May I have the letter now?"

Jeremy swallowed hard as he gave it to her.

The first thing that Camille saw when she looked at it was Meredith's name. The sight sent an electric current through her body that momentarily weakened her knees. After regaining her footing, she read the rest of the message in silence; too startled by the words to give them an immediate voice.

"What does it say?" she heard an impatient Pratt ask. She ignored the question and continued reading. After a second pass to ensure that the words weren't something conjured up by the worst that her imagination had to offer, she looked at Crawley. "We need to get these people out of here."

The concern on Crawley's face was evident as he turned his attention to the media pool. "Okay, listen up. I need all cell phones and recording devices shut off immediately. If you don't comply, your devices will be confiscated. Is that understood?"

Most were rendered speechless by the shock of the moment, including Will Freeman, who managed nothing more than a nod.

"Good," Crawley said. "Now please clear the room."

At this, Jeremy Durant spoke up. "What about me?"

"You stay with us until we can get this sorted out," Camille answered.

"That's not what I mean. The instructions were clear that the camera was supposed to record everything. What if he thinks I didn't give Meredith the message? What happens to me? To my family?"

Before Camille could respond, she was forced to shield her eyes from the camera light that was suddenly pointed at her.

"I thought I told you to turn that off!" Crawley shouted with a ferocity that startled even Camille.

Shaken by the directive, the cameraman promptly pressed a button, and the light went dark. "It's off, it's off."

"I need everyone to leave, now," Crawley repeated in a slightly more measured voice. "The next time I have to ask, you'll be arrested for obstruction."

The still frazzled cameraman didn't even bother to break down his tripod as he scurried out of the room.

"It's obvious that something serious is happening here," Will Freeman said as he made his way to the door with the others. "Do you plan to brief us once you figure out what that something is?"

"Have a nice day, ladies and gentlemen," was all that Crawley said.

Before he crossed the door, Freeman turned to Camille. "We're not all bad, Agent Grisham. Some of us are actually here to help." He pulled out a card and handed it to her. "Just in case you need it."

Camille eyed him warily as he walked into the hallway. In her experience, they were all bad, and she doubted Will Freeman would be any different. Resisting the urge to rip the card into tiny pieces, she gave it a cursory glance. On the front was his name, along with the title Managing Editor. On the back was his handwritten cell phone number.

The weekly publication he worked for was little more than a tabloid rag, hardly on par with the city's more established news dailies; and as such, Camille couldn't foresee an instance when she'd take him up on the offer. Unable to find a trashcan to toss it in, she slipped the card inside her pocket without giving it another thought.

Once Freeman and the others were safely out of sight, Crawley closed the door and immediately turned his attention to the letter that was still in Camille's hand.

"Gloves?" he asked Wells. After receiving his own pair, he took the letter from Camille and began reading aloud. "Hello, Meredith. I regret that you have to read this message, almost as much as I have regrets composing it. Things should have never escalated to this point, but because of your unfortunate decision to involve Jacob in a matter that didn't concern him, we find ourselves here." Crawley paused to look at Camille.

"It gets better," she said solemnly.

Crawley continued. "I want to assure you that Jacob is safe, as is Camille Grisham's father. But I can make no guarantees that they will remain that way. For now, they are serving a purpose, as will you. Consider this letter a guideline for how you are to proceed. Do not, under any circumstances, deviate from this guideline. Failure to comply will have the gravest of consequences, both for you and my two guests. This isn't a trick. This isn't a ploy. This is the result of Camille Grisham's blatant carelessness, and the price she will pay for her cowardice. The price is hers to pay and hers alone. There is no reason for anyone else to suffer, least of all you. Simply do as I ask."

Crawley stopped reading to look at Meredith.

"Looks like your abundance of caution was justified," she said in a strained voice.

Unable to find a suitable response, Crawley turned back to the letter. "Before you read your directive, there are three rules you must abide by. Do not show it to anyone aside from Camille, do not discuss its contents with anyone aside from Camille, and do not take no for an answer. For every one of these rules that you break, at least one person will die."

"What's the directive?" Mendoza asked.

Crawley quickly scanned the rest of the letter. "He's demanding that Camille give a statement to the press, and he wants Meredith to facilitate it."

"But she's already given a statement," Wells said.

"He wants something very different."

"How different?" Pratt asked.

Crawley turned to Camille for the answer.

"He wants me to take full responsibility for the murders that Daniel Sykes committed." She paused to clear the lump in her throat. "Including Agent Sheridan."

"He can't be serious," Wells said.

"He's plenty serious," Crawley countered. "He's even included a script." He held up the five-paragraph statement that Camille was to read. "He says that she has to follow it word for word. If she doesn't..." He didn't bother finishing the sentence.

There was a drawn-out silence as the group caught its collective breath.

Pratt was the first to ask the question they were all likely thinking. "What the hell are we supposed to make of this?"

"It's obviously the communication we've been waiting for," Mendoza said before looking at Jeremy Durant. "If he's to be believed."

"And I'm not so sure that I do," Pratt said.

Jeremy fought back tears as he responded. "I swear to you, I don't have anything to do with this."

"Then tell us what the other note said," Crawley demanded.

Jeremy hesitated before answering. "It said that if I didn't deliver the message to Meredith exactly as instructed, or if I tried to warn her beforehand, my wife would be killed, and someone would be waiting at my house to do the same to me. He had our home address. He had my wife's work address. I didn't have a choice."

"Where's the other note?" Wells asked.

"Inside the envelope."

"Even if it happened the way you said it did, any whack-job off the street could've written that message," Pratt asserted.

"It would be easy to dismiss it as a hoax if it weren't for one thing," Camille said.

"Daniel MacPherson," Crawley added.

Pratt still appeared skeptical. "Are you saying he wrote the message?"

"I don't see how that's possible," Wells said. "Even if he could send correspondence, which he can't, that letter never would've made it past the security check. Not to mention the fact that he doesn't have access to a typewriter or computer."

Meredith let out a shallow breath. "So, do you have *any* idea who could have written it?"

"No," Crawley answered bluntly. "But if we're lucky, the letter itself can give us some answers." He turned to Pratt and Mendoza. "We need to get this to the CBI lab."

"We'll run it over right now," Pratt said with an excitement that Camille hadn't heard in his voice up to this point. He found an empty manila folder on a nearby table and handed it to Crawley. "You can put it in this." Once the letter was inside, Pratt and Mendoza quickly made their way out of the room.

"I'll escort Mr. Durant back to his office for the envelope," Wells said. "I can collect his prints then work on finding the courier."

Crawley nodded his approval. "We'll arrange to send DPD units to Mr. Durant's house as well as his wife's place of business. And Mr. Durant, you keep trying to get your wife on the phone. If there really is a threat here, we'll make sure the two of you are protected."

Jeremy could only nod as Wells ushered him out of the room.

Meredith grew agitated as she watched them leave. "What if he really is expecting Camille to read his statement today? Shouldn't we be talking about that?"

"That obviously can't happen," Crawley insisted. "We

have no idea who he is or what he has planned. And the possibility still exists that this is all a bluff anyway."

"I don't think it's a bluff," Camille asserted.

"We still can't risk it, not until we know more."

"You mean not until he makes good on his threat," a now trembling Meredith said. "You read the letter, and you know what he says will happen if we don't do what he wants. You can't risk putting Camille out there, and I get that. But what about the risk to me? Or to Jacob and Paul? Or to that reporter who was just here? If this is real, it's going to be one of us who ends up paying the price. And forgive my selfishness, but I fear it's going to be me."

"We can't assume that you'll be in any less danger if Camille complies with his demands, despite his promises to the contrary. And as far as your safety is concerned, the two officers we've assigned to you aren't going anywhere until the situation is resolved."

"From what I can see, you're nowhere near having the situation resolved."

We couldn't possibly be further away, Camille thought, wisely keeping the opinion to herself.

Fighting to wrangle in her frayed nerves, Meredith began pacing. "So what's your plan in the meantime?"

Camille looked to Crawley for the answer.

"I think we should hold tight for now. There must be more to this than having Camille go on television to apologize for Daniel Sykes's crimes. That wouldn't be enough to motivate someone to do the things he's done, especially because she's already openly expressed regret for how the investigation concluded. He doesn't want Paul or Jacob dead. Otherwise, we would've found them by now. They're being used for leverage, and until he gets what he wants, he'll continue to use them, despite his threats. If anything, not giving him what he wants may give us an advantage, at least temporarily. If he's frustrated enough, he'll attempt to reach out again; possibly expanding his communication to include us directly. The more he makes himself known, the higher the chances that he'll make a mistake that leads us to him."

It was little more than conjecture on Crawley's part, but Camille understood that conjecture often steered the direction of cases like this more than hard evidence. The grieving daughter in her wanted to do exactly as the message demanded. The FBI consultant knew that it would be the wrong move. Despite every cell in her body screaming at her to do otherwise, she sided with the consultant.

"I agree. He obviously wants more from me than some statement to the press, and I'm sure it won't be long before he asks for it. What we can't afford to do is sit around and wait."

"Speaking of the press, I'm guessing that some version of what happened here is going to end up on the news very soon," Crawley speculated.

"That might actually work in our favor, especially with Daniel."

"So you suggest we keep pushing him?"

"Right now, it might be our only chance at staying a step ahead. How he knew this was going to happen is irrelevant. What matters is that he knew. Now we have to focus on getting him to tell us what happens next."

"And you have faith that your person in Homicide can do that?"

"Right now, Detective Sullivan's ability is about the only thing I have faith in."

Crawley nodded. "I'll call Lieutenant Hitchcock to let him know what happened here and that we're on our way back. Once we're there, we can hook-up with Meredith's security detail and arrange an escort back here."

"If it's possible, I'd like to stay with you," a still shaken Meredith said. "I'd go crazy sitting in my hotel room not knowing what was happening. I promise I won't get in the way. I just can't be by myself right now."

Camille completely understood the sentiment. "Of course."

"Okay then," Crawley said as he led the way out of the room. "Let's go see what Mr. MacPherson really knows."

10

THE MONSTER

AGENT WELLS HADN'T FELT trepidation about the task ahead of him as he followed Jeremy Durant back to the Denver Daily Mail offices, though keeping up with his beat-up Ford Expedition as it lurched in and out of downtown traffic had proven to be a challenge.

Jeremy's disregard for the rules of the road made the trip much more hazardous than it needed to be, and he would certainly hear about that once they reached their destination, but his sense of urgency was understandable. Wells was given the relatively straightforward directive of securing an envelope; an envelope that could contain evidence critical to his team's investigation. Jeremy Durant had been charged with the much more formidable task of ensuring that his wife was safe from a threat that no one could adequately assess. Because the source of the threat was unknown, there was no reasonable way for Wells to predict its imminence, or if the threat had even existed at all.

But for Jeremy, the threat was very real and very imminent. It was his wife who was mentioned in that letter, and it was his world that was in danger of being turned upside down. No speculative risk assessment or flimsy suspect profile was going to mitigate the all-consuming instinct to protect what was most important to him.

That same instinct fueled Agent Wells more times than he cared to admit.

Despite his best efforts at stress management and psychological self-care, the nature of his work lent itself to furious bouts of paranoia, particularly when he found himself separated from his wife and six-year-old daughter for extended periods of time. The home security app on his cell phone allowed him to check the surveillance cameras posted around his property whenever the mood struck. It provided some measure of reassurance, especially when a long stint away from home was coupled with considerable distance, as had been the case now. But that reassurance was rarely enough.

Of the many law enforcement credos that Wells and his fellow agents were encouraged to live by, the ability to keep the work from coming home sat firmly atop the list. But there was a glaring caveat to that credo that was rarely mentioned; one that caused him more sleepless nights than he could count. What if the work that Wells took such care not to bring home decided to make its way to his doorstep without his knowledge or consent? What if the work intended to inflict more than psychological harm? What if it came for his family too?

Behavioral Analysis exposed him to the worst elements of the human condition; elements that existed far beyond the feeble grasp of restraint, reason, and morality. The monsters he dedicated his life to chasing weren't capable of distinguishing between the FBI agent trying to capture them and the innocent family member whose only real stake in the outcome was that FBI agent's safe return home. For Wells, every moment spent in the field posed a risk not only to his own life but to the lives of Emma and Riley as well. And in the same way that Jeremy Durant's all-consuming instincts pushed him to ignore every posted speed limit and fellow commuter that crossed his path, Wells was prepared to do anything to bring about the only outcome that mattered more than capturing the monster: ensuring that the monster never followed him home.

As they pulled into the Daily Mail parking lot and he watched the reporter rush inside without closing his car door, an uncomfortable feeling came over Wells that he couldn't explain. Perhaps it was empathy for Jeremy's situation. Perhaps it was the fear that he would one day find himself in a similar situation. Perhaps it was a sudden realization that his directive might not be as straightforward as he assumed. Unable to conjure up a definitive explanation for the feeling, he attempted to dismiss it. But it was too late. The trepidation that had eluded him for much of the trip here was firmly settled inside his gut where it began its slow expanse into every corner of his body.

Don't complicate the situation with your overwrought emotions, he thought angrily as he walked in behind Jeremy. *The job is simple. Get it done.*

Aside from the understandable questions and expressions of concern from colleagues upon Jeremy's arrival, the envelope and second letter were secured without incident.

The envelope was unmarked except for Jeremy's neatly-printed name on the front. It hadn't been sealed, ruling out the already remote possibility of DNA extraction through saliva, and there were no visible markings or print smudges. After calls to the CBI lab and the courier service that delivered the letter, Wells informed Jeremy that they would be riding together for the short trip to the real estate agency where Amber Durant was employed. Jeremy didn't put up much of a fight as he slid into the passenger's seat.

Several attempts to reach his wife by phone had already

been unsuccessful, and with each subsequent attempt, the glint of panic in his eyes burned a little bit hotter.

"Why in the hell isn't she answering?" he said as shaky fingers attempted to redial her number again.

"Is it possible that she's been showing houses all day and hasn't had time to check her phone?" Wells asked as reasonably as he could.

"She always checks her phone, even when she's in the middle of a closing," Jeremy retorted. "I'm telling you, something's happened."

"We don't know that. Let's just get to her so we can–"

"I know something's happened, okay? I know it." He looked at the speedometer reading of thirty-six and sighed. "Can you please step on it? You're driving like this is a weekend trip to the goddamn park!"

The slow-burning fuse that was Wells' patience had finally reached its end. He couldn't account for what would happen if he allowed the bomb to detonate, so he kept his frustration bottled up tight. "We'll be at your wife's office in less than three minutes, Mr. Durant. There's no need to endanger our lives or anyone else's before we can make it."

Jeremy was preparing to respond in what Wells was sure would be a forceful way when his cell phone rang. His eyes widened when he saw the name on the screen.

"Oh my god, Amber. Where have you been?"

Wells strained to hear the response. "Put her on speaker," he instructed.

Jeremy quickly complied.

"—left my phone at home and I was caught up in a closing for most of the morning, so I couldn't call you back," they heard Amber Durant explain. "Your messages sounded so crazy. What's going on?"

"Where are you now?" Jeremy asked in a still frantic pitch.

"I just got home. Why?"

"We need you to stay right where you are, Mrs. Durant," Wells directed. "We'll be there shortly."

"Who's that, Jeremy?" Amber's pitch now matched her husband's.

"He's with the FBI."

"The what?"

"Honey, have you watched the news at all?"

"No."

"Don't," Wells advised. "Just sit tight until we get there."

Amber sniffed as if she were on the verge of tears. "Why are you with the FBI, Jeremy?"

"I'll explain it when I get there, okay? Everything will be fine. I promise."

Amber sniffed again. "Okay."

When Jeremy hung up, he looked at the speedometer again. Wells saved him the trouble of protesting by stepping on the accelerator.

Jeremy's home was a brick bungalow located on an idyllic street lined with elm trees that were coming to life with the first signs of spring foliage. The tiny house was set back from the curb by a sizable front yard and largely hidden from view by a swath of neatly-trimmed evergreen bushes and a tall Blue Spruce. An ideal set up for privacy. And isolation.

Wells pulled up behind a silver Land Rover parked in front of the house.

"Your wife's?"

"No. We have a garage around back. It's probably someone visiting one of the neighbors. Street parking is at a premium around here, so there's always someone in front of our house."

Wells nodded as they got out of the car.

He noticed nothing out of the ordinary as he and Jeremy walked the long path leading to the front door, but his senses were heightened.

"Nice place you have here," he said in a banal attempt to normalize the moment.

"It's all Amber's doing. She picked the house, designed the landscape. She even brokered the sale."

"Sounds like there isn't much she can't do."

"She can't do yard work. That task, she leaves to me."

"We husbands have to be good for something, right?"

Jeremy's nervous chuckle told Wells that he'd needed this moment of normal too. "I suppose so."

Upon reaching the front door, Jeremy pulled out his key to unlock it. Before he could attempt to insert it, Wells noticed that the door was ajar.

The mood that they'd fought so hard to lighten immediately went dark.

"Amber?" Jeremy was calling her name before he even stepped through the door. Wells stayed behind him as they entered, resisting the instinct to push his way in front.

The tidy house was cold and quiet, like one of the unoccupied show homes that Amber was likely familiar with. Aside from the leather throw pillow resting on the floor near the couch, nothing looked as if it had been disturbed.

The open floor plan provided a clear look throughout the small space, from the bright living room to the dining room, and into the kitchen. There was no sign that anyone had been here.

"Amber, where are you?" Jeremy's voice cracked with uncertainty as it rose. "Amber? Honey, we're here." His pace quickened as he moved through the dining room and into the empty kitchen. "Amber?"

Before Wells could attempt to calm him, Jeremy darted into a short hallway that led to three closed doors. He opened the first door and turned on the light. With no sign of his wife, he quickly moved to the second door, which appeared to be a small storage closet. From there, he moved on to the third. When Wells saw that it was their bedroom, he followed Jeremy inside.

The room was as neatly staged as the rest of the house had been. It was also just as vacant.

Having been inside enough living spaces that were transformed into crime scenes, Wells had become adept at using a room's energy to help tell the story of what may have happened inside of it. In his days as a D.C. patrol officer, he could sometimes walk inside a room and guess where a suspect was hiding based solely on the residual warmth that his body heat produced.

If Amber Durant had been inside this house, she wasn't here anymore.

"Where did she go?" Jeremy asked, his wide eyes probing for an answer that Wells couldn't give.

"Do you have a basement?"

"Yes. But we only go down there to do laundry and change the furnace filter. Amber hates being down there alone."

Maybe someone is keeping her company.

Burying the thought before his eyes could give it away, Wells walked out of the bedroom and into the kitchen, where he saw a dark entryway adjacent to the back door. "Is it here?"

Jeremy nodded. "But you don't think she could be..."

"No, I don't," Wells said, mindful that any expression of

doubt would send Jeremy into a panic. "But in the interest of being thorough, I need to check."

Wells quickly moved toward the entryway. Before he could walk through, Jeremy brushed past him.

"Amber, are you down there?"

The ear-splitting force of his words sent Wells back on his heels. He gathered himself just in time to prevent Jeremy from racing down the staircase. "Step away," he demanded, using a strong hand to pull him backward.

"Goddamnit, if you think she's down there we have to get to her!" Jeremy attempted to push back, but he was no match for Wells' formidable six-foot four-inch frame.

Wells forced him backward a few more feet until he no longer put up a fight. "You have to calm down."

When Jeremy put his hands up in surrender, Wells released him.

"I'm sorry," Jeremy said before turning to the sink.

"It's fine. I just can't have you running down there without–"

"Oh God."

"What?"

Jeremy pointed at the kitchen window. "That shouldn't be open."

Wells walked over to the back-door window and looked outside. He immediately noticed the small storage shed at the far end of the yard. The wooden door was swinging freely in the brisk wind. "Is it normally closed?"

Jeremy nodded. "And locked."

"Does your wife have a key?"

"I gave her a spare, but she lost it months ago. I keep the master with me."

Wells ignored the sinking feeling in his gut as he opened the back door and stepped onto the patio. Once there, he noticed something on the grass near the shed. Its mirrored surface reflected the afternoon sunlight directly into his eyes.

He could no longer ignore the sinking feeling.

"Can you call your wife's phone again?"

Jeremy stood frozen in the doorway. "What? Why?"

Wells stared at the thin silver rectangle, hoping like hell he was wrong. "Please, just call."

Less than a second later, the sound of cosmic chimes filled the air.

Wells rushed to the phone. When he reached it, he saw Jeremy's name on the screen.

He reached inside his jacket for the Glock 9 holstered on his hip and turned to look inside the shed.

The shadow edged across the periphery of his vision before he could draw the weapon. As he spun his head to catch up to the movement, he felt the blow come down on his left ear.

Through the pain and confusion, he heard Jeremy's muffled voice cry out from behind him. "Oh my God, no!"

Before Wells could react, he was blinded by a searing white light that instantly plunged his world into darkness.

With the last thread of consciousness that he could summon, he conjured up an image of Emma and Riley. They were arm in arm. They were smiling. They were safe. And in that final moment, he knew that he'd done his job.

He'd kept the monster from following him home.

11

DESPERATE TIMES

B Y THE TIME CAMILLE MADE IT BACK to the Admin Building, the raw footage of her statement had been uploaded to four different local news websites.

"They certainly didn't waste time," she said as she watched the video on Lieutenant Hitchcock's computer alongside Crawley and Meredith Park. "I guess it won't be long before it goes national."

Crawley nodded. "Whether or not that's a good thing remains to be seen."

When the clip ended, Hitchcock opened a new browser and typed the words *Mile-High Dispatch*. A video thumbnail of Jeremy Durant's distressed face was embedded on the homepage underneath the headline MESSAGE FROM A KILLER.

"From where I'm sitting, it doesn't look good at all," Hitchcock said as he played the choppy cell phone recording posted by Will Freeman.

The unedited clip documented the tense exchange between Camille and Jeremy Durant. Will took special care to zoom in on Camille's face as she read the letter. The moment felt almost cinematic in its surrealism.

She instantly regretted not ripping up the reporter's card the moment he gave it to her. "And we were worried about news cameras and satellite trucks."

"Modern technology at its finest," Hitchcock said with a tight smile.

"You mean at its worst," Meredith countered.

"We should've collected their phones before the presser even started," Crawley grunted.

"That letter was going to find its way into the public domain no matter what you did," Camille told him. "I wouldn't be surprised if another video of Jeremy shows up someplace much more significant than the Mile-High Dispatch."

"And how do you plan to deal with the questions when that happens?" Hitchcock asked.

"I'll deal with the questions by not addressing them. At least not until we get our own questions answered."

"So what am I supposed to do when the hounds show up here? Because they will."

"You tell them that your investigators are following up on every tip and piece of evidence they receive and that you're fully confident in their ability."

"And who's supposed to supply us with these tips that you're speaking of?"

"With any luck, the man sitting in Interview Room Three."

Hitchcock shifted in his chair. "I had a feeling you'd say that."

"How has it been going in there?" Crawley asked.

"Sullivan has gotten him to talk some."

Crawley looked at Camille. "You figured she would."

She never had a doubt.

"What has he told her so far?" Camille asked.

"He seemed to know about your statement, or at least he suggested that he did."

"That's not possible. I hadn't even considered making that statement until long after I interviewed him. There's no way he could've known."

"He knew something. He even told Sullivan that it would start at one P.M. Said he couldn't wait to see it."

Camille and Crawley exchanged a worried glance.

"That was the start time," Crawley confirmed.

"So he was aware of it," Hitchcock reiterated.

"He was aware that a news conference was taking place at one. But it wasn't me he was looking forward to seeing," Camille said.

"Who did he think he'd be seeing?"

Camille pointed to the image on the computer of Jeremy Durant.

Hitchcock shifted in his chair again.

"What else did Daniel tell Detective Sullivan?" Crawley asked.

"Unfortunately, nothing. When she informed him that she couldn't arrange for a television to be brought into the interview room, he shut down."

"Is he still in there?"

"Yes. Unfortunately, Sullivan and Greer aren't doing anything more than keeping him company at this point."

Camille wrung her hands to relieve the nervous energy that had suddenly built up in them. "I'd like to see him."

Hitchcock nodded. "How much stock are you putting into the letter being authentic?"

Camille looked at Meredith. "At this point, we have to assume that the threat is legitimate."

"We'll need to place Ms. Park in protective custody until we can find out for sure," Crawley added.

"Of course. I have the detail on standby." Hitchcock turned to Meredith. "They can escort you back to your hotel."

"She'd like to avoid going back if possible, at least for now," Camille said, saving her the trouble of protesting.

"Okay. We'll keep you here, for the time being. Then we can make arrangements for protective placement later."

Meredith breathed a sigh of relief. "Thank you."

Hitchcock nodded then turned back to Camille. "Right now, Daniel gives us the best chance of figuring out who wrote that letter. Am I correct in assuming that?"

"Yes."

"In that case, we'd better not waste another second in here."

Camille found the monitor the instant she entered the observation room. Daniel's affected composure was on full display as he sat across from the two weary detectives who had clearly grown frustrated with his silence.

"How long has this game of chicken been going on?" she asked Hitchcock.

"Ever since they went back in after I pulled them out to watch your statement. Daniel suspected that something was up and I don't think he took too kindly to not being told what it was."

"Petulant little asshole, isn't he?" Crawley snapped as he joined Camille at the monitor. "He didn't get what he wanted, so he's taking his toys and running home."

"Certainly looks like it," Hitchcock agreed.

Camille was anxious to talk to him, but she feared that his heavily-fortified wall would only be tougher to penetrate now. "Let's bring them out so we can discuss where to go from here."

Hitchcock nodded and walked out of the room.

Camille watched the monitor as the door opened and

Hitchcock stuck his head inside. The relief on Chloe's face was apparent as she and her partner quickly stood up and followed him out. Daniel sat in place as if nothing were happening.

She heard chatter in the hallway as the trio approached.

"No wonder the guy hasn't lawyered up," Detective Greer said. "The torture sessions are a lot easier when he has us all to himself."

"If I had to endure much more of that, I would've been the one seeking legal counsel," Chloe quipped as she walked into the observation room. Her smile widened when she saw her friend standing inside.

"Hey, Camille."

"Hi, Chloe."

The hectic nature of the day hadn't allowed for the phone call that Camille intended to make prior to her arrival at Major Crimes. She knew that Chloe would've appreciated the heads-up and worried that she'd felt slighted at being the last one to know of her presence here. Much to Camille's relief that hadn't appeared to be the case.

"You must be Detectives Sullivan and Greer," Crawley said, extending his hand to both. "I'm Special Agent Peter Crawley with the Behavioral Analysis Unit. It's a pleasure."

"Likewise, Agent Crawley," Greer said. The corner of his mouth curled upward as he turned to Camille. "We haven't officially met, but I feel like I know you already. Chloe talks about you all the time."

"Good things I hope," Camille replied, hopeful that her face wasn't as visibly flushed as it felt.

"Great things." Greer's warm gaze traveled from her eyes to the scar on her cheek, before dropping nervously to the floor.

Camille quickly turned her attention to Chloe, anxious to

put the slightly awkward exchange with Greer behind her. "It's good to see you."

"You too. From the looks of it, you've had a hell of a day."

Camille nodded, trying to shake the feeling that the hell of this day was only getting started. "I'm not the only one, I imagine. Dealing with Daniel is no stroll on the beach."

"Not unless that beach is lined with burning hot coals."

The line inspired a smattering of polite laughter that momentarily lifted the tension.

Crawley saw to it that the reprieve was short-lived.

"I understand you were briefed on the details of Camille's statement," he said to Chloe and Greer.

Chloe nodded. "We watched it along with the lieutenant."

"And did you share any of those details with Daniel?"

"We were told to wait until you arrived before we went forward with that."

"Has he made any further mention of it?"

"No. He asked for a television in the hopes of seeing a live feed, but after we turned him down, he didn't ask about it again."

"Lieutenant Hitchcock says he shut down altogether," Camille said.

"Aside from a request for coffee, he hasn't said a word," Greer confirmed.

Camille looked at the grainy image of Daniel, then back at Chloe. "I think it's time we show him."

"Everything? Including your statement?"

"Especially my statement."

"How do you think he'll react?"

"I don't think his heart will exactly bleed for me, but he also won't be expecting to see it, which could throw him off just enough to expose a crack in the armor."

"You'll be hard-pressed to find a crack anywhere in that armor," Hitchcock said.

Chloe shook her head. "I disagree."

Camille wanted to echo the sentiment, but she was curious to hear how much Chloe's read on Daniel matched up with her own.

"There's no question that he knew about the press conference before it started," Chloe continued. "There's also no question that he knew about the letter that was in Jeremy Durant's possession, along with the threat contained within it. Based on some of his statements to Camille during their Q and A, he knew that the author would demand a full mea culpa. He basically told us everything we needed to know about his involvement in our subject's initial plan: It was significant."

Hitchcock sighed. "But I thought we'd already established Daniel's connection to the abductor. Why does any of this matter if we already know?"

"It matters *because* we know," Chloe answered. "It would've been easy for him to withhold everything. He could've sat back, waited for the plan to unfold, and watched us deal with the aftermath. But he didn't. He warned Camille about what was coming. Do you think he believed that she'd sit on her hands and wait for it to happen? Of course not. He knew that she'd do everything she could to stop it."

"Maybe he wanted to taunt her," Hitchcock reasoned.

"He could've easily done that after everything blew up in our faces. He didn't want to taunt her. He wanted to help her."

Hitchcock turned to Camille.

"I agree."

"Then why wouldn't he just come out and tell you where your father and Jacob Deaver are?"

"He obviously enjoys being courted," Chloe said.

"And he's really good at playing hard to get," Greer quipped.

Hitchcock's chuckle was peppered with frustration. "With all the trouble we're going through, he damn well better put out."

"He will," Camille predicted.

The lieutenant still didn't look convinced. "What makes you think you can–"

Hitchcock was interrupted by Detective Krieger's sudden appearance in the room. The deep creases on his time-worn face were further accentuated by an expression that Camille could only interpret as troubled.

"What's going on, Alan?" Hitchcock asked, seemingly aware of the detective's distress.

"We just heard from the patrol unit assigned to monitor the Durant residence. There's been an incident there."

An alarmed Crawley shot up from his chair. "What kind of incident?"

"Jeremy Durant and his wife were found in the backyard, each of them shot multiple times. They were already dead when the unit arrived."

Camille suddenly felt frozen to her chair, the shock of Krieger's words rendering her immobile.

"What about Agent Wells?" Crawley asked in a breathless voice.

"He's being transported to the Denver Health Medical Center as we speak. There hasn't been an update on his condition, but we understand that he was also shot."

A subdued silence hung in the air for several seconds before Crawley broke it with a heavy fist against the wall.

"There was a typewritten letter found on Mr. Durant's jacket," Krieger continued.

"A letter?" Chloe asked.

Krieger nodded. "We believe it was left by the assailant."

Crawley made an abrupt bee-line for the door.

"Where are you going?" Camille asked.

"I have to see about Stephen."

"Peter, wait."

He stopped before he reached the doorway.

"I know how you're feeling," Camille continued. "We're all concerned about Agent Wells. But right now the most important place for us to be is at that crime scene."

"But I can't leave him there alone," Crawley replied, his voice laced with guilt.

"He's not alone," Krieger interjected. "There are multiple units following him to the hospital, and they've been instructed to contact you directly with any updates."

Crawley took a long moment to steady his nerves before turning to Krieger. "You said there was a letter?"

"Yes, attached to Mr. Durant with what we presume was a nail gun. Parsons is already on scene, and I'm heading there now."

Camille looked at Crawley. "We need to be there too."

Crawley nodded his agreement then quickly left the room.

With her mind still reeling from the news, Camille stood up to follow. Before leaving, she turned to Chloe. "I think it's time to show Daniel the footage, then tell him what happened to the Durant's and Agent Wells. The guilt could be enough to get him to talk. If not, he can stew on it in his cell. There's only so much begging we can do."

"If he doesn't talk, I'll make sure to leave him with plenty to think about."

Chloe's firm declaration was enough to convince Camille not to pursue the task herself. Considering the swell of rage that was surging inside her, it was best for everyone if she didn't.

"Be sure to keep us updated," Hitchcock said as Camille trailed Detective Krieger out of the room. "And be safe."

Camille turned to Hitchcock and nodded. Then she took one more look at the monitor. Daniel's smile was subtle, but it was enough to make her wonder if he could somehow sense the sudden chaos in the room next to him. She knew better than to doubt it.

12

CAPTIVE AUDIENCE

"THAT'S TWICE YOU TWO HAVE run out on me without the courtesy of a warning," Daniel said when Chloe and Greer walked into the interview room. "I was starting to think you weren't enjoying the uncomfortable silence nearly as much as I was."

"It certainly wasn't the best use of our time," Chloe snapped as she set down the laptop that she'd carried in. It hit the table with a heavy thud that reverberated through the tight space. "Fortunately, I have something here that may inspire a little conversation."

Daniel eyed the computer with a hint of apprehension. "What is it?"

"Camille Grisham's statement," Greer answered.

"Camille gave a statement?"

"That's right."

Daniel's apprehension grew. "What did she say?"

Chloe cued the video clip, pressed play, and turned the screen to him.

He appeared to hold his breath as he watched Camille speak to her father's abductor. Chloe studied his face for any emotional cracks that she could exploit, but the only expression he seemed capable of producing was shock.

When the statement ended, Chloe stopped the video. "Is that why you were so anxious for a television earlier?"

A flustered Daniel sat back in his chair without responding.

She took the opportunity to pull up the Mile-High Dispatch website. After finding the clip, she turned the monitor back to Daniel. "Perhaps you were expecting to see this instead."

He tensed at the frozen image of Jeremy Durant.

"Do you recognize him?"

Daniel swallowed hard before answering. "Is this from…"

"Camille's press conference? Yes, it is."

"Was it carried live?"

"No."

Daniel shook his head.

"Disappointed?" Greer asked.

"It's what he would have wanted."

"You mean Paul and Jacob's abductor."

Daniel's anxiety appeared to mount as he continued watching the screen. "Are you going to play it?"

"Not until you tell us how it is that you know so much about him," Chloe said.

"You're very good at finding different ways to ask the same question, Detective Sullivan."

"If you're tired of hearing it, perhaps you should answer."

Daniel took time to frame his response. "He and I share a similar worldview. We were shaped by similar experiences. I know what he wants because I want many of the same things."

"Including this man's death?"

When Chloe pointed at the screen, the first crack appeared in Daniel's face.

"He and his wife were found shot to death outside their home less than an hour ago. An FBI agent was also shot."

Daniel shuddered as if hit by a sudden, violent chill. "Camille?"

Chloe and Greer exchanged a glance, silently agreeing to let the question remain unanswered. Chloe then turned back to the computer screen. She skipped ahead to the moment in the video when Jeremy appeared with the letter, then she pressed play.

"You can't leave yet," she heard him say through the speakers. *"Not until you hear what he has to say."*

Daniel shifted uncomfortably as he watched the chaotic scene.

"I really need you to know that I didn't have a choice. He knew things about me. About my wife. I couldn't risk it."

Chloe stopped the video. "He sounded pretty frightened."

"Obviously his fears were well-founded," Greer added.

When Daniel didn't respond, Chloe skipped to the moment in the video when Jeremy attempted to give the letter to Meredith.

"And he says he'll be watching."

After Jeremy's prophetic words of warning, Chloe stopped the video again and turned to Greer. "He'll be watching. That's basically the same thing that Daniel said to us before the press conference even aired."

"That's right. It's almost like he wrote that letter himself."

"But we know that's impossible, don't we Daniel? Whoever did this is operating on a level that none of us here seem capable of understanding."

"Speak for yourself," Daniel said sharply.

"I feel very comfortable speaking for you," Chloe replied with equal sharpness.

With Daniel successfully agitated, she continued the video.

His eyes narrowed as he watched a shaken Camille read the contents of the letter silently. Chloe stopped the video for the final time just before Camille's directive to clear the room.

Daniel inched his way to the edge of his chair in anticipation of what was coming next, but Chloe would offer no resolution to the cliffhanger. Instead, she closed the web browser and shut down the computer.

The look of disappointment on Daniel's face could not have been more profound. "Isn't there more?"

"There's a lot more," Chloe confirmed. "But what's the point? We've already told you how it ends."

Daniel's face contorted with the burden of a heavy thought as he slid back in his chair.

Greer immediately sensed his discomfort. "What's on your mind?"

"You still haven't answered my question about the FBI agent."

"Would you be upset if it was Camille Grisham?" Chloe asked.

Daniel's jaw tightened. "I didn't think that was part of the plan."

"Plans can change in ways we don't like," Greer said, playing along with his partner's ploy. "Especially when someone else is in charge of making them."

Chloe pushed her chair up to the table and sat. "What was supposed to happen, Daniel?"

"That reporter and his wife shouldn't have died. They didn't do anything wrong."

"Neither did Paul Grisham or Jacob Deaver," Greer countered forcefully.

"Why were the Durants killed?" Chloe asked, ignoring her partner's justifiable outburst.

The corner of Daniel's mouth quivered slightly. When he

bit down on his lip, the quivering stopped. "Something happened at that press conference that shouldn't have."

"Any guesses as to what that something was?" Greer asked.

"Camille Grisham showed up," Chloe answered.

Daniel let out a heavy sigh. "That letter was for Meredith Park to read. No one else was supposed to be there."

"But other people were there, and they were there because of you. And now…"

"What?" Daniel asked anxiously.

"Now there's no more end game. He's obviously changed the script, so it doesn't really matter what you know anymore. Whatever plan you thought there was is completely out the window. Now he's making it up as he goes, which also means that any measure of satisfaction you thought you were going to get out of this is gone. He took that from you by what he did today."

Chloe knew she was stepping out on a limb with a narrative that led Daniel to believe that Camille had possibly been killed, and she was well-aware of its potential to completely blow up in her face. But in her mind, this was the only hand available to play. She had to go all-in.

"When Camille interviewed you, you told her that you were willing to spend the rest of your life in here for the right cause. What you now need to understand is that the cause you were all-too-eager to give up your life for was never undertaken with you in mind. Whoever is doing this could care less about your vision of justice for Camille or the grief you feel over your sister's death. Whoever killed those four girls, whoever killed an innocent man and his wife today, whoever shot…" She purposefully let her voice trail off. "… did so for his own purposes, not yours. Think about that when you're sitting here smugly declaring to us what you know about *his* plan. Your purpose is to be in this room, so he doesn't have to be. You've served your usefulness to him. Hopefully, he doesn't find out that he was forced to kill those people because of what *you* did. Because if he does, and he has any kind of reach, that tiny cage you call home won't be enough to keep you safe. Unfortunately, I've seen it too often to believe otherwise."

She paused to study Daniel's reaction. His eyes were wide with a mix of fear, confusion, and anger, just as she'd hoped they'd be.

"So here's what's going to happen," she continued. "Detective Greer and I are going to leave so we can get on with the business of catching this man. And we will catch him. You'll be taken back to county, and whatever is waiting for you there, and we'll never speak again. Greer and I will be around for your trial, of course, but we sure as hell won't be there to help you. So I hope you enjoyed wasting our time today. We're the last captive audience you'll probably ever have."

With that, Chloe rose from her chair. Greer followed, a wide grin creasing his square, brown face. "Nothing more to add to that except, have a nice day, Mr. MacPherson."

The detectives reached the door before Daniel was able to summon a response.

"For the record, I don't agree at all with what happened to those four girls. It's just as bad as what happened to my sister."

"Those girls were likely someone's sister too," Chloe said as she backed away from the door. "There are a lot of people out there who are feeling the same pain you are. And if this guy has his way, there will be a lot more. Think about them, Daniel."

He lifted his cuffed hands up over his face. When he took them away a moment later, he revealed a pair of strained, watery eyes. Chloe searched for signs of vulnerability. Before she could find any, Daniel turned away from her.

"This doesn't have to go any further," she said as she approached him. "Help us end it before more people are hurt."

When Daniel looked at her, his eyes were no longer strained. His stare was ice-cold; its weight powerful enough to penetrate the core of her being. The emotion that she was searching for became fully evident at that moment, and it was bleaker than anything she could've imagined. "What's the point of telling you anything? He's changed the script, remember?"

"It hasn't changed completely," Chloe said, bracing for the admission that was coming next. "Camille wasn't the agent who was shot."

Daniel appeared unfazed by the revelation.

"She's on her way to the Durant residence as we speak."

"Exactly where he wants her to be," Daniel said matter-of-factly.

"What is she going to find when she gets there?"

"Jeremy Durant's body, I imagine."

"The officers on scene reportedly found a typewritten letter attached to his jacket," Greer said. "Any idea what's in that letter?"

"I don't know anything about it. If I had to wager a guess, I'd say it's intended for Camille. And if it is for Camille, I seriously doubt that she's going to like what she reads."

"Tell us who wrote it!"

The sheer force of Chloe's words forced Daniel backward in his chair. After gathering himself, he forced a tight smile. "I'd like to go back to my cell now."

Chloe closed her eyes and took a deep breath. It did nothing to calm her nerves. "That would be a mistake, Daniel."

"My only mistake was leading you to believe that I give two-shits about what happens to Camille Grisham or her father or any of the rest of them."

Chloe sat down next to Daniel, looking him directly in the eye. "You do care."

Daniel held her eye contact with an unwavering glare. "I'd like to go back to my cell."

Chloe abruptly stood up from the table. "Rot in there for all I care."

"I hope you don't mean that, Detective Sullivan. Just like I hope you didn't mean it when you said I'll never hear from you again. I need someone to keep me updated on what he has planned for the good Agent Grisham now. I promise you, I don't know what it is. But I do know that it's going to make for one hell of a show."

"We'll do that, Daniel," Chloe said as she opened the door to walk out. "But only if you promise to remember us when those tiny cell walls start closing in around you. Because they will start closing in. Probably a lot sooner than you think. And when that time comes, and you finally realize just how much you do care, you'd better hope like hell that we're still here to listen."

13

A NEW DIRECTIVE

CRAWLEY WAS QUIET for most of the car ride to the Durant residence, though the fury simmering just beneath his hardened exterior occasionally surfaced in the form of a grunt or an angry murmur.

Sensing his troubled emotional state, Camille had extended multiple offers to drive, but he rebuffed her each time, arguing that his focus was better directed at the road than on the image of Agent Wells alone in the hospital fighting for his still-too-young life. He'd put in a call to Denver Health the moment they left the Admin building, but updates on Wells' condition were difficult to come by. Camille wondered if he would bypass the Durant scene altogether in favor of a trip to the hospital. She wouldn't have begrudged his decision to make such a detour, but she couldn't have been more relieved when he opted not to.

Crawley's forced restraint was abruptly shattered by a hard fist against the steering wheel. "Why in the hell did I send him out by himself?"

"You arranged for back up."

"A hell of a lot of good it did."

"You can't blame yourself for any of this. It's not your fault."

It was a line similar to one that Crawley used on her in the aftermath of Agent Sheridan's murder. She hoped her version would be better received.

Crawley's heavy sigh told her that it hadn't been. "I obviously should've taken that letter more seriously." He barely had time to complete the thought before he was overtaken by another one. "And Emma. My God, I'll have to call her. She's going to completely fall apart."

From Camille's vantage point, Crawley was the one falling apart. The sight shook her to the core.

"He'll be okay, Peter. We have to believe that."

The words sounded empty as she spoke them, and the blank expression on Crawley's face left no doubt about their ineffectiveness. As much as she felt compelled to offer a comforting gesture, the reality was that she'd known Wells for less than a day. And while she'd seen enough to know that he was a good agent, she didn't know the man behind the shield. Not like Crawley did. Her grief was for a fallen colleague, one that she barely knew. Crawley's grief was for a friend. It wasn't her place to convince him that everything would be okay. It was her job to maintain focus, even if she had to do so for both of them.

"I know how horrible this feels, and I know how concerned you are for him. So if you want to drop me off at the Durant's and head over to the hospital, I completely understand. But it's imperative that I be at that scene. It's taken everything I have to keep my thoughts on the investigation and not on the fear for my father's safety that follows me every second of the day. But I do it because I have to; because my father and Jacob need me to. I'm sorry, but I can't get sidetracked by Agent Wells or anyone else. Not even you."

The words were enough to lift the fog that had settled over Crawley. His white-knuckle grip on the steering wheel softened while his puffy eyes slowly regained their usual laser-like focus.

"You're absolutely right to think that way. But you won't have to get sidetracked because of me. I'm here for you a hundred percent." Crawley let out one last sigh of emotion. "Stephen will pull through."

Camille put a gentle hand on his shoulder, choosing not to echo the sentiment this time.

The street on which the Durants lived was blocked off by a barricade on one end and a convoy of patrol cruisers on the other. Crawley was allowed entry through the barricade by a young female officer who took off her DPD cap as the car drove past. A sign of respect and condolence that Crawley acknowledged with a nod of thanks.

The block was peppered with shell-shocked neighbors milling around their yards and porches; the muddled details of the events that occurred at the Durant's no doubt filtering through their ranks.

It was an atmosphere eerily similar to the one that greeted Camille as she approached the roped-off crime scene that had once been her best friend's house. But the circumstances were drastically different, as evidenced by the FBI visitor's badge hanging from her lapel. She couldn't have been any further removed from her life as an agent on that fateful day three months ago, and she couldn't help but reflect on just how much had changed since then.

And yet, some things hadn't changed at all.

The sight of yellow crime-scene tape instantly brought it all back: Julia's murder, Candace and Jessica screaming for help in Sykes' basement, the warm trickle of Agent Sheridan's blood on her hands, and the spontaneous closing of her airways as the anxiety snuck up on her like a silent predator eager to snatch the life away from its prey.

She'd long-since stopped blaming herself for those murders (though Julia's was still fresh enough to unleash its wrath on her unsuspecting psyche whenever she let her guard down), and the little blue pill her doctor prescribed was enough to keep the anxiety at a manageable distance. But the memories would never be buried deep enough to spare her the agony of complete recall at a moment's notice.

The sound of Crawley's voice interrupted the stream before any more unwanted memories could pour through. "This will be the first time you've seen anything like this since Pennsylvania, right?"

You mean the day I decided to never step foot in a crime scene again?

"Yes."

"Are you sure you're ready?"

Hell no, I'm not ready.

"Absolutely."

Fortunately for Camille, Crawley couldn't read minds. "Okay, let's go inside."

They were greeted by Detective Krieger before they reached the front door.

"I'm really sorry about Agent Wells," he immediately said to Crawley. "We're all praying that he pulls through."

Crawley nodded, his tightly pursed lips not allowing for a verbal response.

Krieger then turned to Camille. "Nice work on MacPherson. Getting him to talk has been like trying to pry open a bear trap. I admire the way you handled him."

The air between them felt heavy despite Krieger's words. Her involvement in a recent case that exposed possible high-level corruption within the DPD meant that she wouldn't be received warmly by many in the department. She hadn't given that fact much thought before arriving at Major Crimes this morning. But with the reminder now staring her in the face, she immediately put her guard up. "Thank you."

"I've known Paul for twenty years," Krieger continued. "He's a great man. Whatever Parsons and I have to do to get him back to you safe and sound, we'll do it."

And just like that, her heavily-fortified wall of protection came crumbling down. "I really appreciate that, Detective Krieger."

"You got it. Now, if you want to come with me, the Durants are this way."

Camille and Crawley followed Krieger into the house. Forensics was already setting up shop in the living room while crime scene photographers lit the tight space with a barrage of flash pops.

When the trio entered the kitchen, they saw two young officers sitting at the table. The official-looking woman sitting across from them was writing something in a notepad.

"These are Officers Bradley and Stanton," Krieger said of the pair. "They discovered the Durants and Agent Wells. Guys, this is Agent Crawley and Agent Grisham with the FBI."

The introduction annoyed Camille, but she did her best to brush it off.

"You were the detail assigned to monitor the house?" Crawley asked in an edgy tone.

"Yes," Officer Stanton answered.

"Where in the hell were you when all this was happening?"

"We'll be finished here soon," the woman with the

notepad interrupted before the shaken officer could answer. "If you'd like a briefing after you're finished out there, feel free to come back." With her stern tone implying that no further interruptions would be tolerated, Camille, Crawley, and Krieger proceeded out the back door.

The first image that Camille saw as she stepped into the backyard was Jeremy Durant's lifeless body curled up near the edge of the patio. He looked unrecognizable as the man she'd promised to protect less than three hours ago. His right hand was covering his face as if he were attempting to shield himself from the flurry of bullets aimed at him, which according to the shell-case markings on the ground, totaled seven.

When she took a step closer, she saw the paper attached to the sleeve of his field jacket.

"Sick puppy we're dealing with here," Camille heard an unfamiliar voice say.

She looked up to see the man she'd recognized from Major Crimes as Detective Krieger's partner. Unlike Krieger, his round face brightened the moment he saw her. "Jim Parsons," he said with an extended hand. "Pleasure to finally meet you, Agent Grisham."

Camille shook his hand, resisting the futile urge to tell him that she wasn't an agent. "Likewise, Detective Parsons."

"Your dad talked about you all the time. He had your FBI stuff all over his office. Sometimes he worried that he gushed too much, but if my boy was in the Bureau, you best believe I'd do the same thing."

While Camille appreciated the polite gesture, hearing such stories only made her feel worse. "That's very kind. Can you tell us where Mrs. Durant is?"

Parsons' demeanor stiffened. "She's in the storage shed. Forensics will be tending to her first. They were instructed not to disturb Mr. Durant until you arrived."

"Have you read the note yet?"

"Yes." Then after a long beat, Parsons added, "It's addressed to you."

Camille had figured as much, but she still looked at Crawley with a concerned eye.

"Has it been print-tested?" Crawley asked.

"Not yet. The techs found another note inside Mr. Durant's jacket pocket. Same font style. It was addressed to him."

Camille looked at Crawley. "The note that Wells retrieved from Durant's office."

Crawley nodded then turned back to Parsons.

"Anything else?"

"Yes."

Parsons' shift in demeanor was subtle, but it was enough to alarm Camille. "What?"

She held her breath as Parsons bent down to pick up something on the ground next to Durant. When he stood up, she could see the plastic evidence bag in his hand. What she saw inside the bag made her heart skip more than once.

"Durant was a reporter. He'd naturally keep a voice recorder with him," Crawley said when he realized what it was. "He probably carried it everywhere he went."

"It wasn't his," Parsons said, immediately confirming Camille's suspicion.

"Who did it belong to?" Crawley asked.

Parsons looked at Camille. "I suggest you read the note first."

She took a step toward Durant, then stopped. "Not while it's still on him."

Parsons nodded then motioned to a nearby CSI. "Robert, can you remove the note now? And get Agents Grisham and Crawley some gloves."

"Of course."

It wasn't until she made eye contact with him that Camille recognized Robert Franklin as the crime scene tech that Chloe had brought to her father's home in the immediate aftermath of his abduction.

He offered a thin smile as he approached her with a pair of latex gloves. "Hello again, Camille." The baritone in his voice was strikingly similar to her father's.

"Hi, Robert." She took the gloves and quickly put them on.

Franklin then turned to Durant and removed the legal-sized piece of paper from his jacket, careful to minimize the tearing as he pulled each corner from the nail it had been attached to. "Watch the blood on the top edge," he said before handing Camille the paper. "And I'll need to bag it as soon as you're finished."

She nodded her understanding as she took the letter and began reading.

The small font was identical to the letter that Durant gave her at the press conference, as was the author's confrontational tone. Only this time, his ire was aimed directly at her.

"Well?" she heard Crawley say from a place that seemed far away.

When she looked up to see the group staring impatiently, she read the letter aloud.

"Hello, Camille. I had hoped you wouldn't have to read this because if you are, more people have died. And just like all the others, they died because of you. Jeremy Durant's death could have been avoided had he simply followed my instructions. But because of your interference, he didn't." Camille stopped reading and looked at Crawley. "He obviously saw Will Freeman's video."

"If so, this was quick work on his part. The clip has only been up for a few hours. He really had to scramble to pull this off."

"Unless he planned for the possibility ahead of time," Krieger suggested.

Camille believed that to be the most likely scenario. He wouldn't have gotten this far without an unusual amount of planning and patience, and because of that, he'd managed to stay a solid step ahead. She now worried that the steps between them were only widening.

Pushing the thought aside, she turned back to the letter and continued reading. "I'm assuming by now that Meredith Park is safely in your custody. Very fortunate for her. But there are others who are not so fortunate, and your actions today have only put their lives at greater risk. In the unlikely event that you don't know who the others are, there is a recorder inside Mr. Durant's jacket. After you have finished reading this, I urge you to play it." Camille looked at Parsons. "Have you listened to it?"

When he nodded, Camille continued reading. "In the meantime, I have detailed your new directive. It is very simple. Follow it exactly as instructed, and no one else will have to die. Deviate from it in any way, and the result will be worse than anything that you can possibly imagine."

Camille stopped reading aloud to scan the rest of the letter. She let out an audible groan upon finishing.

"What is it?" Crawley asked.

She gave him the paper without answering. The nightmare scenario that she'd imagined after reading the first letter – a scenario so crazy that she refused to give it voice – suddenly became a reality, and she couldn't bear the thought of reading the confirming words again.

Crawley took the letter. His reaction after reading it wasn't nearly as restrained as Camille's. "This has got to be a fucking joke."

"I read it five times looking for a punchline," Parsons said solemnly. "Unfortunately, I couldn't find one."

"Would someone kindly fill me in?" an aggravated Krieger asked.

"He's demanding that Camille give a press conference with the original script that he provided," Crawley reported. "But now he wants her to give a second press conference, and for that one, he's expecting someone else to join her."

"Who?"

"Daniel Sykes," Camille answered flatly.

Krieger laughed. "That is a joke. How in the hell does he expect that to happen?"

"He only says that Camille will receive further instruction after the first press conference is complete," Crawley said.

There was a second nightmare scenario currently playing out in Camille's mind, one that she fully expected to encounter whether she spoke of it or not. "I'd like to listen to the recorder now," she told Parsons.

He gave it to her and she immediately pressed the play button.

The first voice she heard was distant, and much to Camille's surprise, female.

"Whenever you're ready, it's recording."

The next voice she heard nearly fractured her soul.

"Hi, Camille. I hope you can hear this."

"She can hear you, Paul," the female voice assured him. *"Just keep talking."*

"Camille, it's Dad." He attempted to clear his dry throat, but his voice only became hoarser. *"I'm so sorry, sweetheart. I know you've been worried sick about me. Just know that I'm still here, I love you, and I'm always thinking about you."* After a long pause, he continued. *"I saw you on TV today. Thank you for saying what you did about me. You're right about one thing, I'm certainly not a saint."* His chuckle quickly devolved into a furious bout of coughing. He composed himself and continued. *"But I do love you, more than life itself, and I want you to do*

whatever you need to do to keep yourself safe. That means not worrying about me. No matter what happens here, I'll be okay knowing that you're okay."

"*Tell her what she needs to do,*" the distant female voice said.

Paul waited a long time before answering. "*Do what you know is right.*"

"*Paul, tell her what she needs to do,*" the woman repeated.

Her father's voice suddenly grew stronger and more defiant. "*Do what I taught you to do, Camille. Do what the Bureau trained you to do.*"

The woman's voice lost its soft edge. "*Jesus, Paul. What are you doing?*"

Camille heard the squeaking of door hinges, then another male voice. "*Turn him around and get that blindfold on.*"

The sound of a brief scuffle ensued, then there was silence.

After a few seconds, the male voice spoke again. "*If I were you, Camille, I wouldn't listen to him. He's been under a lot of stress, and he probably isn't thinking clearly.*"

The voice was unfamiliar, but Camille knew exactly who it was.

"*If you have any designs on seeing him again, don't dismiss me a second time. Paul won't get a third chance. Neither will Jacob Deaver. Neither will you. I expect to see that lovely face of yours on television by tomorrow afternoon.*"

With that, the recording ended.

The group was silent for a long time afterward, no one able to articulate the appropriate response.

Camille didn't need to hear their response to know what was appropriate. The option to do anything else had officially been taken off the table.

"How do we go about setting up another press conference?" she asked Crawley.

"You can't be serious."

"Of course I'm serious, Peter. That was my father's voice

we just heard. You said it yourself, we didn't take the first letter seriously enough, and look what happened. I'm not making the same mistake again." Camille could feel the pressure in her chest expanding with each word she spoke. "If he wants me to go on television and read his damn script, then I'll go on television and read the damn script."

"But that's not all he wants you to do, Camille. Or did you forget about the part where he mentioned Sykes?"

She'd done her best to forget that part. "There's no way I'm going anywhere near him."

"Really? Because he sure as hell expects you to."

"Isn't Daniel Sykes locked up in some prison in Pennsylvania?" Parsons asked.

Camille nodded.

"That would present one hell of a logistical nightmare, even if you wanted to do it."

"Maybe going through with the first press conference would buy you enough time to at least figure it out," Krieger suggested.

"I don't have any other choice," Camille said.

Crawley bit down hard on his lip, his mind clearly grasping for a suitable counter-argument. Unable to find one, he turned to Franklin. "We'll need to take the recorder and envelope to the CBI lab. I have agents there working the first letter for prints. If they get a hit, they'll want to do a cross-match."

"Let me bag them, and they're all yours. What about the letter?"

Crawley looked at Camille.

After thinking about it, she said, "He's giving us until tomorrow. There's time to work it for prints before we do anything else."

Crawley nodded, then handed the letter to Franklin. "Bag this too."

"You got it."

Crawley turned back to Camille. "Does this mean you're willing to take some time to rethink this?"

"It means that I'm not willing to break the chain of evidence."

The hopeful glint in his eyes disappeared. "I'll let Pratt and Mendoza know that we're on our way."

"Krieger and I will monitor things here," Parsons chimed in. "If we find anything else, we'll be in touch."

"Thank you," Camille said.

"Do you want me to talk to Officers Bradley and Stanton? Figure out what went wrong?" Krieger asked Crawley.

"No. Those guys are dealing with enough. If anything, they deserve an apology. I was out of line to go after them the way I did."

Camille agreed that he was out of line, but she also knew that once he realized it, he'd find a way to make things right. He always did.

As Crawley stepped away to make the call to CBI, Franklin returned with the letter and recorder. "Here you go, Camille. Bagged, tagged, and sealed."

Not only did he sound like Paul Grisham, he smiled like him too.

She wanted to take this as a sign that her father was somehow with her, guiding her through the maze of uncertainty that made the end of this nightmare feel as if it were still a million miles away.

"Thank you, Robert."

Franklin mouthed a reply as he handed her the evidence bag. But it was her father's voice that she heard.

"Do what I taught you to do, Camille. Do what the Bureau trained you to do."

She knew exactly what those words meant.

He wanted her to fight. For him. For Jacob Deaver. For herself.

And she would. Until the very end.

She could only pray that he had the strength to do the same.

14

A SMALL PIECE OF HUMANITY

THREE WEEKS AFTER BEING TAKEN from his home with no warning or explanation, Paul Grisham still had no memory of how he'd actually ended up here.

He did remember the frantic woman showing up at his front door earlier that day, searching for a man he'd never heard of. Her name was Meredith Park. His name was Jacob Deaver. Neither name meant anything to Paul then. They meant a whole lot to him now.

He remembered Camille rushing to his house to meet Meredith. He remembered the relief when Camille informed her that she'd met with Jacob no less than an hour prior, and the subsequent horror when they realized that the man she met was not Jacob Deaver at all.

The fear didn't actually hit Paul until Camille made the decision to pursue this Jacob Deaver imposter without his or anyone else's help. She bolted out his front door with Meredith Park in tow - without an ounce of hesitation.

Any mistake that Camille ever made as an agent, including her decision to quit, came as the result of an impulsive nature that she sometimes had difficulty controlling. It made Paul fear for her more times than he cared to. In most cases, the fear was unjustified.

In this case, it wasn't.

Aside from the plea to contact him immediately should anything happen, he couldn't remember the last words he spoke to her. Was there a hug? Was there an '*I love you, please be careful?*' Did she know how proud he was that she still had the fight that made her such a formidable agent? He couldn't bear the thought of her not knowing that. But given his current plight, the very real possibility existed that he'd never again have the chance to tell her.

So when the opportunity came to speak to her through a recorded message, Paul didn't give a moment's thought to ignoring the words written for him in lieu of his own. And even if he'd been afforded the luxury of prolonged reflection, his decision would've ultimately been the same.

"Do what I taught you to do, Camille."

He repeated the words to himself exactly as he'd spoken them into the recorder, partly because he wanted to ensure that the weight of the message was as substantial as he'd hoped it was, and partly to reiterate to the woman sitting next to him that he had no regrets in saying it.

Rather than respond to his sudden outburst, she looked at him with a tired expression. Her bright green eyes were burdened with a concern that Paul couldn't place. She stood up from the chair that she'd put near his cot, walked over to the heavy door that kept him contained, and knocked three times. She then turned back to Paul, staring at him with a morbidly solemn expression that momentarily shook him.

"You know the drill," she said softly.

He did indeed.

Standing up, he slowly made his way to a corner of the tiny, dimly-lit room where he faced the wall, bowed his head, and closed his eyes. Within seconds, he heard the door open, then felt the subsequent change in temperature as the two men entered. The rigid cloth of the bandana he'd grown sadly accustomed to was gently folded around his eyes before being tightened around his head with a violent force that sent him reeling backwards. He wasn't as solid on his feet as he once was - advancing age and retirement from active duty softening most of his sharp edges - but the time here had also weakened him considerably, and he was incapable of mounting any physical resistance.

Once the blindfold was firmly secured, Paul was turned away from the wall toward the door.

"Don't move," he heard a young, familiar voice say. Once, in the beginning, when he tried to wrestle himself free of a grip that he deemed unnecessarily tight, he felt the cold steel pressed against his temple and heard the lever-action as the gun was cocked. He knew then that total compliance was the only option.

A hard tug on his arm told him that it was time to go.

The air grew colder as they walked, and he knew that he was being guided out of the room. He'd only left that room twice before, each time he was blindfolded, and each time he met with *him*. Before today, Paul didn't know the first thing about him, his motives, or his intentions. Paul did know that he was being held here along with someone else - the writer whose disappearance brought Meredith Park to his doorstep. But in neither of their brief interactions did Paul's captor offer a reason for Jacob Deaver's presence, or Paul's for that matter.

That all changed this morning.

"Hold on a minute."

The woman's sudden directive stopped the guide dead in his tracks, causing a sightless Paul to stumble. A gentle hand on his arm helped him reclaim his footing.

Paul could detect the light aroma of her lavender perfume, and he knew she was standing in front of him.

"You're such a smart man. Why would you insist on doing something so thoughtless? And so dangerous?" Her despondent tone suggested that she was worried for him. Her current actions, of course, suggested otherwise.

"I gave it plenty of thought," Paul countered with a forced defiance. "I told Camille exactly what she needed to hear."

"You told Camille exactly what *you* needed to hear. You hoped that your words would inspire some heroic leap of faith that couldn't possibly play out under the current circumstances. You want to think that she's capable of more than she is, and I completely understand that. But what you have to understand is that no one survives this - not you, not Jacob, not Meredith Park and certainly not Camille - if she doesn't do exactly as he says.

She put her hand on Paul's shoulder and squeezed lightly. "You're her father. You love her, and you want what's best for her. Abe wanted the best for his daughter too. He couldn't be there for her the way he wanted to, but that didn't mean he didn't care. There wasn't anything in the world he wouldn't have done for her. But he was powerless to help when she needed him the most. You can still help your daughter, Paul. If you get another opportunity to do so, please don't throw it away. There's still a chance for everyone to walk away from this, but we need your help."

Paul had detected sympathy in her tone before but quickly dismissed it. Now he suspected the sentiment may have been real. From the moment he was brought here, she was the only consistent human interaction he'd had, and she'd always gone out of her way to make sure he had some measure of daily comfort in the otherwise hellish environment he'd found himself in. From the warm, freshly-cooked meals, to the trivial attempts at conversation, to the fact that she didn't force him to wear a blindfold in her presence, she was clearly interested in establishing the trust between captor and captive that was so crucial in executing a broader objective.

Paul knew that Stockholm Syndrome was a very real thing, and it was rarely achieved without careful design and manipulation. What he now needed to figure out was whether she was attempting to manipulate him or if her kindness was rooted in some deeper emotion; an emotion that could possibly be exploited. Without the means to physically fight back, a psychological counterattack was the only avenue of hope left available to him.

"You've been good to me throughout all of this, and I want you to know that I appreciate it." The words almost physically hurt as they came out of his mouth, but he felt satisfied that he'd manufactured the appropriate authenticity. "I'm assuming Jacob Deaver has received the same treatment."

"He has." The woman took a step toward him. "But he's also been more cooperative. A little cooperation goes a long way."

"I realize that, and going forward, I'll do whatever I can. I just want you to know that your kindness hasn't been unnoticed. And it won't be forgotten."

She quietly cleared her throat, a sign to Paul that his gesture made her feel uneasy. It was exactly the feeling he'd hoped to inspire.

"Thank you." Then after a short beat, she added softly, "It's time to go now."

Paul felt the guide's hand tighten around his arm. "Just one more thing," he said before he could be led away.

"What?"

"Can you tell me your name?"

Hesitation. "Why do you want to know my name?"

"You know my name. It's only fair, isn't it?" He thought about adding the fact that she'd already let the name Abe slip out, but decided against it. He instead offered a light chuckle that quickly deteriorated into another bout of coughing that his dry throat was all too adept at manufacturing.

"Clearly you're not drinking enough water," she said sternly before putting the bottle in his hand.

After a few swallows, the coughing subsided. "Thank you."

She said nothing as she took the bottle from him.

Paul's gratitude was replaced with a brief swell of anger. "You have me here against my will, you're threatening my life, and more importantly, my daughter's life, and you can't offer me something as simple as your name?"

"I'm doing everything I can to make you comfortable, Paul. That's my job, and I'm happy to do it. But I don't owe you anything beyond that." Aside from a heavy breath, her tone was measured. "What good would it do to tell you my name anyway? It's not like we'll be friends when this is over."

Paul struggled to swallow the hard lump that formed in his throat. "Because this moment right now is all that I have. And in this moment, I don't need friends. I need to know that I'm in the presence of other human beings. I need you to recognize my humanity by offering me some small piece of yours."

She hesitated for a long time before responding. "Listen, Paul. If I tell you my na-"

Before she could finish, a familiar voice infiltrated the space.

"Bring him in. Now."

Paul had always been aware of the loudspeaker mounted in the corner opposite his cot (just as he'd been aware of the camera mounted directly above him), but he never heard anything come from it until now.

The man he now knew as Abe had been watching the entire exchange. And based on his tone, he wasn't the least bit pleased with what he saw.

"I'm sorry, Paul," the woman said quietly.

"I know."

She swallowed hard. "It's time to go."

This time, Paul was the one to hesitate. "I know."

15

PLANTING CLUES

AGENT PRATT WAS STANDING in front of the CBI conference room TV monitor when Camille and Crawley walked in. Crawley had briefed him on the Durants and Agent Wells prior to arriving, but based on the look of disbelief that clouded Pratt's sharply handsome face as he watched the on-scene report, the reality had yet to fully settle in.

"They haven't given any details on the shooting yet," he said with a slight crack in his voice as he looked away from the screen.

"Any mention of Wells?" Crawley asked.

Pratt shook his head. "They've only confirmed that there were three victims and that as of now, they're still unidentified."

"That will change soon enough," Camille speculated. "Once they make the connection that the victims were the reporter at my news conference and his FBI escort, the shit officially hits the fan."

"And there may not be anything we can do to contain it," Pratt followed.

Camille held up the evidence bags containing the two letters and the voice recorder. "That's why I need to go through with this while we can still stay ahead of it."

Pratt's heavy eyes lit up with curiosity. "Are those the items that the perp left at the scene?"

"Yes," Crawley confirmed. "And before we do anything else, we need to get them to the lab."

"Do you mind if I take a quick look?" Pratt asked, holding his hand out to Camille.

She thought about telling him no purely out of spite, but then remembered her vow not to let her horrible first impression taint any working relationship she would have with him going forward. "Where is Agent Mendoza?" she asked after giving him the bags.

"A hit came in on the letters after Crawley and I spoke. Allison went down to retrieve them."

Camille and Crawley exchanged a nervous glance.

"If the first set of letters don't tell us anything, it's highly unlikely we'll get anything from the second," Crawley asserted.

Camille nodded as she watched Agent Pratt put on a pair of latex gloves.

"The font type is the exact same as the first letter," he said as he eased the paper out of the evidence bag and held it up. His icy blue eyes widened as he scanned the words. When he finished, he looked at Camille. "This guy is kidding, right?"

"It's definitely not a joke," Camille answered as she pointed at the recorder. "He told us so himself."

Pratt promptly took the recorder out and pressed the play button. He visibly tensed at the sound of Paul's voice.

So did Camille.

When the recording ended, Pratt looked at her. The hard edge that she was met with after their first encounter had all but melted away. In its place was something much kinder.

"I can only imagine how hard it was to hear your father's voice like this. "But hearing it is the best thing we could've hoped for. He's alive, and because of that, this has a good chance to end the way we all want it to."

Camille took in a deep breath and quietly let it out. Based on their tense interactions before now, she would've expected his words of optimism to ring hollow. But one look in his eyes told her that the words weren't hollow. She knew it shouldn't have mattered what he thought either way, but she felt a palpable sense of relief at the appearance of the human being behind the gruff exterior. "I hope you're right, Agent Pratt."

Pratt allowed a tight half-smile to infiltrate his face. "Okay, I'm officially calling for an end to the formalities. From now on, I'm Gabe, you're Camille, and he's Peter. If I'm going to be spending this much time with you in the foxhole, we should all feel comfortable with first names."

"Fair enough," Camille said, allowing a half-smile to crease her own face.

"Fair enough," Crawley echoed, straight-faced as ever.

Agent Mendoza entered the room, quickly taking note of the relaxed air between the group. "I apologize in advance for killing the mood."

Camille looked at the manila folder in her hand. "Are those the lab results?"

Mendoza nodded as she set the folder on the table and opened it.

Pratt's smile promptly went away. "Your silence always worries me, Al. Tell me you've got good news."

"I certainly have news. Whether or not it's good remains to be seen." She took the lab report out of the folder and began reading. "There were two sets of prints on each of the letters. The first set belonged to Durant."

"And the second?" an anxious Crawley asked.

Mendoza looked at the report again, as if to ensure that

the information was correct. "The second came back as a match for Jacob Deaver."

Of all the results Camille expected to hear, that one would have been dead last on the list. "That can't be right."

"It is. We cross-referenced both sets of prints in the IAFIS database. Durant's were indexed from a routine background check two years ago. We found Deaver's from a DUI arrest back in 2012."

"What about the envelope?" Crawley asked.

"Three sets," Mendoza reported. "One belonging to Durant, one belonging, once again, to Jacob Deaver, and one still unidentified. DPD has tracked down the courier who delivered the letter, and they're in the process of collecting his prints. If the third set does belong to him, we're basically back at square one."

"There was a second letter found at the Durant crime scene along with a voice recorder," Camille told Mendoza. "We need them cross-checked ASAP."

"I can run them down right now," Mendoza said as she took the evidence bags from Pratt.

"I'll need a copy of the letter for myself," Camille told her.

"I'll have the lab tech scan one for you."

"Thanks."

"No problem. Let's hope the perp actually left us something to work with this time."

"At this point, the odds of that are pretty slim," Camille admitted. "But we have to try."

Mendoza nodded her understanding and quickly made her way out of the room. "Again, sorry for the buzz-kill."

Crawley turned to Camille. "Jacob Deaver?"

Camille took a moment to consider her response. "First the recording from my father, now Jacob's prints. He clearly wants us to know that they're alive."

"A power play to get you to do what he wants," Pratt added.

"Exactly. And that's why I have to do it."

Crawley was slow to respond.

"You can't still be on the fence about this," Camille chided. "What else does he have to do to get our attention? Kill one of them? I can't let that happen, Peter. I don't care what I have to do."

"Excuse me if I'm not anxious to throw you to the wolves without knowing what could happen. This press conference is a smoke-screen, Camille. He's obviously leading you into something else."

"Obviously," Camille replied firmly. "But I'm willing to take the chance. Besides, we have the advantage of knowing that the press conference is a smoke-screen. Our best move is to play along for now and prepare for the probability of escalation. If we don't play along, escalation won't be a probability. It'll be a foregone conclusion."

Crawley let out an aggravated sigh as he began pacing the room.

"At the risk of pissing you off even more, I think Camille is absolutely right," Pratt said. "As much as we hate to admit it, this guy is holding all the cards, and he's already shown us that he's not afraid to play his hand aggressively. Does that mean we give in to him completely? Of course not. But we're fumbling around in the dark right now. Throwing him the bone of this press conference ensures that he'll continue to engage with us. If we want to catch this guy, we need him to continue engaging. We've got Paul's recording and Jacob's prints, but something tells me he's done planting clues." Pratt turned to Camille. "I hate to use the word bait, but the inescapable truth is that you're the only chance we have at actually catching him."

Camille felt a shudder as she looked at Crawley. He'd

stopped pacing long enough to glare at Pratt before turning to Camille.

"I'm doing this, Peter," she said resolutely. "With or without your help." She paused to pick up the letter that contained the statement she was to read. "I'd prefer your help."

Crawley was silent for a long time, his standard response when finding himself on the losing end of an argument. When he finally did speak, it was short and to the point. "We keep the environment tightly controlled, you read the words on that paper, and then we shut it down. No reporters, no questions afterward."

Camille nodded, allowing Crawley's sharp directive to hang in the air. He needed to maintain some semblance of control, and in this case, she was not above letting him have it - or at least the illusion of it.

"Just how tight do we want the environment?" Pratt asked.

"Since this guy is so hellbent on creating a show, we'll need a cameraman, someone from the normal pool that you trust."

"I have someone in mind," Pratt replied.

"We also need to keep the location in-house this time," Crawley added. "We can even have it in this room."

"It might be good to have the CBI seal in the shot," Pratt concurred. As long as we're making a show of it and all."

Crawley nodded at Pratt's suggestion then turned to Camille. "Nine A.M. tomorrow. That'll give the lab time to do its work, and allow you time to sleep on this."

Even if she needed time to contemplate what she was doing, which she didn't, sleep wouldn't be an option. "Nine A.M."

"What happens in the interim?" Pratt asked. "We're in stasis here until those print results come back."

"You and Mendoza keep monitoring the lab work," Crawley answered. "I need to get to the hospital to see Stephen." He checked his phone. "Still no update."

"Let us know as soon as you hear something," Camille said. "In the meantime, I'll get with Chloe to see how the follow up with Daniel went."

"Jesus, in all the chaos, I completely forgot about him," Pratt admitted. "Do you think they're making any headway?"

"I don't know," Camille answered. "But if anyone can bring him around, it's Chloe."

"I'd say you did a pretty fair job of that," Pratt countered, his half-smile returning. "You employed my reverse psychology ploy much better than I ever could have."

Camille resisted the urge to return his smile this time, though she did appreciate his admission. She responded with an admission of her own. "I give you full credit, Agent Pratt. I was obviously wrong to think that your idea wouldn't work."

"I thought we'd agreed to drop the formalities."

"Sorry. Gabe."

Pratt's smile broadened.

"Unfortunately, we're going to need more if we want to crack MacPherson," Crawley interjected. "I'll be curious to hear Detective Sullivan's report."

As the trio made their way out of the conference room, Camille was struck with a thought. "We've been rightfully focused on the man who we think is orchestrating all of this. But who's the woman in the recording with my father?"

"Must be an accomplice," Pratt answered quickly.

"Yeah, but to what extent?" Camille asked. "Was she involved in the abductions directly? Did she take part in the murders of those girls? Moreover, does she even know about the murders? If she's a wife or a girlfriend who's directly involved, then she's on the extreme end of the spectrum. I've personally never profiled a woman who exists there."

"It's very rare," Crawley added.

"Whoever she is, she's clearly playing a vital role," Pratt said. "Hers was the first voice we heard on the recording, which means that she most likely facilitated it. She's also spending significant time with your father and presumably Jacob, maybe even more than he is. And if she is on the extreme end of the spectrum, it doesn't bode well. One extreme head-case is bad enough. Two makes things a hell of a lot tougher."

"Then we'd better hope that she's not on the extreme end of the spectrum," Crawley said.

The thought made Camille's blood run cold.

"You can't always tell from a voice alone, but she sounded older, at least middle-aged," Pratt speculated. "Depending on the connection, it could give us a little more insight into our main perp as well."

"Makes sense that they're older," Crawley added, "given the planning they've put into this. I'm sure it's taken a lot of patience and restraint to hold Jacob and Paul as long as they have, much more than our perp probably has at this point. That could explain her involvement."

It had been three weeks, and despite everything, Camille's father, and presumably Jacob, were still alive, which meant that they were at the very least being sheltered and fed. The only solace that Camille could take right now was that this woman, whatever her other motives, was also serving as a de facto caretaker. She knew for sure that the man behind those letters was not.

He was something else entirely; the kind of something that she knew all-too-well. Entire libraries could be filled with profiles written about animals like him. Unfortunately, none of those texts ever offered guidance on how to deal with the animal when he's trapping the person you love the most under his demented grip.

To figure that out, Camille would have to improvise and pray for the day when this particular animal's successful capture could be tucked away in the annals of BAU history alongside all the others.

Right now, that day felt very far away.

16

A GAME OF CHANCE

THERE WAS SO MUCH TO LOVE about Sabrina Noble. She was kind, loving (to a fault sometimes), and incredibly patient. Most importantly, she listened before she spoke and never made the mistake of asking too many questions.

But the very things that fueled Abraham Noble's intense love for his wife were also the things that infuriated him the most.

Her capacity for generosity was boundless, so much so that it made her more susceptible to manipulation than most. She'd been a victim of his manipulation more times than he cared to admit, but every instance was undertaken with her best interests in mind. Whether she was unaware of the tactics being used against her or an all-too-willing participant was a conversation he never saw fit to initiate before now. But given the interaction he'd just witnessed between her and Camille Grisham's father, Abraham was beginning to think that a serious heart to heart on the subject was in order.

Her critical role in keeping Paul and Jacob alive notwithstanding, he felt no need to discuss the matter of their captivity beyond what inspired it in the first place. Even if she didn't agree with the means (which he never would've suspected before now), she most certainly agreed with the end. She loved Madison like she was her own daughter. And even though the circumstances always dictated that she did so at a considerable distance, she didn't feel any less connected to her.

Abraham had also learned to love his daughter from afar. He was never allowed to be the ever-present father that he wanted to be - his witch of an ex-wife, the courts, and the police saw to that. But he was her father nonetheless; her flesh and blood. And her presence on this earth, though far away from his, provided the only reassurance that his own presence here actually meant something.

When that reassurance was brutally snatched away from him six months ago, he was left with nothing but hatred for those who took it away, a burning desire to inflict twice the pain that he was made to endure, and a wife of fourteen years - a soulmate, he once dared to think - who'd been sufficiently scarred by the atrocities of her own life to completely understand his design. Not only did she understand his design, but she also encouraged its implementation; fully aware of the costs involved, the lives that could be lost, and the necessary abandonment of a soft, generous spirit that would only succeed in clouding her judgment.

Unfortunately, her judgment, as he witnessed not only today but for the duration of Paul and Jacob's time here, was still very cloudy.

But at this moment, Abraham's was never more clear.

He kept Paul blindfolded as he pulled the Ruger SP101 six-shot out of the drawer and loaded the single Federal Magnum round that he'd marked specifically for this occasion. He left the cylinder open and instructed Paul to remove his blindfold.

His trembling hands struggled to remove the tight knot.

"Do you need help?" Abraham asked with a complete absence of empathy.

Paul was silent until the knot was undone and the cloth fell from his face.

"I show a lot of trust by not requiring you to be hand-cuffed," Abraham said as Paul squinted at the pale white light shining in his face. "That's a lot more trust than I normally offer to our friend over there." He motioned to a blindfolded Jacob Deaver. He'd been set up in the corner of the otherwise empty room with a small desk, folding chair, and old fashioned typewriter. He'd also been instructed before Paul's arrival to type everything he heard.

"It's remarkable that he can do all of that with a blindfold on," Abraham said over the clatter of the keys. "I've checked his work thoroughly too. Barely a mistake to be found."

Paul's eyes widened when they finally adjusted to the light, and he realized who was in the room with them.

"I believe this is the first time the two of you have actually been in the same space, so allow me to do the honors. Paul Grisham, meet Jacob Deaver. I'm sure you'll be fast friends in no time, with everything you have in common."

Paul's eyes widened even more when they found Abraham. He wasn't sure if it was the unsightly scar that nearly split his weathered face in two, or if it was the silver revolver in his hand. Based on the furrowed look of disgust, Abraham guessed that Paul was stuck on the former. For good measure, he gave the cylinder a quick spin and flipped it closed, just like they did in the old westerns that his father used to take him to.

At the sight of the gun, Paul's entire body grew rigid.

"Do you remember the circumstances that brought you here?" Abraham asked in as measured a voice as he could summon.

His eyes still trained on the gun, Paul shook his head.

"Apparently it was really something. I say apparently because I wasn't actually there. But the second-hand account was quite memorable. From what they said, you put up a bit of a fight, at least in the beginning. Two random assholes show up in my living room uninvited, and you bet I'd be putting up a fight too. But old guys like us can't fight for long, so eventually, they got the better of you. My wife thinks you suffered a concussion after the head blow that knocked you out. That would probably explain why you don't remember anything. What a smart one my wife is. Most kind-hearted person you could ever hope to meet in a situation like this. But I'm sure you already figured that out. Just like you figured out that I'm not nearly as kind-hearted as she is."

Abraham raised the gun and pointed it in Paul's direction before lowering it again, a move that didn't appear to faze Paul in the least.

"Not the first time I've had one of those pointed at me," he said flatly.

"Could be the last."

"Why haven't you done it already?"

"You know."

"I'm being used as bait."

"Bait is such a cliche word. I like to think of you more as a tool. You can only use a good piece of bait once, maybe twice, but a good tool can be used over and over again, sometimes for many different things." He pointed the gun at Paul again. "Sadly, even the best tools can eventually outlive their usefulness."

"If you're going to do it, just do it."

Even though it physically hurt to do so, Abraham couldn't resist a smile. "I admire your courage. I'm curious how much of it you passed down to your daughter."

"You'll find out soon enough."

"Perhaps. But what good will that courage do her if she makes it here only to find you with a bullet in your head?"

Paul's stiff resolve slowly began to falter.

"You're a certified badass, so I'm sure you could handle seeing such a thing. But Camille…"

"Leave my daughter alone. She didn't do anything to you."

"She did plenty. And she has to answer for it." Abraham paused to allow the tide of emotion welling up inside him to recede. "All I want her to do is answer for it. She doesn't have to die. Neither does anyone else. I'm asking her to do a simple thing. Just like I asked you to do a simple thing. But like her, you're turning a simple thing into something very complicated."

"If you think for a second that I'm going to help you do anything to—"

"I'd be sadly mistaken. I get it. I once had a daughter too, so I understand the obsessive need to protect her. But you're going about it the wrong way. All you had to do was read what I had Jacob write for you. We went through a lot of trouble composing that message. Didn't we Jacob?"

A trembling Jacob paused long enough to nod.

"Why didn't you read it?" Abraham asked Paul.

"Because I knew she needed to hear something else."

"And you know better than I do what Camille needs to hear right now?"

"I'm her father. Of course I know better."

"Of course you know better. Well, in all of your infinite wisdom, did you ever stop to think that there could be a consequence for not doing what I asked?"

"At the time, it wasn't even a consideration."

"Is it a consideration now?"

Paul looked him square in the eye before boldly answering, "No."

Abraham allowed a long silence to settle between them before pointing the gun again. "Are you a gambling man, Paul?"

"I told you, that doesn't scare me."

"You're definitely a gambling man. Tell me, what's your vice of choice? Poker? Blackjack? Spades?"

Paul was silent.

"No. None of those predictable card games for you. You strike me as a guy who likes a simple, old-fashioned game of chance. So how about we play one right now?"

Without saying another word, Abraham turned the gun on Jacob and pulled the trigger. The click of the empty cylinder reverberated through the room like a shotgun blast. An audible groan escaped Paul's throat before he could suppress it.

The sound also caused Jacob to stop typing. "What was that?"

"Don't ask questions, Jacob," Abraham barked. "Write."

Jacob said nothing as he began typing again.

Abraham eyed the cylinder before cocking the hammer again.

"What are you doing?" a visibly shaken Paul asked.

He pointed the gun at Jacob and pulled the trigger. Another empty click. "That's two out of six, Paul. As a gambling man, you should know that the odds are only getting worse. So tell me, what do you want to do?"

"What do you mean?"

"Do you want to keep playing this game, or do you want to comply?"

"Comply with what?"

Abraham sighed, safetied the gun, then slid the cylinder open. He took the bullet out, held it up so Paul could see it, then dropped it back in. He spun the open cylinder. "Round and round she goes. Where she stops, nobody..." He slammed the cylinder shut, cocked the hammer back, aimed the gun at Jacob, and pulled the trigger. He smiled once again at the sound of an empty click. "Knows."

Paul froze, unable to move a single inch of his tall, broad frame.

"I haven't hurt a hair on your head since you've been here," Abraham proclaimed. "I've kept you alive. Kept you fed. Warm. Comfortable. And *this* is how you repay me? By making me threaten you? I asked you to do one thing, Paul."

"Do you really think I'd knowingly send my daughter into harm's way?"

Abraham smiled again. "You really don't care about what happens to you here, do you?"

Paul didn't respond.

Abraham then motioned to a typing Jacob. "Do you care what happens to him?"

When Paul didn't answer, Abraham cocked the hammer again and lifted the gun toward Jacob.

"Enough," Paul shouted.

Abraham lowered the gun. "I'll take that as a yes."

"Why are you doing this?"

"Don't bother asking about my motives. Don't ask about Sabrina's either. I know you wanted to know her name, so I saved you the trouble of asking her again. I'm aware that she told you mine. I swear, she's too damn sentimental for her own good sometimes. But God help me if I don't love her more than life. She really does mean well. Doesn't make her smart, though. It doesn't make her your ally either." Abraham took a deep breath and slowly exhaled before raising the gun again and pointing it at Paul. "Stick to the script next time."

"And if I don't?"

Abraham turned the gun on Jacob.

"Alright, alright," Paul finally relented.

"Wise man." Without warning, he turned the gun on Paul

and pulled the trigger. Paul's defensive reflexes sent him flailing backward in his chair as another empty click filled the room.

"So much for you not caring about what happens. Fortunately, you'll live to comply another day."

Abraham opened the cylinder and removed the bullet. He took a long look at it before saying, "The irony is that you never had anything to worry about. This particular beauty was never meant for you or Jacob anyway." He held it up high enough for Paul to read the name he'd written across the smooth silver surface.

The tiny script was crude and smudged, but he was certain that Camille's name was clearly legible.

After giving Paul ample time to let the image sink in, he put the bullet back in the gun. Then he pulled out a small ammunition box and set it on the table in front of him. He removed the four bullets inside, which he also labeled, and held them up for Paul to see.

"This one, in case you can't read it, is for Daniel Sykes. This one is for…" he pointed silently at a still typing Jacob. "This one is unmarked, just in case I have to improvise. And this last one is very, very special because this is the one I've saved just for you."

He put the bullets into the cylinder and slammed it closed, knowing there was no need for the theatrics of spinning it this time. "Let's pray I don't have to use them."

Paul looked like he wanted to speak but wisely kept his mouth shut. Abraham then turned to Jacob.

"You get all that, son?"

Jacob sniffed softly as he nodded.

"Good," Abraham said, then yelled, "Ok boys, you can come in now."

At the sound of the heavy door being opened, he looked

at Paul one more time, confident that the message had finally been received.

"I hope you get a lot of rest, my friend. Tomorrow should be an extremely action-packed day. Until then, you know the drill."

17

ONE LAST TOAST

THE DIAMOND HEAD BAR & GRILLE wasn't nearly as pretentious as the name implied. In fact, it was something of a dive, with its sparse clientele, dimmed house lights, neon sign accents, deep southern-blues soundtrack, and limited beer selection. And it was the perfect place for Camille to be right now.

When Chloe agreed to meet up with her, Camille insisted that it be in a public place, since quiet, intimate spaces allowed the voices of fear in her mind too much free rein. Hence, her trip to the Diamond Head. There weren't any suits or uniforms inside as far as Camille could see, so she assumed it wasn't a cop hangout. Perhaps this was the place Chloe came to get away from cops.

Despite the professional firestorm that had engulfed her life since Camille entered it less than four months ago, Chloe's hazel eyes were always brightly optimistic; the function of an unwavering confidence that Camille found remarkable. She wondered how much of it was a defense mechanism. She was quite adept at constructing them herself and recognized the signs. But Chloe was a special breed - a kind-spirited warrior who could make your entire day with a heartfelt gesture or ruin it completely with a single glare. Thankfully, Camille was never on the receiving end of the latter.

Despite everything happening in her own life, she worried for Chloe. She knew that optimism would take the young detective only so far, given the current state of the DPD and the unfair scrutiny that she'd been subjected to since her partner's murder. She knew there were forces against her that no amount of self-confidence could overcome should those forces decide to take up the cause.

But she also knew that if anyone was capable of weathering a professional firestorm with nothing more than a graceful smile at her disposal, it was Detective Chloe Sullivan, and that gave her hope.

That graceful smile was on full display when she found Camille seated at the furthest booth in the back. Camille had chosen this spot for its privacy. But the few scattered patrons inside told her that unwanted attention wasn't going to be a problem.

"How'd you know this was my favorite booth?" Chloe quipped as she removed her black leather jacket and slid into her seat. She wore the stress of the long day well. Her fitted thermal henley was tucked neatly inside a pair of dark-washed blue jeans that accentuated a shapely, athletic frame. Her detective's badge was still clipped to her belt, but there was no sign of the duty Glock. Camille looked at the ensemble and felt a twinge of envy. What she wouldn't have given to be so comfortably dressed during her Bureau days.

Chloe was a self-professed workout junkie and yoga enthusiast, and it showed. She'd extended multiple invitations for Camille to join her for a session; nothing beats the stress better, she said. Camille certainly knew her way around a gym, and could undoubtedly give the slightly younger detective a run for her money should the opportunity for physical competition ever present itself. But the idea of being in a space with meatheads throwing weights or young girls standing on their heads for two hours at a time wasn't Camille's idea of stress relief.

"Cozy little spot," she said as she handed Chloe the one-page drink menu.

Chloe immediately waved it off. "No need for that. This place makes the best Old-Fashioneds in the city. You like a good bourbon?"

"At this point, I'm not especially picky."

"You'll love it then."

A young, friendly waitress took the order. When she walked away, Camille and Chloe had the entire rear section of the bar to themselves.

"Hell of a crazy day," Chloe began, the smile fading from cheeks that were still red from the outdoor chill.

"I'm afraid you might be underselling it."

"I'm afraid you're right. Any updates on Agent Wells?"

"I talked to Peter a few minutes before I came here. Wells was in surgery for hours, but they managed to remove the bullets from his chest and abdomen. Apparently, he was very lucky. Had one of those rounds gone a few centimeters deeper, it would've struck his heart. As it stands, he's still in critical care. Crawley said he won't leave until Wells's wife gets there. He'll probably stay long afterward."

"Crawley seems like a really good agent," Chloe said.

"He's a really good man too. He's looked after me my entire career. I owe him a lot more than I can ever pay back. Same thing I say about you."

A rush of blood reddened Chloe's cheeks again. "I don't know about that."

"You literally saved my life, Chloe. If that doesn't qualify as an unpayable debt, I don't know what does."

Chloe smiled with pride as if the memory, long-forgotten, suddenly came back to her. "I did do that, didn't I? Well, you literally saved my career, so I guess that makes us even."

The waitress returned with the drinks just in time for them to toast the moment.

"We're really swimming in the deep end right now though," Chloe continued after taking a sip. "Your press conference is all over the country."

Camille figured it would be. "The country hasn't seen anything yet."

"Can I take a look at the letter?"

Camille pulled the folded paper from her coat pocket and gave it to her.

After quickly scanning it, Chloe looked up at her with concerned eyes. "Are you really doing it?"

"I have to."

"But what he's telling you to say is a complete lie."

Camille wasn't sure if it was a *complete* lie. "Small price to pay to keep my father and Jacob safe."

"There's going to be more to it than this statement. You have to know that."

"I absolutely know that." Camille pulled out the second piece of paper from her pocket and handed it to Chloe. "A photocopy of the letter we found at the Durant crime scene."

Chloe read it then looked back at Camille, her concerned eyes widened with shock. "A joint press conference with you and Daniel Sykes? What the hell for?"

"I couldn't begin to guess."

Chloe took another sip of her drink, this one bigger than the first. "Krieger and Parsons told me what went down at the Durant's."

"I'm sure the description didn't do it justice."

"They also told me about the recording."

Camille took a drink. The warmth of the whiskey momentarily soothed the aching in her chest. "I almost lost it when I heard his voice. Right there in the middle of that crime scene in front of all those detectives and forensics guys and photographers, I nearly made myself the main attraction."

"Frankly, I don't know how you kept it together, or how you continue to keep it together. I would've lost my shit a long time ago."

Camille smiled. It was strained and painful. "I haven't kept it together, Chloe. That's the punchline. I'm dying on the inside. And every second I'm away from him, every quiet moment that allows my mind to wander to the worst-case scenario, every time I think back to the day he disappeared and how irresponsible I was to just go chasing after Daniel MacPherson without making sure he was okay, I die just a little bit more."

"It wasn't your fault, Camille. You had no idea what you were dealing with."

"All the more reason to be cautious. Maybe if I would've stayed around, I would be the one there instead of him."

"And *both of you* could be dead right now," Chloe countered sharply. "Your father's abduction was part of the plan all along. It was going to happen one way or the other. All we can do now is figure out his plan before he has the chance to fully execute it."

Camille felt her eyes watering and attempted to blink the onslaught away. She'd cried herself to sleep nearly every night since her father's abduction. And on the nights she couldn't sleep, tears were a constant companion. Despite the frequency with which she shed them, she knew there were plenty left in reserve, and those reserves could be tapped at a second's notice. She was tired of crying. She was tired of feeling helpless. But the grip of sadness was relentlessly tight.

"This really is delicious," she said with a shallow breath as she took another sip of her Old-Fashioned. "But I feel guilty that I get to sit here and drink it while he's out there suffering. I can't seem to shake the feeling that I should be doing more."

"Right now, you're being asked to do more than anyone in your situation should have to. And you're doing it a hell of a lot better than anyone else would, despite your thoughts to the contrary." Chloe paused. "With that said, are you sure you're not taking on too much with this statement?"

"No, I'm not sure," Camille answered truthfully.

"He wants you to go in front of the world to essentially say that you're responsible for all of Daniel Sykes's murders. How can you be okay with that?"

"I'm not. But I really don't have a choice."

"Why this? I mean, why go through all this trouble just to get you to read some ridiculous statement on television?"

"The statement is just the setup, a way to get me, and by extension himself, into the spotlight."

"But he'd already achieved that by killing those four girls."

"He did that to get my attention. He wants a bigger audience now."

Chloe allowed a moment to process Camille's statement. "Tell me what else you know about him."

"He's much older than Daniel. The amount of planning he's displayed so far necessitates experience and patience. He's obviously killed before, so it isn't a worst-case scenario for him. It's the go-to option. He considers himself to be connected to Daniel Sykes in some way, either through Sykes's M.O. or his actual victims. The fact that he killed those girls in a fashion similar to Sykes tells me for sure that the former is true."

"But his connection to Daniel MacPherson could mean

that the latter is true as well," Chloe added. "Do you think he could be linked to one of the victims directly?"

"It's a strong possibility. The problem is that Sykes killed twenty-six people. We interviewed as many family members and friends as we could. None of them raised red flags at the time. But with so many, it's safe to say that a few could have slipped through the cracks."

"Like Daniel MacPherson."

Camille nodded. "It's a smaller pool than if we'd started from scratch, but we're still talking dozens of potential suspects. Without any concrete link between them aside from Sykes, it's a wild goose chase at best."

"We do have a concrete link," Chloe said. "Unfortunately, he isn't talking."

"Were you able to get anything else out of Daniel?"

Chloe shook her head. "We showed him your statement, told him about Durant and his wife. We also mentioned that an FBI agent was shot. We let him assume it was you for a while, and that really seemed to shake him. But he eventually dug his heels in. We sent him back to county without getting anything new."

"Did you at least plant a seed or two?"

"I definitely gave him a lot to think about, just like I promised I would. But at some point, we have to inspire him to do more than think."

"And we're running out of time to make that happen."

Chloe sank a little bit in her seat. "I'm sorry we couldn't crack him more."

"Don't you dare apologize, Chloe. I know you're not done with him yet."

"It was you who recommended that I be put back on MacPherson, wasn't it?"

"Yes, and with good reason. We have some really good people working this. From where I'm sitting, you're the best. I know things are challenging for you in the department right now with all the fallout from Graham, but I guarantee that Hitchcock knows how valuable you are. Otherwise, he never would've put you back on."

Chloe's chest expanded, and she sat up straight in her seat. "It means a lot that you want my help on this. And I promise I won't stop until we nail the bastard."

Camille raised her half-empty glass. "Cheers to that."

"Cheers."

After taking a long drink, Chloe asked, "How does it feel to be back with the Bureau?"

"I wouldn't say that I'm back," Camille answered with what was now a permanently ingrained defensiveness.

"The badge may not be official, but for all intents and purposes, you're leading this investigation," Chloe countered.

Camille had never thought of herself as leading the investigation. She was here because she couldn't bear the thought of sitting on the sidelines while others - most of whom she neither knew nor trusted - did all the work to find her father. It was true that she knew what the copycat was capable of better than anyone else, but that was Crawley's justification. Her own justification for coming back was that it was personal, and it wasn't permanent.

"Crawley's the best in the Bureau as far as I'm concerned. He's leading things, and he should be."

"Really? And how many times have you already told him no?"

Camille stared at her for a long time, hesitant to confirm the obvious. "Next question."

"What about the rest of the team?"

"Aside from Agent Wells, I like Mendoza the most. She doesn't say a whole lot, but she sees a lot. Really keen eye. She's more than suited for the job."

"And Agent Pratt?"

Camille was afraid she'd bring him up. "Had you asked me when I first met him, I'd say he was a total douchebag."

"That charming, huh? What do you say now?"

Camille gave herself time to legitimately consider the question. "I'd only call him a partial douchebag now."

"Sounds like he's growing on you."

Camille wasn't ready to admit that quite yet, though she was ready to concede that her first impression may have been wrong.

"At the risk of being shallow and completely inappropriate, he's pretty cute," Chloe blurted out of nowhere.

The proclamation left Camille stumped for a response. It wasn't Chloe's observation, but the timing of it that threw her. She'd longed for the day when they could engage in normal girlfriend conversation without the specter of some personal crisis looming over them. But that experience had eluded them thus far, and she wasn't prepared for its sudden arrival.

Chloe had apparently picked up on her discomfort. "Sorry, Camille. It's just hard not to notice."

It was hard, but she still wasn't ready to acknowledge it. "I thought you were head over heels for that guy in homicide. What's his name? Priest?"

Chloe nodded. "Yes. And I am head over heels."

"How are you managing that with everything going on in the department?"

Her eyes lost a bit of their sparkle as she nervously blew a stray lock of curly brown hair off of her face. "Let's just say it's complicated."

Camille knew a sore spot when she saw one and decided not to pry. "Talk about it another time?"

Chloe's smile returned. "Sure. By then I'll be expecting some details about your first date with Pratt. Juicy ones."

Camille wadded up the napkin that came with her drink and tossed it at her. "You're so ridiculous."

They shared a good laugh. For Camille, it was like much-needed oxygen.

"Will you be there tomorrow?" she then asked.

"If you want me to be, then absolutely."

"I do. Nine A.M. CBI headquarters."

"Okay. But if Hitchcock knows I'm there, he'll want to be there too."

Camille shook her head. "The fewer people I have to look at, the better. He can watch on television with everyone else."

"Fair enough. What's the plan after you read the statement?"

"We dig a little deeper into Daniel, even if he's not willing to offer anything up himself. We have to find out who he was talking to before he came out here and what connections he could have to Sykes's other victims or their families. Crawley's team had already pulled phone and email records with no luck. We have to look again, and hope that something was missed the first time around."

"What if the perp comes back right away with a demand for the second statement? The one that supposedly involves Sykes?"

It was a possibility that Camille couldn't even bear to consider at one time, but the luxury of denial was gone. "I guess I'll cross that bridge when I get to it. For right now, I have to focus on what's directly in front of me. After that, we can start to flesh out each cog in the wheel, find the weakest one, and hopefully crush it."

Chloe nodded. "We both know who that weak cog is. Let's just hope that between the two of us we've chipped at Daniel's armor enough to leave a few cracks."

Camille raised her glass. "One last toast to that."

Chloe met Camille's glass with her own. "We're going to end this."

Camille finished what remained of her drink in one swallow. The subsequent head rush made her next words much easier to accept. "Damn right, we will."

18

CLOSING IN

WHEN DANIEL MACPHERSON was first brought inside, he was placed in an open cell block with a few dozen other men. He had no idea what their offenses were, and he didn't bother to ask. But he'd suspected those offenses ran the gamut from petty to the downright scary.

The petty criminals, with their wide, darting eyes, rigid demeanors, and excessive bunk time, made themselves easy marks for the scary ones.

The scary ones, the wolves as Daniel called them, with their constant chest-beating and fear mongering, ran the show; outnumbering the petty marks four to one.

Jail was the wolves' natural habitat, and they were at their best when they were confined to its tight, suffocating space. In here, they could rule freely as the animals that polite society deemed unfit to exist in their world. In here, the wolves were kings, and the others only existed to bow down.

Daniel had survived his week in the common area by being neither a king nor a subject. He opted instead to keep to himself, engaging only when he had to (mostly fielding intrusive questions about his criminal history), and staying calm.

Calm was Daniel's biggest ally. Purpose was his greatest strength.

And he'd had a purpose for being here. He sacrificed himself, willingly and without reservation, so that others could perform the necessary work of vengeance. The thought of having such a purpose kept him calm, gave him peace of mind, and helped him sleep soundly inside this zoo full of nocturnal animals who did unspeakable things when the lights went out.

He was arraigned three days after his arrest. The charges: kidnapping and attempted extortion. The police had no physical proof that he'd kidnapped anyone. But because he'd assumed Jacob Deaver's identity for the purposes of engaging Camille Grisham, they found a way to make the charges stick. They knew he hadn't put a finger on Jacob or Paul Grisham. But they needed a fall guy. And Daniel was all-too-willing to oblige.

His bail was set at a cool one million dollars - the extortion charge driving up the price of his freedom considerably. He was grateful for the large sum. No one he knew was capable of coming up with that kind of money, which meant his continued residency at the Denver County Jail was assured.

Daniel's parents, the poor lost souls who now mourned the loss of two children, pleaded with him to cooperate with the police, arguing that his reasons for doing this, whatever they were, weren't worth the personal cost to himself, or to them. He vehemently disagreed. The fact that they couldn't understand that he'd done this for them infuriated him all the more, and he decided it was best to cease all communication.

He told himself that Candace would've understood. They were siblings, after all. Close siblings. Born eleven months apart, she felt more like his twin. Both were somewhat shy and reserved, yet affable when the situation demanded it. Both had a flair for the dramatic: Candace with her theater-arts training and Daniel with his multiple stints on debate and mock trial teams in high school and college. He had to channel Candace's acting chops for his initial meeting with Camille. Based on the results, he'd done a fine job.

Both he and Candace took too many chances and were at times too trusting for their own good. Daniel didn't know it for sure, but he suspected that it was Candace's trusting nature that allowed Sykes to get close enough to do his evil work. Daniel's own trusting nature had essentially cost him his life too, but unlike his sister, he was a willing participant in his own demise.

There were, however, parts of Daniel that Candace would never understand. Parts that no one would ever understand. Daniel didn't always understand them himself. Before her murder, those parts of him remained hidden from the world, and himself. But Candace's death shattered much more than his emotional well-being. It shattered the protective barrier that existed between him and the thoughts of anger, hatred, and violence that roamed unchecked in the quiet corridors of his mind.

He'd attempted to channel this newly unearthed side of himself in a healthy manner by joining a private support group aimed at victims of Sykes and their families. The experience only proved to him that there was no healthy manner in which to channel this side of himself.

But he did succeed in attracting a kindred spirit.

Through their exchanges on the group's private messaging system, he came to learn that this kindred spirit shared the same thirst for revenge that he did. And like Daniel, his thirst could never be quenched by Sykes's incarceration alone.

When Daniel read the article about Camille Grisham on the Washington Times website - an article that detailed the events leading to Sykes's capture, and more importantly, his sister's murder - he immediately shared it with his new friend in the support group. His reaction told Daniel that their friendship had the potential to extend far beyond the virtual intimacy of a chatroom.

In their mutually agreed upon desire to make Camille brutally pay for what she'd done, they had a purpose. What they didn't have was a design.

An unexpected encounter with a true-crime writer from New York City provided that design.

Jacob Deaver showed up on his doorstep one random Wednesday afternoon to inform him that he was writing a book about the man who killed Candace and so many others. Jacob claimed that he wanted to honor the victims and their families by telling their side of the story, but Daniel could see through that bullshit right away. He wanted to use Candace for his own selfish purposes. In that way, he was no better than Sykes. And because he was no better than Sykes, he could never be allowed to do it.

He asked Daniel for his help. He didn't need much, he said, just insights and anecdotes into the person that his sister was. He said he wanted to paint a complete picture of the damage inflicted by Sykes on all those he impacted.

When he informed Daniel that another of Sykes's 'victims', Camille Grisham, was also slated to be interviewed, Daniel knew he'd found the design.

His friend from the support group, noble visionary that he was, completely agreed.

From that moment on, the design was no longer his. He was content instead to merely play his role. And he played it well.

When his sister was murdered, Daniel's trusting nature died along with her. He learned through her death that trust was a liability that could betray you in the blink of an eye. Daniel decided then that he could only trust himself. Given the dark thoughts that were now allowed free rein inside his psyche, he would wonder at times if that trust wasn't misplaced.

But his noble friend from the support group was worthy of trust. He understood Daniel in ways no one aside from Candace had. Though his understanding was much different, it was just as meaningful. He'd lost someone to Sykes too. A daughter. Madison. Barely a year older than Candace, she had the same blonde hair, the same easy-going, trusting spirit, and the same place in her loved one's heart that could never be touched by another. He knew Daniel's pain because he lived with it every day. The pseudo-psychologists who ran that stupid support group couldn't even say that. So when he spoke, Daniel listened. When he directed, Daniel complied. When he explained that sacrifices would have to be made in order to achieve their purpose, Daniel offered himself up first. And when he promised that his sacrifice would not be in vain, Daniel believed him.

But now, as he sat in his quiet, empty, lonely cell with its dingy white walls - walls that Detective Sullivan warned would close in on him, Daniel began to wonder if he ever should have trusted the man from the support group, or his intentions.

He now realized that the characteristics that initially drew him to Abraham Noble - his vision, his cunning, his cold indifference to anything that didn't serve the design - were also the characteristics that could be used to quickly dispose of him.

From what Detective Sullivan said, that quick disposal was already taking place.

He knew better than to believe anything a cop ever told him, especially a cop who was as closely affiliated with Camille Grisham as Sullivan was. But the fact that the plan as he'd always known it had changed so suddenly and so drastically troubled him. Daniel knew there had already been casualties, and he'd prepared himself for the probability of more. The news that he received about Jeremy Durant and his wife, and the FBI agent, however, was unexpected. From what he understood, only those directly connected to Camille Grisham or Jacob Deaver were potential targets. He hadn't agreed to hurt anyone else. He certainly hadn't agreed to hurting those four girls. But he was far removed from that situation and had no personal stake in it. His personal stake in what happened today could not have been higher.

The fact that Detective Sullivan allowed him to believe that the targeted FBI agent was Camille Grisham certainly didn't help. For as much as the thought shook him, it was also illuminating. Daniel had assumed that he and Abraham shared the exact same vision of Camille's eventual fate. That fate was written in a script that they'd mutually agreed upon. In fact, Abraham said he wouldn't sign off on *anything* that Daniel hadn't agreed to.

But an innocent reporter and his wife were killed. An FBI agent was shot. And there was no one left to account for it except for Daniel.

The script was most certainly changing, and it was changing in a way that he would have never agreed to.

Silence filled the tiny cell and the hallway outside of it, allowing Daniel to hear the rapid drumming of his heart just as clearly as he felt it. The calm that had been the source of his strength up until now was slowly abandoning him. In its place was an acute sense of dread, the same dread that the Midwest farmer feels when his otherwise calm, windless night is suddenly interrupted by the wail of a tornado siren. Daniel was sure something terrible was coming. He just couldn't see it yet.

Before he could even begin to process what that something might be, a heavy rap on his cell door scrambled his thoughts.

"Last call for dinner," a voice on the other side of the door told him. "The line closes down for the night in five minutes."

Daniel hadn't eaten all day, including the nearly five hours he spent inside that interrogation room. Despite the picture of calm he displayed for Camille, he instantly lost his appetite at the sight of her. It had yet to return.

"I'm not hungry," he reported to the guard.

A second voice outside. "Since when do you miss dinner? You on a hunger strike or something?"

This voice was more familiar than the first. In this case, familiar was not good.

"You wanna go check on Philips and Avery? I'll see what's going on with our friend MacPherson."

"You got it," the unfamiliar voice said.

A key in the lock. A quick turn and then a loud snap.

Daniel sat up in his bed as the steel door slowly swung open.

A face he knew very well, narrow and pock-marked as it had always been, peered in at him. He'd seen that face on the outside, before the design dictated that he find his way here. He'd called himself John then, but that sounded trite and made up. As a C.O., he never wore a name tag, so there was no way to know his true identity. But Daniel did know why he was here.

"Are you sure you're not eating tonight?" he asked in a voice loud enough for his colleague down the hall to hear.

"I'm sure," Daniel answered in a matching tone.

When John spoke again, his volume was considerably softer. "Did you see it?"

Daniel nodded.

"How? You were with them all day."

"They showed it to me."

John looked over his shoulder to ensure that it was still safe to talk, then turned to Daniel with a hard glare. "What the hell did you tell them?"

"Nothing."

"Bullshit. It wasn't supposed to play out like it did. They got tipped somehow."

The quivering in Daniel's lip momentarily rendered him speechless. It was just as well. He wasn't prepared to admit that he had indeed said something. And even if he was prepared to admit it, he couldn't offer a suitable explanation for why he did it, other than to rattle Camille. He knew that explanation wouldn't fly.

He certainly wasn't prepared to acknowledge the possibility that there was another explanation; an explanation that had to do with his sister, and his guilt, and the stinging disappointment that he was now certain she would feel over his actions.

"Candace deserves better."

More than anything he heard today, Camille's words stuck with him the longest. Candace did deserve better. From everyone. The thought that he could be added to the long list of people who let her down was almost more than he could handle.

So he told Camille about Meredith Park and the press conference. And if he were honest with himself, he would admit that he did it for Candace, because she would have wanted it.

But Daniel had a very hard time being honest with himself these days.

"You're telling me they kept you there for half the day, and they didn't get *anything* out of you?"

Daniel bit down on his lip to stop the quivering. It didn't work. "That's exactly what I'm telling you."

Footsteps, as the other guard approached the cell.

"Suit yourself, Mr. MacPherson," John said in his affected voice. "Just don't come crying to us when you want a midnight snack." Then, in a quiet whisper, "I told him it would be a mistake to keep you in the loop, but he wouldn't listen to me. He's got a soft spot for you. I don't. If anything else goes wrong, I'll know why. And so will he. I'm here to protect you. But I can also make sure it ends badly for you. It's your choice."

"Everything good in here?" the other guard asked as he stuck his head inside the cell.

"I don't know," John said, looking at Daniel. "Is everything good in here?"

Daniel nodded.

John turned to the guard. "Daniel doesn't like the chicken Alfredo. Can't say I blame him."

With that, the two guards walked out and closed the cell door.

Daniel didn't sleep that night. He kept his eyes focused on the bare white walls around him. The longer he stared, the more he was convinced that they were indeed closing in on him, just as Detective Sullivan said they would.

And they were closing in very fast.

19

MINDSET

CAMILLE WAS AWAKENED from a troubled sleep by an early morning phone call from Crawley.

"Change your mind yet?" he asked when she picked up.

"Good morning to you too, Peter. And no, I haven't changed my mind."

Crawley grunted. "One last-ditch effort on my part. I knew it would be fruitless."

"Then why did you bother trying?"

"Because I'm stubborn, and hard-headed, and can never seem to take 'no' for an answer, even when I know I should."

Camille imagined him smiling. The thought made her smile too.

"The lab work on the second letter and voice recorder came back late last night," Crawley continued. "I figured you needed the rest, so I didn't bug you."

"You wouldn't have bugged me," Camille said as she rose in bed to stretch her stiff legs.

"Just as well that I didn't. The letter and recorder scored the same single print. Jacob Deaver's. A latent partial was lifted from the top edge of the recorder. Enough points to rule out Deaver, but not enough for further comparison."

Camille had expected that and decided to move the conversation along. "How is Wells?"

Crawley cleared his throat before answering. "He's still heavily sedated and hooked up to a ventilator, at least until he wakes up. Otherwise, he's stable. Emma made it in late last night. I arranged to have her flown out on one of the Gulfstreams. You can't imagine the headache that was to set up. But it was worth it because she's with him. I know he can sense it too. The connection between those two is undeniable. She's going to help him come out of this."

Crawley sounded sure of that. It warmed Camille's heart to hear him speak of Wells in such personal terms. She always knew that he had it in him, but most people didn't inspire him enough to reveal it. She took great pride in knowing that she was on the shortlist.

"I prayed for him last night," she said truthfully.

"So did I." Crawley paused. When he spoke again, the formality had returned to his voice. "Have you had coffee?"

Camille yawned. "I'm still in bed, so no."

"Oh. Sorry if I woke you."

"You didn't really. Are you buying?"

"Absolutely. I'd like to go over a few things ahead of this statement reading."

"Like?"

"Mindset."

She knew what that meant and didn't bother to probe for details. "I can meet you at the City Perk Cafe in forty-five minutes. Do you know where it is?"

"I'll find it."

Camille dialed Meredith Park's cell phone as she made the two-block walk to the coffee shop.

She answered after the third ring.

"Camille," she said with relief.

"Hi, Meredith. I would've called to check on you sooner, but.."

"You've got bigger fish to fry right now. I completely understand. Don't worry about me. I'm good."

"Those officers keeping a close eye on you?"

"Like a couple of hawks. They're nice too." Meredith chuckled nervously. "Both of them are readers, so we've bonded over our mutual love of literature. Officer Evans is working on a novel. Wants me to represent him when he finishes it. I told him I would. I'd tell them anything at this point."

"How's the safe house?"

"Is that what this place is called? A safe house?"

"Police term," Camille explained.

"The neighborhood is a little sketchy, but the house is clean and quiet. I guess that's all I can ask for." A beat, then, "When can I leave?"

"Soon," Camille said before she could stop herself.

Meredith chuckled nervously again. It was obvious she didn't believe that. "Are you going through with the statement?"

"Yes. This morning at nine."

Meredith was quiet for what felt like a long time. "I'm so sorry."

"Me too. But I have to do it."

"Do you want me to be there?"

"Better that you stay put for a while. We'll be inside a secure building, so I don't anticipate an actual threat, but I can't be sure enough to take the chance."

"I understand. Call me when you're finished. Let me know you're alright."

"I will."

"Damn this bastard. I hope they fry him when this is all

over. No interrogation, no trial, just straight into the fire. Burnt to a goddamn crisp."

As surprised as Camille was by Meredith's outburst of emotion, she understood it. And she couldn't disagree entirely.

Crawley was waiting for her inside the cafe with two coffees in his hand. "I took the liberty of asking for extra strong. I assumed you wouldn't mind."

"Thank you," Camille said as she took a steaming mug.

"It's pretty crowded in here. Let's find a table outside. Less chance of prying ears."

Camille nodded her agreement and followed Crawley to the empty patio. It wasn't until she sat across from him that she noticed how heavy and bloodshot his normally bright blue eyes were. It was clear that she wasn't the only one who'd had a terrible night of sleep. She could only hope that she wore it a little bit better.

Crawley glanced at his watch. "We don't have much time so I'll cut right to the chase. I don't agree with this course of action, as I've made pretty clear. But I'm in no position to prevent you from doing it. What I can do is help navigate you through it."

Crawley was by far the best instructor Camille ever had. No one knew the literature as well as he did. No one put more effort into building reliable case studies. And no one better prepared her for the actual work. She more than welcomed his guidance right now. "I'm listening."

"What he wants to see when you read that statement is a victim. He wants tears, he wants remorse, he wants a plea for mercy. You gave him all of that the first time around. What you need to give him now is understanding."

"Understanding?" Camille replied with a furrowed brow.

"Not compassion. We already know that won't work. I'm talking about empathy. Pure empathy. You need to deliver his words like you agree with every single one of them; like you personally wrote them. Ask yourself, why would *you* write those words? Why would *you* hate Camille Grisham so much? Most importantly, what would be your immediate motive? You wouldn't want to kill her. You could've done that a long time ago."

"I'd want to psychologically torture her," Camille said with no feeling. "Just like Sykes did."

"Why?"

"To make her feel the same pain I feel."

"And what's the source of that pain?"

"That's what we're going to have to figure out if we have designs on catching him. We don't have evidence. He's careful enough not to leave any. We don't have facts, other than Jacob Deaver's fingerprints and my father's voice to tell us they're still alive."

"But we have him, and we have you. The predator and the prey. When you gave your statement yesterday, you were the prey, he was the predator. If you're really going to do this, you have to change that." Crawley took a long drink of his coffee and allowed the words to settle over them.

Camille was quiet, her racing mind betraying her calm face. She knew what Crawley was asking her to do. His hesitation in seeing her get to this point now made perfect sense. He knew where she'd have to go, and he was worried that she couldn't handle it. She was suddenly worried too.

"This is dark stuff, Camille."

The darkest. "I know."

"You can't read that statement unless you're willing to access that dark stuff. Otherwise, you're playing his game, and we're wasting our time."

Camille could feel the folded-up statement in her pocket. It felt heavy, like a burden that had suddenly become too much to carry. Then she took it out of her pocket, unfolded it, laid it on the table in front of her, and studied the words. Crawley watched her in silent anticipation.

When she was finished, she looked at him. Though she couldn't accurately gauge the intensity of her stare, it felt powerful. Crawley averted his eyes for a brief moment, allowing the energy to subside.

In that instant, something began to change. She felt unanchored yet clear-minded. Her nervousness was now tempered with anticipation. It was dark, just like Crawley said, but she knew she could handle it. The darkest point was yet to come.

Instead of retreating from that reality, as she'd grown accustomed to doing, she slowly relaxed into it, until her mind offered no more resistance.

"Between the three letters he's already written, we have enough to catch him."

Crawley nodded at her sudden declaration. "We just have to know what to look for."

Camille took a long, hard breath, then folded the statement and put it back in her pocket. "Do you mind if we take this coffee to go? I need some quiet time in the environment before the reading."

"Are you sure? You know what I'm asking you to do."

"You're asking me to be a profiler again."

"Under the most trying personal circumstances imaginable."

Camille felt the weight of her gaze return as she stood up. She could gauge its intensity just fine this time. "Right now, I can't think of a better reason. Can you?"

Crawley stood up to join her. He looked relieved, as if his own burden, heavy and long-endured, had finally been lifted. "No."

20

THE PLAYBOOK

CHLOE WAS ESCORTED to the conference room by a CBI employee who nervously watched her out of the corner of his eye. He didn't speak, aside from his rote instructions for wearing the visitor's ID she'd been given. Instead, he walked, and he watched.

At first, Chloe chalked it up to inter-agency mistrust. She'd worked a few cases with CBI assistance, and the road wasn't always smooth. Territorial beefs were par for the course. Being so far from her home turf, as she was now, certainly didn't help.

"How's your day going so far?" she asked in a weak effort to break the tension.

"Just fine," he mumbled, avoiding direct eye contact.

"Seems a little quiet around here," she added as they passed an empty office space of desks and cubicles. "Is everyone playing hooky today?"

This made him turn to look at her. He started at her feet and slowly moved up to the crown of her head, swallowing hard as he did. He strained his neck to briefly hold her gaze.

"In the field probably," he said without humor. When he turned around, his eyes fell back on the floor.

It was then she knew the source of the tension.

At nearly five-feet-ten-inches, she was taller than a surprisingly high number of men she came into contact with. But she had her escort beat by a good half-foot. Chloe was well aware of her intimidation factor, and she used it to her advantage on the street as often as she could. But in normal situations, with ordinary people, it made her feel awkward and self-conscious. Sometimes she simply wanted to move through the crowd, unnoticed and unaware. But her physical presence came with judgments and expectations that she could rarely escape. A blessing and a curse, she knew. People had much worse to deal with. She saw it every day. But personal issues were personal issues, whether they could be dismissed as first-world or not.

When they reached the conference room, she turned to him with an extended hand and an extra twinkle in her smile. "I appreciate the escort, kind sir. I hope you have a really great day."

It was pure affect on her part, but it worked. He offered a crooked but disarming smile as he shook her hand.

"You do the same," he looked at the visitor's badge as if he'd forgotten her name, "Detective Sullivan. And good luck with whatever it is you're working on."

One unnecessarily tense encounter defused by a smile and a handshake. Why couldn't it always be this easy?

The tension returned when she entered the conference room, but for much different reasons.

Camille was alone in the room. She sat at the far end of the conference table with her head buried in her hands. She looked like she'd been crying.

Yeah, Chloe. Your first-world problems really don't mean shit, she thought as she took a tentative step inside. Camille raised her head at the sound of the footsteps.

Her eyes were red and damp. Not tears of sadness, though. Nothing faltered in Camille's delicate brown face as she looked up. There had been no breakdown. It was a release of anger, Chloe had concluded. When you were really pissed off, and you weren't inclined to put a balled fist through something solid, a heavy stream of tears was often enough to relieve the pressure.

"I'm sorry. If this is a bad time, I can-"

"I'm done," Camille replied, wiping the last remnant of moisture from her cheek. "Come in."

Chloe took a seat in the chair opposite her. "Are you okay?"

"I had to purge a few things. I'm better now. Focused."

Chloe nodded. Something in Camille's eyes was different from last night; different from every other time she'd seen her, in fact. The distant, searching stare, with its glaze of uncertainty, was gone. These eyes, alert and fixed, had seemed to find what they were long searching for.

Determination was the word that came to mind when she looked into those eyes; the kind of determination that could frighten a person if they were on the wrong side of it. She was relieved when Camille finally smiled.

"Thanks for coming."

"Of course. Things did get a little awkward with the guy at the front desk, but I made the best of it."

"You mean Arthur? I think he's just a little shy. He signed me in last night. Once he realized I didn't bite, he opened right up."

Chloe appreciated that she could find humor in a moment like this. That part of her was different too. And most welcomed. "I'll keep that in mind for next time."

Camille glanced at the blue spiral notebook that had been

opened in front of her. Every inch of the page, including the margins, was filled with her words. She wrote down one last thought before closing it. Then she placed the statement written by her father's abductor on top of it. Her eyes were light now. She looked ready.

"Do you mind if I ask what needed to be purged?"

"The victim," Camille said without blinking.

"The victim?"

"The victim that's been living inside me since…"

"Sykes's basement. And your partner's death. And Candace and Jessica."

Camille nodded.

"Did it work? Is she gone?"

"The most destructive parts of her are. We'll see what's left."

Chloe didn't know Camille the FBI agent. She'd met her in the aftermath of her resignation, the tragedy that preceded it, and the bigger tragedy that followed it. Camille had experienced more than her fair share of hardship in the past year. Many lesser people would've been broken completely. But Camille endured, even through this, the worst of it all.

Chloe had known her for only a short time, but she'd never met anyone she respected more. She never met anyone she wanted to emulate more either. There were very few mentors in Major Crimes that she could personally relate to. She never could've imagined that she'd find such a powerful mentor in a broken-down, washed-out former profiler with the FBI whom the universe deemed to be on the wrong end of the karma scale. But that was exactly who she chose. And as the sole witness to the startling transformation that had taken place inside this room, she couldn't have been more proud of that choice.

"What now?" Chloe asked after she realized that an extended period of silence had settled between them.

Camille checked the time. "It's eight twenty-two. The cameraman will be here at eight-thirty to set up. Crawley and the rest of the team should be back any minute for a final briefing. Then I do it."

"Do you plan on adding to the script?" Chloe asked in reference to the notebook.

"I'm not sure yet." She pulled the notebook close. "This is what I do - what I *did* - when I needed to understand the person I was dealing with. I tried to get inside their head to figure out what drove them. Sometimes that meant empathizing with them, even to the point of wanting what they wanted. It's a mind-fuck that most sane people can't even begin to rationalize, but when I was in the zone with a killer, and it's only happened twice, there were times I woke up at night thinking I *was* him. I dreamed about his victims, what I'd done to them, and how it felt. That's why there weren't a lot of us in Behavioral Analysis. It's easier for most cops to demonize killers rather than humanize them. And I totally get that. But that's not what we do - not always. It's hard, lonely, gut-wrenching work. And once you fully commit, once you leap from that precipice into the blackest of black, you aren't ever truly the same."

"Did you make that leap with Sykes?"

"Yes."

Chloe didn't have to ask how it changed her. "Are you leaping again?"

"Crawley led me to the edge this morning, but I haven't jumped. I don't know enough about this guy yet." Camille paused a few beats. "But I'm getting there."

Chloe knew how significant 'getting there' was for her. "Do you need more time? I can wait in the hall until you're ready."

Camille shook her head as she turned her attention to the door. "No need. The cavalry's back."

Chloe looked up to see Crawley, Mendoza, and Pratt entering the room.

"Good morning, Detective Sullivan," Crawley said when he noticed her. "Camille filled me in on the MacPherson interview."

"I wish there would've been more to report."

"You got him to talk. That was a lot more than your colleagues were able to do. Something tells me you'll get another crack." He turned to Camille. "Get all the time you need?"

"I did the best with what I had."

Crawley nodded and checked his watch. "Eight-thirty. The cameraman should be here any second."

A hint of nervousness flashed across Camille's face as she stood up from the table. "I'm going out for a little air. Be back in five."

No one in the group spoke as she walked out.

With Camille gone, Chloe suddenly found herself alone with the other agents for the first time. Mendoza was quick to greet her.

"I don't think we've officially met. Allison Mendoza."

"Chloe Sullivan. I've seen you around, but it's nice to officially meet."

"Likewise. And this is Gabriel Pratt."

Pratt extended his hand. "Camille speaks very highly of you."

She does not *speak very highly of you,* Chloe thought before going with the much more diplomatic, "Nice to meet you, Agent Pratt."

"I take it you had a hard time talking Camille out of this too," Crawley said to her.

"I didn't try to talk her out of it, Agent Crawley. She's doing what she feels is best for the situation. I can't imagine any of us making a different decision were we in her shoes."

Crawley didn't say anything.

"She seems to be going about it in a very interesting way though," Chloe continued.

"Interesting?" Crawley said.

"The empathy part."

"With all due respect, Detective Sullivan, there's a world of difference between what you do and what we do. We play for the same team and want the same outcomes, but we operate from a much different playbook."

Chloe folded her arms across her chest, unsure if she should be offended by the comment.

"If it's any consolation, we don't understand it either," Mendoza said with an understanding smile. "Our plays look a lot like yours."

"All that matters is that we want the same outcomes," Crawley reiterated.

"Camille was good when she was with the BAU," Chloe said to him.

"She was very good, with the potential to be outstanding. I personally think she still can be."

"Sykes really derailed her."

"She caught Sykes. People seem to forget that."

"Including the asshole who's doing all of this," Pratt said.

"Do you think he's related to a victim of Sykes?" Chloe asked the group.

"We believe so," Pratt answered. "But there haven't been any firm connections to bear that out."

"What about a direct connection to MacPherson? Perhaps he's another family member or one of Candace's boyfriends."

"We investigated those angles weeks ago," Crawley said. "Phone records, emails, and social media accounts were all pulled. It didn't lead us anywhere useful."

"Daniel had to communicate with this guy somehow."

"We agree," Mendoza said. "But we haven't found a

record of it yet. He was very good at cleaning up his digital footprints."

"Unless he went old-school and did his business offline," Chloe said. "The smart ones do that these days. Say what you will about Daniel, but he's smart."

Her eyes were drawn to Agent Pratt. She could see the gears turning in his mind.

"We're assuming that our unsub is connected to a victim of Sykes, the same as MacPherson," he said. "How would the two of them link up in the first place?"

"How *wouldn't* they link up?" Mendoza asked. "In this wonderful information age of ours, the possibilities are limitless."

"And we've already vetted most of those possibilities," Crawley added.

"The traceable ones," Pratt said. "But what if they went old-school like Detective Sullivan said? How would they connect off the grid?"

After a moment of silent contemplation from the group, Chloe asked, "Are in-person support groups still a thing? I know A.A. is around, but there used to be a weekly group meet-up for every demographic of problem you could imagine."

"Sadly, they aren't as common as the online variety, but they do still exist," Mendoza said.

"We do know that there were online forums for Sykes's victims and their families," Crawley said. "According to the IP addresses on his phone and two computers, MacPherson never visited any of them."

"I'd be willing to bet that someone, somewhere, organized an in-person group," Chloe said. "That may not leave you with anything more than a paper sign-up sheet to work with, but it would be a hell of a lot more than what you've got now."

The trio of agents looked at one another. All of their gears were turning now.

"It's a little bit out of our jurisdiction, but Allison and I can start researching it," Pratt offered.

Crawley took a moment to consider it before saying, "Start in Reading, Pennsylvania where MacPherson lived and slowly make your way out. If he did attend local meetings, it's likely he'd want to stay close to home."

Pratt and Mendoza nodded their understanding.

"Maybe you can ask MacPherson about it directly," Crawley said to Chloe.

"Will do."

Just then, the cameraman walked into the room. He was carrying a tripod and a large camera bag. "Where should I set up, Gabe?"

"In the corner by the TV," Pratt directed.

Camille walked in behind him. Though the nerves were evident, her chestnut-colored eyes were still alert.

"Did the team crack the case while I was gone?" she joked with a light, easy smile that momentarily cut the tension.

"The team is working on it," Chloe replied with an easy smile of her own.

And for the first time, it felt like they were operating from the same playbook.

21

HIDDEN IN PLAIN SIGHT

T HE SETUP LOOKED SIMPLE, even though Camille and Crawley took great pains to create it.

She sat at the head of the conference table, the statement laid out neatly in front of her. The camera was positioned precisely to show it. Fearful that a tabletop microphone would appear too formal, she tucked a wireless lapel mic discreetly inside her blouse. As Pratt had suggested, the blue and gold seal of the Colorado Bureau of Investigation was partly visible on the white wall behind her. Crawley had insisted on it, lest their unsub forget who he was actually dealing with. Camille didn't agree with the tactic but didn't fight it. Her silky black hair was pulled back into a tight bun to reveal as much of her face as possible. *The truth will be in the eyes*, she thought, and she wanted him to look into them without distraction. Her black blouse (symbolic of mourning and regret) was buttoned to the neck, another move to frame the eyes. Chloe, Crawley, and the others were seated to her left and out of the frame.

She'd gone through several dry-runs before the camera began recording, each take exhausting her emotion more than the last. When the emotion was finally used up, she informed the cameraman that she was ready to begin.

The words were repeated in her head so often that she'd had them completely memorized by now. But she needed to read from the paper anyway. He would demand the respect of hearing every word exactly as it was written. Respect for the words and the sentiment behind them meant everything. She understood this about him.

His statement was written as a message to the world. But Camille knew that it was personal. When she looked into that camera, it wasn't the world, with its pity and judgment, that she was speaking to.

She was speaking directly to him.

He came to her as a distant, formless silhouette of a man sitting in a remote, formless void in the earth; far away from her physical reach, yet close enough to touch with the empathy in her eyes, and the understanding that she alone was to blame for what Sykes had done, and she alone had to pay. Convincing him that she actually felt that way would be the challenge, and she prayed that she had the acting chops to pull it off.

She clutched the paper with both hands and held it a few inches off the table as she began reading.

"I want to start by addressing the issue of my father's abduction. Many people are working behind the scenes to ensure his return home, and I have full faith that he and Jacob Deaver will be found alive and brought back safely. What I am about to read has nothing to do with them. It has everything to do with me, and a long-overdue admission of guilt. The following is my admission.

"By reading this, I hope to make things right, not only for Jacob Deaver and my father, but also for the more than two-dozen other victims and their families who have had their lives ripped apart because of my actions, or in some cases, my lack of action."

Camille paused to look at Chloe. She couldn't stomach the deeply wounded expression on her face and turned back to the camera less than a second later.

"Much has been made of the serial killer Daniel Sykes and his horrendous crimes. What hasn't been talked about as much is my role in those crimes. As most of you know, I was the lead agent in charge of the Circle Killer task force, the unit dedicated to finding Sykes. As I admitted in an interview released shortly after my resignation from the FBI, I came into contact with Sykes months before his eventual capture. He assisted in a search and rescue operation for a Virginia woman that he was responsible for killing. Despite the extensive profile I had built on him, when we came face to face, he was nothing more to me than another concerned volunteer."

Camille took a breath to steel herself for the next part.

"What that interview didn't mention... what I was ultimately too cowardly to admit, was that upon his capture, Daniel Sykes revealed to me that he came to Alexandria on that day with the intention of being caught. He knew from news reports that I was the lead investigator in his case, and he wanted to find me. He was convinced that I would take one look at him, and I would know. He said he did everything short of a full-blown confession to raise the red flag. Yet, it wasn't enough."

At this, Camille stopped. She had no intention of stopping. It was completely involuntary. She'd read the statement several times, and it only now occurred to her. Sykes's revelation about wanting to get caught *wasn't* mentioned in that infamous Washington Times interview, or anywhere else for that matter. There was no way that anyone outside of the Bureau or her father could've known about it.

So how did *he* know?

Camille briefly allowed for the possibility that her father supplied the detail under duress, but she dismissed it almost as quickly as it came. Knowing how traumatic and life-changing the incident was, there was no way he would've allowed anyone to use it against her, even under the threat of his own life. That left no other explanation; not one that was readily available anyway.

But there was an explanation, and she had faith that eventually she would see it. She hadn't come this far not to.

Mindful of the need to keep her emotions safely in check, Camille stifled the warm rise of excitement in her chest until it subsided. She turned back to the statement without blinking.

Don't be too brisk with the poker face. Just relax. You're doing great. Read this psychopath's words and get on with the real work.

"Because of my failure in Alexandria, nine people were killed. I realize now that I bear just as much responsibility for those deaths as Daniel Sykes does. The blood is on my hands just as much as it is on his."

Blood that will never completely wash off, she admitted silently.

She felt the rise again as she paused to scan the next paragraph. There was something else she'd missed. It was subtle, but it was significant. She read the passage as calmly as she could.

"I was there when Sykes was finally captured; three months after our encounter in Virginia. Special Agent Andrew Sheridan, my partner, and friend was with me. I let... I let Agent Sheridan die in Sykes's basement, along with the last two victims, Jessica Bailey, and Candace MacPherson, while I kept helpless watch in a corner, too overcome by the chaos to intervene."

It was the last point that mattered. No one outside of the Bureau, her father, or her best friend Julia Leeds knew of the panic attack. The only other person who would've known was Sykes himself. She'd caught a glimpse of him through her blurred periphery as she knelt over Sheridan's bleeding body, trying to comfort herself and him at the same time, and failing miserably at both. She recalled the streak of silver extending from Sykes's hand; the streak of silver he momentarily pointed at her before walking away to shoot Candace and Jessica instead. Lancaster police stormed the basement seconds later. By then the gun was resting harmlessly on the ground as Daniel knelt before them in full surrender.

But again, how did *he* know this?

She continued without an answer.

"Candace's brother, Daniel MacPherson, is currently in police custody in connection to my father's disappearance. Regardless of his role, Daniel's anger should be... should be understandable to anyone with an inclination for justice. It's understandable to me now too."

Breathe deep, girl. Don't lose it.

"All I can do is ask for their forgiveness. I'm fully aware that I may be deemed undeserving, and that will be the cross I have to bear. But I can't begrudge their justifiable anger. They are the ones who have lost, not me. They have lost husbands and wives, girlfriends and sisters. Mothers will never again have the chance to hug their children. Fathers will never walk their daughters down the aisle, or hold their grandchildren, or make amends for all the times they weren't there, including that final moment when they were needed the most."

The last sentence was one that caught Camille's attention the first time she read it, and it made even more sense now. No matter how much thought they put into their crimes, no matter how carefully crafted the execution is, killers always leave clues, often hidden in plain sight. At first glance, those clues are elusive. But once you know what you're looking for, they scream for your attention.

Camille heard the screaming loud and clear.

One more paragraph. She blinked a few times to regain her wandering focus.

"Do I deserve forgiveness for letting Candace and Jessica and so many others die? I'll let that judgment fall where it may. By the time you hear from me again, and if all goes as planned you will, that judgment may have already been passed down, and the closure that so many have been yearning for will finally come to pass. Time will tell."

When she was finally finished, Camille put the paper down and gently slid it across the table, an intentional move to let him know that they were now speaking directly. She kept her eyes fixed on the camera.

"I understand you now." Her tone was laced with an affected resignation that masked her true feelings. She was anything but resigned. "No matter how this ends, always know that I *completely* understand you."

Her emphasis on *completely* was also intentional. It was a subtle way of communicating what she'd learned about him without actually saying so. He would surely pick up on that, and it would leave him unsettled, but not in a way that he could easily articulate.

If her time in the Bureau taught her anything, it was how to mind-fuck with the best of them. This was her first offensive move, and it felt good.

With that, she gave a quick wave that signaled the cameraman to shut it down.

When the camera light went dark, Camille let out a loud sigh, unclipped the lapel mic from her blouse, and threw it across the room.

"My God, that was worse than I thought it would be," Mendoza said as she and the others made their way to

Camille's side of the table. "I can't believe how well you handled it."

Camille opened a large bottle of water and finished it before responding. Her throat still felt raw as she spoke. "I'm sure he expected me to break down at some point. It was important that I didn't."

"I'm glad you didn't give him the satisfaction."

"It was more than that. I needed to analyze the meaning of his words, not feel the emotion of them. Emotion hampers judgment. He knows that, and I think that's why he felt safe to tell me so much about who he is. He didn't think I'd be able to see anything beyond my own pain and embarrassment."

"What did his words tell you?" Crawley asked.

Camille waited as the cameraman finished breaking down his equipment. Suddenly aware that all eyes were on him, he quickly dismantled his tripod, picked up his camera bag, and headed for the door. "I'm assuming you'll be in touch with instructions on what to do next?" he asked Pratt on the way out.

"I'll let you know once we decide. It shouldn't be long, so for now just hold tight."

"And it goes without saying that you aren't to show that footage to anyone," Crawley added. "Don't even rewatch it yourself without one of us present."

The cameraman nodded at the terse directive, added, "Completely understood, sir," then padded out the door.

Once he was gone, the group turned back to Camille for her response to Crawley's question. With the elusive answer finally revealing itself, she was eager to reply.

"Two things. First, he's the father of one of the victims killed *after* I met Sykes in Virginia."

"How did you come to that conclusion?" Pratt asked.

"Considering its prominent mention in the statement, he's

clearly preoccupied with that period of time. If his daughter had been killed before Alexandria, he would never have brought the incident up."

"And the second thing?" Crawley asked.

Camille was suddenly hesitant to reveal it, even though she couldn't have been more certain about it. She worried that giving voice to it would add a weight that she couldn't easily handle. "He's been in contact with Sykes."

Crawley looked as surprised as Camille thought he would. "What do you mean?"

"He mentioned things that no one outside the Bureau, my father, or Sykes himself would know. My reasons for quitting, the panic attack, that stuff wasn't public information. And as far as I know, it hasn't been leaked to the media. That leaves him with either a direct line to Sykes or someone in the BAU."

"And I can most certainly tell you that it isn't the latter," a suddenly defensive Crawley said.

"What about your father?" Chloe asked. "Do you think it's possible he could've been forced to talk about it?"

"I'd considered that immediately. But I'm a hundred percent certain it wasn't him."

"So not only is our unsub a Sykes copycat, but you think he might also be a direct accomplice?" Pratt asked.

"It could explain the insane idea to have Camille and Sykes sit down for an interview," Mendoza said. "This could've been their plan from the beginning."

Camille shook her head. "Serial murderers usually work alone. Sykes was no exception. I doubt he'd have an accomplice, then or now."

"So how else do you explain the information getting out?" Pratt followed up. "Were they penpals or something?"

"Sykes wasn't allowed correspondence of any kind once it was discovered that he'd sent a letter to his one surviving victim asking how she was adjusting to life with a colostomy bag," Crawley said. "It was the first and last letter he wrote."

"Maybe he had a contact on the inside who was able to smuggle things in and out for him," Chloe speculated.

"It's the only possibility that makes sense," Camille agreed.

"Where is he being housed?" Mendoza asked.

"Fairfield State Correctional, a max lock-up about thirty miles outside of Philadelphia," Crawley answered.

Mendoza looked at Pratt. "While you're researching support groups, I can get in contact with Fairfield to get a sense of Sykes's monitoring protocol and his interactions with fellow inmates and staff."

"Works for me," Pratt said before turning to Camille and Crawley.

For his part, Doctor Ice looked less than convinced. "It just seems like a big leap."

"Isn't that exactly what you asked me to do?" Camille said. "I took a leap, and this is where I landed. If you weren't going to trust the result, you shouldn't have asked me to do it."

Crawley's face reddened. "I did ask you to leap, and I do trust your judgment. Don't ever doubt that." A deep breath to calm himself, then, "Maybe we'll get a clearer view after Allison gets the report from Fairfield."

Camille knew that was Crawley's version of an apology. She accepted it and moved on.

"I'll need to access the files of Sykes's last victims," she said to him.

"You mean the murders he committed after Alexandria?"

"Yes."

"You got it. What brought on the hunch about our perp being the father of one of the victims?"

Camille reached across the table to grab the statement.

After a quick scan, she found the sentence. "It's the second to last paragraph." She began reading. "They are the ones who have suffered, not me. They have lost husbands and wives, girlfriends and sisters. Mothers will never again have the chance to hug their children. Fathers will never walk their daughters down the aisle, or hold their grandchildren, or make amends for all the times they weren't there, including the final moment when they were needed the most.

Camille put the paper aside. "I'm not sure how much conscious thought he gave to the passage as he was writing it, but it was probably the most revealing piece in the entire statement. Then there's the wording itself."

"May I?" Crawley said as he reached for the paper.

Camille gave it to him and continued. "The first two points about the father not walking his daughter down the aisle or holding his grandchild are pretty general and could be applied to anyone. But the final point is very specific."

Crawley reread it aloud. "Or make amends for all the times they weren't there, including the final moment when they were needed the most."

"He feels guilt for what happened to his daughter," Camille said. "Not only for what Sykes did to her but for what *he* did by not being present in her life. I'd go so far as to say that he believes his absence directly contributed to her death. Perhaps if he'd been there, Sykes could never have gotten to her."

"Which we know is ridiculous, unless he planned to lock her in a closet," Pratt said.

"Exactly. But for someone lacking rational thought, it makes perfect sense, as does his lashing out by attacking and murdering girls in the same fashion his daughter was attacked and murdered."

"Those girls couldn't have been the first," Chloe speculated.

"Most likely not," Crawley affirmed. "But we researched cold and open-case murders of young women in each of the three states where his victims were found. None of the patterns matched."

"So what are you looking for in the files?" Chloe asked Camille.

"Of the nine people killed after Alexandria, eight of them were women, including Candace and Jessica. We know Candace's story. And Jessica was an only child whose father is a pastor in some Baptist mega-church. We can certainly look at him again, but I think it would be a waste of time."

"That leaves six other possibilities," Crawley said.

Camille nodded. "From what I remember, family and friends were interviewed immediately after the victims were ID'd, but only those who were easily accessible. There weren't any attempts to locate distant or estranged relatives. Is that right?"

"That's right," Crawley said.

"Then that's where we have to start."

The sudden quiet that overtook the room was interrupted by Crawley's heavy sigh as he sank back in his chair. "Jesus, Camille. If you're right about this…"

She knew there was no 'if'. She was right about it. The only question was what difference, if any, it would make.

"It's only a start. Best-case scenario, we get a positive ID along with a last-known address. But this guy is mobile, most likely settling down here, so the address won't do much good. And without any sort of DNA, that best-case scenario is a long-shot."

"So what do we have going for us at this point?" Mendoza asked.

"This isn't some stone-cold killer," Camille said. "He's not motivated by self-gratification or lust or a hunger to inflict pain. Most serial murders detach themselves from their victims as much as they can. This guy is just the opposite. He's emotionally invested in everything he's doing. That makes him vulnerable."

"Now all we have to do is figure out what that vulnerability is," Pratt said. "Any ideas?"

"Not yet." The admission was a difficult one for Camille to make. With all that she'd discovered about him so far, most of who he was remained safely hidden. She could only hope that the emotional liability she'd detected in him would reveal itself in a lapse in judgment or some other mistake that allowed her to see more.

"If nothing else, you're giving me a reason to be a little less pessimistic," Crawley said.

"Only a little?"

"My cynical nature usually doesn't allow for much more than that," he answered, a light smile creasing his face.

Camille returned his smile before a sudden thought snatched it away. "He'll be expecting to see me soon. How are we planning to get the footage out there?"

"I was thinking we could post it on the CBI website before letting the local TV outlets pick it up," Pratt said. "It wouldn't take long to go wide from there."

"It may take more time than you have," Chloe warned. "And the CBI website will probably be the last place he looks."

"He didn't specify where he wanted to see it. He just wants to see it," Pratt countered.

"Detective Sullivan does have a point," Crawley said. "It's better to post it where his attention is already likely to be."

"So we go directly to the national networks?" Mendoza asked.

"No," Camille answered as an image of Jeremy Durant flashed in front of her. "He's already told us where his attention is."

"The Mile-High Dispatch," Crawley said as if reading her mind.

"You want to give that gutter of a newspaper another crack at this story?" Chloe barked, her soft brow furrowed in disgust. "Didn't they do enough damage the first time?"

"Be that as it may, Will Freeman's cell phone video was uploaded onto the Dispatch website twenty minutes after he left my press conference," Camille said. "Forty minutes before the write-up appeared on the Denver Post website and two hours before the news camera footage appeared on television. Given the amount of time required to record my father, compose the note found on Jeremy Durant, and carry out the shootings, it's a near certainty that the perp saw the Dispatch footage first."

"Which means he'll be expecting to find it there this time too," Crawley added. "Posting it there also gives us a chance to control the rollout of the story a lot easier than if we just handed it off to a network."

Chloe folded her arms across her chest and sat in silence, resisting the follow-up protest that was clearly simmering beneath the surface.

The Mile-High Dispatch's overzealous reporting on the issues inside the police department made Chloe's objection very understandable, and very personal. But while Camille could appreciate her feelings, she couldn't allow herself to be swayed by them.

"I know his paper has come after the DPD pretty hard, but I read Freeman's piece this morning about my press conference and the aftermath with the Durants and Agent Wells. There was nothing out of bounds about it."

The frown lines digging into Chloe's face told Camille that she still wasn't convinced, but her response indicated a willingness to toe the line. "You have to do what you have to do. I respect that."

"I'm sure he'll be positively giddy that we're offering him the exclusive," Mendoza said, cutting the tense silence that had settled over the group.

Camille glanced at Chloe in anticipation of a response. She remained silent, keeping her stare fixed and her arms folded.

"I know you said his piece this morning was fair, but let's make double-sure he stays level-headed this time around," Crawley said. "We need to get the perp's attention, but we don't want to make a public sideshow out of it."

Camille nodded her agreement, knowing the sideshow was unavoidable at this point. But the Dispatch was the easiest, most predictable route they could take. This wasn't the time to play chicken or attempt surprises. This was still his game, and for now, Camille was going to play it precisely the way he wanted.

But that didn't preclude her from scripting a few plays of her own.

"I'll make sure we keep the cluster to a minimum, Peter. But I do have a plan for how Freeman can help us aside from posting the video on his website. It's a bit outside the box, but given what I've learned today, it just might work."

"Screw the box," Crawley said emphatically. "Whatever we can hit this guy with, let's use it."

Camille appreciated the vote of confidence more than she could verbalize. She could only hope it wouldn't prove to be misguided.

"Depending on what the perp asks for next, Freeman might be the perfect person to have on deck," Pratt added. "He's clearly not afraid to stick his neck out there for the right story."

She was counting on that, just as she was counting on the sincerity of Freeman's words as he left yesterday's press conference; words that Camille dismissed at the time but now desperately wanted to believe. *"We're not all bad, Agent Grisham. Some of us are actually here to help."*

Right now, Camille needed all the help she could get, even if that help came in the form of a hungry media shark desperate for the sight of blood.

22

MAKING AMENDS

A S HE WALKED THE UNNERVINGLY QUIET hallways of the Colorado Bureau of Investigation headquarters, Will Freeman couldn't help but think that he was being set up.

He knew the notion was likely the result of an overactive imagination fueled by his days as a crime-beat reporter. But he'd been witness to the bloody aftermath of enough gang-land-style executions to recognize the signs: a seemingly random phone call in the middle of the day, a voice on the other end that you didn't expect but ultimately trusted, a meeting request vague on details in a remote location that you wouldn't otherwise dream of visiting. And in this case, an escort who refused to look you in the eye no matter how much you attempted to engage him.

The little man knows what's about to happen, Will thought of the front-desk clerk who checked him in and gave him his visitor's badge, but otherwise didn't speak.

The instant he'd gotten the call from Camille Grisham, he knew why she'd reached out. Will hadn't given himself much time to consider the ramifications of posting the video of her statement and the subsequent confrontation with Jeremy Durant. He knew that there was more footage of the event out there, and if he hadn't broken the story, someone else would have. Then he received the news about Jeremy Durant, his wife, and FBI Agent Stephen Wells, and suddenly, the ramifications of being first became horrifyingly clear.

His head told him that he wasn't directly responsible for what happened to them. But there were long periods during the sleepless night that followed where his aching heart told him otherwise.

He expected Camille Grisham and her merry band of steel-plated G-Men to feel the same way. For Will, this was a news story, unusual yet highly compelling. But for Camille, it was literal life and death. Durant's death meant that her father could possibly be one step closer to his own.

That particular reality had only sunk in for Will on the drive to CBI, as had the reality that Camille's ambiguous meeting request most likely meant trouble for him.

Seeing Detective Chloe Sullivan's name on the sign-in sheet in the space above his didn't help. Sullivan had once been the partner of a detective who was the prime focus of his newspaper's ongoing investigation into allegations of gross misconduct within the DPD. The now-deceased Walter Graham, from what Will could see, was as rotten as they came, and Detective Sullivan was in the unfortunate position of being guilty by mere association in the eyes of the reporters assigned to the story. Kyle McKenna, his head watchdog, was particularly aggressive in her pursuit of answers. Unlike Will, Kyle gave little thought to the personal entanglements that came with the job. The potential to alter the lives of the people who make the story never much bothered her, as long as the truth of their story was told. The pursuit of that truth was often a hard, messy fight that left many casualties in its wake. Detective Sullivan was one such casualty. Whether she deserved to be or not was a question Will couldn't answer. He only knew that she didn't take very kindly to it, and would take the first opportunity she could to rake him and his little paper across the coals. Perhaps that opportunity was finally presenting itself today.

Will steeled himself for all of the worst-case scenarios he could imagine, and all of those that he couldn't, as his escort knocked on the closed conference room door.

A male voice that Will remembered as Agent Crawley's instructed them to enter.

He was surprised and somewhat relieved to see that Crawley and Camille Grisham were the only ones in the room. Both were seated at the far end of the conference table, facing him, their hands folded in front of them. Their expressions were spitting images of stoic detachment.

Crawley kept his eyes on Will as he spoke to the escort. "Arthur, please check Mr. Freeman."

Before Will could decipher what that meant, he felt the little man's hands cuff him around his shoulders before moving quickly down the sides of his torso, under his arms, across his chest and lower back, down the outside of his legs to his ankles, and back up through his inner-thigh, stopping short of his groin.

"Jesus, do you think I'm carrying a gun?" an irate Will asked Crawley.

"For your sake, we hope not," was how Crawley answered.

"Nothing," the little man reported.

Crawley nodded. "Very good. Mr. Freeman, we'll need you to leave your cell phone and bag with Arthur."

"Excuse me?"

"For our safety," Camille said. "You snuck a recording by us once. We can't allow you to do it again. That was why we had you searched."

"Your cell phone and bag," Crawley repeated with an edge that wasn't present the first time.

Will turned to Arthur, who was awaiting his cooperation with an outstretched hand.

Yep, I'm being set up all right, was his thought as he took the cell phone out of his pocket and the messenger bag from around his shoulder. Arthur took both without saying a word.

"You're carrying my entire professional life there, pal," Will said, his pride compelling him to offer at least a small measure of protest. "Be careful with it."

"Your things will be fine," Crawley assured him before turning to Arthur. "That'll be all. Thanks."

A slight gust of wind caused the red hairs on Will's neck to rise as Arthur closed the door behind him.

A long moment of tense silence settled over the room before Camille finally spoke.

"It's okay, Mr. Freeman. You can sit."

"I'm not so sure it's okay, but I'll sit anyway," Will said as he settled into the chair closest to the door.

"Would you like a cup of coffee?" Crawley offered without an ounce of cordiality.

"I'm good," Will answered, even though nothing sounded better at the moment.

"You must be wondering why we asked to meet with you," Camille said.

There were a million reasons Will could think of for why he'd been abruptly summoned to the Colorado Bureau of Investigation headquarters on a random Thursday afternoon. None of them offered the promise of a positive outcome.

"I'm assuming you won't keep me in suspense much longer."

"No, we won't," Crawley said. "The fact of the matter is that we were less-than-thrilled to see the video on your website. But we're grown-ups, and we've been around long enough to understand how things work. You had a story that you believed would get eyeballs on your paper, and you ran with it. I'm sure anyone in your position would've done the same."

Will shifted in his chair, bracing for the hammer that Crawley was sure to drop with his next statement.

"But your haste to break the story has created something of a quandary for us."

"What do you mean?"

"The timeline of events that occurred yesterday afternoon lead us to believe that my father's abductor watched the statement on the Dispatch website before he saw it anywhere else," Camille answered. "That means he's likely going to look there when he wants to know what's happening next."

"But I found out about the Durants and Agent Wells at the same time as the rest of the media. I wasn't the first to report on it." Will paused, then he turned to Crawley. "I'm really sorry about Wells, by the way. Any word on how he's doing?"

"Are you looking for another exclusive?" Crawley asked through tight lips.

"I'm asking because I'm genuinely concerned."

"It's touch and go right now. But we're praying for a full recovery," Camille quickly answered, knowing it was best not to give Crawley the chance.

"So am I," Will offered, meaning it.

Crawley started to speak, then caught himself. After taking a measured breath, he tried again. "We appreciate the sentiment, Mr. Freeman, and I'm sure Agent Wells's family does too. But back to Camille's point about your website. Our subject has opened up another line of communication with us, and we believe, based on what occurred yesterday, that he'll look to the Mile-High Dispatch for our response."

Will's eyes widened. "What do you mean by a line of communication."

Camille opened the laptop computer that had been sitting on the table in front of her and inserted a flash drive. "When we show you, perhaps you'll understand our insistence on confiscating your cell phone."

When she turned the computer to him, he saw her face on the screen, sitting in the same chair, looking exactly as she looked right now, holding a piece of paper in her hand as she stared directly into the camera.

"No one outside this building has seen this," Camille said before pressing play.

Surreal didn't come close to describing the feeling of watching her calmly deliver the most devastating self-critique he'd ever heard come from anyone, let alone someone in Camille's position. She was a high-profile former FBI agent whose father had been abducted by people with very bad intentions. There wasn't a more sympathetic character in the entire world right now. Yet, here she was, on camera, telling that sympathetic world that she not only understood her perpetrator's motives, but she deserved whatever outcome was to follow.

In his sixteen years of journalism, Will had never seen anything like it. Nothing he'd experienced in that time could've prepared him for it. And no amount of remorse, guilt, or fear he imagined could justify it.

"Tell me this is a joke."

Before Will could get an answer, he remembered Camille's first press conference, and Jeremy Durant, and the letter from Paul and Jacob's abductor, and the stark terror in Durant's eyes as he gave it to Camille. And then it all made sense.

"Those are his words."

"Yes."

"And when Jeremy pointed to the camera and said he'll be

watching, he was referring to this. The perp wants you to read those words on television."

"You don't miss much, Mr. Freeman," Crawley said.

"Are you really going to release this to the public?"

"Yes," Camille answered. "That's why we wanted to meet with you."

Will suddenly knew what was coming and felt the corresponding rise of tension in his stomach.

"Like Agent Crawley said, we weren't exactly thrilled when we saw your cell phone video," Camille continued. "We know you're a journalist doing your job, but going about it that way felt unseemly. To have that video out in the world before we could assess the credibility of the letter or the threat to Jeremy Durant put us at a grave disadvantage. It was irresponsible journalism at best."

Will shifted under the weight of Camille's stare. "Believe me, if I had it to do over again, I wouldn't have posted the video, especially given what happened afterward."

"The benefit of hindsight aside, no one is blaming you for what happened," Camille assured him. "He was coming after them whether he saw the video on your website or someone else's. It just so happens he saw it on yours. And if he looked there once, he'll look there again."

"So the video I just watched… you want to post it on the Dispatch website."

"That's the plan."

Will's adrenaline spiked with excitement at the prospect of scooping the world yet again. Then it abruptly ebbed at the thought of this maniac using him as a conduit for his twisted message.

"But we need you to do more than post the video," Crawley added.

Will was afraid to know what that something was but asked anyway. "What?"

"We need to control the narrative."

"How can you possibly control something like this? The second you release it and the larger news outlets pick it up, it doesn't matter what narrative you try and attach it to. It won't be your story anymore. It'll belong to the public and the talking heads and the greedy news anchors who will dissect every possible angle of the story, every word of the statement, even the clothes Camille is wearing. No one has ever seen anything like this, and they won't know what to think of it. When people don't know what to think of something, their first instinct is to assume the worst about it. And with the public thinking the worst, your best-laid plans can go to shit real quick."

"That's exactly why he's making me do this," an incredulous Camille said.

"Well, it looks like he's going to get his way," Will countered. "As great as the exclusive would be, how can releasing it on my website stem the tide at all?"

"It's true that he wants to make a public spectacle out of this," Crawley said. "We've already taken that fact into consideration, and we're prepared to deal with it. The narrative we're interested in controlling is the one between him and Camille. Right now, he thinks he's in control of that narrative."

"From everything I can see, he's correct in that assumption."

"We have to change that," Camille said.

"But we have to do it in a way that he still thinks he's in control," Crawley added.

"And how do you plan to do that?"

Crawley opened the manila folder that had been sitting on the table in front of him. "We'll need a written piece to accompany the video," he said as he took out the contents and slid them across the table. "You have all the leeway you need to make the article your own, of course. But the bulleted items need to be featured prominently."

Will took the paper and began reading. The bullet points were quotes from Camille to be included in the story. Many of them reiterated the points made in the statement. But several of them struck him as being out of place for a story like this. One quote, in particular, caught his attention, so much so that he read it aloud.

"I think of the families, the loved ones left behind, almost as much as I think about the victims. I remember once finding a diary that belonged to one of the last girls killed. It was filled with passages about her father; a father she hadn't heard from in many years. I'll never forget those words as long as I live, and it broke my heart to know that he would never get to read them. I know she would have wanted him to.

He turned to Camille.

"I don't know much about how the FBI works but isn't this one of those personal details that you wouldn't want floating out there for the sake of everyone's privacy?"

"We wouldn't if the diary actually existed," Camille answered.

"You mean you just made that up?"

"I'm afraid there isn't any time to provide context, Mr. Freeman," Crawley said. "Just know that those words were very well thought out and need to find their way in your article exactly as they're written."

"Okay," Will said, sensing that it would be futile to ask any more questions. "Sounds like I'm doing this, whether I want to or not."

"There are lives at stake, Mr. Freeman. You should want to."

Camille's words hit him like a punch to the sternum. But they also served as a wake-up call. Blind ambition caused him to do something yesterday that he knew he shouldn't have done. And as a result of that decision, he found himself here. But instead of lamenting his unenviable position, Will thought it best to use the opportunity to make amends. Perhaps then, his heart would ache a little bit less when the quiet of night no longer afforded him the luxury of distraction.

"I'm assuming that time is of the essence."

"Absolutely," Camille confirmed.

"Then let's have Arthur bring my things back so I can get started."

23

HIDING THE MONSTER

A BRAHAM NOBLE SAT BEHIND a large oak desk inside the living quarters of the three-story Tudor that now doubled as a makeshift prison. Abraham rarely found himself alone these days. Between Sabrina, her sons, and his two guests, there was always someone around; always a fire to put out, or a warning to issue, or a frayed nerve to smooth over. But right now, the world around him was quiet, and he relished it.

He reached inside the desk drawer and pulled out a small humidor. Even though he hadn't eaten yet today, he took out the richest, most potent cigar he had - a Liga Privada Number 9. Abraham had been an everyday cigar smoker for the past thirty years but saved this particular stash for special occasions.

This was such an occasion. His first real victory in a recent string of bitter and sometimes debilitating defeats.

If nothing else happened, if no other aspect of his plan came together as he'd imagined it, he would always cherish this moment - the moment he forced Camille Grisham to stand in front of the world and take account for all that she'd done, and all that she'd taken from him.

The logical half of his brain reminded him that Camille was merely doing as she was told. She was reading words that were written for her. The logical half also knew that she would've done or said anything to ensure her father's safety, and reading a script into a camera was relatively easy. He would've done the same thing had he been in her position, even if he didn't believe a single word of it.

The other half of his brain, the emotional, untamed, dominant half, didn't care that Camille was simply doing as she was told, or that she was doing so only in her father's best interests. That half of him knew there was more to it. It knew how she felt as she looked into that camera and admitted her guilt. She may not have written the words, but she still owned them. And even as she tried to deliver those words with the cold detachment that had been the trademark of her public persona, the truth behind them clung to her like sand on wet skin.

She'd kept her emotions in check much better than he expected her to. In certain respects, she was almost too calm, even going so far as to claim that she understood him. But quietly, subtly, secretly, he'd gutted her. She may not have felt the pain right away, but she would. And by the time she did, it would be too late to make herself whole again.

The statement may have only represented the beginning, but it couldn't have been a more satisfying beginning.

As he clipped a sliver off the cap of the cigar and began lighting it, Abraham paused, suddenly concerned that he was celebrating too soon. There was still a lot to do after all, and the most important work was yet to be done.

There were several moving parts to his operation, all of which he was responsible for overseeing. His wife, his prisoners, Daniel - they all had to be handled in different ways. So far he'd stayed on top of it. But the further this went, the more he worried that his grip would eventually weaken.

Sabrina had already breached his trust with her obvious sympathy for Paul, all the while ignoring his increasing defiance.

Daniel, his one-time friend, and closest confidant was willingly confined to his jail cell, committed to playing his part and keeping his mouth shut about the rest. But with word that he'd spent a good portion of yesterday inside a Denver police headquarters interrogation room, Abraham now feared that he couldn't be trusted. It didn't help that his interrogation came on the same day as Camille's unexpected appearance at Meredith Park's news conference; a news conference that Daniel was well aware of. The mere idea of Daniel's betrayal saddened Abraham in a way he couldn't quite articulate. He had genuine affection for the boy. With his own father being too much of a coward to do what was right for Daniel's sister, Abraham knew that Daniel had turned to him for the guidance and inspiration that only a true mentor could provide. Abraham was that mentor. He was also a friend and a kindred spirit and trusted Daniel to be the same. Now he worried that his trust in Daniel, as it had been with so many others, would prove to be misplaced.

Daniel hadn't yet been made aware of the price to be paid for betraying his trust. But as it had been with the others, Abraham wouldn't think twice about showing him.

He hoped like hell that it wouldn't come to that.

As he took the first long draw off of his cigar, Abraham thought about something else, equally troubling, yet infinitely more challenging.

Madison had been far and away the most important person to ever enter his life. But she wasn't his only child. When he married Sabrina, two of her three sons were already on the verge of adulthood, while her youngest, Lucas, was finishing his freshman year of high school. Their biological father had been with them during the formative years. As such, the damage he inflicted was permanent. Abraham did his best to stem the tide with the boys, Lucas especially. But as it turned out, his influence wouldn't be much better than their father's.

Lucas, like his mother, seemed the most susceptible to his negative tendencies. Sebastian and Ash, Lucas's older brothers, had already been so thoroughly hardened that nothing new could penetrate them. They feared Abraham, but they didn't respect him. They didn't want to emulate him either. Not like Lucas did. But it was just as well. He couldn't fathom the burden of helping to nurture three serial murderers. Nurturing one was more than enough.

Abraham knew he wasn't directly responsible for what Lucas had become. The seeds had been sown long ago; fertilized by his father's vicious DNA and cultivated by his mother's blatant denial. But Abraham recognized the signs. He'd displayed the same signs himself from as far back as he could remember. The only difference was that Abraham never acted on them until he was forced to.

When he discovered the full extent of Lucas's actions, their shared obsession with Daniel Sykes, and the subsequent murders he'd patterned after him, Abraham wasn't surprised, nor was he particularly alarmed. But he did feel a measure of guilt, not because he failed to stop him, but because his mother, Abraham's wife, continued to believe that the monster she gave birth to was anything but.

She had good reason to deny the monster. He was cloaked inside the most respectable veneer possible. He'd joined the family business of law enforcement, like his brothers and father, before becoming a corrections officer in the Fairfield maximum security prison - the same prison that housed Daniel Sykes.

It was there that his obsession with Sykes was solidified. And it was there that the monster fully emerged. Lucas was determined to keep that monster hidden from everyone, his mother especially. But Abraham knew him all-too-well.

In the quest to spare Sabrina the pain of that recognition, Abraham lied, claiming he knew nothing about the four murdered girls. He wasn't convinced that she'd believed him, but being the serial denier that she was, Sabrina didn't press. Her lack of persistence allowed him to use Lucas's proclivities, and his proximity to Sykes, to his own advantage.

The information Lucas gleaned from Sykes was crucial to the formation of Abraham's attack on Camille. The information he'd learned about Sykes's transfer out of Fairfield would allow Abraham to complete that attack. Lucas had done more for him from seventeen-hundred miles away than his two imbecile brothers in the next room combined.

Lucas was special in so many ways, not only for what he'd done for Abraham but because he'd asked for nothing in return except his assistance in keeping the monster safely hidden.

Keeping Lucas's secret safe from the world was easy. Keeping it safe from Sabrina was proving to be much more difficult. He'd demanded a lot of her over the years; asked her to do more questionable things than he should have. But he never lied to her, except when it came to Lucas.

He came up with a million justifications for why the lie was necessary. But none of them were legitimate. She'd shown more faith and trust in him than anyone else ever had. She'd trusted him to keep her safe. She'd trusted him to always do the right thing by her. And most importantly, she'd trusted him to love her sons like they were his own; to love them the same way he loved Madison. He'd sworn to her that he would do just that.

But the inescapable truth was that he hadn't. And the only

thing that frightened him more than the potential for Sabrina to learn that truth was the inevitability that she eventually would.

No longer finding himself in the mood to celebrate, Abraham stamped the cigar into the ashtray, his chest and throat too tight to handle the thick plumes of sweet smoke. He turned to his computer and pulled up the Mile-High Dispatch website, clicked the video of Camille, and watched. The feeling of satisfaction he felt the first time he watched it was gone. Now he could only think about what was next.

A phone call from Lucas detailing the specifics of Sykes's transfer was imminent. In the meantime, he had other issues to contend with, from the DPD's renewed interest in Daniel to outlining his next directive to Camille, to delivering the news to Paul that his daughter wasn't nearly as headstrong and defiant as he gave her credit for.

But the most pressing issue of them all would remain unresolved, at least for the time being.

He'd gone to great lengths to avoid Sabrina since the incident with Paul, partly out of anger, and partly out of the shame of being reminded of her kindness, her openness, and her general belief that good could still exist - even in a circumstance as dark as this one. Despite everything he'd put her through, he hadn't been able to break her spirit. He'd been grateful for that. But now, for the first time in his entire life, he was scared. He was oh-so-close to achieving his objective of making Camille Grisham pay fully for what she'd done. But he also knew that the closer he got to that objective, the closer he was to crushing the only person still alive that he actually loved by allowing the truth about the one person she loved more than him to be revealed.

He'd always been aware of the probability of such an event actually taking place, and because the cause of Camille's destruction meant so much to him, it was a chance he was willing to take. Now he understood how misguided he was. Only now, it was entirely too late.

The wheels had already been set in motion, and there was no stopping them. The vengeance he spent countless hours fantasizing about was finally within his reach. He always knew it would come with a price. What he didn't appreciate until this moment was just how high that price would be.

He caught a glimpse of Camille Grisham in his peripheral vision, and it momentarily lifted his spirits.

He wondered how long it would be before he saw her on television instead of his computer. He assumed it wouldn't be long. Abraham wasn't particularly savvy when it came to the media, but he knew enough to realize how effective an ally they would be in spreading his message.

There was a reason why popular videos were considered viral. Mass media was a terminal disease spreading unchecked through the body of the world. And the more painful the story, the faster the disease spread.

His story was gloriously painful, and Abraham knew that it would only be a matter of time before its malignant core infected every corner of the globe.

But the Mile-High Dispatch would have to do for now.

Abraham smiled thinly, ignoring the physical pain it caused him, and turned back to the computer to restart the video. He again understood the victory that this represented and he thought about re-lighting his cigar. But before he could, he saw something on the screen that he hadn't noticed before. The sight of Camille's face had rendered everything else around it invisible. But he could see it clearly now. A hyperlink in the sidebar of the screen.

AN FBI AGENT'S BIGGEST REGRET: THE UNTOLD STORY

When Abraham clicked the link, the site moved to a short article written by William Freeman, the same reporter who posted the footage from yesterday's fiasco. After wading through a dull regurgitation of Camille's statement, Abraham found something that stopped him cold.

"I remember once finding a diary that belonged to one of the last girls killed. It was filled with passages about her father; a father she hadn't heard from in many years. I'll never forget those words as long as I live, and it broke my heart to know that he would never get to read them. I know she would have wanted him to."

The words were so unbearable that Abraham had to read them aloud to ensure they were real. After reading the quote a second time, he still wasn't convinced.

A torrent of horrible thoughts tore through his brain that caused the thick scar on the crown of his forehead to throb.

She couldn't have been talking about Madison.

Abraham fought the notion even as the strength of it began to overpower him. It pushed, it pulled, it ripped, until it finally penetrated the armor of his doubt and invaded the core of his being.

It was Madison's diary. It had to be. Which meant the words inside it had to be about him.

Were they words of praise? Anger? Longing? Mockery? He imagined it could have been all of them. But the fact that he would never know for sure nearly destroyed what was left of his soul. He could feel the remaining fabrics of sanity that held him together tear apart, allowing the man that he was before this, and the man he hoped to be after this, to float harmlessly into the ether, never to be accessed again.

He thought about what he would be willing to give up, who he would be willing to sacrifice, to read that diary. Anyone and everyone, he quickly concluded.

Then an image of Sabrina flashed in front of him. Would he really be able to sacrifice her? Even for Madison?

A knock on the door pulled him away from the question before he could answer it.

"Who is it?"

"Sebastian."

Suddenly aware that he'd been slumped over in his chair, Abraham quickly stood, stiffened his slack jaw, and walked to the door. "What is it?" he said when he saw Sabrina's oldest son, a thirty-four-year-old prescription pill addicted burnout who was also a corrections officer like his younger brother.

"I just wanted you to know that I'm on my way out. Ash is here if mom needs any help."

Based on the fact that he was wearing his uniform, Abraham assumed he was on his way to another shift at the Denver County Jail. "Weren't you just on last night?"

"We're short-staffed, and they were looking for volunteers to work doubles. I figured I should volunteer. Gives me more time to keep an eye on Daniel."

"How is he?"

"Shaken up over our conversation last night."

"Do you think he got the message?"

"Yeah."

"Stay on him just in case. If you see anyone sniffing around him that shouldn't be…"

"I'll take care of it," Sebastian said.

"You'll tell me, and I'll take care of it," Abraham clarified. "Understood?"

Sebastian cast his pock-marked face down at his feet. "Yeah."

"Good. Anything else?"

"I saw Camille Grisham on the Dispatch website. What a lying bitch she is."

Abraham bristled at the comment. Even though he shared the sentiment, it sounded ugly and offensive coming from him.

"But at least we can finally take this to the next level," Sebastian continued. "I talked to Lucas yesterday. He's looking forward to coming home, and bringing his new best friend with him." He said that last part with a snicker, like it was the least bit funny. "It'll be nice to finally have it over," he continued. "I'm really getting sick of those two pricks, especially the old man."

Abraham and Paul were nearly the same age.

"What do you suggest we do with them when this is all over?" Abraham asked.

Sebastian thought on it a moment. He was never good for much more than a moment's thought before his brain short-circuited. "We have to kill them, of course."

"If you're that certain, does it mean you're prepared to do it yourself?"

"Hell yes. I'll do both of them right now."

At sixty-two-year- old, Abraham was anything but frail, and even though his step-son stood three inches taller and carried considerably more weight, Abraham had no trouble driving him backward into the door and keeping him pinned there with an elbow to the throat and a knee to the groin.

"Show some goddamn respect," he growled as he drove his elbow deeper into Sebastian's Adam's apple.

Shock had prevented the younger, stronger man from fighting back, even as his eyelids drooped with the first signs of unconsciousness.

"You're not touching them or anyone else. Your brother has done enough of that. Do you understand?"

Sebastian made a gurgling sound that Abraham interpreted as a yes.

"Good." He released Sebastian's throat, grabbed him by his neatly-pressed uniform collar, shoved him out the door, and slammed it in his face.

The violent outburst surprised him, and he realized immediately how unnecessary it was. Sebastian was simply saying what he thought Abraham wanted to hear.

But he soon understood that the outburst wasn't about Sebastian. It was about the boy he tried to love like his own son who grew up to become a man he feared. And it was about the little girl who grew up to become a beautiful spirit that was taken from him before he had the chance to know her.

Abraham failed two children in the worst way imaginable because he couldn't be the father they needed them to be. The first failure resulted in the death of his daughter. The second failure, he now felt with increasing certainty, would result in his own.

24

TETHER

CAMILLE AND AGENT CRAWLEY were escorted through a private entrance as they made their way inside DPD headquarters. The main entrance, they were told, was effectively blocked off by the large media contingent that had congregated outside. A quicker than expected response to her statement, Camille assumed. She understood that she'd have to face them at some point but now was definitely not the time. She appreciated the heads up from Lieutenant Hitchcock, despite his obvious irritation in extending it.

When they arrived at his office, they were greeted by Chloe, her partner Marcus Greer, and Detectives Krieger and Parsons. Hitchcock sat behind his desk, staring at the computer with a grimness that felt all-too appropriate under the circumstances.

"Come in and close the door," he directed without taking his eyes off the monitor. "There are a couple of folding chairs in the corner."

Camille and Crawley made their way inside the cramped space, setting up their chairs behind Krieger and Parsons.

Camille and Chloe exchanged a brief glance, but for a

while, no one spoke.

Crawley eventually broke the silence.

"I'm assuming Detective Sullivan briefed you prior to the video's release," he said to Hitchcock.

"She did. I would've preferred to be consulted beforehand, though." Hitchcock looked up from the monitor and took off his glasses. His eyes were glossy. "Had I been consulted, I would've certainly advised against it."

"I'm sorry, lieutenant, but there wasn't any time for consulting," Crawley said. "And even if there were, the matter wouldn't have been up for negotiation."

Hitchcock attempted a smile, but the bulging in his jaw prevented it. "That's all well and good, Agent Crawley, but the shit's on my lawn now. I gave you the courtesy of a redirect away from the zoo downstairs, but just in case you're curious to see how bad it is, I'd be happy to take you down for a look." He turned his ire to Camille. "Being the star of the show, I'm sure they'd love to get a crack at you anyway."

"Not the role I wanted, lieutenant," she said. "He didn't offer me a choice."

"Since when are we in the business of taking offers from criminals?"

"Since that criminal is holding my father captive and is threatening to kill him. Or did you forget what was actually at stake here?"

Camille's sharp reply forced the tension in Hitchcock's jaw to soften. "Of course I didn't. But you have to remember that we're a part of this investigation too, and we're happy to be a part of it. No one in this room is willing to rest until we get Paul back. But when you do something as major as this," he pointed to the monitor, "and you're not available to publicly answer for it, the hounds start beating down *our* door. Our spokespeople have deflected the questions as much as they can, but they're flat-footed out there. The public perceives that as incompetence. One more feather in the cap of the activists that want to take us down." Hitchcock took a deep breath to collect himself. "I understand why you did what you did, Camille. But you have to keep us in the loop going forward. As much as this is your fight, you aren't a task force of one. Can we agree on that?"

Camille couldn't argue Hitchcock's point. She didn't want to either. She was getting dangerously close to biting off more than she could chew as it was. The consultant was quickly morphing into a full-fledged profiler. That hadn't been the plan. Not even close. And now Hitchcock was accusing her of wanting to take over the investigation entirely, something she couldn't have ever fathomed doing when Crawley asked her to join. She would've bent over backward to defend herself against such an accusation before today. But right now, there was nothing she could say to the lieutenant, or anyone else in the room except, "Yes we can."

Mindful that Crawley was due his own slice of humble pie, she turned to him with an expectant eye. He shifted in his chair as if preparing a protest but quickly thought better of it.

"We can agree on that."

Hitchcock nodded. "That's all I ask."

"Now that we've got that uncomfortable business out of the way, where do we stand overall?" Greer asked.

The group turned to Camille. Apparently, she hadn't shed the 'task force of one' moniker completely.

"Agents Pratt and Mendoza are following up on possible angles in Daniel MacPherson's home town of Reading, Pennsylvania, and Fairfield prison where Sykes is being kept. We believe the perp has connections to both."

Hitchcock raised an eyebrow. "Are you saying he was working with MacPherson *and* Sykes?"

"I'm fairly certain that he and Sykes weren't affiliated directly. But there were things written in the statement that no one but Sykes would know. Mendoza is looking into the possibility that the two were able to trade correspondence without the prison's knowledge."

"Like someone on the inside was helping them?" Parsons asked.

Camille nodded. "It's a long shot, but we have to consider it."

"And what about MacPherson?" Hitchcock asked.

"Daniel's lack of cooperation notwithstanding, we hadn't been able to establish a firm connection between the two of them before now," Crawley said. "Then Camille discovered something fairly significant that they have in common."

"What's that?"

"The perp is related to one of the victims," Camille answered.

"The father of one of the victims to be exact," Crawley added.

"Do you know which victim?" Hitchcock asked.

"I was able to narrow it down to six. The last six specifically," Camille said.

"How were you able to do that?" Parsons asked, shaking his head in wonder.

"Clues he left in the statement."

Parsons looked at Krieger, still shaking his head. "I listened to her statement five times, and I didn't pick up on any of that."

"That's because we don't do what she does," Krieger replied. "Now that you know what the perp and MacPherson have in common, how did they originally connect?" he asked Camille.

"Most likely, through their shared experience of grief. At least initially. We know there were countless online forums dedicated to Sykes and his victims. But MacPherson's internet history before arriving here doesn't show that he visited any of those sites. Burner phone and encrypted dark web activity are both possibilities, but Detective Sullivan suggested another possibility that we deemed worthy of investigation."

The group turned to Chloe, who looked uncomfortable with the sudden attention. She quickly shook it off, cleared her throat, then spoke.

"It's likely that MacPherson and the perp shared a close geographical proximity. The first copycat victim was found forty miles outside of Reading. My thought was that they originally found each other in person through a local support group of some kind."

"An idea that we concurred with," Crawley said. "Agent Pratt is researching victim support groups in Reading and the surrounding area on the off-chance that one or both of them may have left some sort of paper trail. Anonymity is usually a staple of these kinds of groups, but it's worth pursuing."

Krieger and Parsons looked at one another, then looked at Chloe. The corner of Parsons' mouth was curled up with a smile.

"Top-notch detecting, as usual. You and Greer just make sure you don't go running off to the Bureau any time soon. Somebody's gotta run the show after the two of us retire."

Parsons' quip made Chloe smile. "We could never fill your shoes, Jimmy. But we plan on being around to try."

"I doubt I'd pass the Bureau's psych eval anyway," Greer said with a smile of his own. "I'm surprised you guys let me get this far."

A smattering of laughter from the DPD side. Camille and Crawley were silent; the latter understanding why the former wouldn't find humor in such a statement.

Hitchcock quickly redirected the group's focus. "I was just reading the article by Will Freeman. That quote about the victim's diary…"

"It's there to get his attention," Camille confirmed.

"You'd better hope it doesn't provoke him instead."

"I took that into consideration, lieutenant. But the truth is, we have no idea what makes this guy tick. For all I know, he could've been set off by the color blouse I was wearing. I played on what I perceived to be his weakness. He won't be expecting it, and like anyone confronted with an unpleasant surprise, it could very well piss him off. But it's also going to spark his curiosity. He's going to want to know what I know, perhaps more than anything else that he wants. It could be enough of a wrench in his plan to force a mistake."

Hitchcock nodded his understanding.

"Were you guys able to dig up anything more at the Durant scene?" Camille then asked Krieger and Parsons.

"No," Krieger answered. "Forensics finished their last sweep early this morning but didn't uncover anything new. There was no sign of forced entry into the home, and the gate leading to the backyard was locked. It's possible the perp followed Mrs. Durant home and confronted her as she was pulling into her garage, but there was no sign of struggle. Did I hear right that the only print found on the letter and voice recorder belonged to Jacob Deaver?"

"That's right," Crawley confirmed. "This guy is obviously careful. Deaver's print was intentional."

"Maybe Deaver is the one writing the letters," Greer said. "The perp comes up with the content and forces Deaver to type it out."

"It makes sense with Deaver wanting to write a book about Sykes," Parsons said. "Could be the perp's twisted way of granting the guy his wish."

Camille had already concluded as much but didn't feel the need to steal the moment. "We certainly can't discount that, Detective Greer."

Greer flashed a quick smile before diverting his gaze to the floor.

"What's happening with MacPherson?" Crawley asked Chloe and Greer.

"We plan to pull him out of county again today," Chloe said. "It's a good bet that he's already seen Camille's statement. All the better if he hasn't. Either way, we'll show it to him to see how he reacts. Then we spend the rest of the day pressing him."

"Make sure he's aware of the article," Camille said. "I want him to know about the diary. If I'm right that the perp is the father of one of the victims, and Daniel believes that this diary belonged to her, he might start to crack."

"Understood."

"Did you say that DPD forensics finished their sweep of the Durant residence?" Crawley asked Krieger.

"Yes."

Crawley turned to Camille. "We might want to pay another visit now that the scene is quiet. It was tough to get a good feel for it with all the techs running around."

Camille nodded, even though it was the last place she wanted to be.

"We can make sure you get in," Parsons offered. "We'll get out of your hair when you're ready to look around."

"That's fine," Crawley said, though Camille knew he'd rather not have them there. When it came to collaboration with the locals, Crawley put the 'I' in team. But in this case, he chose the wise route of diplomacy.

"At what point do you plan to address the media?" Hitchcock asked them. "It's only a matter a time before the chief rips me a new one for not getting rid of them."

"I took a huge risk with the article," Camille said. "I'm not going to compound that by going on television again to answer a bunch of random questions. I don't know much about what triggers him, but I guarantee you, that will."

The look of grim desperation that painted Hitchcock's face as they walked in made a sudden reappearance. "You realize the longer it takes for you to speak, the more likely it is that they'll start speaking for you. Next thing you know, there's a tidal wave of misinformation out there. Do you really want that?"

"You watched the statement, lieutenant. They can't say anything about me that I didn't already say about myself."

Hitchcock put his fingers up to his temples and sank back in his chair. "As if one PR nightmare wasn't enough."

A brief silence settled over the office that was broken by the buzz of Crawley's cell phone. He quickly pulled it out of his pocket and looked at the screen. "It's Allison," he told Camille.

When he answered, she could hear Mendoza's faint voice on the other end. Her pitch sounded high.

Crawley's face contorted as he attempted to absorb her rapid-fire delivery. "Alright, Allison. Just hold on a second. I'm in a meeting with Lieutenant Hitchcock and the team from DPD. I need to put you on speaker." He pressed a button and turned up the volume until the staccato rhythm of Mendoza's heavy breathing could clearly be heard. "Can you hear me?" he said as he held up the phone.

"Yes, I can hear you."

"Repeat everything you just told me. I don't believe I heard you right the first time."

"You heard me right, sir," Mendoza said. "Daniel Sykes is being moved out of Fairfield."

Camille felt a rush of adrenaline that plummeted almost as quickly as it came. She felt light-headed and queasy. "Where is he being moved to?"

"The SuperMax facility in Florence."

Crawley looked at Camille before saying, "When?", though she couldn't be positive that was what he said. She only saw his lips move. The ringing in her ears didn't allow for anything else.

"Apparently the transfer paperwork is being drawn up as we speak. It shouldn't take more than forty-eight hours to go through."

Camille looked at Crawley with eyes that were desperate for clarification. What she was hearing couldn't possibly have been true.

"How did you find out about this?" Crawley asked.

"The warden. When I called to inquire about Sykes's correspondence, he asked if it had anything to do with his impending move to Colorado. He must've assumed it did since I told him I was a CBI agent. He told me that Sykes was being moved because Fairfield could no longer accommodate him due to the scrutiny the prison received as well as issues related to Sykes' safety, the safety of his fellow inmates, and a recent rash of unrelated escape attempts that exposed major holes in both staff and operational security. He said he couldn't elaborate on what that meant due to an ongoing investigation by the Pennsylvania Department of Corrections. There are major-league problems there."

"Why not just transfer him in-state?" Crawley asked. "There's a Supermax a few hundred miles away in Greene county."

"No room," Mendoza reported. "And for as good as Greene might be, Florence is considered one of the most secure prisons in the country. They'd send him to the hole for even contemplating an escape attempt."

The United States Penitentiary located in Florence, Colorado, a Supermax facility referred to as "The Alcatraz of the Rockies" was opened in 1994 and is home to some of the country's most notorious inmates; homegrown criminals and international terrorists alike. Prisoners there spend twenty-three hours locked in their cells, and when an individual is allowed to move about during their limited recreation time, it's under the close supervision of at least three corrections officers. Camille was already responsible for the placement of one inmate at the facility, a California physician who killed nineteen people, including five elderly patients under his care. But she hadn't given Dr. Myles Garrett a second thought since he'd been locked away. Daniel Sykes was a much different story.

The only safe barrier between them had been distance. If the thought of Sykes being locked in a cell helped Camille fall asleep at night, the thought of his cell being seventeen hundred miles away helped her stay asleep.

Now she was being told that they would be separated by less than a two-hour drive. And if that really were the case, the extraordinary security measures would ultimately mean nothing. There wouldn't be a physical wall high enough to keep Sykes out of her nightmares.

By the time Camille's awareness brought her back to Hitchcock's office, Crawley had taken his phone into the hallway. Parsons, Krieger, and Greer were huddled around the lieutenant's desk, engaged in a conversation she couldn't hear. Chloe had moved next to her, though Camille didn't know that until she felt a hand on her shoulder.

"I said, are you okay?"

Camille took Chloe's hand and squeezed it. The move was unplanned and involuntary. She needed something solid to hold on to. The tether that kept her from drifting into the endless black had come dangerously close to snapping, and the warm grip of Chloe's hand was the only thing in that moment capable of bringing her back. And with her return came a second, more devastating thought.

"It all makes sense now."

25

EMBRACING THE DARKNESS

C AMILLE FOUND CRAWLEY INSIDE an empty break room, pacing furiously as he shouted into his phone.

"I don't give two shits about DOC protocol, Travis! Somebody should've let us know what was happening!"

Camille knew Travis to be Executive Assistant Director Travis Spaulding. From what Crawley told her, it was Director Spaulding who signed off on her involvement in the investigation. Having someone that high up the food chain give his seal of approval was a big deal that wasn't lost on her. Knowing how the Bureau worked, she also realized that it was a likely precursor to the more formal request for her reinstatement that Crawley was eventually hoping to make.

Based on how he was talking to the director right now, Camille had grave concerns that he wouldn't be around long enough to make that request.

"I am calm, sir. But I'm telling you that transfer cannot happen. The perp's second letter mentions Daniel Sykes specifically. We still don't know what he has planned, but we can't discount the possibility that this move is part of his plan." Crawley paused to listen to the director's response. "I don't know how he would've been privy to the move. But he obviously was. That's why we need to put it on hold until we know more.

After pausing again, the tension in Crawley's voice softened. "Thank you, sir. I'll report back as soon as we learn more." He hung up and turned to Camille. "They were apparently just as surprised by the transfer as we were."

"Can they stop it?"

"Director Spaulding is putting in a call to the Pennsylvania Department of Corrections right now. He's not making any promises."

"But the perp's letter about Sykes…"

"Pure conjecture as far as Fairfield is concerned. We'll have to twist their arm to convince them otherwise. Fortunately, the director has a hell of a grip."

Just then, Chloe and Greer walked into the break room.

"Any further word on the transfer?" Chloe asked.

"The Bureau is working on a hold," Camille said. "But we can't wait around to see how it turns out."

"We've already contacted county to let them know we want to talk to Daniel again," Chloe reported. "He should be here in half an hour. We've got the video of your statement ready, and Marcus printed a copy of the article. We'll let Daniel look at both before we even ask the first question."

"Good plan," Camille said.

"We can't let him go back before he gives up something significant," Crawley said, the tightness returning to his face. "It won't be long before we hear from this guy again, and God only knows how he plans to deliver the message this time. We need to head him off before he can. Daniel is going to help us do that."

"Okay," Chloe said. "What's next for you guys?"

"I'm putting in a call to the warden at Fairfield. It might help to hear about the particulars of the investigation from someone directly involved," Crawley said before turning to Camille. "While we're at it, we should start a probe on the staff. The information Allison received just might support your theory about Sykes having a collaborator on the inside."

Camille was sure of it at this point. What she couldn't fathom was how Sykes was ever granted enough leeway to have unmonitored conversations of any sort, let alone conversations about her. For the safety of everyone involved, perhaps a transfer out of Fairfield was the best course of action. But of all the places in the world he could've landed, why in God's name did it have to be here? With the probability of a suitable answer ever revealing itself being less than zero, she resolved never to ask the question out loud. "I'll hook up with Pratt and Mendoza to see what they've already learned and then go from there," she said instead.

Crawley nodded. "The clock is ticking, and it seems like it's only moving faster with each second that passes, so let's get to it. Detectives, you'll keep us posted on your progress with MacPherson?"

"Absolutely," Greer said.

With that, Crawley made his way out of the break room with Greer following. Camille started out behind them when Chloe stopped her."

"Hold up a second. I need to ask you something."

"Okay."

"The thing you said back in Hitchcock's office about it all making sense. What did you mean?"

The stream of trepidation that Camille had attempted to shake off instantly came flooding back. "He knew that Sykes was going to be moved here."

"Your father's abductor?"

Camille nodded. "The demand for a joint interview with Sykes was his way of warning me about what was coming."

"Do you think he intends to follow through with it?"

"At this point, I have no choice but to believe that he does. It was easy to dismiss the idea before now because of the logistics of Sykes being so far away. But the logistics just got a whole lot less challenging."

"The Florence Supermax would never sign off on it. He has to know that."

"As long as he's holding Jacob and my father, he believes he's got all the leverage he needs to change their minds. He's certainly changing mine."

Chloe's eyes grew wide with disbelief. "Don't tell me you're considering going through with it."

"If that's what it takes to keep my father safe."

"But what about your safety? If he's really in a position to facilitate a meeting between you and Sykes, who knows what he'll be able to do once you're there. You've already said it, this is about more than a simple press conference. He's got something much worse planned. And if you insist on this meeting with Sykes, you could be walking right into it."

"Then we'd better catch him before I have to make that decision."

"How much time do we realistically have?"

"Less than forty-eight hours if the transfer is allowed to go through. Unfortunately, that's the best-case scenario. If the transfer is stopped, and he gets word of it, we may have even less time. Pratt and Mendoza could catch a break with the support group angle, but we need something that helps us break this open right now."

"That something is on his way here as we speak," Chloe declared.

"This has to be it. We can't send Daniel back without getting what we want."

"Do you want to be there?"

Camille took a moment to consider it. "If I could promise

to hold myself together, then I'd absolutely be there. But I can't make that promise."

"In that case, you have my word that Daniel will give us what we want."

"Thank you," Camille said, understanding full well that her entire existence was riding on it.

26

THROWN TO THE WOLVES

D ANIEL HEARD THE BUZZ about Camille's statement before he had the chance to see it. Most of the comments from the inmates who'd watched it were on par with the profane, sexually-charged fare that he'd become accustomed to. But they offered little in the way of content or substance.

Since the rec-room television was restricted to repeat viewings of daytime courtroom shows and sports highlights, Daniel wasn't hopeful that he'd see a recap, and he wouldn't dare ask one of the wolves on rec-room duty to change the channel for him. So he cut his free time short and returned to his cell.

He didn't know the specifics of what Abraham had told her to say, but he was able to paint with enough broad strokes to conjure a crude image of what she looked like when she said it. The thought of her emotional anguish should've summoned an immediate rush of satisfaction. It didn't. Much to his surprise, he felt nothing.

He'd wanted to attribute this to the fact that he hadn't

actually seen the statement and therefore couldn't adequately align with the emotion behind it. But that wasn't the truth.

The truth about his feelings of emptiness was that they had nothing to do with Camille.

Last night, as he lay staring at the barren white walls closing in around him, he finally came to appreciate just how alone he was. There were no pictures of his family on those walls, no letters or phone calls, no assurances that the life he once had could ever be a reality again.

Instead, everyone he'd ever trusted, including the man he trusted the most, had turned their backs on him.

Daniel always knew that he'd have to sacrifice in order to achieve everything the two of them imagined. But he didn't appreciate the depths of that sacrifice until now. In the blink of an eye, he'd gone from being the architect of the design to becoming a victim of it. Thrown to the wolves, just as Camille had been. Her wolves were symbolic. His were very real.

The emptiness, Daniel came to realize, had been his way of finally empathizing with her.

Unfortunately for both of them, that empathy had likely come too late.

Daniel knew he couldn't save himself. His fate had already been sealed. But he wondered what could've been for Camille had he told her and Detective Sullivan everything he'd wanted to. He wondered if the reporter and his wife would still be alive. He wondered if Paul Grisham and Jacob Deaver could've been found by now. Most of all, he wondered if the act of saving them could've been enough to ensure his own salvation.

The threats made against him last night were a clear indication that his days were numbered. Harm would most certainly come to him, whether by Abraham's hand or by someone else's, and he feared that the only person willing to protect him had already delivered the last words she planned to speak to him.

So when the two corrections officers who escorted him to DPD headquarters yesterday opened the door to his cell, ordered him to put on his shoes, and proceeded to outfit him in the heavy restraints that indicated a trip outside was imminent, Daniel could barely contain his relief.

"Your presence has been requested at Major Crimes, Mr. MacPherson," the tall black guard told him. "In case you didn't know, you're a really popular fella right now. Has anyone asked you for an autograph yet?"

Daniel didn't want to know what that meant, so he stayed silent.

The other guard, a short blond with a much harder disposition, stared coldly at Daniel as he secured his leg shackles.

But Daniel's relief didn't waver.

This was an opportunity, a gift, and he knew what he had to do with it.

He prepared himself for the possibility that his life would be no different when this was all over. The world might still deem him unworthy of salvation.

But even if the wolves did eventually feast on him, he would be reunited with Candace knowing that he did everything he could to finally make her proud.

The thought nearly made him smile.

As the two guards led him out of his cell, he caught sight of someone at the far end of the corridor, fast approaching them.

Once Daniel realized who it was, he put his head down and cast his eyes to the floor, hoping not to be noticed. But an inmate in leg shackles flanked by two burly C.O.s is difficult to miss.

"Where are you taking that one?" the man Daniel knew as

John asked the officers, his acne-ravaged face beaming. "From the looks of it, he's been a naughty boy."

"We're actually taking him over to DPD Admin," the blond guard said. "The detectives in Major Crimes want to talk to him again."

John's face darkened. "For what?" He looked at Daniel as if expecting him to answer.

"My guess is he's ready to sing," the black guard said with a chuckle. "How about it, Daniel? You gonna belt a few bars for us now?"

This caused the blond guard to join in the laughter. John didn't appear to find it the least bit funny.

"You're not turning rat, are you Daniel?" he asked with a light tone that did nothing to mask his anger. "You know how that goes over in this place."

Daniel kept his eyes on the floor, hopeful that there were no other inmates within earshot. If so, there was a better-than-average chance that he wouldn't make it through the night before being confronted by one of the wolves. Perhaps that had been the plan.

"We don't know what's going down, and unfortunately Danny here isn't willing to tell us," the black guard said. "But if self-preservation is on his mind, I can't say that I blame him."

"I'm sure that crazy FBI agent giving him a shout-out on TV didn't hurt," the blond guard followed. "Maybe they're ready to give him a pass altogether."

Still afraid to know what they were speaking of, Daniel stayed silent.

"Yeah," John replied, keeping his glare on him. "Sounds about right."

"In any case, we gotta go," the blond guard said. "He's supposed to be there already."

"Mind if I tag along?" John asked.

Daniel's blood suddenly ran cold with fear.

"I know he looks like a handful, but I think we can manage it," the black guard said, still chuckling.

"It'll give me something to do," John insisted. "I came in for an extra shift thinking we'd be short-staffed. Turns out we're not. I've been standing around for an hour picking my nose. If I'm gonna get time and a half, I should at least earn it."

"Fine," the blond guard said, his patience for the conversation ebbing. "But we gotta go."

The two guards led Daniel down the corridor without saying another word.

John quickly fell in line behind them.

Daniel could feel the heat of his stare penetrating the back of his skull, and at that moment, he wanted to blurt out everything he knew about John and Abraham and all the other goddamn things he had no business getting mixed up in. But now was not the time, and these two guards were certainly not the audience.

He was less than ten minutes away from reaching that audience. But John's presence, and his apparent desire to prevent his meeting with Major Crimes, made that ten minutes feel infinitely longer.

27

INTERVENTION

ALL THREE OF THEM WOULD HAVE TO DIE.
As he followed Daniel and the two guards through
the maze of jailhouse corridors leading to the parking garage,
Sebastian Gideon knew he had no other choice. He couldn't
stop to consider how impossible the notion was under the
circumstances, or the fact that he'd worked with Prescott and
Irving for over a year and had beers with them on multiple
occasions, or that he once promised to show Irving's son how
to shoot a bow and arrow when the thirteen-year-old learned
of Sebastian's passion for archery. None of that mattered
now.

These men, friends and colleagues that they once were,
had become impediments to his objective. It was an objective
born out of necessity but fueled by rage and frustration. And
he had to see it through.

From the moment Abraham entered the picture, he'd gone
out of his way to make Sebastian and his brother Ash feel
unworthy of his time and attention. Not that his time and
attention mattered. Sebastian hadn't received much of that
from anyone, not even his own mother. But the constant belit-

tling, combined with his increasingly destructive influence over Sebastian's mother and younger brother Lucas, were taking a toll.

Sebastian played along the best he could. He did so for his mother's sake, and because his two kid brothers still looked to him for some measure of guidance and support. He also did so because, deep down, he still hoped to gain the respect of the man who'd come into his life with the promise of being the father-figure he mistakenly thought he never needed.

But after years of prodding, years of challenging, years of making him feel small, Abraham had finally gone too far.

In the hierarchy that he'd decided to create for their family, Lucas was the strongest of the lot; the chosen one capable of doing no wrong. Sebastian and Ash were merely inferior imitations; always chasing the glory, but never attaining it. And today, Abraham showed, once and for all, just how inferior he believed Sebastian to be.

But Sebastian was going to prove, right here, right now, that he wasn't inferior to anyone.

It wasn't only Abraham's doubt that he needed to erase with this act. It was his own.

His doubts manifested in many forms: drug addiction, blind obedience, fear that he looked too much like his father to ever earn his mother's love and trust. But the biggest doubts came when he looked in the mirror. What had the person staring back at him ever done to earn anyone's respect? The hard edges of his muscular physique certainly made him look like a man. But when he pressed his hands against his rock-hard chest, he couldn't feel the heart that he knew was required to actually be a man. He stood in front of the mirror every morning and pressed as hard as he could in search of a pulse. Yet, for years on end, he could find no evidence that it actually existed.

This lack of heart and the courage that eluded him as a

result, allowed Sebastian to risk his freedom, his very life, for a fight that wasn't his. Camille Grisham had done nothing to him, neither had the two men who were being held captive in her name. But because of the empty cavity in his chest where his conviction should've been, he was not only smack dab in the middle of this fight, he was dangerously close to finding himself on the losing end of it.

Had Sebastian been honest with himself, he would've admitted that he was already on the losing end of it. Once Daniel stepped foot inside Major Crimes for a second time, it would be all over for him, and his brothers, and worst of all, his mother. But the intensity of the moment hadn't allowed time for honesty, or reflection, or hesitation. The moment only allowed for action.

He'd have to make his move before the van left the lot. Irving would most likely be the driver with Prescott in either the backseat with Daniel or riding shotgun. The latter would be much more convenient.

Either way, he could take out all three of them with his service pistol before anyone saw it coming. Unfortunately, Sebastian couldn't guarantee that the van's robust insulation would be enough to drown out the noise.

He'd have to use his pocket knife instead. He hated the thought of getting up close and personal, but there was no other viable option.

He'd disable Prescott with the knife as he was getting Daniel situated in the rear cabin. Quick and quiet. Daniel would be next. Irving would most likely be alerted by then. The shock of it all would allow Sebastian a brief advantage, less than a second. He'd have to make the most of it.

The screams of panic in his head didn't allow room for the logical voice that would've told him just how ill-conceived his plan was, so he pressed forward into the parking garage with his hand cradling the knife, and his heart, the one that had been missing all these years, beating wildly inside his chest.

"Where do you want me?" Sebastian asked the guards as he spotted the van on the far end of the lot.

"You can ride in the back with your buddy," Prescott said. "I'm sure he'd love the company."

I'm sure he would too, Sebastian thought, suppressing a smile.

Daniel walked along quietly as if Sebastian's presence hadn't bothered him. Perhaps he felt safe, thinking that Irving and Prescott were there to protect him. A false sense of security that would make the actual end that much sweeter.

Less than twenty feet now before they reached the van. Aside from a DPD patrol cruiser parked some distance away, there wasn't another soul within earshot. No one around to hear the screams. Sebastian wished he could record them, solely for the satisfaction of seeing the horror on Abraham's already hideously contorted face. He never admitted where the scar came from that nearly split his head in two. But Sebastian suspected that it had something to do with his brother. A real shame that Lucas didn't finish the job. After today, perhaps Sebastian would have the fortitude to do it himself.

He didn't bother suppressing his smile this time.

When they arrived at the van, Prescott reached for the rear door handle with one hand while keeping the other wrapped around Daniel's scrawny arm. He pulled the handle, and the first door swung open. Irving opened the second as he made his way around to the driver's side, just as Sebastian predicted he would.

"Alright, Mr. MacPherson. Your chariot awaits." Prescott gave a nudge, and Daniel proceeded to the bumper step that would lead him inside.

A voice from behind stopped him before he could reach it.

"Hey, is that Daniel MacPherson?"

Sebastian and the others turned around. The voice belonged to a DPD patrol officer. His female partner stood next to him. Both were taking dead aim at Sebastian with their eyes.

"Yeah," Prescott said. "We're taking him over to Major Crimes right now."

"We can take him in," the female officer said.

Irving came from around the driver's side of the van. "What's the issue with us taking him in?"

Sebastian tensed when the female officer looked at him again before turning to Irving.

"We were instructed to deliver him ourselves," she said. "I'm not sure why, but as far as I know, there's no beef with you guys."

"We have instructions too," Irving said. "Besides, the van makes for easier transport, with the restraints and all. If you guys want to follow us to make sure we get there safe and sound, be my guest." He put his large hand on Daniel's shoulder. "What could be better than giving our VIP here a police escort all the way across the street?"

Unmoved by Irving's thin attempt at humor, the female officer cast another hard look at Sebastian before saying, "Does it normally take three of you to execute transport for one inmate?"

"No," Prescott said. Just as he prepared to say more, Sebastian interrupted him.

"They were humoring me. It was a little slow in there today, so they allowed me to tag along. It might be the only action I see all day." He attempted a smile, but quivering lips forced it back.

"That's great, but I think the four of us can handle it from here," the male officer said before turning to Irving and Prescott. "You guys can drive him over, and we'll see to it that he gets inside."

"Works for us," Irving said. Then he turned to Sebastian. "Sorry, chief. Maybe next time."

Realizing he had no choice but to stand down, Sebastian eased his hand off the handle of his pocket knife and took a step away from the group. "Yeah."

"Hell, if they really don't need you in there, you should blow this place and go enjoy the rest of the day. Maybe we can all hook up for a beer later."

Sebastian swallowed hard, nodding at Irving's offer like he was actually considering it. Then he looked at Daniel. Though he obviously fought hard to contain it, the relief in his eyes was apparent. He could sense what was being planned here, Sebastian was sure of it. Yet he said nothing. As appreciative as he was for the hesitation, he couldn't understand it. Perhaps Daniel had simply been resigned to his fate. More likely, he was biding his time, hoping for the miraculous intervention that eventually revealed itself. In either case, Sebastian couldn't help but admire the boy's resolve, even as he felt his own slipping away.

There wasn't anything left to do but stand and watch as Prescott loaded Daniel into the back of the van, climbed in beside him, and shut the doors.

"You two want to lead the way?" Irving then asked the officers.

"We trust you," the male officer said with a crooked smile. "Give us a minute to bring our car around, and we'll follow you out."

Irving nodded then gave Sebastian a quick pat on the shoulder. "Don't forget about those beers later."

"Wouldn't miss it."

Sebastian watched as Irving climbed into the van and

started the engine. By the time his attention was directed back at the officers, they were halfway to their cruiser. It was then that he noticed the second group of DPD uniforms.

He wasn't sure where they came from or how long they'd been there. He only knew that they were staring at him, and it took everything he had not to give in to the fight or flight instinct that would result in him doing something foolish.

They don't have a reason to stare at you, he told himself. *Don't give them one.*

Sebastian held his breath as the two officers made their way to the group. After a brief discussion, the officers climbed inside their cruiser. When they approached, Irving started the van, gave Sebastian one last wave out the window, then pulled away, taking the cruiser with it. He watched until they disappeared out of the garage.

Suddenly desperate to make his own escape, Sebastian quickly assessed his options. His car was parked in an adjacent lot. The only way to get to that lot was to go back inside the building to use the elevator or staircase. And the only way to get inside the building was to walk past the officers.

In a half-hearted effort to avoid interaction, Sebastian pulled out his cell phone as he slowly approached them, his eyes cast down at the blank screen. He could feel their eyes on him but resisted the temptation to look up.

When he got within earshot of their conversation, he slowed his walk. He certainly hadn't intended to, but the nature of their discussion made his desire for a hasty escape suddenly feel a lot less urgent.

"I heard that Camille Grisham and the dicks in Major Crimes worked him pretty good yesterday," one of the officers said. "Apparently they stashed Meredith Park in the safe house because of what he told them."

"Based on that shit-show of a press conference today he obviously didn't tell them enough," another officer said.

"Not yet. I don't know much about Detective Sullivan aside from her beef with IA. But I worked patrol with Greer a couple of years ago. He jokes around a lot, but he's a beast when it comes to the job. It'll only be a matter of time before they break the kid down."

Sebastian felt a ringing in his ears that momentarily drowned out the conversation. His hands trembled as he pretended to type something into his phone. After a moment, the ringing stopped. But his hands still shook.

Fearful that his nervous display would alert the officers, he continued slowly toward the building entrance with his head down, struggling to recapture his bearings.

"If they don't catch this guy soon, the shit-show's gonna get a whole lot worse," the third officer said. "McClellan and Evans say the lady in the safe house is paranoid as hell. She's convinced that whoever is after her will get to her there."

"If McClellan and Evans were protecting me, I'd be paranoid as hell too," the first officer quipped.

The trio shared a laugh.

"Where are they keeping her?"

"The dump over on thirty-eighth and Vine."

"You mean that corner house next to the old crack palace?"

"That's the one."

"Jesus, no wonder the lady's so paranoid."

Sebastian stopped again, his eyes growing wide with a shock that he couldn't suppress. Had he really just heard Meredith Park's name along with an address? He couldn't imagine such a stroke of good fortune ever being visited upon him, and for a moment, he believed it to be nothing more than a trick of his eager imagination.

But he also allowed for the possibility that the drastic change he'd witnessed in himself today could very well have brought with it a radical shift in fortune; a shift that allowed a piece of information that others around him would've killed for to fall effortlessly into his lap.

Still unconvinced that such a shift had actually taken place, he continued listening.

"She seems a little high-end for that neighborhood," one of the officers continued. "I figured they would've stashed her in a penthouse at the Four Seasons."

"All the more reason to keep her locked up in the hood. No one would think to look for her there."

One of the officers chuckled. "Yeah, I trust the gang-bangers to keep her safe a hell of a lot more than I trust Evans and McClellan."

The other two joined him in laughter.

"How long are they keeping her there?" one of them asked.

"Evans said that if they can't crack this thing today, they'll move her out in the morning. You can't be there more than a couple of days without the natives getting suspicious. Who knows where they'll put her after that, but knowing the department, I doubt that it'll be an upgrade."

"They'd just better make sure Camille Grisham's boyfriend doesn't get to her first."

That was the last thing Sebastian heard before the ringing started up in his ears again. When the ringing stopped, there was no thought left but one.

Abraham will never get to her.

Reason took an immediate backseat to expediency as Sebastian's thoughts turned to Meredith Park and what should be done with her. Reason dictated that he leave right now, get Abraham on the phone to share what he'd just learned, and let him deal with the aftermath. Expediency dictated that he act immediately and in his own self-interest, absent any thought of the potential consequences.

To cower to Abraham's will and influence now would

nullify everything he'd discovered about himself: the heart, the conviction, the courage. All of it. If that happened, there would be no coming back, no starting over at square one. It would be far better to lose everything on his own terms than to continue living as the impotent moron that Abraham assumed him to be.

Sebastian knew that Meredith Park had done nothing to him, and killing her would serve no purpose other than his own ego-fulfillment. He also knew that the cost-to-benefit ratio was exceedingly high. But he didn't care.

Dismantling Abraham's plan ultimately meant disman- tling Abraham. Considering the amount of pain visited upon himself and his family, it was the least that Sebastian could do.

The thought made him smile in a way that nothing else ever had.

The euphoric rush that followed hadn't allowed him to notice the trio of officers approaching him until they were only a few feet away. He also hadn't realized until now that he'd been staring at them much longer than he should have.

"Something we can help you with, friend?" the first officer asked with a terseness that Sebastian wouldn't have expected. The officer's tight blue eyes were hovering around Sebast- ian's chest, undoubtedly searching for the name tag that he'd removed prior to his encounter with Daniel.

He did so before every encounter with Daniel, and so far, no one else seemed to notice. It certainly wasn't a full-proof way of keeping his identity hidden. If Daniel really wanted to know his real name, all he had to do was ask another guard or inmate. After what happened today, Sebastian wouldn't have been surprised if he did just that. But at this point, he knew it wouldn't matter.

"Sorry, guys. I wasn't trying to pry. I overheard you talking about that FBI agent who was on TV today, and I got a little curious. I haven't had a chance to see it yet. I heard it was insane, though." It was the best Sebastian could come up with under the circumstances. He hoped it would be enough.

"It's all over the news," the officer replied, his hard edge softening somewhat. "I'm sure you won't have a problem catching a replay. It's definitely worth watching."

"I'm sure it is," Sebastian said with an overcooked smile.

"Speaking of which, were you part of the crew transporting Daniel MacPherson?" another officer asked.

"I was, but once your colleagues showed up, my services were no longer required," Sebastian said, wishing immediately that he'd thought of something else to say.

A nod from the officer was followed by an extended silence that made Sebastian feel very uncomfortable.

"Well, I'm sure they need you back in there," the first officer finally said.

"I'm sure they do. You guys take care."

The trio eyed him silently as he turned to walk inside the building. He cursed himself for so carelessly drawing their attention, and for a moment, he wondered if it was a sign that he was out of his depth.

He let the thought pass without an answer, choosing instead to hold tight to the image of Abraham that had formed so clearly in his mind's eye. The shock and devastation he'd feel at the news of Meredith's murder - news that Sebastian vowed to deliver personally - would only be the beginning.

The real satisfaction would come later when Abraham would finally get to experience first-hand the power of the man he'd deemed so unworthy of his time and attention. He'd finally have no choice but to stand up and take notice.

But by then, if Sebastian had his way, it would be entirely too late.

28

A CRACK IN THE ARMOR

C HLOE AND GREER STOOD BY in the parking garage as the transport van carrying Daniel MacPherson pulled up in front of them. The DPD cruiser sent to escort Daniel trailed close behind.

"They thought it would be easier to bring him in the van," one of the officers said as she stepped out of the cruiser.

"Perfectly fine," Chloe responded, keeping an eye on the van's rear cabin door.

The police escort had been her idea. Daniel needed to know that this interview session was going to be much different than the last, and she thought that the drastic change in transport protocol would be the first step in communicating that.

She had expected to feel an air of resistance once Daniel saw her. Based on the conclusion of yesterday's interview, he would have neither expected nor wanted such a quick return trip. But much to Chloe's surprise, he looked alert, refreshed, and somewhat relieved. Knowing his penchant for mind games, she was careful not to jump to any conclusions.

"Hello, Daniel," she said as he stepped out of the van.

He surprised her again by promptly returning her greeting. "Hello, Detective Sullivan. Detective Greer. Good to see you."

Chloe turned to her partner, wondering if the dumbfounded expression on his face matched her own.

"Would you like us to bring him in?" the tense-looking guard accompanying Daniel asked.

"We can take it from here," Chloe answered. "I'd tell you guys to remain on standby, but we might be a while." She looked at Daniel after she said this. He seemed unfazed by the words. "We'll call you when he's ready to be transported back."

"Okay. You can reach us at this number," the guard replied before handing her a card.

A second guard, much friendlier, peered around from the driver's side of the van. "You be sure and behave yourself, Daniel," he said with a grin. "And use that singing voice of yours for some good this time."

Daniel looked at him like he knew exactly what the directive meant.

Interview Room One was the biggest of the interrogation spaces in Major Crimes. Unlike Room Three, the chairs were well-cushioned, and the temperature sat at a comfortable sixty-eight degrees. It was essential to make Daniel feel as relaxed as possible this time around.

Playing up the good cop routine, Greer extended an immediate offer for coffee upon their arrival, which Daniel gladly accepted.

While Greer was away, Chloe busied herself by setting up the laptop computer on which she'd uploaded Camille's statement.

Daniel shifted in his chair, appearing somewhat unnerved by the silence.

Once Chloe cued the video, she turned the computer to him. "Have you had the chance to see this yet?"

A deep breath, and then, "No."

"Is there anything you want to know before I show it to you?"

"Will the walls start closing in tighter?"

Chloe was caught off guard by the question. "What do you mean?"

"I mean am I really going to be locked up in here for the rest of my life?"

Greer returned with the coffee, allowing Chloe the necessary time to formulate her response.

Daniel's handcuffs rattled as he reached for the cup.

"I think we can undo those," Chloe said to Greer.

He looked at her with surprise. "Are you sure?"

"We should be able to trust him at this point." She looked at Daniel. "We can trust you, right?"

The surprise in Daniel's eyes matched Greer's. "I don't know. Can I trust you?"

Chloe pulled a set of keys out of her pocket. "I'm willing to take a chance if you are."

Daniel tensed as she unlocked his restraints and let them fall to the floor.

"You'd better drink up," she continued. "That stuff turns to sludge once it gets cold."

With his hands now free, Daniel took a long pull from the styrofoam cup.

After a beat of extended silence, Chloe returned to his initial question.

"When you were asked yesterday if you were worried that you would spend the rest of your life in jail, you indicated that you weren't. Has something changed?"

Daniel's hand trembled as he set the coffee on the table. "A lot has changed."

"Tell us about it."

"Not until I know that you're willing to help me."

"Are you asking us to make a deal?" Greer asked.

"Yes."

"I'm afraid that's a conversation for the lawyers."

"I don't have a lawyer. I only have you."

Chloe and Greer exchanged a glance. Fully aware that there was no time for a conference to discuss it, Chloe nodded her approval.

Greer turned back to Daniel. "What did you have in mind?"

"I can't be in there anymore. It's not safe."

"Jail isn't designed to be a picnic," Chloe said.

Daniel shook his head. "It's not the other inmates I'm worried about."

Chloe immediately thought back to their conversation yesterday. He'd already referenced it once with his comment about the walls closing in. And now this. She took a quick breath to contain her enthusiasm at the discovery, knowing that an *I told you so* would be completely inappropriate under the circumstances. "Did you hear from him? The man you're protecting?"

"Not directly."

"How then?" Greer asked.

A pained expression suddenly cut across Daniel's face. Chloe had seen that look dozens of times on the faces of suspects who said way more than they intended to, only to realize that it was too late to backtrack.

"You haven't addressed my deal yet."

"What kind of deal do you want?" Chloe asked.

Daniel waited a long time before answering. Chloe took this to mean that he hadn't considered the answer before now, or he didn't think that he'd get far enough to ask the question and needed time to process his emotions.

"Full immunity," he finally said.

"In exchange for what?" Greer asked.

"Everything that I know."

"Full immunity is a lot to ask for," Chloe told him. "Despite what you may see on television and in the movies, the request is rarely granted."

"I believe the information I'm willing to share warrants it," Daniel declared.

"Why don't you let us be the judge of that," Greer countered.

"In other words, you want me to tell you what I know before you agree to a deal?"

"Yes," Chloe said.

Daniel's eyes darkened. "That doesn't work for me, detective. I didn't do a goddamn thing to anyone, yet I'm the one whose life is at stake. It's not fair."

"It's a little too late to play the victim card," Greer said coldly. "There's blood on your hands whether you want to admit it or not."

"I didn't kill anyone."

"But you collaborated with someone who did. In the eyes of the law, that makes you just as guilty as him."

"Information alone doesn't give you leverage," Chloe added. But your willingness to proactively offer that information, absent any pre-arranged deal, could work in your favor."

The feigned composure on Daniel's face faltered as he folded his arms across his chest. He bit down hard on his bottom lip as if stopping himself from saying something that he didn't want to. If Chloe didn't know better, she'd think he was on the verge of tears.

"I can't do that. Not until I know you can do something for me. My life is in danger."

"So are a lot of other people's," Chloe countered sharply. "That didn't seem to bother you before. But now that you've been threatened, you're suddenly ready to take this seriously?"

Daniel sat back in his chair, unwilling to respond.

"Okay, so you can't talk. I'll tell you what you can do," Chloe said as she restarted the laptop. "You can watch this video. Then you can read this article." She put the Mile-High-Dispatch printout in front of him. "And then you can decide how much further you want to see this nonsense go. Something terrible is about to happen, Daniel. And the only way that you survive it is if stopping that thing matters more to you than saving yourself. Which one matters more?"

She started the video of Camille's statement without waiting for an answer.

It took Daniel twenty minutes to watch the video and read the accompanying article, and in that time, he said nothing. When he finally finished, he closed the laptop and slid the paper across the table to Chloe and Greer.

"Thoughts?" Chloe asked.

"It's a lot," he said unemotionally.

Everything you expected?" Greer asked.

He hesitated. "No. There was something there that I didn't expect at all."

"What was that?" Chloe asked.

"The diary."

Chloe felt a surge of excitement course through her. The diary was precisely what Camille hoped he would pick up on. "Why did that stand out to you?"

"Because I know it would have stood out to him."

"Camille is talking about his daughter. Isn't she?"

"I don't know," Daniel answered, his voice suddenly strained with emotion. "But if it is, he's going to want to know what's in that diary, probably more than anything he's ever wanted in his entire life. And he should know what's in it. Madison was his life. Everything he did, he did for her. Just like everything I did, I did for Candace."

When Chloe looked at Greer, he took out a small notepad and began writing. Daniel had become so lost in his thoughts that he hadn't appeared to notice.

"You feel sorry for him," Chloe said.

"I did." A tear began to pool under his eyelid. "I knew we shared something; a pain that most people wouldn't even imagine, let alone experience. I thought that meant something to him. I thought that I meant something to him."

"And you were willing to look past all of the awful things he did because you thought he cared about you?" Chloe asked.

When Daniel nodded, the tear that had been dangling from his eyelash broke free. "I guess that confirms your belief that I'm no better than him."

"We wouldn't mind being proven wrong," Greer said.

"That's right," Chloe followed. "And you still have the opportunity to do that."

"How?"

"You can start by telling us why you don't feel sorry for him anymore."

Daniel blinked, and a second wave of tears rushed down his cheek. "Because he's trying to kill me."

"Through one of the inmates at the jail?"

"No."

"How, then?"

Daniel quickly wiped the tears from his face, cleared his throat, and sat up straight. All traces of uncertainty had vanished from his eyes. What remained was a look of clarity that hadn't been present before. Chloe could tell at that moment that he'd finally made the decision.

"A guard."

And with that, the crack in the armor that she'd been patiently waiting for finally revealed itself.

29

SMALL WORLD

CAMILLE'S CELL PHONE RANG as she made the walk from the CBI parking lot to the cubicle inside the Special Crimes Section where Agent Pratt had situated himself. She answered Crawley's call immediately.

"Great news," he said before she had the chance to greet him. "Director Spaulding's grip was even tighter than I thought it would be."

Camille felt an instant wave of relief wash over her. "Did he get a hold on the transfer?"

"Yes. It's not indefinite, but it should buy us some more time."

"How much?"

"As much as we need. But Spaulding made it clear that once the case is settled, Sykes will be moved here."

In the grander scheme, the news was still dire, but Camille saw no benefit in communicating that, so she stayed silent.

"Where are you now?" Crawley asked.

"On my way to meet up with Gabe."

"It's nice to know that you're finally on a first-name basis.

I didn't think you'd ever get over that horrible first impression."

"He's been trying to make up for it. The least I can do is extend a little grace."

"You've always been better about that than me."

"You make people earn it. Nothing wrong with that. It's one of the things that makes you a great leader. I certainly didn't have an easy road with you in the beginning."

"And look at how incredible you turned out as a result."

Camille certainly hadn't felt incredible lately, but she saw no benefit in communicating that opinion either.

"Do you remember when I made you promise to tell me if this was getting to be too much for you?"

"Yes, and I promised that I would."

"Well, with everything that's happened since then, I'd be remiss if I didn't ask again."

"My answer is the same as last time. I'm fine."

"Even with the news about Sykes?"

"The thought of Sykes being so close devastates me, but if it's meant to be, there's nothing I can do about it."

"We're on the verge of a break, Camille. I can feel it. I know you can feel it too. I just don't want the news about Sykes to derail you before we can get there. If you tell me it won't, I'll believe you, and I won't bring it up again. But if you think there's any chance-"

"My personal feelings about Sykes aren't a factor, Peter. Not when it comes to this."

Crawley allowed an extra moment to pass before responding, as if he needed to test the resolve of Camille's declaration. It wasn't until he finally said, "Okay, it won't come up again," that she knew he believed her.

All that was left now was for Camille to believe it herself.

When she found Agent Pratt, he was huddled over his desk, furiously typing notes into his computer.

"Hey, Gabe. How's it going in here?"

He immediately stood up to greet her, his wide-eyed excitement communicating the significance of the news he was about to deliver. "Camille, I'm glad you're here. I think I just scored a major hit on the Pennsylvania support group."

Camille followed him to his computer where she could see the lengthy report that he'd already begun compiling.

"I started with a basic search of in-person support groups in the state," he said before Camille could ask about it. "To my surprise, there were hundreds of them. When I filtered for grief and trauma counseling, I whittled it down to a couple of dozen. Of those, eleven were located in the greater Philadelphia area, six were in Pittsburgh, and the rest were scattered throughout the state. I ruled out the Pittsburgh sites right away due to the considerable distance. Philly was a possibility even though the group closest to Reading was still over an hour away.

"When I searched for groups within a twenty-five mile radius, I narrowed it down to three. The first was a women's-only group and the second catered to parents whose children had passed away from terminal diseases. That left only one.

He clicked a hyperlink in the report that opened the website of an organization called *New Horizons Counseling Services LLC.*

"It's located in a town called Blandon, which is only ten miles outside Reading," Pratt continued. "They specialize in grief counseling for families of missing or murdered loved ones. They hold sessions twice per week, and their policy is to keep the groups small, with no more than five attendees at any one time."

"That would make it much easier for them to remember Daniel if he were there," Camille said.

"Exactly. But when I called the lead counselor to explain the situation, he claimed that there were never any attendees who mentioned having a connection to the Sykes murders, and even if there were, he was bound by confidentiality not to reveal their names."

"Did you explain to him that we could issue a federal subpoena for the names if necessary?"

"I most certainly did. The good news is that it didn't take him long to find the attendee list after that."

"What's the bad news?"

"Daniel's name wasn't on it."

Camille could barely mask her disappointment. "But I thought you came up with a hit on something."

"I did." Pratt reopened his report and scrolled down a few pages. "I wanted to keep pressing, so I emailed the counselor a picture of Daniel. He recognized him right away."

"From the news reports?"

"No, from a group he put together a few months ago. According to the counselor, Daniel only attended two sessions, and he did so under the name Michael Barber."

"Is that name significant?"

"Not as far as I can tell. Allison put in a request to have it run through the IAFIS just to be sure."

"What did the counselor remember about Daniel?"

"When he introduced himself, he revealed that his sister was murdered recently and he was having a hard time forgiving the people involved. But he didn't say much after that. He was attentive when the other two group members were speaking, though. He actually started crying when one of the ladies finished her story. I personally can't see Daniel having that much empathy for anyone."

Camille could see it quite clearly. "What about the two other attendees?"

"This is where it gets interesting," Pratt said, his wide-eyed excitement returning. "The counselor identified the other attendees as Brenda Ellis and Sabrina Noble. Brenda identified herself as a local while Sabrina told the group that she was originally from Reading."

"The same as Daniel. What are the odds?"

"Yeah, it struck me as being a hell of a coincidence too. Anyway, the counselor was able to supply me with an address and telephone number for Brenda because she subscribed to the group's monthly newsletter. He didn't want to, of course, so I had to play the subpoena card again. Worked like a charm."

"What about Sabrina Noble?"

"According to the counselor, she didn't leave any contact information except for an email address. I've sent her a message requesting that she contact me. It feels like the proverbial needle in a haystack, but I had to give it a shot."

"Since Daniel didn't use his real name, is it safe to assume that he didn't leave behind any viable contact information?" Camille asked, already knowing the answer.

"No telephone, no email, nothing."

Camille sighed, doing her best to temper her disappointment. "Great work anyway. Daniel may have hidden his tracks, but at least we have a specific trail to follow now. And there's still a chance that something could pan out with one of the other attendees."

"I think it already has," a voice from behind them declared.

Camille turned to see Agent Mendoza fast approaching. The excitement in her eyes mirrored Pratt's.

"Allison, I was getting Camille up to speed on where we are so far. Something tells me you have more to add."

"A lot more," Mendoza said as she took the chair from a nearby cubicle to sit next to them. "I just got off the phone with Brenda Ellis. She was definitely an attendee of the New Horizons victim's support group, and she did remember a young man fitting Daniel's description by the name of

Michael Barber. She couldn't tell me much about him, other than his hyper-sensitivity when anyone had a question about his sister. So I asked her about the other woman in the group, Sabrina Noble."

"What did you come up with?" Camille asked.

"Turns out the two of them struck up a brief friendship after the support group ended, speaking mostly over the telephone. According to Brenda, they wanted to keep the dialogue going that they'd created in the group."

"Why were they attending in the first place?" Pratt asked.

"Their daughters were both murdered. In Brenda's case, it was her daughter's ex-boyfriend. In Sabrina's, it was her step-daughter, and her murder was still apparently unsolved. They'd been trading daily phone calls for a couple of weeks when Sabrina announced out of the blue that they'd likely had their last conversation because she was moving to Colorado."

"Colorado?" Camille asked, her senses suddenly heightened.

"Yes."

"Why so abrupt?" an equally intrigued Pratt asked.

"Sabrina told Brenda that she and her husband had to make an emergency move out here to attend to some family matters that involved her son, who was a corrections officer inside the Denver County Jail."

"Wow. Small world," Pratt said.

"A little too small if you ask me," Camille followed.

Mendoza nodded. "I thought the same thing, so I recruited a couple of agents in the Identification Unit to see what else we could find out about Sabrina. Between the three of us, we were able to locate her last-known residential address in Reading, her previous place of employment, and an email address. She worked at the *Free Your Space* storage facility in Reading for over ten years before abruptly submitting her resignation letter seven weeks ago.

"According to her employer, she didn't offer an explanation other than she needed to move to Colorado to be with her husband. When we asked about him, the employer was able to supply the name Abraham Noble based on emergency contact information. Sabrina's son, Asher Gideon, who lived in Reading, was also listed. We attempted to call them, but Sabrina's and Abraham's numbers were disconnected, and Asher's belonged to an auto body repair shop. That was where we hit the wall.

"Before I came here, I put in a call to Reading PD to see if they could send someone out to talk to Sabrina's neighbors on the off-chance that they knew more. They said they'd get back to me if a unit was available to pay a visit, but the brass didn't seem too warm on the idea, so I'm not holding my breath."

"What about her son, the correction's officer?" Pratt asked.

"The guys in Identification are running checks in the DOC database for anyone with the last name Gideon or Noble. They haven't come up with anything yet."

Something about the name Noble struck Camille as familiar, but she couldn't yet put her finger on what it was.

"Excellent work. Both of you," she said to Pratt and Mendoza. "There's definitely more to Sabrina's story. The shared support group experience with Daniel, her abrupt move to Colorado at the same time as him, her son working as a corrections officer in the same jail that Daniel is being kept, not to mention the fact that they both lived in Reading. Even if I did believe in coincidence, which I don't, it all lines up a little too perfectly to be random."

"I couldn't agree more," Mendoza said.

"If nothing else, perhaps she can tell us more about

Daniel's life in Reading than Brenda Ellis could," Pratt added. "If Sabrina struck up a friendship with Brenda, it's certainly possible that she would've reached out to Daniel too. Their proximity to one another would make it relatively easy."

"For sure," Camille said. "Now, all we have to do is find her."

"We're working on it," Mendoza assured her.

Camille nodded, reflecting once more on how impressive Agent Mendoza was. And though it took her some time, she could now freely admit that Pratt was pretty damn good himself. She was beyond grateful for the team around her and the enthusiasm with which they took up her cause.

For the first time since leaving the Bureau, she was reminded of her love for the job, the bright-eyed idealism that led her to believe that she would never quit, and the reality that she simply wasn't built to do anything else.

"Let me know when you've got something," she told them. "I'm heading back to Major Crimes to check in with Detective Sullivan. Hopefully Daniel is ready to help us connect a few more dots."

Camille didn't realize it then, but Daniel MacPherson was ready to do a lot more than that.

30

THE PHANTOM

DETECTIVE GREER REENTERED the interview room with a huff after leaving twenty minutes earlier to make a phone call.

"I tried Officers Prescott and Irving five times. They're not answering," he reported to Chloe as he dropped their card on the table. "I managed to reach their supervising officer Kevin O'Dell, but as far as he knew, Prescott and Irving were the only officers assigned to Daniel today. There are rarely more than two C.O.s assigned to transport a single inmate unless that inmate is high-risk, which Daniel isn't."

Chloe didn't want to dismiss Daniel's story about the mysterious corrections officer who came into his cell late at night to issue threats on behalf of the madman she so desperately wanted to find, but she also couldn't deny how far-fetched the entire notion sounded.

"You need to tell us a lot more about this man than you already have," she informed Daniel. "Because right now we can't find one person to confirm that he even exists."

"What about the police officers who escorted me here?"

Daniel asked, his eyes burning with desperation. "They saw him. Just find them, and they'll confirm everything."

"They'll confirm that he came into your cell last night and threatened to kill you if you met with us again?"

Daniel sighed loudly. "No, they obviously weren't there for that. But they saw him with me today. They were the ones who told him not to come. Please, find them and ask."

"Okay, Daniel. Suppose we do find them, and they do confirm that a third C.O. was there with you today. What does that prove?"

Daniel sank back in his chair; his shoulders slumped in defeat. "So you spend all this time begging me to talk, and now that I do, you don't believe me?"

"It's not that we don't believe you," Chloe said, unsure if that were true. "It's just that you've gone on about this officer for nearly an hour without giving us any useful information about him other than his first name - a name that you think might be made up. But you haven't told us one thing about the man who you claim is putting him up to all of this. That's who we're interested in learning about, Daniel. And with every minute that you avoid talking about him, the closer we are to concluding that you're making all of this up so we'll feel bad for you."

"I'm not making any of it up, Detective Sullivan."

"If that's the case, tell us everything you know about Paul and Jacob's abductor. And I do mean everything."

"Okay," he said after a long hesitation. "But before I do, just know that the story I've told you about the correction's officer is true, and at some point, possibly very soon, you're going to realize that. Hopefully, by then, you're prepared to do something about it."

"Fair enough," Chloe conceded. "Go on."

"His name is Abraham Noble. I met him through his wife,

Sabrina, who I got to know through a therapy group we both attended back home."

Chloe felt the air momentarily leave her body. She'd had a strong hunch about the support group, but to hear that hunch now being corroborated as a fact made her dizzy with satisfaction. Ever mindful that self-congratulatory pats on the back didn't solve cases, she allowed the feeling to linger for less than a second before casting it aside.

"When did you meet Sabrina?" she asked.

"About three months ago, shortly after my sister's murder. I joined that support group because I didn't know what else to do. My parents were barely talking to me. They were barely talking to anyone, not even each other. They were just numb. We were all numb. I thought that I would be able to process my feelings by talking to someone."

"And did it work?"

"You tell me."

Chloe let the statement hang in the air without addressing it. "Tell us more about Sabrina."

"I didn't think much of her when I first joined the group. She was just another sad woman mourning the death of someone she loved. But the more she talked about what happened to her step-daughter, and how she was murdered, the more I realized the two of us had something very significant in common."

"Daniel Sykes," Chloe said.

Daniel nodded.

"Is she involved in this?"

"I don't know. But she's a very kind woman, so if she is involved, I can't imagine that she's too happy about it."

Chloe immediately thought about the woman in Paul's recorded message. She didn't sound happy to be there at all.

"Where is Abraham now?" Greer asked.

"I honestly don't know. We both arrived in Colorado at roughly the same time. I've only seen him three times, always in public places. Any other time we spoke, it was by cell phone."

"You're telling us he never made any mention of where he was staying?" a skeptical Chloe asked.

"He did joke once that he needed a lot of space for all of his guests, so I'm assuming he must be living in a large house somewhere."

"Pretty shitty joke," Greer scoffed.

"I didn't laugh. Trust me."

Chloe sighed. None of this helps us, Daniel. How are we supposed to catch him, and this C.O. of yours, if we don't know where to find them?"

"I don't know, Detective Sullivan. But I can't give you any more information about them than I already have. You have to believe that."

"Do you at least have Abraham's phone number?"

"It was blocked. He always called me."

"Tell us what he's planning to do next," Chloe said, her patience officially exhausted. "Or do you not know that either?"

Daniel took in a hard, shallow breath and sat back in his chair. "At this point, I'm more than happy to tell you. I just don't think you'd believe me."

"Try us."

"He's planning to kill Camille."

"You have to do better than that," Greer barked.

"He's planning to kill Camille *and* Daniel Sykes. Live on television. In front of the entire planet. Is that better?"

"And how does he intend to do that?" Chloe asked with the best facade of calm that she could muster.

"His son."

"You mean John? The phantom C.O.?"

"Not John. He has another son."

"What's his name?"

"Abraham never told me."

"It sounds like he didn't tell you a lot of things," Greer said with a tense smirk.

"Compartmentalization, I suppose. The less I knew, the less I could tell."

"So how did you come to learn of the plan to kill Camille and Sykes?"

"Abraham's son is a corrections officer at the Fairfield Maximum Security Prison. Guess whose an inmate there?"

"We know," Chloe said. "Go on."

"His son was one of the C.O.s assigned to look after Sykes. They interacted with one another every day. Eventually, they started talking. Not too long after that, they came to realize that they shared certain characteristics."

"What characteristics?" Greer asked.

"Abraham's son killed those four girls."

"And how do you know this?" a suddenly shaken Chloe asked.

"Abraham told me, in a round-about way. I was with him and John once, and I overheard them talking about it."

"So how does this relate to him killing Camille and Sykes?" Chloe asked, knowing that she had to keep her suddenly scattered thoughts on the task at hand.

"Did you know that Sykes is being transferred to Colorado?"

"Yes, we know," Chloe confirmed.

"Too bad. I was hoping I could break the news."

"Get to it, Daniel," an impatient Greer ordered.

"Abraham told me that his son was selected to accompany Sykes on the trip in order to brief the new staff that would be looking after him. Once Sykes arrived, Abraham planned to have Camille go on television and demand a joint press conference with Sykes. He figured that holding Jacob and Paul captive would be all the leverage he needed to get the powers that be to sign off on it. Being an expert on how to handle Sykes, Abraham's son would insist on escorting him to the interview, then remain on close standby to watch over him. Once Sykes and Camille were together, and the cameras started rolling, he would wait for his opportunity. Then, well, you can probably guess what would happen from there."

"And Abraham told you all of this?" Greer asked.

"Some parts of it. I extrapolated the rest. Given all the facts, it was pretty easy to figure out."

"Good detective work," Chloe said with a forced smile meant to mask the almost overwhelming sense of dread that Daniel's story inspired. "Unfortunately, there's a major problem with your theory."

"What's that?"

"Sykes's transfer has been put on hold."

"Daniel's already ashen face lost another shade. "For how long?"

"We don't know for sure," Greer admitted. "But given everything that's already happened, plus the new information you provided here, it could be indefinite."

"That's terrible news for Jacob and Paul."

"Why?" Chloe asked.

"Because that interview was the only chance they had of staying alive. Once Abraham finds out, he won't hesitate to kill them. And when he does, it's only a matter of time before he comes after me too. He'll know that I'm meeting with you, and he'll think that I'm the one who tipped you off. You can't let him get to me."

"We won't," Chloe assured him.

Daniel sank back in his chair, suddenly appearing overwhelmed by the moment. "Do you really want to keep me safe?"

"Of course," Greer said.

"Then find John. Please. Because if you don't, and I'm allowed to go back there tonight, I can guarantee that I won't be around to see how this ends."

31

PUTTING THE PIECES TOGETHER

C AMILLE HAD ATTEMPTED TO REACH Chloe several times ahead of her trip to Major Crimes. Unable to do so, she placed a call to Lieutenant Hitchcock instead.

"I have some news about Daniel," she said when he answered.

"I have some news about Daniel too," Hitchcock said before she could continue.

Based on the uncharacteristically high timbre of his voice, Camille suspected that his news might have trumped hers.

"You first, lieutenant."

"Sullivan and Greer have finally gotten Daniel to crack."

"What does that mean?" Camille asked, her grip on the wheel tightening.

"It means that he's willing to deal in exchange for telling us everything he knows."

Fortunately, Camille was stopped at a red light as Hitchcock said this, otherwise, she would have needed to pull over to collect herself. "What has he told them?" she asked in a breathless voice.

"So far, he's given us two names, Abraham and Sabrina Noble, some details on the perp's motive - which you're not going to like, and a connection that Sykes had at Fairfield that might help explain why he's being transferred here." After a pause, he added, "And there's something else, though we don't quite know what to make of it."

Camille could barely contain her happiness at the news he'd already delivered, and she was unsure that she could process anymore. "What?"

"Daniel claims that he's being harassed by a C.O. inside the jail who has connections to our suspect, Abraham Noble. Daniel said that he knew him through Noble while he was still on the outside and that it was this C.O. who fed him the information about Meredith Park's press conference a few days ago. He also believes that the C.O. was given orders to kill Daniel because he's been meeting with us."

There was so much to unpack from Hitchcock summary that Camille wasn't sure where to begin. But she couldn't help but fixate on the last part. "Did Daniel tell you the C.O.'s name?"

"He said it was John, but he believes that could be an alias."

"And have you been able to confirm anything through County?"

"We've been working on it, but so far, we haven't found anything that would substantiate his claims."

Camille took a deep breath, hopeful that she wasn't going to regret her next words. "We may have found something."

"What do you mean?"

"I'm not entirely sure yet. Just sit tight, lieutenant, I'm on my way."

Camille and Hitchcock sat in silence for what felt like a long time, each processing what the other had told them. On the monitor in front of them, Chloe, Greer, and Daniel appeared to be doing the same.

"We've got a lot of pieces," Hitchcock finally said. "Now we have to start putting them together."

Camille nodded. "From the look of it, they're hitting a wall with Daniel. They may have gotten everything they're going to get out of him at this point."

"Do you believe his story?"

"One hundred percent."

"Even the part about the perp wanting to get you and Sykes in the same room to kill you both?"

"Especially that part. I'm sure he couldn't think of a more poetic ending for us."

"Shakespeare would've been proud," Hitchcock said with an uncomfortable smirk. "This guy is more twisted than we thought."

"In his mind, he's doing the right thing. In his mind, he's merely the victim. In his mind, I'm the twisted one. It's all a matter of perspective, lieutenant."

Camille looked up to see that Hitchcock had been staring at her, his eyes registering confusion that bordered on disgust. She'd seen that look a million times before from locals unfamiliar with what she did, and unprepared for how she thought. Her playbook, as Crawley rightly pointed out, was very different.

Thankfully, Hitchcock chose not to press. "Assuming Daniel doesn't have anything more to tell us, how do we start putting the pieces together?"

That was the hard part. They had names, they had motives, and they had timelines. But they didn't have anything concrete to link them. In many ways, it was more frustrating than not knowing anything. At least then they could use ignorance as an excuse for their lack of progress.

"The best we can do now is run Abraham and Sabrina Noble through the IAFAS database to see if anything comes up. If we can get a hit on anything significant, we can hand them over to the media as persons of interest, attach an award for any information on their whereabouts, and see what it leads to."

"Let's just hope it doesn't lead to another needle in a haystack," Hitchcock replied sharply. "We need more, Camille. And right now, we don't have it."

Frustrated by the stark truth of Hitchcock's statement, Camille stood up and began pacing the room. She'd managed only a few steps before the sound of her ringing cell phone stopped her cold.

Anticipation swelled as she pulled the phone out of her pocket. She answered it without checking the number. "This is Camille."

"Hi, Camille. It's Gabe."

She'd hoped it was him, and exhaled with relief at the sound of his voice. "Tell me something good, Gabe."

"We found Sabrina Noble's son."

Camille immediately put the phone on speaker. "We got another name, possibly the C.O.," she told Hitchcock as she sat down next to him. "Go on, Gabe."

"His name is Sebastian Gideon. He's been with Denver County as a corrections officer for two and a half months. Clean record, obviously. He was a patrol officer with Reading P.D. for six years before taking a personal leave of absence early last year. There was no official explanation for his departure, and he never returned."

"And the connection to Sabrina Noble?" Camille asked.

"We've confirmed it. We checked his personnel file, and she's listed as his first emergency contact. Same Reading, PA information that we already have."

"What about Abraham?"

"No. The only other listed contact is his brother, Asher."

Camille looked at the monitor, keeping her focus on Daniel. "Can you send me his picture?" she then asked Pratt.

"I'll message it to you right now."

A few seconds later, Camille's phone dinged with the sound of an incoming text message. She quickly opened it and saw the photo that had likely been taken from Gideon's personnel file, which meant it was recent. His face was long and lean, punctuated by deep acne scars that would surely make him stand out in a crowd of his middle-aged peers. Camille suspected he would stand out to Daniel too. She showed the photo to Hitchcock, then said, "I think we finally have more."

Hitchcock nodded his agreement. "Time to get Sullivan and Greer back in here. We'll need to show this to Daniel ASAP."

Seconds after Hitchcock left to retrieve them, Chloe and Greer raced inside the monitoring room.

"Hey, Camille," Chloe said upon seeing her. "The lieutenant said you have something important to show us."

"Sebastian Gideon," Camille said as she gave Chloe her phone. "He's a corrections officer at the Denver County Jail whose mother happens to be one Sabrina Noble."

Chloe's mouth fell open in disbelief. "Which means he's connected to Abraham Noble." She promptly turned to Greer.

"Which means that Daniel is telling the truth."

"It appears so," Camille said in response to Greer's assertion. "Did you find an address for Sebastian?" she then asked Gabe.

"1345 Monroe Street, apartment 205."

"I'll dispatch a unit out there now," Hitchcock said before leaving the room.

"We have to show this photo to Daniel," Chloe said.

Camille nodded, then spoke into the phone. "Gabe, I need you and Allison to get here as soon as you can in case we have more questions."

"We're on our way," Pratt replied. "But there is one more thing you should know."

"What's that?"

"We also got a hit on a name at Fairfield Prison. Lucas Gideon."

Chloe put a finger up to her mouth as if to stifle a gasp. "Sebastian's brother?"

"We don't know yet," Pratt reported. "At this point, we've only got the name. Allison is working on digging up more. We can hand it off to the Identification Section to keep looking while we head over there."

"Good idea. I'll get Crawley on the phone. He's been in close contact with officials at Fairfield. Maybe he can fast-track the search for you."

"Okay. Allison and I will get there as soon as we can."

"Thank you. And great work on this."

"We're just doing our small part to help your dad. Save my pat on the back for when he's home with you safe and sound where he belongs."

Camille felt a large knot of emotion plug her throat as she disconnected the call. She fought hard to push it down, hopeful that no one noticed. After taking a quick moment to collect herself, she gave the phone to Chloe.

"Jesus, if this Lucas Gideon angle pans out…"

"Let's not get ahead of ourselves," Camille cautioned. "We have to make sure Sebastian pans out first."

Chloe nodded as she took Camille's phone. "Do you want to come in with us?"

Camille knew that she would be due for another face to face with Daniel before this was all over, but now wasn't the time.

"You and Greer got us this far. It's only fair that you be the ones to bring it home."

32

SAFE SPACE

DANIEL FLASHED A SHEEPISH GRIN as Chloe and Greer reentered the interview room. "Here we go again with the disappearing act. If I were the paranoid sort, I might think that you two were talking about me behind my back."

Chloe sat down next to him. "We need to show you something."

The grim look on her face made his forced smile disappear. "What is it?"

She promptly held up the phone.

Daniel didn't blink as he stared at Sebastian Gideon's photo. In fact, he didn't move at all. But Chloe could see the tension building up in his face. When she spotted the involuntary twitching of the muscle just below his left eye, she knew she'd hit the right nerve.

"Do you recognize this man?"

The fluttering under Daniel's eye intensified. "Yes."

"Who is he?" Greer asked.

"John." Then, as if freeing himself from the grip of a powerful trance, Daniel blinked. When he did, the twitching stopped. "But I bet you're going to tell me that's not his real name."

"His real name is Sebastian Gideon," Chloe said. "We've confirmed that Sabrina Noble is his mother, though we've found no official relation to Abraham."

"Abraham referred to them as his sons, but they weren't his."

"Same with Lucas?" Greer asked.

Daniel looked at him with genuine confusion. "Who is that?"

"The guard at Fairfield Prison," Chloe said. Then, she upped the ante by adding, "Sebastian Gideon's brother. Sykes copycat. Camille's would-be killer."

Daniel shuddered at her words. "I never knew his real name. I've never even seen a picture of him. But Abraham had plenty of stories. The only time I ever saw anything that looked like happiness on his face was when we talked about..." he paused. "Lucas. Do you know where he is?"

"No," Greer said.

"What about Sebastian?"

Chloe stood up from the table, with Greer quickly following. "You've done a lot to help us here, Daniel. We told you that we're not going to let this guy get to you, and we intend to keep our word."

Daniel kept his eyes on them as they walked out of the room. Chloe thought that she might have heard the words, "Thank you," coming from the other side of the door, but she couldn't be positive about that.

When they reconvened in the monitoring room with Camille and Hitchcock, Greer took out his cell phone to attempt another call to Officers Irving and Prescott.

"Another step in the right direction," Camille said to Chloe after she took back her cell phone. "Pratt and Mendoza should be here any minute, and Agent Crawley is working

Fairfield for more information on Lucas Gideon. He'll report back as soon as he learns something."

Greer stopped Chloe before she could respond.

"Officer Irving? Yes, this is Detective Greer with DPD Major Crimes. Right, we're the ones interviewing Daniel MacPherson. No, he's not ready to be picked up yet, but we do have some questions about his transport. If it's okay, I'd like to put you on speaker so my colleagues can hear the call. Thank you."

Greer nodded at the group and pressed the phone's speaker button.

"Can you hear me, Officer Irving?"

"Yes, I can," Irving reported.

"Were you and Officer Prescott the only two assigned to Daniel's transport this morning?"

"We were the only two officially assigned to him, yes."

"Was there anyone there who wasn't officially assigned to Daniel's transport?"

"Yes. Another guard wanted to come along for the ride over here. We were overstaffed inside, and he said he needed something to do. He was all set to ride with us, but when your buddies from the DPD showed up to tell us that they'd be bringing Daniel over, it was decided that he wasn't needed anymore."

"And what is your colleague's name?" Chloe asked.

"Sebastian Gideon."

A wave of relief washed over the group as they acknowledged one another with silent nods and subdued smiles.

"And where is Officer Gideon now?" Greer asked.

"I'm not sure. Since we were overstaffed, and he was pulling an extra shift, I told him he should probably head home."

"We just heard back from the unit on scene at Gideon's apartment," Hitchcock said as he entered the room. "The property manager says that he's always paid his rent on time, but he never sees Gideon around the complex and he rarely seems to be home. He always assumed that it was due to the work hours he kept. They knocked on his door and got no answer. When they entered the apartment, it was mostly empty, and it hadn't looked like anyone had been there for a while."

"Is there something going on with Sebastian that we should know about?" a suddenly concerned Irving asked over the phone.

"Have you ever noticed anything unusual about him?" Chloe asked. "Any reports of misconduct or interactions with inmates that may have raised red flags?"

"Not at all," Irving said. "He's solid as far as I know. I've spent some time with him outside of the job. He's always been a decent guy to be around." A long pause, then, "I guess there was something this morning during the transport, but I didn't think much of it."

"Tell us about it," Greer said.

"There was another group of DPD officers there along with the two you sent over to bring in MacPherson. I'm not sure why they were there, but I did notice one of them staring down Sebastian pretty hard. I thought it might have been a personal beef or something, so I didn't say anything to Sebastian about it. I don't even think he noticed. I told my partner Prescott about it, and he said he overheard one of the officers saying that something about Sebastian creeped him out. He's a pretty intense-looking dude, and I've heard other people say that about him. That was why I didn't think anything of it. We all left after that, and it never came up again."

"Do you know who the other officers were?" Chloe asked.

"No. I couldn't see their name tags. But they seemed pretty friendly with the team you sent over, so I suppose you could ask them."

"Who were the officers assigned to pick up Daniel?" Camille asked Chloe.

"Reed and Eckhart."

"I'll see if I can find them," Hitchcock said before leaving the room.

He led the officers back inside the monitoring room a few minutes later. Agents Pratt and Mendoza came in behind them.

"Thanks for coming in, guys," Chloe said to the officers.

Eckhart looked nervous as she spotted Camille but still extended her hand to greet her. "Kate Eckhart," she said. "This is Micah Reed. We're really sorry about Sergeant Grisham, ma'am. We're all praying that he gets home safe."

Camille smiled as she shook her hand, clearly moved by the warm gesture. "Thank you, Officer Eckhart."

"How can we help, Agent Grisham?" Reed asked.

Camille pulled out her phone. "Do you recognize this man?" She held up the photo of Gideon.

Officer Reed nodded. "He was one of the guards with Daniel MacPherson this morning."

"His name is Sebastian Gideon," Greer said.

"He wanted to make the trip here with the other two guards," Reed continued. "But Officer Eckhart and I vetoed it."

"Was there a reason for that?"

"Three guards for one inmate transport felt like overkill, especially since we were there."

"Was there any other reason?" Chloe asked.

"I'm not following, ma'am."

"One of your fellow officers was heard to say that something about Gideon made him uncomfortable," Hitchcock explained. "I believe the term he used was *creeped out.*"

Reed smiled, then looked at Eckhart. "Oh yeah. That was Stanger."

"Right," Eckhart said with a smile of her own. "He said he didn't like the way the guard was lingering around, burning a hole into everyone he looked at. He seemed to have it in for MacPherson. I didn't notice it, but Stanger said he looked like he wanted to kill the guy."

"Did Officer Stanger say anything else about that?" Chloe asked.

"No," Reed answered. "We left shortly afterward. But they apparently stuck around. Stanger used to be a C.O., so I think he's pretty sensitive to the issue of inmate mistreatment. I don't know if they had any words after we left, but knowing him, I wouldn't doubt it."

"Do you know where Officer Stanger is now?" Greer asked. "We'd like to talk to him."

"I just saw him down in the squad room," Eckhart reported. "I'll be happy to grab him for you."

Stanger's thick jaw bulged when Camille showed him the photo of Gideon.

"Yep, that's the guy," the young officer said with a faint Brooklyn accent. "I knew something was up the moment I laid eyes on him."

"Did he make any gestures toward MacPherson or anyone else that you interpreted to be threatening?" Chloe asked.

"Nothing overt. It was just an overall vibe. Dude was wound up tighter than a steel drum. When the van carrying MacPherson drove off, the guy just stood there staring until it left the lot. I don't know what was so important about that van, but I can sure tell you that he wanted to be on it."

"Did you interact with him at all after that?" Camille asked.

"Yes, ma'am. Once the van left, he was standing there for another two or three minutes, just staring at nothing. After that, he started walking toward the building. He was walking fast at first like he was in a hurry to get somewhere. But then as he approached the three of us, he slowed down. Actually, he damn near stopped in his tracks."

"Did he engage you first?"

"No. He kept his eyes on his phone, but it was obvious that he was listening to our conversation."

"What were you talking about that would pique his interest?" Greer asked.

"We were just shooting the shit... I mean, we were just talking about random stuff."

"This is a safe space, officer. Feel free to swear as much as you need to," Chloe said with a light smile.

The officer's beet-red face softened, allowing him to offer a smile of his own.

"Just try your best to remember exactly what you were talking about," Chloe continued.

Stanger paused to search his memory. "At the point I noticed him paying attention to us, we were talking about a couple of other officers, just joking around about them. It wasn't anything serious."

"Who were the officers you were talking about?" Camille asked.

"Rasheed Evans and George McClennan."

"You mean the officers assigned to the Meredith Park detail?" an alarmed Hitchcock asked.

"Yes, sir."

"What specifically did you say about them?" Greer asked.

A visibly nervous Stanger paused again. "We'd just watched your statement on TV," he said to Camille. "And we're speculating about the perp. Rollins asked who was working the security detail for Meredith Park. That's when Evans and McClennan came up."

"Did the conversation go any further than that?" Camille asked.

"Other than Rollins asking where the safe house was, no."

Camille and Chloe exchanged a worried glance.

"Did you disclose the location?" Chloe asked.

Stanger swallowed hard before answering. "Yes. I only mentioned it in passing, though. We moved on pretty quickly after that."

"And you believe that Gideon was within earshot of the conversation?"

"Yes, ma'am."

"Oh, God," Camille cried.

"You don't think he's headed there, do you?" Chloe asked her.

"I don't know. But I don't think we can wait to find out." Camille turned to Hitchcock. "Lieutenant?"

"I'll alert Evans and McClennan right now," he answered.

"It might be a good idea to send additional units out there," Pratt suggested. "Agent Mendoza and I will come along too."

As the group scrambled around him, Stanger's eyes bulged, as the gravity of the moment suddenly hit him. "Do you think Sebastian Gideon is connected to all of this?"

"We don't know yet," Greer answered.

"But you think he's going after Meredith Park." He paused to collect himself. "And I told him exactly where she was." His stiff, square jaw suddenly flattened. "Jesus. I'm sorry."

"No need for apologies," Pratt said as he and Mendoza followed Hitchcock out of the room. "Just suit up so you can help us find him."

When Stanger rushed out of the room behind Pratt, Chloe turned to Camille.

"I hope to God that you're wrong about this."

"I hope I'm wrong too," Camille replied, doing her best to ignore all of the instincts that told her she wasn't.

33

THE LAST LAUGH

T HE SINGLE STORY CORNER HOUSE was a run-down shit hole, just as the officers described it, though it was probably the best-maintained house on the block. Sebastian suspected that he'd dealt with quite a few inmates from this war-torn section of the city, and imagined what it would be like to run into one who had recently been set free. That thought frightened him far more than anything he imagined encountering inside that house. If the young, aimless boys he saw roaming the streets around him were anything like the men he saw on the inside, he knew it would be wise to handle his business here quickly.

That business would likely mean killing three people, including the officers assigned to protect Meredith. As had been the case when he thought about Irving and Prescott, Sebastian didn't allow himself to be deterred by the challenging logistics of the operation or the fact that the men he would be forced to kill both wore a badge, just like he did. Aside from the uniform, they had little in common.

That uniform, elaborate costume that it was, would be used as a means of engaging the officers. There would be no sneaking around the property, looking for an open window to crawl through. The surveillance cameras would make that impossible anyway. Instead, he would walk right up to the front door and announce himself as a colleague sent to warn them about Daniel MacPherson's escape from the Denver County Jail and his possible plan to come after Meredith Park.

The officers would have questions, of course. They would wonder aloud why they weren't notified by their superiors beforehand. And they would promptly inform Sebastian of the need to radio in the confirmation before they could allow him inside.

That was when Sebastian would make his move.

With the officers out of the way, he could take his time with Meredith if he wanted; making sure the entire episode was documented for Abraham. It promised to be one hell of a show, and he didn't want the old man to miss a second of it.

He'd parked his car one block over and decided to make the rest of the trip on foot. Had the officers been watching the street and saw him getting out of his civilian car, this little operation would've been over before it even started. Thankfully, he'd regained some semblance of the common sense that had been absent with Irving and Prescott.

He could see no signs of activity in or around the house as he approached it. Blackout curtains covered windows that were fortified by heavy security bars. The camera posted above the front door could be clearly seen, as could the doorbell security camera; its soft blue light letting all would-be intruders know that they were being watched.

Walking across the dead, weed-infested lawn that led to the front door, Sebastian knew he was being watched too. The doorbell sensor had likely alerted those inside to his presence. Knowing this, he went to great lengths to ensure that the

Department of Corrections seal on his sleeves and lapel were clearly visible.

Mindful that the presence of his duty Glock could put the officers on edge, he left it in his car in favor of the smaller .38 that he was able to conceal neatly in the small of his back.

One more run-through of the story before he stepped onto the porch. *Daniel MacPherson. Escape. Manhunt underway. It's believed that he's aware of Meredith Park's location, and will attempt to confront her. Back-up units en route.* The officers will be confused by his presence, and even more confused by his story. But their guards would be down just enough.

The plan wasn't full proof, but it was the best he could hope for under the extraordinary circumstances.

And he was ready to see it through.

He rang the doorbell first. When no one answered, he knocked. It was a cop's knock; the soft side of his closed fist pounding hard against the rusted metal of the security door.

One set of knocks, then another, harder this time. Still, no answer. A swell of panic rose in his chest as he stepped to the edge of the porch, putting himself in full view of the security camera above him.

He stood quietly, listening for any sounds of activity on the other side of the door. Hearing none, he stepped off the porch and followed the cracked cobblestone walkway along the side of the house until he came to the fence. He gave the gate a light tug. Realizing it was locked, he stepped away and made the walk back toward the front porch.

He'd barely rounded the corner when he saw the shadow casting long against the dead lawn. Even though he hadn't heard anything, he knew someone was there. And based on the extension protruding from the base of the shadow, he knew that someone was holding a gun.

The panic that had seized him earlier suddenly vanished. In its place was a calm sense of resolve that he'd never experienced before this moment. It was then that he fully understood the importance of this moment, and how everything up until now, and everything that he would be remembered for afterward would be defined by it.

"Officer Evans? Officer McClennan?" Sebastian was careful to keep his tone even as he said the words. Even as he rounded the corner and saw the short, stout officer pointing the gun, his swollen, tattooed arms gleaming with perspiration, Sebastian kept his head.

"Stop right there," the officer said with a shaky voice that betrayed his gruff exterior.

Sebastian put his hands up slowly. "It's okay, sir. I'm here to help."

The officer took a tentative step off the porch. Behind him, the front door stood open. "Help with what? Who the hell are you?"

"My name's John Willis. I'm a corrections officer at the Denver County Jail. I'm afraid there's been a major incident involving an inmate, and we've been dispatched to assist the DPD in locating him."

As Sebastian predicted, the officer's face registered confusion. "What are you talking about? What kind of incident?"

"Daniel MacPherson, the man in custody in connection to the Camille Grisham case, escaped from the jail about an hour ago. Based on conversations he had with fellow inmates prior to his escape, we believe that he may be trying to contact Meredith Park, the woman you're currently holding in protective custody. We can't be sure of his intentions, but-"

"Bullshit," the officer barked as he took another step off the porch. "Get down on the ground. Now."

He was close enough now for Sebastian to read his name tag. "Officer McClennan, please. This is serious. Back-up units are already en route, but we have to make sure this area is completely secure right now. If you don't believe me, put in a call to your superiors. But we can't be out here like this making a scene. If MacPherson does show up, and he sees us, we may not get another crack at him."

"I've already been in contact with my superiors. They told me that there was an incident at county, but it didn't have anything to do with Daniel MacPherson escaping."

When the officer got closer, Sebastian could see the fiery focus in his eyes, and he knew there was only going to be one way out of this.

"On the ground, Mr. Gideon. Face down, with your hands on top of your head. I'm giving you one opportunity to comply."

The gun was steady in McClennan's hand now with his index finger comfortably on the trigger. Sebastian thought about the .38 tucked in his back and the amount of time it would take to reach behind him, unholster it, and squeeze off a shot. He estimated that he'd need at least three seconds; two seconds more than he had before McClennan could empty half a clip into his chest.

He raised his hands higher before slowly extending them toward the ground in front of him. He attempted one last-ditch effort at diplomacy before making the unavoidable decision that would end it all for him.

"I have no idea who Mr. Gideon is. I told you, my name is Officer John Willis. Please, you're making a terrible mistake here." Sebastian felt his voice rising with each word he spoke; the even-keeled tone he fought so hard to maintain now abandoning him.

"I've seen your picture, asshole. I know exactly who you are. I just can't believe that you were actually stupid enough to show up here."

The chaos of the moment hadn't given Sebastian time to reflect on the fact that the officer not only knew who he was, but that he was also expecting him to show up here. There was no way to fathom how he could've known that. Not even that rat Daniel would know.

He supposed it didn't matter how they knew. Based on the measure of his life up to this point - the mistakes, the failures, the constant shadow that his younger brother cast over him - it should have come as no surprise to Sebastian that it would end this way. He'd led himself to believe that, for once in his life, he wasn't completely in over his head. He told the ultimate lie to himself. And it was about to cost him what remained of his pitiful existence.

Abraham, as it turned out, would have the last laugh after all.

"That's it," Officer McClennan said. "On the ground, slowly. Hands on top of your head. Don't move a muscle."

As Sebastian laid on the ground, he heard the officer speaking into his radio.

"Suspect is secure outside. Once I get him cuffed, I'll call it in to dispatch. The cavalry is supposedly on their way, but hopefully, this will force them to double-time it. Everything okay inside?"

"Roger that," the voice from the other end said. "Mrs. Park is secure."

"Good. Stay inside with her until you get the all-clear out here."

"Roger that. Good work, my man."

"Thanks," McClennan said as he took his final step toward Sebastian.

"Oh shit! That cop's about to smoke that other cop! Grab your phone and record it!"

The loud voice from the street behind them tore through the air like a sonic boom, causing McClennan to spin around.

What happened next took less than the three seconds he predicted he'd need to execute it. But for Sebastian, the event unfolded in slow motion; every moment captured as a single frame that could be dissected, analyzed, and wholly appreciated.

In one fluid sweep, he'd drawn the .38 from his waistband, took aim at McClennan's chest, and fired two shots. They hit dead-center of his sternum, causing micro-explosions of red splatter that dotted his black uniform.

McClennan fell backward onto the lawn. Because his attention was directed at the boys on the street, he never saw the shots coming.

For their part, the two teenagers high-tailed it out of there, the one with the phone taking off on foot, while his friend pedaled away on a blue dirt bike.

Sebastian flashed a quick smile of thanks at his unlikely saviors as they disappeared from view, then he turned his attention to the house.

Content with leaving Officer McClennan to bleed to death on the lawn, Sebastian raced up the stairs to the front porch, and through the front door that, much to his surprise, was still open.

The instant he walked in, he heard footsteps ambling across the creaky wooden floors, fast-approaching him from the other side of the house.

He immediately took cover inside the coat closet near the door, sinking into a soft, cashmere overcoat that smelled of expensive perfume.

From the sliver of an opening, Sebastian could see the front door. The fast-approaching footsteps most likely belonged to the second officer, and his first course of action upon reaching the door would be to look outside, see his colleague, and attempt to render assistance. With the officer distracted by his own panic, Sebastian would burst through the door, rush him from behind, and disable him with the pocket knife he now held firmly in his left hand.

The footsteps were much louder now. He was close.

Sebastian's grip on the knife tightened as the footsteps abruptly stopped. The officer was somewhere nearby, but he hadn't gone to the front door as Sebastian had predicted.

Instead, the footsteps doubled-back in the opposite direction. Much slower and more deliberate now. These footsteps weren't reacting. They were searching. For him.

Shit.

"Dispatch, this is unit five-eight. I have a code ten, officer down. Repeat, code ten, officer down. Multiple shots fired. Suspect may still be on the premises." The officer spoke in a whisper, but his voice was calm.

"Copy, five-eight," a voice from the radio said. "Additional units have already been dispatched and should be arriving shortly. Sending emergency personnel as well. What's your current position?"

Sebastian held his breath as he waited for the officer to respond. But there was no response.

"Five-eight, do you copy? We need to know your current position."

Just then, Sebastian saw something through the sliver in the door. A quick burst of bright light. Then darkness.

The sound of the front door being slammed shut caused Sebastian's heart to jump. He regained his bearings in time to see the bright light again. It was a flashlight.

"Officer McClennan is outside the residence. I'm inside with Meredith Park. She's secure, but I have to assume that she's the target of whatever is happening here, so I'm staying with her until back-up arrives. Get them out here quick!" More panic in the officer's voice now.

"Roger that, five-eight. Just hold tight."

When the radio went silent, Sebastian could hear the officer's heavy breathing nearby. The labored, staccato rhythm matched his own. Against the backdrop of the darkness came more darkness as the black mass of the officer's silhouette moved past the closet door. It settled near the front window, where Sebastian saw a crease of sunlight appear as the officer parted the blinds to look outside. The light allowed Sebastian to see the Glock in his hand.

The officer's position at the window gave him a clear line of sight to the closet, meaning he would see Sebastian coming the instant he emerged from it. He had to make his move in spite of that. He knew the longer he allowed this to drag on, the worse it would be for him.

He took in a deep breath, held it tight, and pulled out the .38. He kept the pocket knife in his other hand for good measure.

When he nudged the door, it gave the slightest squeak. But he doubted the officer had heard it. The sound of Meredith's high-pitched voice echoed through the tight space with the force of a loudspeaker.

"Officer Evans? What's happening out there?"

"Stay where you are, Mrs. Park," the officer said in a strained but firm voice.

"Why hasn't help arrived yet?"

"Help is on the way, Mrs. Park. Please, just stay back."

Now or never, was Sebastian's final thought before he burst through the closet door, firing his .38 into the darkness. The muzzle flash of the first shot allowed him to gauge the officer's position adequately. The next two shots, fired a split second later, caused the officer to scream out in pain.

With only one shot left, Sebastian descended upon the wounded officer lying in a heap near the window. In the darkness, he could see the whites of his eyes; bulging and fearful. Without a word, Sebastian plunged the knife into the base of the officer's throat. In an instant, his shouts of pain became gurgles of suffocation, as blood filled his larynx and trachea. His body thrashed violently, then seized. A second later, the gurgling stopped.

When it did, the only sounds that remained were Meredith Park's screaming and the drumming of his own heart.

Despite the physical exertion required to finish off Evans, Sebastian felt light on his feet as he stood up. Abraham once told him that clarity of purpose brings with it a drive that nothing else can inspire. He'd never felt such clarity before now, and the electric current of energy that began at the base of his spine and radiated through every bone, artery, and muscle in his body, was a testament to the truth of the old man's words.

He followed Meredith's screaming to the rear of the house, where she unsuccessfully attempted to open the back door, then down the staircase, where she disappeared into the tight, inescapable corridors of the basement.

Exactly where Sebastian wanted her.

He exhaled as he stood at the top of the staircase, allowing himself to relish the moment. Before he went down after her, he pulled out his cell phone and opened the camera app.

He began by pointing the lens down the staircase, then turned it on himself. Even though he hated the sight of his reflection, he smiled. This was a moment of triumph, and Abraham needed to know that.

"I'm sure you can't guess where I am right now," Sebastian said to his stepfather. "But as you can tell, it's someplace very dark." He paused at the rustling he heard in the basement. "I don't know if you can hear that," he said as he pointed the camera back toward the staircase. "But Meredith Park is somewhere down there all by herself." He turned the camera back. "Well, she's not totally by herself."

Sebastian started down the staircase, taking each step slowly in an effort to draw out the time as long as he could. When he heard the sirens in the far off distance, however, he was reminded that his time was coming to an end.

"I'm sure you'll hear the news reports about what I've done here. But I wanted you to see it for yourself. I wanted you to see what you've done - what you've made me do. And I wanted you to see how the end begins for you. It begins right here, in this basement, with the death of Meredith Park. It continues with my own death. And it finishes with Camille Grisham finding you. I only wish my mother and Ash didn't have to get caught up in this. But they made the choice to follow you. We all did. And now we all have to pay for that choice."

As he descended to the last step, Sebastian turned the camera toward the darkened space in front of him. "I've got some very important business to finish, so I'm afraid I'll have to say goodbye now. But I'll leave the camera rolling for you. The cinematography may leave a lot to be desired, but you'll get the essence of the story." He turned the camera back on himself and gave Abraham one last smile. "So sad that it took this for you to realize that Lucas wasn't the only capable one among us. Enjoy the show."

Sebastian felt along the wall until he came upon a light switch. He flipped it on, revealing a small but well-kept space, with a washer and dryer separated by a basin, a free-standing pantry with fresh towels and cleaning supplies, and a large refrigerator. There was a closed-door about ten feet in front of him, and two more down the short hallway to the left.

"Well, Abe, let's see what's behind door number one, shall we?" Sebastian chuckled at himself as he propped the still-running camera on a bookshelf near the staircase.

"It's okay, Meredith," he said as he approached the closed door directly in front of him. "I know how you're probably feeling. You're scared. You're confused. You thought those officers would keep you safe. At this point, you probably just want it all to be over. Believe me, I understand, more than you realize." He struggled to clear the hard lump that unexpectedly formed in his throat.

Ignoring the spontaneous outburst of emotion, Sebastian set his sights on the door directly in front of him. The linoleum under his feet was sticky, causing his shoes to squeak when he walked. Seeing no need to announce himself before he was ready, he took them off.

Putting an ear against the door, he heard nothing on the other side. "Are you there?" he asked in a quiet voice. "It's okay if you are. Why don't you come out so we can talk? I know you're afraid. But there's no reason to be. For either of us."

He pressed his ear harder against the door and waited. Still hearing nothing, he turned the doorknob and pushed his way in.

The small room was mostly empty except for a work desk, two folding chairs, and a large computer monitor that displayed images of the home's interior. But there was no closet or dark corner for Meredith to hide in.

Sebastian closed the door and quickly made his way to the other side of the basement and the two remaining rooms.

He gripped the knob of the first door he came to. It turned, and he gently pushed it. He opened the door a few inches and then stopped. He turned to the other closed door a few feet away. He walked over, placed his ear against it, and listened. There was a gentle hum coming from the other side, though he couldn't place the sound. Unlike the others, this door felt warm to the touch. There was life in there. Life that now belonged to him.

When he turned the knob, it caught, just as he thought it would. Meredith had locked herself inside. *Why would she think that would be enough to keep me away?*

"Door number two it is, Abe." He turned back toward the

shelf on which he'd mounted the camera. "I do hope you're seeing all of this."

The wailing of sirens that were once distant had now grown louder. There was no more time for theatrics.

He pulled the .38 out of his waistband. This would have to be over quickly. One shot in the head. He'd considered saving the bullet for himself, but the courageous warrior he'd discovered inside himself today would not allow it. The new and improved Sebastian Gideon would go out fighting.

He gave the door a hard push with his hand, then a harder push with his shoulder. "If you opened the door, this would be a hell of a lot easier," he said as he drove his shoulder into it. He could feel the wood buckling more and more with each blow.

With the sirens getting louder now, Sebastian began kicking at the door, only to be painfully reminded that he'd removed his shoes minutes earlier.

With the door not opening, and his panic starting to build, Sebastian stepped back a few feet to get a running start, then drove his body hard into the door. That was when he finally heard the first substantial crack. He repeated the move. This time, the door frame split at the top. One more time and he'd have it. He stepped back, planted his feet as much as his smooth socks would allow, and hurdled himself into the door one last time.

He crashed through in an explosion of splintered wood and landed hard on the floor.

Through a swirl of dizzying stars, he looked up and saw the ceiling fan spinning above him. That had been the source of the hum. The space heater at the foot of the twin-sized bed had been the source of the warmth.

Rising to his knees, he pulled the long string attached to the fan. The room was flooded with bright light.

The bed was neatly-made, with basic white sheets and a

brown quilt. An open closet revealed a large suitcase with loose articles of women's clothing inside. An NYU sweatshirt and a pair of pink pajama bottoms were folded on top of the bed.

This was Meredith's room. But Meredith wasn't in here.

Clever girl, he thought as he realized what she'd done.

The thought hadn't yet cleared his mind when he heard footsteps behind him. By the time he turned around, Meredith had cleared the hallway and was rounding the corner to the staircase. The door to the room she'd been in - the unlocked storage closet that he walked away from - stood wide open, taunting his stupidity.

"Much more clever than you, Sebastian," he said out loud.

He ambled to his feet and immediately gave chase. Meredith had made it halfway up the staircase before he got to her. He stopped her with a hard hand on the cuff of her jeans and pushed her down until he could get a firm hold on her ankle. She flailed and kicked, but couldn't escape his grip.

He heard her scream before he saw her face. The sound excited him, and he felt a rise. Maybe he was more like Lucas than he realized.

He pulled Meredith down far enough to grab her by the belt using one hand, while the other held tight to the .38. As his knuckles rubbed against the soft skin of her torso, he regretted not having the time to do what he'd originally planned. When he turned her around and saw those beautifully terrified brown eyes staring back at him, he regretted it even more.

What a fitting thing it would've been to capture on video. He glanced at his phone and was relieved to see that it was still recording.

Through the screen, he saw something that he hadn't seen when he was facing Meredith.

The object in her hand was long, slender, and cylindrical. And it looked heavy. With all of her flailing and thrashing, he must've missed it. Lucas wouldn't have missed such a thing. It was then that he knew for sure that he was nothing like his brother.

Sebastian felt a hard blow on his shoulder before he had the chance to turn around. He attempted to raise the gun, but his arm was suddenly limp. The blow to his head came next. It was a glancing shot, the cold, sharp edge of the pipe scraping his forehead and temple.

Before Meredith could raise the pipe to attempt another blow, Sebastian grabbed it with his good hand and pulled it away from her while simultaneously pushing down on her with every ounce of bodyweight that he had to prevent her from moving.

There was a noise upstairs that sounded like a boom, followed by the unmistakable sound of shattered glass. Footsteps, lots of them, were moving toward him in a mad rush.

"I'm afraid this is it," he whispered in Meredith's ear. The warmth of her heavy, panicked breathing on his neck made him rise even more, and it was all he had not to kiss her. Instead, he turned to his phone for what would be the final time. He wanted to say something to Abraham, but he didn't know what to say. At this point, Sebastian doubted that he would even see this. And if he did, what difference would it make? What difference would *he* make?

He decided to let time answer the question for him. Time, after all, had a way of elevating a man's trivial existence into one of merit, should it choose to. Sebastian could only hope that his trivial existence would receive such consideration. The thought that it would made the end much easier.

He saw the flashlights, and the black uniforms, and the drawn weapons bearing down on him. Then he looked at Meredith, the woman who had done nothing to him during this ridiculous fight that was never his to begin with. And he realized something that killed him before the cop's bullets ever got the chance.

He was exactly where Abraham would've wanted him to be.

34

SURVIVORS

WHEN AGENTS PRATT AND MENDOZA made it past the gauntlet of officers lining the basement staircase, they saw Sebastian Gideon's lifeless body curled up against a nearby bookshelf. The silver .38 that he used to kill Evans and McClennan was beside him on the floor, covered in the same dense blood splatter that stained his uniform and the surrounding walls.

Meredith Park was sitting on the floor a few feet away, cradling shaky legs that she'd pinned against her chest. The basement was cold, and she shivered.

"Somebody get her a blanket," an angry but relieved Pratt said to the group of officers huddled beside her. The group quickly dispersed in search of the blanket.

He and Mendoza walked up to her. Specks of blood dotted her gray blouse and blue jeans.

"Are you physically hurt?" Mendoza asked as she crouched down beside her to get a closer look.

"The blood is his if that's what you're asking," Meredith said in a surprisingly strong voice. "The officers shot him while he was still on top of me. They said they didn't have a choice. Jesus, I felt the bullets whizzing past my head."

"He had a gun, Mrs. Park," Pratt said as he knelt down beside her. "Had the police not acted as decisively as they did, you might not be here." He put a gentle hand on her shoulder. "Personally, I'm glad you're still here."

"You're not the only one, Agent Pratt," Meredith said with a heavy smile. "Those men saved my life. I hate the way they did it, but I'll always be grateful." She cast a quick glance in Gideon's direction as more officers surrounded him. "Is that…"

"No," Pratt answered. "We're confident that he had a role, but we're not sure of the full extent of it."

"So Paul and Jacob. They're still… this isn't over yet?"

"Not yet."

"But it will be soon," Mendoza quickly added.

"How did you learn about this man?" Meredith asked. "How did you know he would come here?"

"We learned about him from Daniel MacPherson," Pratt answered. "He's also told us a lot about the man we're still looking for; the man responsible for all of this."

Meredith took a shallow breath and blew it out in short, uncontrolled bursts. "What's his name?"

"Abraham Noble," Mendoza answered. "Is that name at all familiar?"

"No."

"What about Sabrina Noble or Lucas Gideon?"

"Are they suspects too?"

"Yes," Pratt answered.

"I've never heard of them until now. How close are you to catching them?"

"Close," Pratt said.

Meredith took another hard breath. "Pardon me for not feeling any better."

"We understand," Mendoza said. "But at least you're safe now."

"I was supposed to be safe with Officers Evans and McClellan." A long pause, then, "Did either of them make it?"

"No," Pratt answered.

Meredith's eyes welled up with tears at the news. For the first time, she appeared to be on the verge of breaking. "They were so nice to me. They didn't deserve this. No one does." A hardened resolve suddenly came over her as she looked at Gideon. "Except for him."

Pratt looked at Mendoza, unsure of what to say next.

An officer appeared with the quilt from Meredith's bed and draped it around her shivering body. "There you are, Mrs. Park," he said. "The paramedics are on the way down. They're going to make sure you're looked after properly."

Meredith nodded, then looked up at the officer. "I'm sorry about Evans and McClellan."

The hard lines in the officer's brown face deepened as he attempted to blink away the pain in his eyes. "Me too. I'm glad you're okay."

After a tense silence, Meredith turned back to Pratt and Mendoza. "Promise me you'll help Camille get Paul and Jacob back alive. I can't bear the thought of them going through what I just went through. Not even a fraction of it. Please, promise."

The agents exchanged a glance, the pleading desperation in Meredith's eyes rendering them momentarily speechless.

Pratt knew the consequences of making a promise that he wasn't sure he could keep, but after what happened here, on their watch, it was the least he could give her.

"You have our word, Mrs. Park. We're going to finish this, and bring them home."

Meredith barely had time to respond before one of the officers huddled around Gideon interrupted her.

"Agents, we have something over here you'll want to see."

Pratt and Mendoza quickly got to their feet and made their way to the officer. He was holding a cell phone in one hand and a wallet in the other.

"What did you find?" Mendoza asked him.

"We normally wait for forensics or the homicide dicks to arrive before doing something like this," he explained. "But given the circumstances, we knew we couldn't wait."

"I'm sure the dicks will forgive you, officer," Pratt said without a smile. "What did you find?"

"When we came down, there was a cell phone propped up on the bookshelf here. The video camera on it was running. We started the video from the beginning. The suspect makes mention of the name Abraham several times as he's looking into the camera. Does the name mean anything to you guys?"

"Yes, it does," Pratt answered, suppressing his mounting excitement. "Play the video again, please."

The officer complied. While the recording ran, the officer pulled a piece of paper out of the wallet and unfolded it. "We immediately searched him. We found his driver's license, as well as this Department of Corrections I.D. The names on both are a match. Sebastian Gideon."

"What's the address on the driver's license?" Mendoza asked.

"1345 Monroe street."

"The same address we've already checked out," Mendoza said to Pratt. "Dead end."

"I continued looking through the wallet and found something else," the officer reported. "It's a receipt for a rather large food delivery order taken out two days ago." He gave the receipt to Pratt. "There's enough Kung Pao chicken there to feed General Tso's entire army."

Pratt took the receipt, noting the large order size and dollar amount. "China Dragon Restaurant," he read from the top of the receipt. "1471 Windhurst Court. Windsor, Colorado."

The officer nodded. "Which is over an hour from here. Do you see the last four digits of the credit card number?"

"Yeah."

"They match a Visa we found inside the wallet. Belongs to Mr. Gideon."

"So what the hell was he doing in Windsor?" a perplexed Pratt asked.

Mendoza shook her head, then turned to the officer. "Did you say the receipt was for a delivery?"

"Yes, ma'am. Says so right there at the top."

Mendoza took the receipt from Pratt. "No delivery address, unfortunately."

"We could always call the restaurant," Pratt suggested. "I'm sure they log every delivery. We have a partial credit card, delivery date, and time. That should be enough for an address."

Mendoza paused to contemplate her response. In Pratt's experience with her, long contemplation usually led to positive results. "I may be able to do you one better," she finally said. "If Gideon was tech-savvy enough, we can find the information right now. May I have the phone, officer?" After he gave it to her, she scrolled through the various apps until she found the one she was looking for. "All the cool kids have food delivery apps now. Never mind the hassle of calling, you don't even have to visit the restaurant's website anymore. Just plug in the type of food you want, and they do the searching for you. Works just like ride-sharing, only lazier." She opened the app, then showed it to Pratt and the officer. "This gives you everything. Participating restaurants, menus, order history, even your choice of a driver based on their profile picture."

"I'd never get any business based on my pic," the portly officer bellowed. "One look at my pie hole and they would know why there weren't any extra fries at the bottom of the bag."

Normally all business in situations like this, Pratt smiled in spite of himself.

"Here's what we want," Mendoza said as she finished navigating the app. "Order history. It looks like our guy had a real hard-on for China Dragon. In addition to his most recent delivery, there were two deliveries last week, and one the week before. They were all sizable, and he paid for them all with the same credit card."

"Sounds like he's spending a lot of time up there," the officer said.

Mendoza nodded. "It explains why he's been MIA from his apartment."

"Can you find a delivery address?" an anxious Pratt asked.

After scrolling for a moment longer, Mendoza found it. "16825 Deer Trail Lane, Windsor, Colorado. No apartment number."

"The houses aren't cheap out there," the officer said. "I seriously doubt he could afford one on a C.O.'s salary, even if he was renting."

"I'm pulling it up on Google images right now," Pratt said as he typed the address into his phone. When he found the house, it was all he could do to keep his jaw from hitting the floor. "It's huge," he said as he held up the image of the three-story mansion built atop a large, empty parcel of land.

"And from the looks of it, very remote," Mendoza added. "Let's get the address plugged into the database, check for phone numbers, and cross-reference them against Gideon's contact list."

"We've already checked it," the officer reported. "His only contacts were Darryl Irving, Lee Prescott, and the main number for the Denver County Jail."

"Irving and Prescott are fellow guards," a frustrated Pratt said. "Are you sure there was nothing else?"

"No calls in or out, no text messages, and nothing in his email except spam."

"He's obviously been instructed to cover his tracks," Mendoza said.

"He didn't cover them well enough," Pratt said in reference to the delivery app.

"It could be a wild goose chase," Mendoza warned.

"Or it could be what finally breaks this thing open. Think about it. Large food orders, huge house in a remote location, Gideon on video referencing Abraham Noble in a personal and exceedingly hostile way. None of this is a coincidence. Our perp is in that house, Al. And if he's there…"

"Paul and Jacob are there too."

"I'll get Camille on the phone. She'll obviously want to know what's happened here."

Mendoza flashed that '*I told you so*' smile that he'd been on the receiving end of more times than he could count. "Nice to see that you've come around on her."

Pratt returned her smile. "I think she was the one who had to come around on me. It may take a while, but I eventually win most people over."

"I'm still firmly on the fence, Agent Pratt."

"That's why I said *most* people."

After a fist bump that had been their way of acknowledging a job well-done, Mendoza went upstairs to phone CBI HQ with news of the address, while Pratt prepared to make the same call to Camille. Before dialing, he locked eyes with Meredith as she was being examined by a trio of paramedics.

"We have an address," he said, nudging past the paramedics to kneel down beside her.

"I heard. Does Camille know yet?"

"I'm calling her with the news right now. Would you like to talk to her? Let her know you're okay?"

"You tell her for me. She's got enough going on."

Pratt nodded. "I saw the pipe. Yours?"

"It was the only thing I could do to protect myself."

"You were very brave."

"I didn't feel very brave, but I appreciate you saying that."

"I know a fighter when I see one. You're definitely a fighter. That's why you survived."

Meredith smiled despite the pain in her eyes. "What about Camille? Do you think she's a fighter?"

"She's a hell of a fighter."

"And do you believe she'll survive this?"

At this point, Pratt didn't even have to consider his answer. "Once she finds her father and Jacob, and this is all over, she's not only going to survive. She's going to come out swinging harder than she ever has."

35

CONVICTION

CAMILLE'S HEART DROPPED as Pratt relayed the news about Sebastian Gideon and the two police officers he'd killed. It dropped even further when she learned just how close Gideon had gotten to Meredith before he was finally taken down.

"How is she?"

"Bruised and shaken. But physically, she's going to be fine. Mentally and emotionally..."

"Not so much."

"Not for a while, at least."

Camille knew that it would be much longer than a while. "Are you still on-scene with her?"

"Yes. They're preparing to take her to the hospital for an eval. Allison and I will stay close by."

"Tell Meredith I'm sorry. For everything."

"She doesn't blame you."

"It doesn't matter. I need her to know anyway."

"I'll tell her. What do you plan to do now?"

"Call Crawley to tell him what you told me, and to let him know what has to happen next."

"You're going to the Windsor house," Pratt said as if he'd already known. "Will you need us there?"

"I'd feel better if you stayed with Meredith. I'm sure she'd feel better too. I have some pretty formidable backup here should I need it."

"I'd certainly trust Detective Sullivan to watch my six," Pratt said with a light chuckle. "Just make sure you're careful out there."

Though Camille didn't know Pratt well enough to vet the sincerity of his emotions, he sounded genuinely concerned.

"I appreciate that, Gabe. Thank you for being there for Meredith."

"You're welcome."

She felt gratitude at the notion of having one less enemy in the world. "I guess I can officially admit that I was wrong about you."

"I'm happy you think so, as long as you don't mind putting it on the record. Since you're being so official."

Camille imagined him smiling. In her mind, it looked plenty sincere. "I don't mind at all."

After her call with Pratt, Camille convened with Chloe, Greer, and Lieutenant Hitchcock in the monitoring room. She'd conferenced Crawley into the meeting via phone.

"Put in a call to Windsor P.D. before you head out there," he advised. "I want those guys going in ahead of you. If there's a collar to be made, I'd prefer they make it."

"Understood," Camille said, fully aware that what he was asking wasn't standard protocol in such a situation. But her involvement in the collar wouldn't exactly be standard protocol either, and he suggested it out of a need to protect her. While she understood the sentiment, she wasn't sure if she would be either willing or able to take a backseat once she was actually there.

"Is Daniel familiar with the location?"

"We haven't asked him about it, yet," Chloe said. "But he claims to have only met with Noble in public places."

"Try and jog his memory one more time before you go," Crawley said. "I want to know what we're walking into if at all possible."

"What's happening on your end?" Hitchcock asked.

"I'm still working the Lucas Gideon angle. I'm going through his file now. Pretty slim outside of his time at Fairfield, but I was able to confirm his assignment to Sykes's detail, along with eight other guards. There isn't anything here to suggest that he was any closer to him than any of the other guards, but there are also several redacted sections of the file that I want to get some clarification on. The warden has been tied up in a Pennsylvania DOC meeting regarding Sykes's transfer and hasn't been available for questions. I'm looking for a workaround."

"Hopefully you can find it soon," Camille said. "If Lucas is the connection to Sykes and the perp that we're looking for, it's probable that he's already tried to contact him. Once he does, all bets are off."

"I'll let you know the second I have something."

"Parsons and Krieger are on standby in case you need their assistance," Hitchcock said to Crawley. "They're chomping at the bit to jump back into this."

"They just may get their chance, Lieutenant. As I said, I'll be in touch." A brief silence, then, "Camille, can we chat for a minute?"

She immediately took him off speaker. "It's just you and I, Peter. Go ahead."

"I understand why you feel you have to do this, and I won't even attempt to stop you. But I need you to be prepared for the possibility that this may not lead to anything."

"I am prepared for that. Just like I'm prepared for the possibility that my father is there."

"And if that is the case, you have to stay back as far as you can. You have Detectives Sullivan and Greer, and you'll have the locals. Let them handle the takedown. If our suspect is there, and he sees you..."

"I know what could happen. And I promise I'll be careful."

"I'm insisting on it for your sake as much as anything else. I didn't ask you to come back with the intention of exposing you to this kind of action."

"But you knew damn well that it could happen."

When Crawley didn't respond, Camille realized that her measure was faltering.

"I know you're only looking out for me, and I appreciate it," she said in a calmer voice. "I'll let the guns and badges do their work."

"Thank you."

When Camille finished her call with Crawley, she turned to Chloe and Greer.

"I think now would be a good time to have a few words with Daniel."

The look of concern in Chloe's eyes was palpable. "Do you want us to be in there with you?"

"No. We don't have much time, so I don't plan to be long. But I need some closure. So does he."

Camille felt a jolt of nervousness when she entered the room. Daniel wasn't handcuffed, and she was on the defense, both mentally and physically, just in case she'd need to protect herself.

The moment she got close enough to see the look in his eyes, she knew such measures wouldn't be necessary.

"You almost look relieved to see me," she said as she sat across from him. "That's certainly not what I was expecting."

"What were you expecting?" Daniel asked, his lack of a direct rebuttal instantly confirming Camille's notion.

"We have something of a history, Daniel," she said with a wry smile. "Our dynamic has been pretty consistent."

Daniel nodded. "Dynamics have a way of changing when they need to."

"But not always for the better."

"Indeed. I guess we'll just have to see where this moment of change takes us."

"Fair enough. I have two pieces of news for you."

Daniel leaned forward in anticipation.

"We've found the guard you told Greer and Sullivan about."

"You did?"

"Yes. His name was Sebastian Gideon."

"*Was?*"

"He's dead. Shot by police as he was attempting to kill Meredith Park. Unfortunately, he was successful in killing the two officers assigned to protect her."

Daniel visibly shook as he covered his face with his hand.

"We were able to catch him before he killed Meredith," Camille reiterated. "And we were able to do so because of you."

"I'm not a hero, Camille. I was only trying to save myself."

"Is that why you told me about Meredith's news conference? To save yourself?"

Daniel looked down at the hands he'd rested on the table. "I don't know why I did that."

"Yes, you do. It's the reason you're here now. Self-preservation is only part of it."

Daniel brought his hands up from the table, then ran them through his thick mane of dark brown hair and down his face. He took them away to reveal a pair of red eyes strained with worry. "I just want this to be over."

"So do I, and we could be close."

"Is that your second piece of news?"

Camille nodded. "We may have located Abraham Noble."

"Jesus Christ. Where?"

"In a town called Windsor, about an hour from here."

"Is it a big house?"

"From the picture, it looks rather large."

"And isolated?"

"Yes."

"That's where he said he'd be."

Camille felt a hard thud in her chest as her heart skipped several beats. "Tell us what we are walking into."

"I don't know anything specific about the house. I was never there."

"But you know a lot about him."

Daniel sat back in his chair and quietly contemplated his answer. "He thinks he has this all figured out. He thinks he's in control. That's the only reason why Jacob Deaver and your father are still alive. Once he figures out that he's no longer in control, he'll become desperate. And when he's desperate, he's exceedingly dangerous. I've seen him turn from cool and methodical to out of his mind psychotic on more than one occasion. He can flip as fast as a light switch, and when he does, no one around him is safe. No one. The moment he sees you, he's going to flip. And if that happens, you'd better make sure you get to your father before he does."

"We plan to," Camille answered in a voice incapable of producing the conviction that she'd wanted.

"For what it's worth, I hope you're successful. I know a simple apology isn't nearly enough, and I feel stupid for saying something is trite as I'm sorry. But I am."

Camille paused to gauge the conviction in Daniel's eyes.

She knew that all of this could've been nothing more than a
ploy for the camera, and the prosecutors who would eventually watch this interview. But she wanted to believe that
something else was at work inside of him, prodding the
human being who existed beneath all of that pain and anger,
until it finally decided to emerge. She wasn't sure if she'd
witnessed that emergence yet. But she was sure it was
coming. And if the circumstances allowed, she would do her
part to help the world see it.

"An apology isn't nearly enough, Daniel. But it's a start."

"Thank you." For a brief moment, Daniel's face brightened. "Now stop wasting your time here with me and go
catch him."

When Camille looked into his eyes this time, she had no
more doubts about his conviction.

36

WORKAROUND

"I'M SORRY, AGENT CRAWLEY. I'm afraid Mr. Bradley is still unavailable."

The receptionist, who up until now had been fairly understanding of Crawley's persistence, could hardly mask her irritation this time around. "As I've mentioned several times already, the moment he's available, I'll pass along your message."

"I'm afraid the situation has changed since you and I last spoke," Crawley said. "It was urgent then. It's twice as urgent now."

The receptionist sighed. "Even if I wanted to pull him out of the meeting, I wouldn't know how. His cell phone goes straight to voicemail every time I call, and he didn't leave any information about where the meeting was taking place. My hands are tied, sir."

"There has to be someone else I can speak with about Mr. Gideon."

"Mr. Bradley was insistent that any questions about personnel be answered only by him."

"Mr. Bradley's insistence doesn't mean a damn thing when

he doesn't make himself available to me, does it?" Crawley barked. It took less than a second to realize the depth of his mistake, and he quickly backpedaled. "I apologize for the outburst. I was out of line, and you did nothing to deserve it."

"You're damn right on both counts," she replied, meeting his unprofessional jab with one of her own. "Under the circumstances, I accept your apology. But there still isn't anything I can do about the warden."

"Can you at least direct me to someone who worked with Gideon? A superior? A colleague? Give me a name, and I'll do the rest. They'll never know that I got it from you."

The receptionist was quiet for a moment. "Okay. His lieutenant's name is Odell Hamilton. Unfortunately, Mr. Hamilton is in the DOC meeting along with the warden."

Peter pounded his desk with a hard fist, realizing it was better to take his frustrations out on the faux wood then risk pissing off the receptionist again.

"In the interest of sparing you a trip to the ER with a broken hand, there may be someone else I could connect you with," the receptionist said. "But if I do, you have to promise never to mention my name."

"You have my word," Crawley promised. He'd forgotten her name anyway but figured it was best to keep that tidbit to himself.

She proceeded to give him the telephone number of Caleb Foster, the senior officer specialist in charge of Gideon's unit, on the condition that Warden Bradley was never notified. Crawley once again gave her his word, along with a healthy thank you for sparing him that trip to the ER.

Much to his relief, it only took 10 minutes for Foster to respond to his voicemail. Aside from explaining that he was an FBI agent investigating a case loosely connected to Daniel Sykes, he kept the details of his inquiry vague. He didn't want to give Foster any reason to report back to Bradley, who he assumed by now was stonewalling him.

"How can I help you, Agent Crawley?" Foster asked after polite introductions.

"I have some questions about one of the officers on your team. Lucas Gideon."

Foster responded with an irritated sigh. "Yeah, I have some questions about him too."

"What do you mean?"

"I mean, he was supposed to report back here, and he hasn't shown up. No phone call, no text, nothing."

"Report back from where?" Crawley asked.

"He was on his way to the airport along with the rest of Daniel Sykes's transport detail when we got the call about the transfer being put on hold. Some of the team hadn't made it to the airport yet, but Gideon and two others had. When we got the news, we called them with orders to report back here for an immediate briefing. We heard back from everyone except Gideon."

"He didn't make the trip back from the airport with the other two officers?"

"After he was informed of the change, Gideon contacted his colleagues to tell them that he'd arrived at the airport early and had already made it through security. He ended the conversation with plans to meet them back here."

"How long ago was he due back?"

"Four hours ago. It's not like him to pull something like this for no good reason."

"Do you think he could've gotten on the flight anyway?"

"He was ordered specifically not to. If he got on that plane, he did so for his own reasons. Not ours."

Crawley grew quiet as he attempted to process the torrent of thoughts swirling in his head.

"What are you interested in talking to him for anyway?"

he heard Foster ask. "You said there was a case involving Sykes. Is that why his transfer was stopped?"

"Mr. Foster, if Lucas Gideon did get on that flight, when would he have been due to land in Denver?"

"According to the itinerary, it would have been at six-twenty-seven P.M. Accounting for the two-hour time difference, that's four-twenty-seven your time.

Crawley immediately checked his watch, noting the time of three-nineteen. "What's the flight number?"

"Wait. You don't really think he could be-"

"The flight number, Mr. Foster."

"United Airlines, 502. But I don't understand why he would want to go out there without Sykes."

"You've been a tremendous help," Crawley said, refusing to address the question. "I'll contact you in the event there's any follow-up."

Crawley disconnected the call before Foster could ask another question.

His next call was to Detective Krieger.

"Are you and Parsons still available?" Crawley asked when Krieger picked up.

"Absolutely."

"Good. I'll be by to pick you up in fifteen."

"Why? What's going on?"

"I'm not entirely sure yet. But we're starting with a trip to the airport."

37

A DIRE MESSAGE

ABRAHAM FELT AN ACUTE SENSE of finality as he
made the short walk from Jacob's room to his office.
The feeling was as mysterious as it was sudden, and he had a
difficult time tracing its source.

What he did know for sure was that it left him hollow and
weary, and longing for a sign, any sign, that the ending he'd
worked so hard to create was still the one that destiny had in
store for him. Despite his broad smile and confident stride, he
had serious doubts.

"I'd call this a significant turning point in our relationship," he said as he turned to Jacob. He hadn't gotten a true
appreciation for how tall and gangly the kid was until he
walked beside him. A full head taller than Abraham's five-
feet, ten-inches, Jacob could easily pass for one of the emaci-
ated supermodels used to sell murses and men's skirts. Fortunately, this didn't make Abraham despise him any more than
he already had.

Jacob had developed a full-grown beard since coming
here, and his dark blond hair was in need of a major trim. But
he refused to let Sabrina anywhere near him with a razor,

despite her assurances that she wouldn't hurt him. Abraham never offered any such assurances, which was probably why Sabrina's was met with skepticism.

"I never would've thought the day would come when I could trust you enough to leave the blindfold and handcuffs off. But here we are."

The decision not to handcuff Jacob had been an intentional one, meant to instill the sense that trust had finally been earned, that familiarity, even cordiality, was possible, and, most importantly, that there was still a scenario where Jacob could make it out of this situation alive.

None of those things were actually possible. But if Abraham wanted to use him to the extent that he'd always plan to, Jacob had to believe that they were.

"It must be nice to make this walk without a gun pointed at your head," Abraham continued as he unlocked the office door.

"I'm assuming there's one very close by," Jacob said in a dry, strained voice.

"Let's not dwell on the negative, son. We have some important work to do."

Abraham opened the office door and allowed Jacob to walk inside first. Entering the room with an unsteady gait, he immediately found the table and chair in the corner that was his customary workstation, and he slowly made his way over to it.

"Not yet," Abraham said.

Jacob stopped in his tracks.

"I'd like to have a chat first." Abraham pointed to the large leather armchair that sat opposite his desk. "Please, join me."

Jacob swallowed hard as he followed Abraham to the desk and promptly sat.

When Abraham sat behind the desk, he opened the mini-refrigerator beside him and pulled out two water bottles, one of which he gave to Jacob. "I have something stronger if you'd prefer," he said with a smile. "It might help to take the edge off."

"Water is fine," Jacob answered as he twisted the cap and took a hard pull. He choked, and water dribbled out of his mouth onto the oversized *Cowboys from Hell* t-shirt that once belonged to Lucas. Sabrina brought along a duffel bag full of his old clothes, explaining that it was her way of keeping her baby close. She had no idea how far away her baby truly was.

"I'm okay," Jacob said before Abraham could ask.

"Thank goodness. The irony of you choking to death on water would be too criminal to believe at this point."

His thin attempt at humor managed to coax a quick, nervous smile out of Jacob.

After giving him another moment to compose himself, Abraham continued. "I guess you're wondering what it is I want to talk to you about."

Jacob nodded.

Abraham opened the drawer, pulled out his laptop computer, and placed it on the desk. "I first wanted to commend you for the excellent work you've done so far." He opened the web browser and typed in Camille's name. The initial search results were all links to Camille's statement and were carried by news outlets ranging from The New York Times to the BBC. Creature of habit that he was, Abraham pulled up the original story from the Mile-High Dispatch. "You haven't yet gotten to experience the fruits of your labor." He opened the video and turned the screen to Jacob. "Have a look."

His eyes narrowed as he watched, but he was otherwise expressionless.

"Your words. And I must say they were quite brilliant."

Jacob continued to watch in silence until Camille's statement was finished.

"What are your thoughts?"

Jacob took another drink from the water bottle. "Does this mean it's over?"

Abraham laughed. It was the first time he'd done so in a while, and it felt strange. "Far from it. Camille introduced a new wrinkle that I admittedly wasn't prepared for, and we have to figure out how we're going to respond to it."

"A new wrinkle?"

Abraham brought up the article and turned the computer back to Jacob. "Read this."

He did so, taking in the words slowly and with a measure of surprise not unlike Abraham's. When he was finished, he took another drink, downing the contents of the bottle in two large gulps. "Is she talking about Madison?"

Abraham's face darkened the same way it did every time he heard his daughter's name. "Yes."

"Do you know what's in her diary?"

"Of course not. But I intend to find out."

"How?"

"I think you know."

Jacob sank back in his chair. "Are you planning to kill more people?"

"What makes you think I've killed anyone at all?"

"The reporter who was mentioned in the article. Didn't you kill him and his wife?"

This time, Abraham was the one who sank back in his chair. "If it was me, why should I admit that to you?"

Jacob looked around the empty office. "At this point, who am I going to tell?"

Abraham smiled. "You're right. Besides, you've earned the right to full disclosure at this point. I did kill them."

"And the FBI agent too?"

"Apparently, he survived. Sloppy work on my part. That won't happen again."

"You mean when it comes to Paul Grisham and me."

Abraham let the question linger as he carefully considered his response. "I don't want anything to happen to you and Paul that doesn't have to. Jeremy Durant and his wife needed to die in order to keep the two of you alive. If I intended to kill you, we wouldn't be having this conversation."

Jacob's expression let Abraham know that he didn't believe that any more than Abraham did, but he wisely chose not to verbalize it.

"So, I'm sure the next logical question you have is what I plan to do to keep you alive."

"If it involves killing anyone else, I don't really care to know."

"So you'd rather I kill you instead?"

"I'd rather you cut the bullshit. I'm tired, I'm scared, and I want to go home. You have that woman here, taking care of me, to make me think that going home as a possibility when you and I both know that it isn't. I've done everything you've asked me to do, knowing full well what you have planned for me. I've allowed myself to be manipulated into thinking that I was actually here for a reason beyond your obvious intention to torture me. But now I see that's the only reason I'm here. You want to torture me, just like you want to torture Paul, and Camille, and Meredith, and any other goddamn person you see fit.

"This is nothing but a game to you. You've lined us all up like pieces on your chessboard, not caring at all how your moves affect us. Well, I'm sorry, but I'm not playing anymore. You can write your own story with whatever ending you want. But I won't have any part in it."

Abraham was caught off guard by Jacob's fiery response and needed to give himself time to process it. "I'm impressed with the fight," he said truthfully. "After all this time, I didn't think you had anything left. But I also have to admit that it's a little disappointing."

Jacob suddenly tensed as he balled one of his hands into a tight fist.

"How far are you willing to take this fight, Jacob? Are you prepared to take me on, right here and now? I don't think I'd have to tell you how badly it would end."

"You don't have to tell me," Jacob replied, his fist still coiled. "Physically, you have every advantage in the world. If we fought, it wouldn't last ten seconds. But I have no intention of challenging you physically."

"Then how do you intend on challenging me?"

"By doing my part to ruin what's left of your ridiculous plan for Camille Grisham. You clearly scripted this thoroughly. And the fact that Paul and I are still alive means that you intended to use us and some larger way. I can't speak for Paul, but I can't imagine that he wouldn't give his own life in a heartbeat if it meant stopping you from doing anything else to her. And at this point, I feel the exact same way."

Abraham felt the little remaining composure in him begin to falter. "You have no idea what you're saying."

"Of course I do. You want to kill me, but not before you convinced me that the words I've helped you write were responsible for killing Jeremy Durant, and his wife, and ultimately Camille. But I'm not responsible, just like Camille Grisham isn't responsible for your daughter's death."

"I advise you to stop, Jacob. Right now."

"You've tried to paint yourself as a victim in all of this. The poor, innocent father that was never allowed the chance to see his daughter. You somehow think that you were the only one who lost something when she was murdered. But from what I could gather, you were never much of a father to begin with. From what I gather, you abandoned her. The only person who lost in this was Madison. And whether you want to admit it or not, she lost long before she was murdered. If she did write that diary, and you were in it, do you really think she had anything good to say? Do you really think that reading about how much you let her down is going to make any of this better for you?"

"Shut up."

"She's the victim, not you. And how are you honoring her memory? By manipulating her, just like you're trying to manipulate all of us."

"I said, shut up!"

In the wave of blinding fury that washed over him, Abraham hadn't realized that he raised the gun to Jacob until he saw the sudden fear in his eyes. The cold steel felt heavy in his trembling hand, and he feared that the weight would cause him to drop it. He cupped the barrel with his other hand to secure it.

The look of frozen dread on Jacob's face helped stabilize Abraham's breathing, allowing him to loosen his grip on the .38 slowly.

"This isn't going to happen, Jacob. Not until I want it to."

With one hand still on the gun, Abraham used his other hand to reach into his pocket for his cell phone. He needed to get away from Jacob as quickly as he could and didn't trust himself to escort him back to his room. He needed Ash to do it for him.

He checked one pocket, then the other, then his desk drawer, before realizing that his cell phone was nowhere to be found.

"Shit!"

Struggling to regain control of his frayed nerves, he quickly stood up, took a set of handcuffs out of the desk drawer, and walked over to Jacob.

Worried that he could make a move, Abraham struck him

on the top of the head with the butt of the gun and yanked
him out of the chair. Dazed from the blow, Jacob offered no
resistance as Abraham put a cuff around one of his wrists
before dragging him over to the radiator on the other side of
the room. Once Abraham secured him to it with the other
cuff, he stepped back to take in a deep pull of oxygen. His
breathing was heavy, and he feared losing control of it
altogether.

With his chest still heaving, he quickly left the office in
search of his phone. He found it on the nightstand inside the
bedroom he shared with Sabrina. Before he could leave to
find Ash, the phone's screen lit up. He immediately noticed
the six missed calls from Lucas, and his chest tightened even
more.

When he opened up the phone, he saw four voicemails in
addition to the calls. He'd expected to hear from Lucas as
soon as he arrived in Denver, but the number of calls, some of
them made over four hours ago, troubled him, and he knew
instantly that something was wrong. That notion was all but
confirmed when he listened to the first message.

"Give me a call as soon as you get this, Abe. Something's
happened with the transfer. I don't know what yet, but we've
been told to remain on standby until they contact us again."

The second message was left twenty minutes later.

"Where the fuck are you? Something is happening. I'm at
the airport, but I just got a call from one of the guards I'm
traveling with. He's telling me they might call us back to Fairfield for some kind of emergency. Call me. Now."

With fingers that were trembling uncontrollably, Abraham
played the third message.

"They just told us that the transfer has been put on hold.
Daniel Sykes isn't going anywhere. Damn it, Abe. Where are
you?"

His heavy fist pounding against the wall made it difficult

for Abraham to make out much of the fourth message, aside from the words, "I'm getting on a flight anyway."

After putting several sizable dents into the drywall, Abraham called Lucas, praying to a deity he was convinced didn't exist that his stepson would answer. As he anticipated, his empty prayer went unanswered.

"Lucas, it's me. I'm sorry I didn't get your calls - I was caught up in a lot here. I don't... I don't understand your messages. What did you mean when you said Sykes's transfer was put on hold? Put on hold for a day? A week? Indefinitely? What in the hell does that mean, Lucas?" Abraham felt his anxiety rising with every word he spoke. "If he isn't here, everything I've worked for is officially gone to shit. Everything you've done - those girls, all that time you spent with Sykes, none of it means a goddamned thing. Do you understand that, Lucas? Sykes has to be here. It doesn't matter that you're coming now. If anything, you should've kept your ass there until you made sure that Sykes could come with you." He paused to allow his anger to subside.

"Look, I'm sorry, okay? I just wasn't expecting this. Of course, I want to see you. But we've got to figure out this thing with Sykes. Otherwise... I don't know what I'm going to do. Call me back as soon as you can."

When he disconnected the call, he threw his phone against the bed and began pounding on the walls again.

Once his hands were sufficiently battered, and the anxiety and desperation were drained from him, Abraham grabbed his phone and started for the door. His mind was beginning to clear, and he knew there wasn't any more time to waste. There hadn't been a legitimate Plan B before this moment. He had to create one. And he had to do it fast.

Jacob and Paul.

At this point, it was his only play. He'd been content to use them as background players until the end when they were of no further use to him. Now, they would be forced into starring roles; second-rate stand-ins for the real stars who were, sadly, no longer available for the top billing that they deserved.

He opened the door with his sights set on Jacob and Paul but was instead met with the ice-cold stare of his wife.

She'd been standing on the other side of the door. Abraham couldn't be sure how long she was there, but he suspected that it was his pounding on the walls that drew her attention.

"Not now, Sabrina." Abraham barked as he attempted to brush past her.

Sabrina grabbed him by the forearm with such force that it physically hurt. "Yes, now." Her eyes were red and glassy as if she were near tears. But her voice was calm and resolute.

Abraham attempted to pry free of her grip. She responded by tightening it.

"What the hell are you doing? Let me go." Abraham attempted to mask the shock on his face with the intensity of his voice, but Sabrina appeared to be unmoved.

"Not until you tell me what you were talking about in there."

"I'm sorry, Sabrina. But that isn't any of your business."

"If you were talking to Lucas, you better believe it's my business."

Abraham grabbed her wrist and squeezed, just hard enough to force her hand away. "I told you, it's none of your concern."

"Daniel Sykes? The prison? Those girls? What did all of that mean, Abraham? What on Earth does it have to do with my son?"

"*Our* son."

Her bottom lip quivered as her reservoir of strength began a slow, steady drain. "What does it have to do with him?"

And here it was, Abraham's worst nightmare staring him in the face. A greater man, undeterred by the consequences to himself, would have done the right thing and told the woman he loved the truth. A greater man would have known that her need for the truth meant more than his pathetic need for self-preservation. A greater man would have admitted his own role in what Lucas had become, begged his wife for forgiveness, and swore with his life that he would do everything he could to make her whole again.

But Abraham was not a better man, in this instance, or any other. And the greatest lie he ever told was that he could be that man once this was all over.

"Don't ask questions you don't want the answers to," was all he could bring himself to say before he walked away.

38

THE OTHER SHOE

T HE DRIED ROSE PETAL was pressed neatly between pages ninety-one and ninety-two of Ralph Waldo Emerson's *Society and Solitude*.

The petal, plucked fresh from a Valentine's Day bouquet over eighteen years ago, had been an ever-vibrant symbol of new beginnings and the intoxicating allure of courtly love.

The book, Sabrina's favorite since high school, was a bleak reminder of the past. It was a past rooted in misguided idealism and bitter disappointment and nourished by failure, abandonment, and a never-ending feeling that the other shoe was always going to drop, like a laser-guided anvil from the sky, at the least opportune moment possible.

Before the rose petal, and the man who gave it to her, there was nothing in Sabrina's life capable of countering that ever-present sense of dread that followed her every waking moment of the day. But then Abraham Noble showed up, with his promises of love and security, and a better life for her sons.

For a time, Abraham's promises helped convince her that the tide of misfortune had finally turned. For a time, she gave herself permission not to expect the worst, or look for the dark lining that hid behind every ray of light. For a time, Sabrina allowed herself to be happy, both for herself, and her three sons, who needed Abraham and his promises just as much as she did.

But experience told her that happiness was never meant to last.

Unlike the breakdown of her first marriage, which had been brutally swift, the end for Sabrina and Abraham came on slowly, methodically, and for a long time, painlessly.

It began, as it often does, with the yelling, but she'd lived with that her entire life and believed it could be managed. Then came the chain of broken promises. Fishing trips with the boys that never came to be. Declarations of his unyielding fidelity broken first by an emotional affair, then by a physical one. Assurances of a peaceful and stable home life shattered by sudden, uncontrolled, and oftentimes unwarranted bouts of anger, that would end with Abraham putting a fist through a wall, or, in one horrifying instance, through a window.

She was never a direct target of his violence, but her sons sometimes were. And though they were big enough to occasionally push back (in her youngest son's case, pushing back meant taking a box cutter to Abraham's face with the intention of cutting it in half), the precedent of victimhood set by their father long ago had instilled in them a numbness to the violence that gradually morphed into acceptance.

Shaped by her own history of brutality, Sabrina also grew numb to Abraham's. There were enough good moments, tender embraces, and tearful apologies, to allow her to stay. But she did so with one eye always trained to the sky, in search of the other shoe that inevitably had its sights set on her.

After all that had happened, after all she'd been through

with him, after all she'd blindly given to him, that other shoe finally dropped. And it dropped hard.

It was Abraham's volatile temper that, not so ironically, alerted her that something was wrong. She'd become accustomed to the sound of his fists echoing through the walls of their home, but she hadn't heard it this bad in a long time - not since his ex-wife called to deliver the news of Madison's murder. She'd never been more afraid for him, or herself, as she was on that day. And she hadn't been so afraid since. Their abrupt move to Colorado hadn't done it. His plans to abduct Paul Grisham and Jacob Deaver hadn't done it. Nor had his obsession with the man who killed his daughter, or her suspicion that he may have known something about the four girls whose murders were perpetrated by a supposed Sykes copycat.

The numbness had allowed her to stay detached from those things, as had Abraham's assurance that no harm would come to anyone aside from the woman he'd convinced her was ultimately responsible for Madison's death.

But as time went on, and the daily sight of Paul and Jacob no longer afforded her the luxury of detachment, her faith in Abraham's assurances began to wane.

She already knew there was a lot he wasn't telling her, both about Camille Grisham, and his plans for Paul and Jacob. But she never could've imagined that he would lie to her about her own child. But what Sabrina heard today told her that he had done just that.

Her default mechanism of denial hadn't allowed her to believe the words at first. The more she replayed them in her mind, however, the less she could deny. Now, the only thing she could think about was getting to the truth of them, even though she knew that doing so would likely mean the end of everything meaningful that the rose petal stood for.

Before Sabrina left the bedroom, she put the book, her

true lifelong companion, back on the bookshelf, and gave the petal one last squeeze. It's warm energy pulsated inside of her palm, before sending its current throughout her body. When she let it drop to the floor, the pulsing stopped. She mourned its loss, but she didn't allow herself to cry. She would save her tears for the end that she now knew was inevitable.

The finality infused her with a sense of power and strength that she never knew she had.

Storming through the long corridor that led to Abraham's office, she ran into her middle son, Asher.

"Where is he?"

Taken aback by what he saw in his mother's eyes, Ash met her question with stunned silence.

"I said, where is he?"

"Mom, what's the matter?"

"Ash!"

"He's in the office with Jacob. He said he wants to be alone."

Without thinking, she pushed him aside and continued her walk until it eventually became a sprint.

From behind her, she heard, "Mom, what is it?" She continued running without answering his question.

By the time she made it back to Abraham's office, he was already coming out. He held Jacob's arm in one hand and his gun in the other. The fury on his face matched hers.

"What are you doing?" she asked as he walked past her.

"Ending this."

She turned to follow him. "Stop, Abraham."

He continued walking without acknowledging her.

Her anger now reaching a fever pitch, she sped up until she positioned herself in front of him. "Tell me about Lucas and Daniel Sykes. What has Lucas done?"

Abraham pushed her aside. "Get the hell out of my way."

She grabbed him by the shoulder before he could walk away. "No. Not until you tell me the truth."

When he turned to her, something shifted in his eyes. A sudden sadness overtook him, and he struggled to hold back tears. Then he blinked, and as quickly as the sadness came, it was gone. "Do you want me to say that I lied to you? That I failed you, and him? Do you want me to tell you that Lucas is something far worse than you or I could've ever imagined he'd become? It's too late to tell you that, Sabrina. It's too late for apologies and regrets. He is what he is, and there's nothing we can do to change that. But what I'm doing now," he pointed the gun at Jacob, "It's not too late to handle it the right way. And I have to handle it. Please, don't get in my way."

"Or what?"

The sadness returned to Abraham's red, narrow eyes. And this time, he couldn't blink it away.

Before she could say anything, he took off down the hall.

The anger that fueled her suddenly ebbed, and her legs felt weak. She struggled to keep pace as he made his way to Paul's room.

By the time she caught up to him, he'd unlocked the door and walked inside. From the hallway, she saw Paul leap off the cot, startled by the sudden intrusion.

Without warning, Abraham shoved Jacob inside. He landed on the floor with a hard thud.

Paul rushed over to him.

"Get back," Abraham shouted, pointing the gun. "Leave him right where he is."

With Ash running in behind her, Sabrina entered the room.

"Abe, what are you doing?"

"Ending this." He took out his cell phone and pointed it at Paul and Jacob.

When she walked up to him, she saw that he was recording them.

"This isn't the final interview I had in mind," he said in a low, strained voice. "But it will have to do." He directed his attention to Paul. "What would you like to say to your daughter before I put a bullet in your head? If you feel at all disappointed that she forced you into this situation, now would probably be the time to let her know."

Sabrina jumped in front of Abraham before Paul could respond. "Put the gun down."

"You don't want to do this," Abraham warned.

"Sweetheart, please." Her only recourse now was to beg, and it made her feel sick to her stomach. "It doesn't have to be like this."

He turned his hard stare back to Paul. "Yes, it does."

Without giving conscious thought to the action, Sabrina grabbed his arm.

In one swift motion, Abraham lowered the gun, then raised it again, this time, directly at Sabrina's head. "I said, don't." His once sad eyes now burned with malice.

And just like that, she felt the end crashing down upon her.

Abraham could have put twenty bullets in her at that moment. The pain would have paled in comparison to the utter destruction he'd inflicted with that single look.

39

KILL SHOT

CAMILLE STOOD IN THE BACKGROUND while Chloe and Greer explained the situation to Windsor PD Chief Jim Lewiston. She had neither the credentials nor the level-headed demeanor to lead the conversation herself.

"This is a big ask based on a very small piece of evidence," Chief Lewiston said in reference to the receipt that Greer handed him. "I think I should have a little more than this before I go knocking on someone's door asking them if they're involved in a kidnapping." He looked at Camille, then promptly looked away.

"We understand the size of the ask, chief," Chloe said. "But we wouldn't be asking if we didn't have good reason to suspect that the people living in that house could provide information crucial to our investigation."

"In other words, you believe your suspect is there."

"There's no hard evidence to prove it as of yet. But yes, we do believe that."

The chief's round, puffy face reddened as he let out a loud breath. "Just my damn luck. We work really hard to keep Windsor off the radar. We're a nice, quiet, family-friendly little enclave that enjoys minding our own business. We don't like to make news, Detective Sullivan. And now you're telling me that we're about to make the worst news imaginable."

"I'm afraid that's a very good possibility."

Lewiston once again turned to Camille. "I saw you on TV, Agent Grisham. It's absolute bullshit what that man is making you do. Pardon the French."

"I agree with you, chief," Camille replied. "But unless we find this man, and find him now, it's going to get a lot worse, for my father and possibly many other people."

Lewiston cast his eyes at his feet and nodded. "I understand. But you have to understand that I can't go unleashing the hounds until I know more about who lives in that house. If I send the entire force, and it turns out there's no one there but a pair of retirees and their pet Yorkie, we'll be digging out of the shit storm long after they give my badge to someone else."

"So you don't know anything about the people currently living there?" Greer asked.

"No. It's in a really quiet area, which means my officers don't have much occasion to drive out that way. As far as I know, the place was vacant for about a year or so. The previous owners put it up for sale, but the asking price was apparently too steep for the condition it was in, so they took it off the market. I wouldn't have known that anyone was in it at all, but my wife showed me the listing a couple of months back. She's real big on the property values in the area and keeps up with all the local real estate. Anyway, the listing said that the house was being rented out. As far as what kind of folks are renting the place, I couldn't tell you. But we haven't gotten any sort of disturbance calls out there, so as far as I'm concerned, they're model citizens."

"Well, we need to ask these model citizens a few questions," Chloe said. "And we would really appreciate your assistance in doing that."

The chief put his hands on his wide hips and let out another loud sigh. "Fine. The house is a few clicks north. I'll have a unit accompany you out there. I'd advise you to let them make the first contact. Feel free to brief them on what they should be looking for. If they smell anything funny, they'll bring you in, and we'll get more boots out there. Fair enough?"

Chloe turned to Camille for confirmation.

She would've preferred that they approached the house with a more substantial show of force, but she understood the chief's position. In the interest of keeping her out of harm's way, Crawley would've understood too.

"Fair enough."

Camille and Chloe waited inside the car while Greer briefed the two officers who would escort them to the house.

"How do you feel about this?" Chloe asked from behind the driver's seat.

Camille took a moment to assess her feelings, but a firm answer eluded her. "I don't know. What I can say is that I'm worried. Maybe even a little bit scared. Everything is riding on this, Chloe. If we come up empty here, I don't think we'll get another chance."

"Don't say that."

"Do you know of another avenue if this one doesn't pan out?"

Chloe contemplated the question before resting the back of her head against the seat. "No." She turned to Camille. "That's why this one is going to pan out."

The thought sent a shudder through Camille's body that she had a hard time controlling.

"I want to give you something," Chloe said after a long silence.

She reached in the glove compartment. When Camille saw what was in her hand, she shuddered again.

"Take this," Chloe said as she pulled the Glock out of the leather holster it had been encased in. "Fully loaded and safetied. You still know how to use one?"

Camille was on the verge of being insulted until she saw Chloe smile. "Of course I do. Crawley would shit a brick if you knew you were giving this to me."

"Agent Crawley strikes me as the type who shits bricks strictly for the challenge of it."

This inspired a genuine outburst of laughter from Camille. "I don't know how you can find humor at a time like this, but God bless you for finding it."

"You can show your gratitude by taking this," Chloe said. "I don't anticipate that you'll need it, but I'll damn sure feel better if you have it."

Camille reached out with a tentative hand and took the gun by the handle. She hadn't held one since she turned in her duty Glock and shield months ago, and the weight of it felt substantial. But as she eased her fingers across the coarsely textured handle and established a full grip, the piece felt manageable.

Manageable as long as she didn't have to use it.

"I won't tell Agent Shit-A-Brick if you don't."

Camille smiled, despite the unnerving thought swirling inside her mind.

But if I do have to use it, I'm shooting to kill.

"Thank you, Chloe."

40

SPLIT-SECOND DELAY

I T TOOK ABRAHAM LESS THAN A SECOND to understand the ramifications of what he'd just done, but by then, any hope he had of ever making the situation right again had all but evaporated.

"Jesus, Sabrina. I didn't mean that," he said as he lowered the gun to his side. "I would never... Oh, sweetheart... I would never hurt you."

Sabrina's chest heaved with anxiety despite the gun no longer being pointed at her. She opened her mouth to speak, but shallow breathing kept the words inside.

Abraham dropped the cell phone, then reached for her with outstretched arms. "Sabrina, please."

"Don't touch me." She had no trouble producing the words this time. "Don't ever touch me again."

"Sabrina, honey, you don't mean that." He took another tentative step toward her.

"If you touch me again, I'll kill you."

At this, Abraham stopped,

"You've hurt me more than I could ever describe," Sabrina

continued. "After everything I've done - supporting you after Madison's death, going along with this plan of yours, risking my life and my freedom to help you get the closure you claimed you so desperately needed - this is how you repay me?"

"Sabrina-"

"First, you lie to me about Lucas, then you stick a gun in my face, with a look of hatred that I wouldn't wish on my worst enemy. And for what? Because I wouldn't let you hurt two men who've done absolutely nothing to you?"

"Because you won't take my side, Sabrina. Because you've never taken my side."

"Never taken your side? For the entire time I've known you I've done nothing but take your side. Who's been there for you through all of this bullshit more than me? And I haven't asked for a single thing in return aside from the truth. I can always handle the truth. No matter how dark it is. What I can't handle are lies. You know that, and you've lied to me anyway."

"You call what I'm doing *bullshit*?"

"Yes, because that's exactly what it is."

"Sabrina, I've never-"

"Lied to me about anything? Fine, then you shouldn't have any problem telling me about your voice message to Lucas."

Abraham long imagined how he'd feel when the time finally came to tell her everything. He imagined the fear, his hesitation, and most certainly, his remorse. But he felt none of that. The vacant look in Sabrina's eyes told him that he no longer had anything to lose by revealing the truth. So when he finally spoke the words he dreaded more than anything else, he felt nothing.

"Lucas killed those four girls. It's entirely possible that

he's killed before. It's absolutely certain that he'll kill again. He was the prison guard assigned to Daniel Sykes. Through their time together, they grew close. Sykes told Lucas of his fantasies about girls, and Lucas carried them out for him. Just like the good little helper that he was. He was a help to me too. Sykes was supposed to be transferred here from Fairfield, and Lucas was assigned to oversee his transition. That's why he was planning to come. Not to see you, but to help carry out my objective of killing Sykes and Camille Grisham. I won't bore you with the details of how that was going to happen. Just know that the plan has now changed." He looked at Paul. "It looks like Camille is going to live to see another day. I'm afraid you won't be so lucky."

Sabrina stood in front of him, staring with no discernible emotion on her face. She appeared to be frozen in time, caught in the void between the life she'd known before this moment, and what would remain of her life after.

"I didn't want this for him," Abraham continued. "I did what I could to stop it early on. But at a certain point, I knew there was no going back."

"So not only did you decide to keep it from me, but you also allowed him to fall deeper into it."

"I'm sorry."

"You're sorry?"

"Yes, I'm sorry. What else can I say?"

Sabrina abruptly turned to her son, who'd been standing quietly in the corner. "Where is Sebastian?"

It took a long time for Ash to answer.

"He took another shift at work."

"Call him, right now. He needs to know what's about to happen here."

"What do you mean, Mom? What's about to happen?"

Without saying another word, Sabrina walked up to Abraham until she was inches away from his face.

"Mom, what's about to happen here?" Ash repeated.

"Yes, Sabrina. What is about to happen here?" Abraham's voice was calm, but his chest throbbed from the sharp stabs of panic.

"You're going to finish the job," she answered in a soft voice.

"Finish what job?

Instead of answering, she put a gentle hand on his shoulder, then slowly eased it down his arm, onto his wrist, and finally around his hand - the hand holding the .38.

Abraham didn't resist as she raised the gun until it was level with her heart. It was then that she said, "You're going to finish killing me."

Every muscle in Abraham's body instantly faltered, and it took all that he had to stay on his feet. "My God, Sabrina. What are you talking about?"

"Do it. I can't go on. Not after this."

Abraham's throat suddenly constricted, causing his eyes to swell up. "I won't."

"You're not going to do as I ask? You're not going to end this misery for me?"

"No." Abraham could no longer feel the gun in his hand. He wouldn't have known that Sabrina had taken it from him at all if she hadn't pointed it in his face.

"Then I guess I'll have to end yours."

"Mom, what the hell are you doing?"

Despite Ash's words, Abraham still couldn't process what had just happened.

"What I should've done when I first realized how much damage he'd done to our family."

The sound of the hammer being cocked finally brought Abraham to full awareness. "Sabrina, you don't have to do this."

She responded by taking four steps backward, aiming the

gun dead center of his forehead. "I gave you a chance, Abraham. Now your death is the only thing that will bring me closure."

With the gun held high, Sabrina took a step toward him. On her second step, her grip tightened around the handle. On the third, her finger found the trigger. Before she could take what Abraham knew would be her fourth and final step, something stopped her. It stopped everyone.

The chime of the doorbell.

"Shit," Ash cried in a panicked whisper.

"Calm down," Abraham said, attempting to calm himself as well. "It's probably some kid selling candy bars. They'll go away."

The doorbell chimed a second time, then, seconds later, a third time.

"Whoever the hell it is, they're not going away," Ash bellowed.

"Check my phone," Abraham said. "It's connected to the doorbell cam. My password is *Sabrina1957*." He looked at her after he said this. The gun was no longer dead center of his forehead.

Before Ash picked up the phone, he looked at Sabrina.

"It's okay," she said.

Ash quickly picked up the phone, entered the password, and opened the security app.

"Damn it!"

"What?" a wide-eyed Sabrina asked.

"It's two cops."

Sabrina and Abraham exchanged a long look.

"What are we supposed to do?" Ash asked.

"Wait for them to go away," Sabrina suggested.

"They won't go away," Abraham countered. "They're here for a reason, and unless they know they shouldn't be here for that reason, they're going to keep coming back. You have to get rid of them, Ash."

"How am I supposed to do that?"

"By being calm and reasonable."

"What if calm and reasonable doesn't work?" an irate Sabrina asked.

Abraham turned to Ash. "If you can talk them off the front porch, do that. If you can't…"

Ash took a deep breath and nodded.

"Ash, no!" his mother ordered.

"Mom, I'm not going to do anything that I don't have to do. It'll be fine." He gave Abraham the phone and quickly ran out of the room. Seconds later, his footsteps could be heard directly above them.

"Give me the phone."

When Abraham looked up, Sabrina had her hand out. With her other hand still firmly wrapped around the .38, Abraham had no choice but to comply.

Thirty seconds passed, then one minute. There was no sound from upstairs. Sabrina's cold stare gave no insight into what she was watching.

Then, he heard it.

"Do you recognize this man?" one of the officers asked.

Ash stammered before answering, "That's my brother."

"Sebastian Gideon?"

"Yes."

Damn it, Ash, Abraham thought.

"Your brother is dead," the officer told him coldly.

"What?" Sabrina yelled.

"He's suspected of killing two police officers. Do you know anything about that?"

Abraham heard the pop on the phone before he heard it in the house. It was quickly followed by a second, then a third, then a fourth, each shot being delayed for a split second as the sound traveled the wide corridors of the house, and into the basement.

The sound he heard next was Sabrina, repeatedly screaming, "Ash, what did you do?"

_____

41

DEAD SPRINT

CAMILLE WATCHED THROUGH A PAIR of Windsor PD-issued Black Hawk Falcon binoculars as the two officers stepped onto the large wrap-around porch, and rang the doorbell.

The young man who answered the door looked a bit skittish, the same as anyone in his position would be, but there was nothing about him that drew immediate suspicion. The young man mostly listened while the officers talked. There were no sudden movements or other visible displays of nervousness, even as the officers pulled out the photo of Sebastian Gideon. This kid was either a very cool customer, or they were barking up the wrong tree entirely.

The longer she watched, the more she feared the latter.

She'd taken her eyes off the house for a brief moment to share her observation with Chloe and Greer when she heard the first pop. Immediately recognizing the sound as gunfire, she directed the binoculars back onto the front porch. By the time she found the officers, one of them was already down. The second officer fell as he attempted to draw his weapon.

Camille, Chloe, and Greer quickly exited the car without a

word, the three of them converging on the porch in a dead sprint.

Before Camille could blink, Chloe and Greer had un-holstered their duty Glocks, and we're taking dead aim at the young man.

He'd already pulled the first officer into the house before they could cover the one hundred and fifty yards between their car and the porch.

When they finally reached him, he'd taken the second officer by the collar to pull him into the open door. The officer was well over six feet tall and solidly built, and the much smaller shooter had a difficult time managing him. The fact that the officer was completely limp likely made the task much more difficult.

The shooter managed to pull the officer halfway inside before Greer reached him.

"Stop right there!"

The shooter stumbled back onto the marble floor, rolled over onto his stomach, and attempted to climb to his feet. The silver automatic was clutched tightly in his right hand.

"Get down!" Greer commanded. "Drop the gun!"

The shooter managed to raise his weapon a few inches from his side when Greer fired. A quick double-tap, dead center of his chest. The shooter instantly fell backward, the gun flying out of his hand and landing several feet behind him.

Giving herself no time to consider the ramifications of what she'd just witnessed, Camille pulled out her gun and ran past the dead shooter and two officers.

She'd just made her way through the large foyer and into the sparsely furnished living room when she heard Chloe.

"Code-ten, code-ten. We have two officers down. 16825 Deer Trail Lane. This is Detective Chloe Sullivan, Denver PD. I repeat, officers down. One suspect is also down, but we believe there may be more on-scene. Request all available units while we attempt to secure the house."

When Camille turned around, she saw Chloe kneeling over one of the officers talking into his two-way radio.

"Code-ten, copy," she heard the dispatcher say. "Sending all available units."

Greer quickly checked the pulses of all three men. When he got to the shooter, he looked at Chloe solemnly and shook his head.

The two detectives stood up and raced inside the living room to meet Camille.

"They're all dead," Chloe told Camille. "Backup is on its way, but we obviously can't wait."

Camille had no intention of waiting. "That wasn't Abraham."

"I know."

"But he's here."

Chloe nodded her agreement. "Are you good with that?" she motioned to the Glock in Camille's hand.

"Yes"

"Okay. There's a lot of ground to cover here, so we'll have to split up. Greer and I will check the upper levels of the house, and you cover the main floor. If we don't find anything, we'll meet up back here. I'm assuming there's a sub-level. If we have to take it, we need to do it together."

"Understood."

With that, Chloe and Greer took off down the hallway that led to a spiral staircase. They quickly climbed it and fanned out to two different sides of the floor.

Camille took a quick moment to catch her breath. The hand that held the gun trembled, and she fought hard to steady it. Once she did, she started down the first hallway that she saw. It was lined with four doors, each of them closed.

For as frightened as she was, she wasn't the least bit surprised that she found herself here. She'd somehow known that this would be the only possible outcome the instant she agreed to come back. She was never here to consult on this case. She was here to end it.

And that was exactly what she planned to do.

42

ONE LAST KISS

S ABRINA WAS SO TRANSFIXED by the horror she just witnessed that she didn't realize Abraham had snatched the gun out of her hand until she looked up to see that he was pointing it at her. Even then, she didn't move, opting instead to keep her attention on the phone and a horrific scene that was playing out in real-time outside her front door. When Ash attempted to pull the officers he'd shot inside the house, she finally couldn't look anymore. Abraham took the phone from her without saying a word.

He watched in stunned silence as Ash was confronted by the two detectives. Instead of using the split-second advantage he had to fire on them, he continued the fruitless task of pulling the second officer inside the house. By the time the instinct to protect himself finally kicked in, it was too late.

With Ash effectively neutralized, a scenario too bleak even for Abraham's nightmares suddenly unfolded. The two officers made their way inside the house, followed closely by an armed Camille Grisham. There wasn't a defense mechanism in his vast arsenal powerful enough to defend against the blinding panic that came over him at that moment. Asher was gone. Sebastian was gone. Sabrina was gone. Those losses, even the latter, could be overcome as long as the plan he'd given them up for was still salvageable. But with the appearance of Camille at his front door, it was doubtful that he would even have that.

Abraham looked up from the phone to quickly assess his options. Sabrina had moved to the far corner of the room, cowering against the wall, too distraught to make a sound. Her tearless eyes were empty and distant as her chest slowly expanded, then fell, expanded, then fell, until it pushed out what remained of her spirit. The chasm left in its wake was darker than anything he'd ever seen.

For their part, Paul and Jacob held their ground near the cot. He figured one of them would've made a move against him by now, but they hadn't. Perhaps he was more successful in breaking them down than he'd realized. More likely, they were heartened by the prospect of help coming and were simply biding their time. Either way, he knew there wasn't much time left with them. He had one last card to play, and he had to play it.

Giving no thought to Jacob, he quickly made his move on Paul.

"You and I are going to take a walk," Abraham said as he grabbed Paul around the collar and pushed him out of the room.

Before he left, he turned back to Sabrina, now a lifeless shell of the woman he once knew. He had a fleeting thought of granting her the mercy of a bullet in her chest. He hated himself for having such a thought and attempted to shake it off.

"I'm sorry, my love. You deserved better than this. You deserved better than me."

He replaced the thought of killing her with the image of kissing her one last time. Her lips were as sweet and kind as they had ever been.

43

CLOSURE

OF THE FOUR MAIN-LEVEL ROOMS that Camille searched, all were completely empty except for one.

The small bedroom was cold and newly furnished, with a crisply-made twin-sized bed, a polished oak dresser, and a lounge chair with a hand-stitched blue and white blanket draped over the top of it. The blanket was embroidered with the initials LFG. There was nothing to indicate that the room was currently occupied, but the neatly-folded men's t-shirts inside the dresser and the *Welcome Home* postcard on the bedside table did indicate that someone was expected.

Camille studied the framed photos on top of the dresser. Several of them featured a young man with a tanned, handsome face. In two of the photos, he stood next to an older woman, probably his mother, likely Sabrina Noble. She beamed with pride and admiration as she stood next to him. The young man's expression offered no hint of affection.

Camille knew then that she was looking into the eyes of the Sykes copycat, Lucas Gideon.

She also knew from the embroidered blanket that this bedroom was meant for him.

He looked to be in his mid-to-late twenties. His tall, athletic body and pointed good looks would cause him to stand out in a crowd, but not too much. The four girls he killed were all around his age, single, and very pretty. Gideon wouldn't have used force or the element of surprise to get close to them the way Sykes would have. Gideon used seduction, fortified with an affected charm that he'd carefully cultivated to hide who he truly was. Based on the photos, that affected charm had clearly worked on his mother.

Camille quickly checked the rest of the drawers in search of anything else that could offer clues into Gideon. Finding nothing, she carefully removed one of the photos from its frame and stuffed it inside her jacket pocket.

She heard footsteps on the other end of the hallway. Assuming that Chloe and Greer had finished their sweep of the second level, she left the bedroom to join them.

When Camille entered the hallway, the footsteps stopped. Her vantage point offered only a partial view of the living room and the three other rooms she'd already checked. She held her ground outside the bedroom door, listening for any sounds of movement. She heard footsteps again, this time above her. Chloe and Greer were still upstairs.

She gripped the Glock tight with both hands and held it out in front of her. The only sound she could hear now was her own heavy breathing. She held it in the best she could and proceeded slowly down the hallway.

The hardwood floor creaked with each soft step that she took. Somewhere close by, a clock ticked, mimicking the rhythm of her movement.

When she reached the end of the hallway, she stopped. A floorboard buckled under the shift of a weight that wasn't hers. Someone was here.

She closed her eyes, listened to the ticking of the clock, then began a silent count.

Five…

Four…

Three…

Two…

One…

She opened her eyes and rounded the corner.

The young man's face was haggard and beaten, and even at the sight of Camille, the terror in his eyes burned hot.

"Jacob," she whispered. "It's okay. You're safe now."

The terror in his eyes quickly gave way to confusion, then relief.

"Camille."

"Where are they?"

"He took your father and just left me. I don't know where they went."

"Are they still in the house?"

He nodded.

"Is there anyone else?"

Jacob struggled to speak through his labored breathing. "The woman, Sabrina. She's still down in the basement. I told her to come with me, but she wouldn't. She tried to help us. She tried."

His face faltered, and he looked dangerously close to breaking down.

"It's okay, Jacob. The police are on their way, but you have to get out of here."

His large eyes darted around the space. It was clearly unfamiliar to him.

"The front door is down that hallway to the left," Camille explained. "There are three men there. They're all dead. Don't look at them. Just keep running until you get outside. The police will be here any minute."

At first, Jacob didn't move. The fear had returned to his eyes. But this time, she knew the fear wasn't for himself.

"I'll find them. I promise. Now please, go!"

In a move that startled her, he grabbed her by the arm and squeezed.

"Paul needs you, Camille. Please hurry."

With that, Jacob took off down the hallway. Seconds later, she heard the front door open, then close with a loud clang.

Hearing no other movement around her, Camille proceeded through the living room and into the large, unfurnished dining room. From there, she glanced inside the kitchen. There was a large sliding door that led to the backyard. Ten feet to the left of that was a dark entryway that opened up to the basement.

She considered calling out to Chloe and Greer, but with no indication that they were close enough to hear, she decided against it. Instead, she backed out of the living room toward the staircase, eventually making it back to the hallway where she started.

She caught a glimpse of the grandfather clock that had been the source of the ticking, but she no longer heard it. She couldn't hear anything over the roaring in her head that came at the sight of her father, standing no less than five feet from her. Tears instantly flooded her vision, making it impossible to see the smaller man standing behind him until he spoke.

"I've always been a sucker for reunions, especially when they're as long overdue as this one is. I would've hated to miss it."

When he emerged from behind Paul, Camille could see the gun in his hand. She instantly raised hers, but without a clean shot to take, she eased her finger off the trigger.

"Good girl. Now, put it down before someone needlessly gets hurt."

"No."

Abraham Noble's narrow eyes widened with surprise before being overtaken by amusement. "A hero to the end.

Where was all of this gusto when you had the chance to save my daughter?"

"Back away from him, Abraham. Slowly."

"It's nice to know that I don't have to bother with the formality of introducing myself."

"I know exactly who you are."

"I gathered as much from your little article. My question is, how much do you know?"

"You mean, aside from the obvious?"

"Are you implying that I'm one of those cartoon characters that you're so fond of profiling?"

"Not at all."

"Good. Because I'm not."

"Right. You're something much sadder."

Abraham laughed.

"I don't find anything funny about that."

"Neither do I," Abraham said, the darkness returning to his face. "What I do find funny is the fact that you, of all people, are attempting to judge me. You, the coward that allowed dozens of people to die. You, the worthless bitch who stood by and watched as my daughter was gunned down in cold blood. You! The phony hero who refused to take account for what you'd actually done until someone with the proper moral authority finally forced you to. You're pathetic beyond measure. And you have the audacity to call me sad."

"And was it your moral authority that allowed you to kill Jeremy Durant and his wife?"

"The fulfillment of every great cause comes at a cost. Jeremy Durant and his wife sacrificed their lives so that you and I could have this moment. They're not victims. They're heroes. Which is more than I can say about you."

"Okay, Abraham. You got what you wanted. I'm here now. It's just us. Let my father go."

Abraham tensed as he looked over Camille's shoulder. "I'm afraid it isn't just us."

Camille turned to see Chloe and Greer slowly approaching them from behind, weapons drawn.

"Drop the gun, Abraham," Chloe barked. "Now."

Abraham responded by pressing the barrel deeper into Paul's temple.

"Chloe, no," Camille cried. "Stay back."

"Sorry, detectives, Camille is right. Unfortunately, this table only has room for three."

"The party is going to get a lot bigger very soon," Greer said, his gun still raised. "This won't end well for you."

"As far as I can tell, I'm the only one here with nothing left to lose. Your threats don't mean anything to me."

"You still have plenty left to lose," Camille said.

Abraham pressed the gun deeper into Paul. "Not as much as you."

Camille saw the pain on her father's face and nearly lost control of her trigger finger. "Much more than me."

"And how do you figure that?"

"I know how much my father loves me. And he knows how much I love him. If this is the last time we see each other, I'll always have that love. If you kill him, you'll die too. And you'll die never knowing what Madison really thought about you. You'll never know if she loved you just because you were her father, or if she hated you for leaving her.

"You wanted to kill Daniel Sykes because you believed that he somehow knew Madison better than you did, because he was the last person to see her alive. You hated him because he was with her at the end when it should've been you. You've imagined countless times what the end was like for her. You've imagined what she was thinking, who she was thinking about, who she believed would come to save her. It killed you to consider the possibility that she never once thought about you, didn't it?

Camille paused to gauge Abraham's reaction. His stone face gave away nothing.

"There's not a day that goes by that I'm not haunted by the fact that I couldn't save her," she continued. "And as the person who helped to give her life, I mourn deeply for your loss. But you've allowed your justifiable grief to morph into something dark and twisted. And because of that, the tragedy of Madison's death has become something even worse now. If you kill my father, that knowledge is the only closure you'll ever have."

Abraham held Camille's stare for a long time before finally looking away. When he finally spoke, his voice quivered with emotion. "Madison's diary. I need to know what's in it."

Before Camille could reveal the truth about its existence, a voice from the kitchen stopped her.

"There is no diary, Abraham. You should know that."

Camille looked up to see Sabrina Noble standing in the kitchen entryway. Her red, swollen eyes burrowed into Abraham with a frightening contempt.

"Don't move," Chloe ordered.

When she and Greer advanced toward her, Sabrina lifted a large knife up to the side of her neck.

Abraham turned to her in horror. "Sabrina, what are you doing? Put the knife down."

"Madison knew who you were, just like I did," Sabrina continued. "The only difference between her and I was that I foolishly believed that you could be something better."

"Mrs. Noble, please, put the knife down."

Sabrina recoiled at Chloe's words. "Don't call me that. I want nothing to do with him or his name. I'm Sabrina Gideon, the proud mother of three sons, Sebastian, Asher, and

Lucas. They were my true family. And because of him, my family is gone."

"You don't have to do this, Sabrina," Camille said. "Jacob told us that you tried to help him through this. We can help you too."

"Camille is right," Paul said, speaking for the first time. "You're not like him. It shouldn't have to end this way for you."

"It's already over for me, Paul. I could have helped you more. I should have. But I didn't. That makes me just as bad as him."

"You're wrong," Paul insisted.

Sabrina shook her head, then pressed the tip of the knife deeper into her neck.

"Don't do this," Chloe pleaded.

Before she spoke again, Sabrina turned her empty eyes to Camille. "Is it really true that Sebastian is dead?"

"Yes," Camille confirmed.

"How?"

"He was shot after killing two police officers, and attempting to kill a woman named Meredith Park."

"Jacob's agent."

"That's right."

"He did that because of you," she said to Abraham.

"I didn't tell him to–"

"Shut up."

"Mrs. Gideon, please. Put the knife down," Greer reiterated.

Sabrina kept her focus on Camille. "Those four girls who were killed. Do you think Lucas killed them?"

Camille hesitated. "We don't know for sure."

"I do," Sabrina responded in a broken voice. "Tell me about them. What were their names?"

"Harley Middleton, Kerrie Wallace, Emily Flynn, and Brianne Thompson. They were all in their early twenties."

"Children, just like my Lucas."

"By all accounts, they were living happy, productive lives before their deaths."

"Just like Lucas. Or so I was led to believe." She again looked at Abraham.

"What would you have done if I told you, Sabrina? It would've killed you."

"At least I would die peacefully, and on my own terms. Instead, I'm going to die like this."

"You don't have to die," Chloe said as she lowered her gun. She motioned to Greer and urged him to do the same. "You can't blame yourself for what your sons did."

"But I knew something was wrong with Lucas. Deep down, I knew. I didn't want to believe it, so I didn't help him."

"If Lucas really is what we think he is, there was nothing you could've done to help him," Camille insisted.

"There was something I could've done," Sabrina said, looking at Abraham one last time. "But it's too late for that. All that's left to say now is that I'm sorry for what happened. And I'm sorry for what may still happen. If you catch him, I pray that you keep him alive. I know he can still be saved."

Sabrina wiped away the single tear that streaked down her face. Then, without warning, she plunged the knife deep into the soft flesh of her neck, the instant severing of her carotid artery causing heavy pools of blood to stream down her body and onto the floor. She fell before Chloe and Greer could reach her.

Abraham let out an agonizing scream of pain, allowing Paul enough time to break free of his grip and push him against the wall. Quickly regaining his footing, Abraham managed only to raise the gun to waist-level before Camille shot him; twice in his shoulder and once in his leg just below the kneecap. He buckled under the pain and fell to the ground, releasing the gun is he did. Greer swooped in to pick it up, then stood to take aim with his own.

Abraham writhed on the ground, holding his injured leg and crying, "Sabrina, no," over and over again.

It wasn't until Camille turned to look away that she noticed the officers from Windsor PD had converged on the house.

She had no idea how long they'd been there.

44

EMPTY SEAT

CRAWLEY, KRIEGER, AND PARSONS arrived at the gate twenty minutes before Lucas Gideon's scheduled flight was due to land. The extra time allowed Crawley to gather as many DPD airport patrols as he could. He spread them out thinly around the gate area, with the idea of not drawing too much attention. Two of them would accompany Crawley and the detectives onto the plane.

The pilots had been radioed ahead and told to keep the passengers seated once the plane arrived. They were also told that Crawley and his team would be boarding, but they weren't told why.

With the help of an airline agent assigned to the gate, Crawley was able to confirm that Gideon had checked in for the flight early this morning, and that his boarding pass was scanned at the gate in Philadelphia. She was also able to confirm that he checked one piece of luggage, carried on one more, and was assigned to seat Eight-A.

That was a break. If he was on board, having a window seat near the front would make it difficult to react quickly once he saw them coming.

The gate agent looked nervous but didn't ask a lot of questions, which Crawley was thankful for. An airport, especially one as large is Denver International, was perhaps the worst location to execute a takedown operation of this magnitude. The presence of police in any capacity was likely to draw interest. A show of force too large could incite panic. Crawley was walking a razor-thin line with this one. A single false move could spell disaster in a million different ways.

"I'll go in first," Crawley reiterated to Krieger, Parsons, and the two officers who would accompany them on board. "The detectives will come in with me while everyone else hangs back on the jet bridge. If he somehow slips past us, you're the last line of defense," he told the officers. "He can't make it to the terminal, under any circumstances. Is that clear?"

The group nodded their agreement.

"Good."

Moments later, the gate agent received a telephone call. "Okay. I'll let them know." When she hung up, she turned to Crawley. "They've just landed and they're making their way to the gate. The pilot estimates it will be five minutes.

"Okay. Remember, we know what he looks like, and we know his seat number," he told the group. "We board the plane quietly. Once we confirm that he's there, we simply make our way to Eight-A, order Gideon to exit the plane, then get the hell out. Don't bother with the cuffs until he's on the jet bridge."

When the plane pulled in, the gate attendant opened the jet bridge door, and the five-man team rushed through it, Agent Crawley leading the way. They stood impatiently at the main cabin door until the flight attendant opened it. She was understandably frightened.

"Were you informed that we were coming?" he asked in a low voice.

"Yes, but we weren't told why."

"A passenger," he whispered into her ear. "He may be dangerous and we need to get him off the plane as soon as possible."

Her bright blue eyes widened. "Oh my God, is it a-"

"No," Crawley said quickly. "But we still need to get him off the plane, quietly if it all possible."

The flight attendant took a deep breath to steady herself. "Okay. What do you need the crew to do?"

"Keep the passengers calm and tell them to remain seated. The person we want is in a window seat near the front. If the aisles are kept clear, we shouldn't have a problem getting to him."

"Which seat?"

"Eight A."

The flight attendant looked confused. "Did you say Eight-A?"

"Yes."

"That's not possible. Seat Eight-A has been vacant for the entire flight."

Crawley couldn't believe what he'd just heard, so he asked her to repeat it.

"It was the only unoccupied seat on the plane," she added.

Crawley felt his stomach drop. "But we cross-referenced the passenger manifest. The passenger assigned to that seat checked in this morning, went through security, then had his boarding pass scanned twenty-three minutes before take-off."

"Are you sure that was the final flight manifest? Because the passenger in Eight-A was never on this plane. And if he planned on boarding, he changed his mind somewhere between the jet bridge and here."

"You don't recall anyone getting on the plane then getting off?" Parsons asked.

"No, sir. If anyone had gotten off the plane, one of us would have noticed, and held the flight until they returned."

"And if they didn't return?" Krieger asked.

"The flight likely would have been delayed until they were accounted for and questioned."

"Do you mind if we take a look?" Crawley asked, still not wanting to believe her.

"Of course. But can it just be you?" she asked Crawley. "No need to alarm the passengers if we don't have to."

"Fine."

He followed the flight attendant, ignoring the murmurs among the passengers until he reached seat Eight-A. Just as she said, the seat was empty.

"Excuse me, Miss," he asked the teenage girl in Eight-B. "Was anyone sitting in the seat next to you at any point prior to take-off?"

"Not while I was here," the girl said in a slow unaffected drawl. "And I was one of the first people on the plane, so…"

Crawley nodded and flashed a tight smile. "Thank you."

On the inside, Crawley wasn't smiling at all. On the inside, he wanted to punch a hole through the first inanimate object that he came across.

After calls to Philadelphia Airport TSA to request camera footage from the security checkpoints and the terminal, and Caleb Foster to confirm that Gideon still had not checked in with Fairfield, Crawley waited in baggage claim for Gideon's suitcase. Krieger and Parsons stuck around, just in case they were needed. Crawley knew they wouldn't be, but he appreciated the company nonetheless.

Before he could retrieve the suitcase, he received a call from Camille.

"Let's hope your news is better than mine," he said when he picked up.

For a second, he heard nothing on the other end. Then came the slight sniffle.

"Camille?"

"It's over, Peter," she finally said.

Dread instantly washed over him. "What do you mean?"

"I mean we got him."

"Abraham Noble?"

"Yes."

Crawley held his breath before he asked the next question. "Paul and Jacob?"

"They're safe."

He exhaled loudly. "Thank God. How are you?"

"Oh…"

Camille proceeded to tell him the entire story, down to the moment when her three shots brought an end to Abraham Noble's time on Earth as a free man. Crawley didn't bother to ask where she got the gun. Frankly, he didn't care.

"I told myself that if I ever got him in my sights, I'd take the kill shot."

"Why didn't you? Were the extremities a safer play?"

"Not at all."

"He had a gun, Camille. You would've been justified if you did."

Camille was quiet for a long time. "I'm not in the business of other people's suffering, but killing Abraham would've given him the easy way out. He doesn't deserve easy."

"No, he doesn't."

After another silence, Camille said, "We're at UC Health Med Center in Loveland. Get up here as soon as you can."

"I will."

Before hanging up, Camille asked, "Any movement on Gideon?"

Crawley watched as the plain black suitcase with Lucas Gideon's name on it dropped down into the carousel bin.

"A conversation for another time."

He let the suitcase spin in the carousel for quite a while after he hung up, hoping beyond hope that Lucas Gideon would emerge from the shadows to quietly pick it up.

After waiting much longer than he should have, Crawley finally resigned himself to the fact that he wasn't coming.

45

HARD TIMES AHEAD

P AUL AND JACOB WERE ADMITTED to the UC Health Medical Center for overnight observation. Aside from mild dehydration, both were in reasonably good physical shape. The doctors stopped short of offering a psychological assessment, however. Such an assessment, they admitted, would require far more expert hands than theirs.

Camille didn't need an expert to tell her how bleak the preliminary results would be.

But now was not the time to fixate on that.

Despite his insistence that he was fine and had no business being here, Camille remained at her father's bedside, doing whatever she could to make him comfortable. After hours of constantly fluffing his pillows, keeping his water mug filled, and harping on him to eat the turkey and mashed potato meal that had thus far remained untouched, Paul was getting understandably annoyed. But Camille didn't care. There were moments where she was convinced that she would never see him again. Now that she had him back, she wasn't sure if she ever wanted to let him out of her sight again.

Despite his irritation at being fussed over so much, the occasional unguarded smile that slipped through told Camille that, deep down, her fussing meant the world to him.

"You really did do what I trained you to do," Paul said after taking a sip of the hot tea Camille insisted he drink. "I was really proud of you."

"Thank you, Dad. I was really proud of you too. The way you kept your composure through all of that. Whenever I felt like it was too much, whenever I felt like Noble might've been getting the best of me, I looked into your eyes. You gave me the strength to get through that, just by being there." She leaned over and put her head on his chest. "Thank you for being there."

Camille heard him sniff.

"Thank you for coming for me."

"Anytime. Just don't be surprised if I request an armed federal agent to follow you around from now on."

Paul chuckled. "Like hell, you will. Do you know how distracting it would be trying to play eighteen holes with some chump in a suit staring me down? No thanks. I'll take my chances."

Camille was being sarcastic. But the more she considered the prospect of Lucas Gideon still being out there, the more serious the notion of armed security became. "Fine. We'll revisit the conversation another time."

She felt a gentle hand on her shoulder. When she looked up, she saw Meredith standing next to the bed. Camille instantly stood up to hug her. "I'm so glad you're okay."

"I'm glad you are too," Meredith replied. "Thank you for everything."

Camille said you're welcome by pulling her in for another hug.

"And you, young man," Meredith said to Paul. "You let

this woman take good care of you. She's a hell of an agent, but when it comes to you, I bet she's an even better nurse."

Paul smiled broadly and extended his hand to Meredith's. "You have a keen eye," he said, giving her hand a light squeeze. He gave Camille a subtle wink for good measure.

The rest of the group had been congregated on Jacob's side of the room to allow Camille and Paul some private time. Unlike her father, Jacob looked to be just fine with all of the extra attention.

"Are you okay?" Chloe asked when she walked up.

"Yes," Camille said. "I'm sure the crash is coming. But for now, I'm hanging in."

"Good."

"How are you?"

"Relieved, but not totally."

Camille nodded. "I know the feeling."

"Greer and I will need to head back soon. There's a lot of inter-jurisdictional red-tape to sort out. The shootings were justified, but still, it's going to be a mess."

Camille would have her own red tape to sort through. She and Crawley would have questions to answer, mostly involving the shooting of Abraham Noble. It could make for a touchy trial, should it go that far, but she trusted Crawley to see her through it.

"I think it's high time I see your dad now," Chloe said with a warm smile. "I need a little positive energy."

"Okay. Let's get a drink soon to regroup."

"Another round of Old-Fashioneds?"

"It's a date, my friend."

They exchanged a fist-bump as Chloe walked away. She meant it when she called her a friend.

"Hey, Paul," Camille heard her say as she approached his bed. "We've got to stop it with these hospital room meetings."

Paul chuckled again. "Tell me about it."

After some time with Jacob, Camille found Agents Pratt and Mendoza huddled in the corner alongside Crawley.

"He looks really good, considering," Pratt said in reference to Paul.

"He's a pit-bull," Camille said with a proud smile. "Tough as nails."

"Now we know where you get it from."

Camille was somewhat embarrassed by the gesture and felt her cheeks warm in response. "I've got nothing on him."

"Don't sell yourself short, Agent Grisham," Pratt continued. "I'd follow you into the foxhole any time."

"So would I," Mendoza added.

Pratt's kindness no longer surprised her. The fact that she wasn't the least bit bothered when he called her *Agent Grisham* did.

"Let's chat real quick," Crawley said.

Camille nodded and followed him into the hallway.

"We didn't find much inside Gideon's suitcase," he began. "Just some clothes, toiletries, and his corrections uniform. There was a razor inside, which should give us adequate DNA. Combined with his prints, we should have more than enough for comparison."

"Now all we have to do is find him."

"Did you suspect that he was our copycat before his mother confirmed it?"

Camille nodded, then pulled out the photo she taken from his room and handed it to Crawley. "As cliché as it sounds, it was in his eyes."

Crawley took the photo and studied it closely. "There's nothing cliché about what we do, Camille."

"What *we* do?"

Crawley didn't respond.

"What do you think this means for Sykes's transfer?" Camille asked after a long silence.

"We may not be able to justify the hold for much longer, especially if it's established that an officer at Fairfield may have colluded with him to commit more crimes. Don't be surprised if Sykes is here very soon. Are you going to be okay with that?"

Camille nodded, unsure if she would be able to vocalize the lie. "And for what it's worth, it never got to be too much," she added.

"That's worth a lot, Camille."

"My father and Jacob are home. Abraham Noble is in custody. Everything should feel right in my world. So why doesn't it?"

She suspected that Crawley knew the answer, but had decided to let Camille come to it on her own when she was ready. In the interest of finding Lucas Gideon, she needed to be ready soon.

"There might be some hard times ahead, but right now, let's celebrate. We worked our asses off to get here. And frankly, I don't want to waste another second of it."

Camille thought back to how far she'd come to get here, what she gave up, what she gained, and the remaining obstacles that she now had the confidence to face. And suddenly, she didn't want to waste another second either.

46

THE LAST GOOD AGENT

T HE NEXT MORNING, Crawley made his way to the Denver Health Medical Center, where Agent Wells was finally moved out of intensive care and into his own room.

The ventilator had been disconnected, and he was breathing on his own. The prognosis was good. A couple more weeks here, then he would go home. Crawley would be here until he did, and probably long after.

"How are Emma and Riley?"

"They're good," Wells answered in a hoarse voice. "Riley's back home with Emma's folks so she can get back to school. Emma finally felt comfortable enough to get a hotel room."

"That's great. You're a lucky guy in more ways than one."

"Ain't that the truth."

Crawley gave him a hearty pat on his good shoulder.

"You look tired," Wells said.

Crawley rubbed his eyes in response. "No time to be tired, my friend."

"Do you have Camille on board to help you find him?"

"I'm not sure yet."

"I don't love your chances without her."

"Me neither. I can tell she likes you, Stephen. Perhaps you could convince her."

Wells chuckled, then winced in pain. "I'm not a miracle worker, Pete. I'm just a broken-down, beat up, BAU soldier who thanks my lucky stars for every breath I take, painful as those breaths are. I'd be the last person to inspire her to come back."

This time, Crawley was the one who chuckled. "You're probably right about that. But I do take exception to your self-characterization. You're as strong as an ox, and you'll be back on your feet in no time."

"It won't be soon enough to help with Gideon."

Crawley nodded. "With you being out of commission, Camille might be the last good agent left."

"She's got me beat by a country mile, Peter, and you damn well know it."

Crawley did know it.

He could only hope that Camille knew it too.

EPILOGUE I

THE STUDIO LIGHTS THAT HAVE BEEN set up in my hotel room are blinding, and I'm self-conscious of the fact that I'm squinting. The man sitting across from me insists that my eyes will adjust with time, but so far, he's wrong.

I've had to make many adjustments in the two months since my time with Abraham Noble and his wife Sabrina came to a violent but merciful end.

There are a lot of people who deserve to be recognized for what they've done to bring about that end. Camille Grisham and the team that she worked with. Paul Grisham, for fueling the fire that kept Camille going. Even Daniel MacPherson, who, unlike Abraham, decided to honor the legacy of the loved one he lost by doing the right thing.

I'm not entirely sure that I could, or should, count myself among this group of heroes. Yet, here I am, being lauded as one.

The irony of my discomfort with my new-found notoriety is that it's the one thing I've always wanted. After years of toiling, I finally have a legitimate story to tell. And the world seems all too eager to hear it. But now that the moment is in front of me, I'm hesitant.

Because of the impending trial, I'm not yet able to release *Ignoble Deeds*. In fact, many of the passages from the book - passages that I dictated directly from Abraham's recordings - will likely be used as evidence in the trial. I've been assured by my attorney that I'll eventually be able to use the material in my book, but it could be several months.

The world at large will have to wait to hear Abraham Noble's full story. But in the meantime, it seems eager to hear mine. People love survival stories, and the story of my survival is more harrowing than most. If this moment represents my fifteen minutes, then I'm going to use every second of it to the fullest. Not to talk about myself, but to thank the men and women who saved me. The heroes. I'll never forget them. And I want to make sure the world doesn't forget them either.

That's my story as it stands today.

As far as what comes next, that part is still to be written. But one thing is for certain. If my wonderful agent and friend Meredith Park has her way, it'll be a runaway bestseller.

"You're finally looking a little more comfortable," the man sitting across from me says. "Are the lights getting easier to deal with?"

"They are."

"I told you so. Hopefully, you can take this as the first sign that you can trust me."

The man sitting across from me is named Will Freeman, editor of the Mile-High Dispatch. From what I've come to understand, Will's involvement with Camille Grisham and her team was crucial to helping them catch Abraham Noble. Because of that, I chose him to conduct my first on-camera interview. As it turns out, it was his first on-camera interview too.

"Are you ready for this?" he asks after blowing out a nervous breath.

"Absolutely."

"Okay. Let's roll."

With that, the camera light is switched on.

After reading a scripted introduction into the camera, Will turns to me and smiles. "We're not live, so you can stop and start as much as you need to."

"Understood," I tell him. "But I don't have any intention of stopping. Not until everyone who tried to hurt me gets exactly what's coming to them."

EPILOGUE II

H E COULDN'T STOMACH the Jacob Deaver interview for more than five minutes before turning it off. The pseudo tough talk about the animals getting exactly what they deserved was downright nauseating. They weren't animals, and he couldn't tolerate the suggestion that they were. Just like he couldn't tolerate the notion that Camille Grisham was some kind of hero. According to Daniel Sykes, she was anything but a hero.

Sykes, for better or worse, had a lot of opinions about Camille.

His own association with Sykes ended long ago, but the fallout from it was just beginning. Because of that association, his face was now known to the world. Because of that association, he would now have to live the rest of his life in the shadows. Living in the shadows would require discipline, patience, and most importantly, purpose – all of which he had.

For too long, he allowed his work to be driven by someone else's vision; someone else's design; someone else's purpose.

Not anymore.

From this moment forward, his purpose would be clear.

Unlike Abraham, he felt no hatred toward Camille Grisham, or for what she'd done to his mother and brothers. When he thought about Camille Grisham, he felt something else entirely.

Watching her from the shadows, as he'd already done more than once, he realized that the stories told to him by Sykes, the ones that fueled his fantasies, did no justice to what Camille had been in real life.

In real life, she was so much more.

And if Lucas Gideon had his way, he would eventually experience every inch of it.

ABOUT THE AUTHOR

Long-exiled from the cut-throat world of politics, John Hardy Bell is the author of the bestselling Grisham & Sullivan series. His debut novel, THE STRATEGIST, has been an Amazon #1 Bestselling Political Thriller and has garnered rave reviews from mystery fans the world over. When he's not spending time with his wife and son, John enjoys reading, forcing himself into new and uncomfortable yoga poses, and, of course, making up stories that entertain people.

To learn more, please visit John at johnhardybell.com

You can also email him at john@johhhardybell.com